Life on A Mountain

Love is a Cabin Series
Book 2

JACQUE JACOBS

Drawings by
Ken Czarnomski

Cover Photo by
Bill Johnston

Drellag Press, LLC

Life on a Mountain
Love is a Cabin Series: Book Two

This is a work of fiction. Names, characters, places, and incidents are products of the author's imagination or are used fictitiously and should not be construed as real. Any resemblance to actual events, locales, organizations, or persons, living or dead, is entirely coincidental.

An imprint of Drellag Press, LLC
Address: 2160 58th Ave. PMB 58 Vero Beach, FL 32966
Website: LoveisaCabin.com

Printed in the United States of America
Paperback book: ISBN 978-1-7373398-2-3
eBook: ISBN 978-1-7373398-3-0

Other Works of Fiction by
JACQUE JACOBS

Love is a Cabin Series
Book One - *High on a Mountain*

Look for:
Book Three – *Settled on a Mountain* (Winter, 2022)
Book Four - *New Beginnings* (Spring, 2022)
Book Five – *The Community Unites* (Late Summer, 2022)
Book Six – *Holidays on a Mountain* (Fall, 2022)

Drawings by
Ken Czarnomski

Cover Photo by
Bill Johnston

An Imprint of
Drellag Press, LLC
Vero Beach FL

Acknowledgements

Thanks does not seem sufficient to those who have given feedback and encouragement in my creative endeavors—nonetheless, thank you. Thanks, with love, to Bonnie Jacobs Coats who listened to me read each and every chapter and encouraged me to keep writing. Dondra Traylor Maney, Ph.D., has graciously read each chapter as it was written—you're awesome. Susan Lovelace, Bonnie MacDougall, Ph.D., and Michelle Wheeler of the *Tuesday Writers* of the Laura (Riding) Jackson Foundation, thanks for sticking with me on this journey and for your time and effort in giving me feedback. Donna Duffy, Mary Ann Klein, Nancy Gorneau, Kate Charbonneau, Ruth Jackson Johnston, Jaye Taylor, Marilyn Burton, Paula Van Hooser, Peggy Jones, Ed.D., and Tom Hall have all been readers and given me thoughtful input for consideration which I deeply appreciate.

Others have encouraged me and asked about my work. Your interest makes a huge difference. Thank you.

Ken Czarnomski's drawings are an asset to the story and help bring the book to life.

Many thanks. Your talents are evident and your kindness appreciated.

William F. (Bill) Johnston, Ed.D. is a decades long friend and colleague whose retirement passion for photography has produced stunning pictures. Thank you for letting me display your work.

A man who has no idea he inspired me to write every day is also critical to this accomplishment. I took a *Master Class* with the author, Walter Mosley, in early December. After years of attending writing workshops in my professional life, and since, someone finally explained to me *why* you need to write every day. I'm paraphrasing his ideas: You write every day because you are not the writer today you were yesterday, and you won't be the writer tomorrow you are today. His second point was equally important: When you write every day words play in your head. Thank you, Mr. Mosley. Your inspiration launched the six books I have written in the last eleven months.

The final stages in bringing this book to print and e-book could not have happened without Elaine Massung, editor extraordinaire at

hello@blueeagleacademic.com

Amazing cover design by
PixelStudio at http://www.Fiverr.com

And book formatting by
Arkonna at http://www.Fiverr.com

Dedication

This book is dedicated to my children and grandchildren and to my ancestors, known and unknown, whose lives and legacy have enriched my life beyond measure.

*Keep close to Nature's heart ... and break clear away once in a while,
and climb a mountain or spend a week in the woods.
Wash your spirit clean ...*
(John Muir, 1838 – 1914)

Drawing by Ken Czarnomski

1

Week Three on the Mountain

Bella stood in the open French doors leading out to the front porch of her cabin, looking towards the ridgeline of the Smoky Mountains. *Time. I have all the time in the world, and I'm home.* The early reds and yellows of autumn were scattered across the mountains and drew Bella outside at every opportunity. The heavy socks she had pulled out during a September cooler than anticipated were definitely welcome inside her fuzzy slippers this morning. Although she wore her silk thermal underwear under her jeans and flannel shirt, the drop in temperature made her reconsider the wisdom of starting this day on her porch. She decided the weather called for a change of venue; the kitchen table would do nicely.

Sipping freshly brewed tea in her favorite dragonfly cup gave some comfort as she read the headline in last week's *The Tuesday*

Tattler: Teen Dies in Meth Lab Explosion. Bella was still reeling from the explosion that took place near her mountain cabin, and she remained troubled by the events of the past two weeks, several of which had happened on her land. She wasn't sure she wanted to read the article, but she was anxious to find out if she was identified in it—she hoped not.

After retiring from her university teaching position, Bella Anderson had recently arrived at her ancestral home in the mountains of east Tennessee with a plan to write and enjoy the land she loved. Although tracks from all-terrain vehicles crossing her road had troubled her, she had assumed it was from curious mountain riders. She never imagined the ATVs would lead to injury, death, and destruction. Now, thanks to the weekly newspaper, everyone knew about the explosion. She stopped reading and looked out the window. *The worst part of all is two young men have died from making and running meth: one in the explosion in the forest and one on my land.*

Although the shock was fading, the sadness lingered. Bella felt more secure now that she knew the sheriff, Chad Oliver. She originally met him in the Valley Store when she arrived back in the mountains for her first extended stay in years, but within two days she was depending on him to keep her and her property safe. She quickly learned the sheriff and his deputies were diligent in their efforts to protect the entire community as much as possible.

She breathed a sigh of relief when she reached the end of the article and saw that neither she nor her property were identified. As she leaned back in her chair, the ringing of the phone on her kitchen wall interrupted the unpleasant thoughts.

"Drellag Caban, may I help you?" She still used the formal greeting she had learned as a child; her mother had insisted it was proper. *It makes me happy to answer by the name I gave the cabin ten years ago, not just "Olivers, may I help you?" After all, I'm only an Oliver in lineage, not by name.*

"Dr. Anderson, this is Detective Williams."

"Good morning, Detective. How are you?"

"Fine, fine." The detective often used the double statements made by many of the local people. Bella's grandmother used to say it was because people were so accustomed to the echo in the mountains it made them think they had to say things twice.

"I'm calling to see if it's convenient for me to come up this afternoon. I want to double-check a couple of things from the ATV that smashed into your shed. Really sorry you have to deal with the damage."

"Me too, but I suspect the owner of the ATV is also pretty upset." She paused. "I'll be here all afternoon, Detective. Is there anything you need from me?"

"Just access to the shed, ma'am. See you around two o'clock, if that works for you?"

"Two o'clock will be fine, see you then." At his goodbye, she hung up the phone and stood at the kitchen counter. *The plywood covering the hole in the side of my shed is a constant reminder of that ATV slamming into it. I need to ask Detective Williams if it's okay to make arrangements to get it repaired. It will be winter soon.*

The way of life for the people in the valley had changed very little in the past century, and Bella cherished the serenity she had known from childhood summers spent in these mountains. But the explosion of the meth lab seemed to indicate that the modern world had managed to encroach upon the valley's defenses. *I wonder what other changes are destined for this part of the world?*

However, she was an optimist at her core, and Bella chose to focus on the positive things that had come from her first weeks back. She was happy to rekindle a friendship with Joshua Johnson and his father, Joe, the owners of the Valley Store. Over the years, she and her late husband, Matt, had visited several times with Joshua and his wife, Jan. Bella was saddened to learn about Jan's recent illness and death; she knew managing grief was unpredictable, and she hoped she could be a good friend to help Joshua navigate his loss.

Bella's goals were to write a mystery novel and create a new life for herself. Perhaps she would do that here in the mountains since she could now stay as long as she wanted. She had begun to toy with the idea of making the cabin her year-round home, but the many changes happening in the valley could affect her long-term decisions. Most of the changes came from the intrusion of housing developments that were redefining the landscape of the hills and the very fiber of the community. She would have to decide how any accompanying changes to the mountains themselves, or dangers like those she had just experienced, would affect her decision to stay. She was also becoming aware that getting to know Joshua and Chad might bring changes in her personal life that would convince her to stay.

Early Monday Morning for the Sheriff

Sheriff Chad Oliver found the quiet of home made it easier to concentrate on the detail of written reports, and he was determined to finish his review of the September activity reports, or the "police blotter" in big city lingo. *I'm not interested in acquiring big city language. I just need to keep a handle on the crimes in my little corner of the world.* When he wasn't reviewing the latest updates from his officers, Chad normally arrived at the station around six o'clock in the morning to catch up with his deputies from the tail end of the midnight to eight shift and the beginning of the eight to four shift. He packed the reports from state and federal agencies which he still needed to read to take to the office.

Even after reviewing the activity reports at home, Chad still managed to arrive by seven-fifteen. As he walked down the hall towards his office, he heard several voices call out, "Morning, Sheriff Oliver," and he responded with his own "Morning" in turn. He had a meeting with Detective Billy Williams at eight, so he would check in with the shift sergeant and still have time to get through some reports he was trying to read before the meeting. As sheriff, he could certainly call the shift sergeant to come to his office, but he liked the little things he picked up about his employees and the general atmosphere of the station by wandering to the front.

He turned on the computer and made a note on a scratchpad while waiting for his login details to process. *Connection??? Sightings of light & Unmanned Aerial Vehicles (UAVs).* He moved the brown leather satchel he used for ferrying reports between his home and the station to the far side of his desk to make room for the day's paperwork. The feel of the weathered leather always made him think of his dad. Chad liked knowing his late father had carried the satchel each day to his small law office near the library. Like his father, Chad had never had any interest in moving to the city. Knoxville was a great place to visit but not to live; at least, not for him.

Thankfully the city was also far enough away that he had literal and figurative distance from Mary, his ex-wife. *Why on earth are you traveling down memory lane this morning?* When he stopped to think about it, he realized it must be due to the picnic he had enjoyed with his daughter and her family yesterday. He was grateful Nora valued his job and was more than willing to postpone her birthday celebration after their original plans were derailed by the meth lab explosion and fire.

As he headed towards the front of the station with his empty coffee mug, he shifted his thinking to the day's work. He saw Sergeant Whitehorse heading towards him.

"Hey, boss, I heard you were in the house."

"Urgent, or can I say good morning up front?"

"Important, but not urgent, I'll grab a cup of coffee and meet you at your door." She kept walking towards the break room.

"Sure thing," he said, "Sure thing." Most folks hardly knew how often they made double statements. It was viewed by some as a way of reassuring the other person that whatever was said was a fact, not important to the circumstance, or not offensive. A kind of mountain reassurance that was too deeply ingrained for most to break the habit. Flatlanders, the local term for people not from the mountains, found it odd how often locals said things twice.

The deputy at the front desk was the only one in his area. "Left all alone up here, are you?"

"Morning, Sheriff. Always good to have a quiet few minutes on a Monday morning. How are you?"

"Right as rain, thanks. Good to see all is quiet." Chad turned to head back to his office, "Let's hope it stays that way."

"Right about that, boss. Right about that. Have a good day."

Chad lifted his hand in a wave. He stopped in the break room and filled his mug. As he approached his office, he saw Sergeant Whitehorse waiting. "Go on in. Have a seat."

She walked to the round table and set her coffee mug down. She looked up at the topographical maps on his wall.

"Saw you with Nora and Fred at Flat Rock Park yesterday. Looked like the kids were having fun."

Chad turned his head to look at her. "How did I miss seeing you?"

"Sleeping on the job?" Chad's sergeants knew he was pretty easy going on the personal side of things, but all business when it came to the law.

"Probably so, Sylvia." He was good natured in his retort. "I was overdue on that birthday picnic. It should have been two weeks ago."

"Boss, if ever there was a daughter who adored her father and cut him the slack you need in this job, it's Nora." Her voice was sincere. "I'm sure she knows you were knee-deep in the meth case."

"I don't know how I'm so lucky in life. She's smart as a whip, beautiful inside and out, a great wife to Fred, and a super mom to my grandkids..." He hesitated. "And a daughter I'm not sure I deserve. I guess it never occurred to me how all her great qualities are obvious to everyone else as well."

"Hard to be a teacher in this area, *and* the daughter of the sheriff, and not be noticed. You're a fortunate man."

"Thanks, Sylvia. I know it. I'm generally good about making sure Nora knows it. Pretty sure you have more things to do than butter up the boss, though. What's up?" His tone made clear the bantering was over; it was time to move into work mode.

"Billy...Detective Williams asked for a couple of deputies to follow a lead on the missing ATV from the meth case. The one that *didn't* run into Dr. Anderson's shed."

Chad sat up straighter in his chair. "And?"

"Couple of the local boys at the high school were talking about one of the new kids from the Mountain Villages..."

She was surprised when he rolled his eyes—he rarely showed any reaction at all. She continued as if nothing had happened.

"Seems one of the boys heard Nick Brown, another local boy, bragging about his new friend. Said he was probably going to give him an ATV that got banged up in a little accident they had. He claimed that the new boy, who goes to the fancy private school over in the Mountain Villages, told him he would just buy himself a new one."

"Any luck talking to any of the boys involved?"

"The deputies were at the school at six forty-five to talk to the principal. Dr. Bennett was cooperative, as always." They both knew Amanda Bennett. Her husband, Ken, was a deputy, and she knew the importance of helping law enforcement to protect her students.

"Apparently Nick Brown turned in a note on Friday from his folks about a doctor's appointment in Knoxville today." Before he could say a word, she went on. "The deputies are on their way to his house to see who might be home."

"Good work, Sergeant." Chad was definitely back into his professional demeanor. "Does Detective Williams know?"

"Yes, sir. Called him. He planned to meet up with the deputies at the boy's house."

"Thanks. He's due here at eight."

She stood. She knew Chad was never one for drawn out dismissals with his officers. "Can you step back then? No need to close the door."

Sylvia left without saying anything and headed back to her office.

Chad saw it was only seven thirty, so he had a good half hour to read the FBI analysis on drones. Or, as Sam was always reminding him, unmanned aerial vehicles. UAVs for short. He was particularly interested to learn how they were used by law enforcement, and likewise curious about the suspected uses and misuses of the increasing number of civilian-owned UAVs. He knew DEA agent Sam Nations believed the light would be gone with the explosion of the mobile meth lab. But Chad couldn't just dismiss the light as being connected to the lab without doing everything possible to verify it. He would hate to find out it signified other activity in the hills.

He was lost in the new world of technology, his scratchpad rapidly filling up with notes, when Detective Billy Williams knocked on the door frame. Chad saw Sergeant Whitehorse beside him. "Come in. Come in. Bring your coffee if you have it. We'll sit at the table." Both walked in with a mug in hand and sat down.

"Be with you in a minute." Chad was suddenly distracted by a message that had popped up on his computer screen. It read: "Remains verification."

"Give me a minute, please."

Sylvia turned to Billy. "So, Billy, do you know the significance of the boss having a round table?"

"Got it out of a warehouse sale? Government budgets for furniture not so plentiful?"

"Just like you, Billy, to assume there can only be one reason for a purchasing decision." She was teasing him, but she became more serious. "In our tribe, as in most, we believe the circle represents life, and this table is an example of a traditional talking circle."

"Hey, Sylvia, I respect traditions, yours and mine, but I'm ashamed to say I don't know much about yours." It was often hard to gauge Billy's level of sincerity, but, in this instance at least, she could tell he meant it.

Chad joined them. "Okay, sorry, I just received notification the remains found in the rubble from the meth lab are definitely those of Edward Calhoun, the college student missing from Round City. It's what I expected based on the tip from Dr. Anderson."

Billy looked at him. "What tip, boss?"

"The one from the article she read several weeks ago in *The Tuesday Tattler* about a missing boy in a U-Haul truck on his way back to college. Thought you knew. The truck he rented matches with the vehicle identification number on the frame. Questions?"

They both shook their heads.

"Sergeant, I'd like you to take care of notifying Calhoun's next of kin."

"Sure thing, boss. I'll take care of it before I sign out today."

Chad looked at his watch. "Feel free to pass it on to the next shift."

"If it's all the same to you, I'll take care of it. I think it's going to involve a grandmother getting the news."

"Fine. Appreciate it." Chad's eyes stared off into the distance.

Sylvia knew this was how he dealt with the loss of life, especially that of a young person. She and Billy remained silent.

Chad cleared his throat. "Now, Billy, did you find out if the Brown kid had a doctor's appointment?"

Billy shook his head. "No one was home, boss, so that part might be legitimate. It could also mean he was hurt in the crash, and this is a follow-up of some kind. The deputies will go back out this afternoon around supper time."

Chad nodded his head. "Where are we overall in connecting these cases?"

"I spoke to Justin Culverson in the jail. He won't admit to knowing anything about the other ATVs being near where his wreck was. Acted like he knew nothing about the backpack of drugs we found on his ATV. No surprise there. Justin hasn't lawyered up yet, just being stubborn. I suspect when he finds out his buddy died in the wreck and then the meth lab blew up, he'll either talk or demand a lawyer."

"Has he asked about his buddy Will?"

"Not a word, boss. I'll keep working him. Once we track down this Brown kid and the fourth ATV, we should be able to wrap this one up. The kids at the high school said that Nick Brown lost his class ring in the accident, so I want to go back up to the Anderson place and check around the shed one more time. I called Dr. Anderson to ask if it's okay."

"Class ring? That's interesting. Good idea to go back and check. I'll go with you."

Billy looked at him, perplexed. "Boss, you think I can't handle it?"

Surprised at Billy's comment, and himself, Chad hesitated for a moment. "I need to check a few things with Dr. Anderson as well. Might as well save her the hassle of each of us going at separate times." *Why am I going? Is it to see her as Bella, or as the property owner?*

Sylvia and Billy looked at each other and shrugged. They had never heard the boss stumble over his words, and both knew there was likely nothing related to the case the sheriff needed to ask. They also both knew the sheriff had been calling her by her first name since the ATVs crashed on her land—so why the formality now?

As the lead detective, Billy had talked with Dr. Anderson several times. *Guess I can't blame a single man for wanting to talk to the new woman in the area, especially when she's good looking and smart.*

"Sure, boss. I told her I'd be up at two. Does that work for you?"

"Two is fine. I'll meet you there." Chad stood.

Billy and Sylvia followed suit. They both knew the signal of dismissal.

Monday Morning at Drellag Caban

Drellag Caban served as a warm blanket protecting the many memories Bella had of Grandmother Hazel, her parents, and her beloved husband, Matt. The heavy timber logs seemed to bear the weight of all the losses the Oliver and Anderson families had experienced over the last one hundred and twenty years. She had such fond memories of her time as a child that she was sure she could bring joy back into this cabin. After all, she had given the cabin a joyful name: Drellag, the Scottish word for dragonfly, and Caban, the

Welsh word for cabin. She was determined to move past the difficult reminders of the recent events; she decided one of the best ways to do that was to enjoy the crispness of the autumn weather and the other seasonal changes happening all around her.

But before she could fully enjoy her land again, the repairs to her shed needed her attention. As she was prone to do, she analyzed the pros and cons of each choice. At the moment, she was inclined to replace the shed and make it big enough to serve as a garage for her Jeep Wrangler and perhaps even include a guest cottage. She could decide later about whether to keep or remove the carport, but she had concerns that the snow load on the carport roof might take it down one of these days. She would decide on her course of action once she knew what the detective needed.

She cleaned up her breakfast dishes and poured another cup of tea. The small table she had ordered to serve as a writing desk was waiting to be put together. It took ten days to reach Drellag Caban. She knew it would have been at her North Carolina home in a couple of days. *Stop comparing. Like Daddy used to say, "Here is here and there is there."*

The partial wall between the dining room and kitchen seemed the ideal place for the writing table, which could also serve as a buffet table when she had guests; she liked the idea of furniture serving dual purposes. *I'm glad I bought a writing desk with drawers so I can easily tuck away papers and my laptop when I want to use it as a buffet.*

Her hair fell in her face as she leaned over the box to open it. She stood and went to the bathroom to brush her long dark brown hair into a ponytail. *Maybe it's time to cut my hair shorter?* She stood for a moment, looking into her daddy's mirror on the medicine cabinet and trying to imagine what she would look like with a shoulder-length bob or even a pixie cut. *A shorter style would need to be constantly trimmed; that's too much maintenance!* She laughed and let the idea go—she knew she was procrastinating.

Returning to the dining room, she carefully lifted each wooden piece out of the box and set it next to her on the floor. The instructions were a single page of diagrams. *That looks straightforward enough.* She fetched her toolbox and set to work. She had just finished attaching the legs when the sound of the phone shook her out of a pleasant state of focus, and she put down the screwdriver to go answer it. *Wonder why the phone ring seems so jarring when it's a landline?*

"Drellag Caban, may I help you?"

"Hey, Dr. Anderson. It's Victoria."

"Hey, Victoria. How are you?"

"Well, thanks. And you? What's up?"

"I'm well too. I'm still settling in here. Everything is..." Bella paused, about to say that things were getting back to normal. But there was no need to worry or distract Victoria by mentioning the meth lab just yet. Bella caught sight of the nearly finished writing desk and smiled. "Everything is coming together. What are you up to?"

"I had a few minutes and just wanted to let you know that everything here is fine. I feel so lucky to be in your home. Thanks for trusting me. Since I didn't know when you might get down the mountain and see a text or email, I decided to call and tell you."

"Glad to hear it, Victoria, and I'm the one who should be thanking you. It's a great comfort to me to have you there in my home. How's your thesis coming along?"

"Working on it ten to twelve hours a day, but it will be worth it."

"I'm sure you'll do a fine job. Remember, if Dr. Carlsen gives you any grief, just call."

Victoria laughed. "Will do. Thanks. I'll let you go, just wanted to say, 'hey.'"

"Thanks. Keep your focus. You'll be finished with that degree soon."

"Sure will. Take care. Bye."

"You too. Bye." Bella slowly replaced the handset. *I don't think I've appreciated the instant communication of a text or email. At least for now, I'm grateful for the break from them.*

Bella stepped out the kitchen door to the smell of smoke as it wafted up from the valley. She could imagine people were starting their day by lighting fires in their cabins to take the edge off the morning chill. She carried the empty shipping boxes out to the shed, making a mental note that all of it could go in the big recycling bin at the elementary school on her next trip down the mountain. She liked supporting the students' project as a way of contributing to the community while recycling at the same time. She knew the traditional way of disposing of trash in the mountains—burning it—was not good for the environment. Deeply rooted mountain folks cared about preserving their land and were doing much less burning than when she was a child.

She left the shed unlocked, deciding to lock up after the detective left. It was time to reclaim her land and the feeling of safety she had always enjoyed as a part of being here. Her leg brushed against her all-terrain vehicle as she turned to walk back to the cabin. *It's time to get back on my ATV and enjoy riding on my eighty acres before hunting season starts.*

Bella walked into the dining room and set the writing table, admiring its simplicity. She decided she wouldn't miss the many trappings of academia in her home office in North Carolina. She found a Mason jar under the kitchen sink to use for her pens and pencils. She stacked the note pads she used to jot her writing ideas, and now had a permanent place for her charging cords. *Just not having to pull the charging cords out of the dresser every time I need to charge the phone or laptop will be a relief.* She hoped she would spend many hours here writing.

She glanced out the window and saw the sun coming over the mountains. It was almost ten and this would become the norm now. *Daylight starts at eight o'clock, sun decides to join it at ten. I wonder who came up with that saying?* It was time to open the windows and French doors to the porch to get some fresh air flowing through the cabin. There wouldn't be too many more days she could open them without feeling the need to light the gas fireplace.

Once everything was opened, Bella returned to sit at her writing table. In the quiet of the cabin, her thoughts drifted to the last two weeks. As had happened many times since Matt's death, tragic events or trauma triggered a return of grief, which she knew she just had to work through.

It was becoming easier to sort out all the intrusive activity that had arisen from her first week back. Joshua had called every few days to ask if she needed anything, but Bella had kept the calls cordial and short. Last Saturday morning she drove down to the valley. It had been good to stop in the Valley Store to get groceries, see Joe and Joshua, and catch up with them before she spent a couple of hours at the library. Both men seemed to sidestep the fact Bella had not been to the store in almost two weeks.

Dona, the librarian, was disappointed when Bella only checked out two of the books on her recommended reading list. Bella was not ready to tell Dona she didn't have time to read. Now that she had a clearer head, she wanted to spend her time developing the elements for a novel. She had a good start on a plot from the night after the fire at the meth lab, but she knew the writing she did then was pure adrenaline. Bella believed she was ready for the true work of creating fiction. She wanted to settle in this time—maybe just not at this moment.

Monday Morning in the Valley

The previous day, Joshua had gone to the small, white clapboard Presbyterian church and tried to set aside the memory of his wife's funeral there last month. *I've hardly been able to go to church in the last two years. It felt good to go with Dad.* He often went to the Valley Store on Sunday afternoon to finish stocking for the coming week. He enjoyed the peace and quiet on the one day of the week they were closed. Yesterday, though, he had spent the afternoon with his dad.

After the service, Joe and Joshua had walked out to the cemetery next to the church to visit the graves of their wives. Joe Johnson's wife had been gone almost two decades, but Joshua's loss was a little over a month ago. Both men took flowers to put in the vases on the markers of the women they had loved for so many years.

On this Monday morning, Joshua was at the Valley Store by six o'clock to finish stocking shelves. He did a fast walk through the aisles to see if he had missed anything in his quick perusal on Saturday evening. Satisfied he could do the stock work in less than

15

thirty minutes, he set about his task. He didn't want to dwell on yesterday.

He heard the bell over the front door jingle and knew it would be his dad.

"Good morning, son. Need help?"

"No, Dad, I'm good. Thanks."

With that assurance, Joe climbed the stairs to the loft over the cash registers and took out one of the cash drawers from the safe in their small office area. As he stepped from the bottom stair to the floor, his foot slipped and the cash drawer went flying.

Joshua heard the noise and ran to the front. He saw his dad sitting on the bottom step.

"Dad! Dad, are you okay?"

"Fine. Fine, son. Must have stepped on a banana peel." He hoped his usual good humor would distract Joshua.

"Not funny, Dad. Not funny at all. Let me check you out."

"No need, son. All my parts are moving." He flung his arms in the air, turned his hands, wiggled his fingers, and moved his legs up and down from his sitting position.

Joshua looked at his dad and in a straightforward tone said. "Dad, look at me."

Joe looked into Joshua's eyes.

Joshua had advanced first aid training and he could see that his dad's pupils looked normal. "I'm going to pick up your foot and move your ankle. Ready?"

"Son, is this really necessary?"

"Yes. Yes, it is." Joshua remained calm. "You can let me check you, or I can take you to the emergency room."

"No need for all that folderol. Here, take my foot."

Joshua watched Joe flinch when he moved his right ankle, but his reaction didn't suggest severe pain. "I'm going to call Doc Smith."

"I said I'm fine." Joe used his parental voice, but Joshua could hear the breathiness of pain creeping through as he spoke.

"Good. Let's keep it that way. You stay right there." Joshua went to the phone by the cash registers. Dr. Fred Smith's personal number was highlighted on the paper taped to the register. Joshua dialed.

"Hey, Doc, Joshua here. Dad took a bit of a fall." He described what he knew and told him how he had checked his dad. Joshua finally spoke. "You're a good man, Doc. Thanks."

Joshua turned to his dad. "Doc was already on his way to the hospital. He'll stop here in about five minutes." Joe nodded, but Joshua could see he was not pleased. "Dad." Joshua waited until Joe looked up. "He said if you're being a stubborn ole coot, he'll call 9-1-1 himself."

Both men laughed.

"In the meantime, he told me to put some ice on that ankle. I'll be right back." Joshua ran to the back and got the ice pack they kept in the storeroom freezer. It was normally used to keep food cold when they carried it home, but it would do in an emergency. He put it on his dad's ankle. The wall clock showed six thirty. Joshua was relieved that Doc Fred would be here before their usual opening time of seven thirty. He picked up the cash drawer and put it in the register, grateful he had bought the new drawers with a locking lid—at least he wouldn't have to track down the coins.

Nora's Day Begins

As she fixed breakfast for her children, Nora Oliver-Smith glanced at the clock above the stove and saw it was seven thirty. Her husband, Fred, had left for the hospital an hour before, and she knew her little ones would be waking up soon. She had been lost in thought about the picnic with her father on Sunday. *Wonder why Daddy asked me if I was going to go back to teaching? Maybe he thinks I need more to do? Ha! A physician's wife and two small children...* She stopped herself and leaned against the kitchen counter. She knew her father only wanted the best for her. *I love him for flat-*

tering me about the students needing the joy of music. He did tell me how much he missed hearing me sing and play the piano.

The sound of small footsteps brought her out of her reverie.

"Mommy, Mommy, I'm hungry," pleaded four-year-old Mac. He looked up at her with sleepy eyes, and she scooped him up and hugged him, grateful for the few minutes the two of them had at the start of the day. They stood cuddling for a minute or two, his head nestled into her shoulder. Then she felt the arms of her two-year old daughter, Lilly, hugging her leg. *This is the way to start a day.* She put Mac on his stool at the kitchen counter and kissed his head.

She picked up Lilly and hugged her. She whispered in her ear, "Your daddy said to tell you good morning and he loves you." Lilly just snuggled in tighter.

"Mac, Daddy asked me to be sure and tell you he loves you."

"I know." Mac was holding his head up with his elbow on the counter.

"We're going to eat breakfast, get dressed, and then we're going to go to the park. So, let's eat. I bet I can beat you around the walking path, Mac!"

"No, you can't," he muttered. She could hear the soft giggle.

After putting Lilly in her highchair, she wrote a note to herself: "Call The Corral—Friday night music."

Checking on Joe

Dr. Fred Smith was met at the door of the Valley Store at 6:45 a.m. with a bear hug from Joshua. "Thanks, Doc."

"Don't tell the Medical Association, they frown on house calls." Joshua nodded.

"That's why I like rural medicine. Do what I think is right; their advice heard but not needed." Fred headed towards the chair where Joe was sitting, his foot propped up on the first stair.

"Out chasing girls this morning, Joe?" Fred studied Joe's face.

"Nah, Doc, must've had an encounter with a banana peel."

Joshua gave his dad a rather stern look.

"Give me a minute here, Joshua, and then the three of us will have a chat."

Joshua nodded and walked to the back to give them some privacy. Although he understood that Joe hated having a fuss made over him, Joshua also knew he was right to be concerned about his dad; after all, he was eighty-five.

Five minutes later, Doc Smith called out to him, and Joshua walked to the front. "As I told Joe, I think he's going to be a bit sore around the ankle for a day or two. Unless any swelling starts, I don't think we need an x-ray."

Joshua let out a quiet sigh of relief. "I've been telling Dad he needs a day or two off, but he won't hear of it. What do you think about me taking him home so he can put that foot up and stay off it for a while?"

Fred nodded. "I think keeping it elevated today with ice on it is a pretty good plan. It's important to keep moving, though. Usually easier to do that at home where you have furniture to lean on as you move around." He looked at Joe. "If the ankle is feeling better tomorrow, and there's no swelling, you can decide where you want to be. Fair enough?"

"Fair enough," Joe said.

Fred looked at his watch. "It's almost seven. You open now, right?"

"No. Not 'til seven thirty. I can put up a sign and take dad home."

Showing his determination—what Joshua's mother used to refer to as sheer stubbornness—Joe said, "I can walk from here."

Fred shook his head. "Not a good plan. Look, I'm headed to the hospital to see a couple of patients. It's not out of my way to drop you off a whole block from here at your place."

Joshua nodded. He was always amazed at how Fred, like his dad, had such a quick wit and could lighten a burden without realizing it.

"Thanks, Doc. I appreciate it. Dad, just take that ice pack. Hold on, I'll get another one from the back. I'll check on you later in the morning but call if you need anything."

"I will, son. I will." Joe stood and walked towards the door with Fred.

Joshua ran to the back to grab a fresh ice pack. He gave it to Fred, then watched as they walked to the car. Joshua was relieved to see Joe didn't seem to be limping or favoring the ankle. *Thank God.*

Breakfast at The Corral

The Corral was busy earlier than usual this Monday morning. Carla, the locals' favorite server, was also half-owner of the restaurant with her brother, James. She heard all the gossip but never spread it. She hated that folks were still speculating about the boys who were running drugs from the meth lab. *'Bout time the gossip moved on to something new.*

Two deputies just coming off duty sat down in her back booth. She grabbed the water pitcher and coffee jug and headed towards them. "Morning, boys. Want some coffee or are you hoping to get some sleep today?"

Both deputies shook their heads, held up their coffee mugs, and laughed.

"Coffee is like blood; can't live without it," one of them said.

Carla filled their mugs and nodded to the booth across from the deputies. It was a well-established signal that they should drink their coffee and listen.

"I know Nick is excited about getting an ATV from that new boy down the road, but our daughter is not, do you hear me, is not going to get on it with him!" The woman glared at the man across from her.

"Fine, fine. I agree."

The woman went on. "I heard the ATV was in an accident already. I wouldn't be a bit surprised if Nick caused it. I don't want our girl on a new ATV, much less one that's been wrecked."

The man just nodded his head.

"Do you even care who our daughter hangs around with or not?"

Taking a deep sigh, the man looked at his wife. "Kids will be kids. She's a good girl and she'll be careful. Just trust her. Now, can we just eat in peace?"

The woman gave a harrumph and picked up her coffee.

The deputies had just come from Nick's house with Detective Williams. They made note of the couple, who they knew lived down the road from Nick Brown.

"Need to let Billy know. He might want us to make a stop by their place," the older deputy said quietly.

The younger deputy nodded agreement, then smiled to see Carla headed towards them with their usual breakfast order.

"Have time to stop by the Valley Store before I drop you at home?"

"Sure, sure." At that moment all the young deputy cared about was eating.

Passing Time

Pleased she had put the table together, Bella worked quickly to finish the email she had downloaded on Saturday. She made a mental note to go to the library in the next couple of days to send her responses. None of them were urgent, and her friends knew she had no internet connection at the cabin.

She opened the folder on her computer desktop labeled "Writing" and looked at the notes she had made of all the ATV activity across her property to make sure she had recorded the important information. There were a total of four ATVs that had crisscrossed her property, and three of them wrecked. One young man had died on her land, and one in the later explosion at the meth lab. She could hear Joshua's voice in her head saying, "It's not your fault, Bella." *I know, I know. Doesn't mean I don't feel terrible that it happened here.* Bella had written for hours the night after the explosion as a way of dealing with the danger and tragedy.

Today, however, she hoped reviewing her notes would spur her to write something; she was more determined than ever to see if she could move beyond short stories to a novel... but a short story would be a good start. She made a few notes as she realized she hadn't included the second set of ATVs in her initial writing. *Those two actually caused the damage to my shed. Why did I block the damage from my mind when I wrote about the events earlier?*

Thinking about the damage to her shed, she couldn't imagine what Detective Williams needed to see. She focused on one more read of what she had written three weeks ago, hoping it might refresh her memory if the detective had questions. Nearly thirty minutes later, she finished the review of her notes and the narrative. She stared at the computer screen; she knew she wasn't going to write anymore today. Closing her laptop and moving it aside, she picked up a pencil and a pad of paper.

She knew the easy choice would be to fix the wall destroyed by the ATV, but she decided to do a rough layout of what she might do with the shed if she replaced it. Her initial concern was that the existing concrete slab might be too old to build on if she decided to add a guest room and bath; she could end up having to start from scratch. She started listing the functions she was considering: garage for her Jeep and Outlander ATV, and a guest cottage. *What would be the purpose of a guest cottage?* As she sat drawing lines on the paper to experiment with the shape and size of a replacement for the current shed, she sat up straight in her chair.

Why didn't I think of it before? It's the perfect solution for what to do post retirement. She thought about using the space for a writer who wanted to have a place for a month or two to work on a special piece. She could also hold small writing retreats in Drellag Caban and use the guest cottage for herself. As the sun showed itself over the mountains and the air began to warm up, she walked on to the porch to sit and think. *This could be a way to convince myself to stay up here year-round.* She smiled and let her mind wander—*a writer's retreat!*

Heading up the Mountain

Chad was surprised Billy had not questioned him when he said he would meet him at the Anderson property. *Guess I used my boss voice.* He stood to get his lunch out of the refrigerator in the break room, but his phone rang before he managed to step away from his desk.

"Oliver here."

"Sheriff, Chief Whitehorse is calling."

I wonder what the chief wants? "Put him through."

"Hey, Chief, to what do I owe the honor?"

"How many times do I have to ask you to call me, Tom?" Chief Tom Whitehorse asked without giving him time to answer. "How's that girl of mine doing? Sure does seem to work more than most folks."

"A leader among leaders, Tom. You already know that." Chad said it and meant it.

"See, was that so hard?" Tom Whitehorse chuckled. "I imagine you know I didn't really call to check up on Sylvia. And you'd be right." Already knowing that Chad was a master of waiting to let people talk, he took a breath and continued, "I'd like to talk to you about the powwow in November and was wondering if we could get together in the next day or two for a chat?"

"Always appreciate being part of the planning, Tom. History shows when we try to anticipate problems, we're better prepared. How about lunch tomorrow or Wednesday?"

"Wednesday works just fine. A late lunch at The Corral might give us a bit more quiet than during the rush. One o'clock work for you?"

"One o'clock it is. Thanks for the call, Tom, see you then."

"Thanks, Chad. See you soon."

Chad sat back in his chair, wondering what was behind the call. *When you haven't heard anything in the wind, don't pounce on the wolf.* It was one of his father's favorite sayings to remember not to anticipate the worst when you didn't have any evidence anything was wrong.

He got his lunch and saw it was already twelve thirty. He would eat and try to be on the road to Bella Anderson's place by one. He wanted to take his time on the county road going up to see if there were signs of any new criminal activity—he hoped not.

Lost in Thought

Billy called dispatch and checked out for lunch. *Left before the rooster crowed. Might as well get a bite to eat at home and put my feet up. Going to be a long day by the time I get back from the Anderson place and head over to Nick Brown's house.* He was running through the pieces of the case that started three weeks ago before literally blowing up with the fire at the meth lab. *How long were those kids running meth?* Making a note on the pad at his kitchen table, he needed to recheck the date the boy's grandmother had rented the U-Haul for him to go back to university. *Pretty good bet the cooking in that location was a new spot. But was it the first?*

Billy recalled his talk with the high school principal after they arrested Justin Culverson, the survivor of the first ATV wreck. Amanda had confirmed that the staff had not reported any behavior changes among the high school kids that would indicate widespread drug use. He made a note to check back to see if the staff had any new concerns that might indicate drugs were moving through the valley.

Billy stared at the ceiling as his thoughts started to move from work to his personal life, or the lack of it. He was envious of any man who had a good woman in his life. *I don't know how Ken and Amanda have much time together with their jobs.* He hoped he would meet the right woman someday. *Can't make it happen when I work all the time, though, can I?* He finished eating and put his notepad in his pocket, washed up, and splashed some water on his face to clear his head. He headed out to check the shed at the Anderson place.

As he drove the switchbacks up the mountain, he tried to shake the feeling of loneliness that comes with all work and no play. *Maybe even the sheriff is interested in a woman now that Dr. Anderson is in these hills. Already got a deputy married to a woman with a doctorate. Could happen for the sheriff too.*

Interesting Moments

Bella decided on her favorite easy lunch choice, a peanut butter sandwich. She wished she'd brought her bread machine with her from North Carolina. It would be nice to have the smell of bread baking in the cabin. *Might be easier to just order one and have it here.* She dismissed the thought. *If I'm truly considering being here full-time then there's no sense owning two bread machines.* She took her sandwich and tea and went to sit behind the shed to enjoy the mid-day sun.

Although her wide porch on the east side of her cabin provided a gorgeous view of the trees and mountain ridges in the Great Smoky Mountains National Park, the sun barely hit that side of the house this time of year. *Might as well take advantage of the remaining days of heat.* She sat down on the grass and leaned against the western side of the shed, sipping her iced tea and enjoying her sandwich.

Climbing a Mountain

As he drove up the county road, Chad knew he could be at the Anderson place in less than twenty minutes if he pushed it, but his goal was to do some close observation. He was particularly interested to see if there were more ATV tracks going off into the woods. Before the start of the sharp switchbacks that curved across the hillside like a child's drawing of a squiggly line, Chad stopped his SUV to investigate some fresh tree breakages in the brush. He stood at the edge of the road and shook his head with annoyance when he saw what caused the trail. *Why can't folks just take their old appliances to the recycle center in Round City? Fifteen minutes to get up here and twenty-five minutes to go to town. Why do they have to throw them over the edge of the mountain and make it hard for the county to clean up?*

Satisfied the breakage of shrubs and saplings was caused by the abandonment of the old stove, not more ATV tracks, he returned to his SUV. He made a note to have dispatch notify County Manager Harold Cooper. Putting the SUV in gear, Chad continued his slow climb up the mountain. It was one twenty.

As he reached the crest of the hill, he marveled at the view of the mountains surrounding the cabin. Approaching the grate that crossed over the small creek, he noticed something on the west side of the shed. Slowing down to avoid startling someone who might be up to no good, he saw the figure stand up. He stepped lightly on the brakes as he sat and watched Bella stretch, wipe the grass off her jeans, and then bend down to pick up a glass. He smiled. *Slow down, fella... You need to wrap up this case before you start thinking about asking a gorgeous woman out to dinner.* He took his foot off the brake and continued across the grate.

A Chat with the Sheriff

Bella turned after picking up her glass and saw Chad's SUV heading up her road. She was surprised she hadn't heard him approach. She waved and hurried to set her glass on the steps to the kitchen door. *Wish I had time to brush my teeth. Nothing much worse than peanut butter breath when you're talking to someone. Oh well.*

"Good afternoon, Chad." He had parked near her carport on the grass, the only place to park at the moment. *Hmmm, I might need a parking area if I do a writer's retreat.*

"Good afternoon, Bella, lovely afternoon, isn't it?"

"Between the crispness in the air, the warmth of the sun, and the view of the valley," she pointed off to the northwest, "what more could you ask? Come look. Do you think there's a more beautiful view anywhere?"

Chad was walking right beside her, so when she stopped and turned, she bumped into him. She looked up. "Oops, sorry, I didn't realize you were right there."

His gray eyes, which had attracted her attention the first time she met him, were looking directly into hers.

"My pleasure." He had an impish grin on his face. *Guess I shouldn't tell her I like the ponytail look.*

She stared at him. The phone call Chad had made to someone named Nora, the day he drove Bella back up from the valley after the ATVs crashed, popped into her head. She cleared her throat and stepped back. "I decided to come soak up some vitamin D while I ate my lunch."

"Nice place to do that. The first tinge of color is on the sugar maples. Before long you'll have a painter's palette of color across the valley." His words caused her to look back into his eyes. Measuring five foot eight, she was almost eye to eye with his at his six-foot frame.

"Yes. Yes, it *is* like a painter's palette." She spoke softly, enjoying his analogy.

Chad cleared his throat. "Headed up a bit early to check out the county road on my way."

"I'm happy to see you, but I wasn't aware you were coming with the detective. Is there a problem on the county road?"

"No, I haven't been back up this way since before the fire. With the strong sun today, I wanted to check and see if there were other ATV tracks heading off the road."

"And?"

"No evidence of any." He sounded confident. "I found one old stove thrown over—"

"Oh, I hate that, don't you?"

"Yes, but I'll let Harold know about it and the county will get it cleaned up."

"I wish it was easier for people to have their appliances recycled. That's a cause I could get behind."

"Could you now?" Chad sounded intrigued. "We could use a champion for recycling besides the elementary principal."

"Well, if I decide to live up here year-round, I might just see what I can do," Bella said with conviction. "Thank you for checking the road."

"That's our goal. We want to solve this so you can put it behind you, and we can bring those involved to justice. Speaking of justice, we're closing in on finding the last two ATV drivers. Once we do, you'll be contacted about the damage to your shed, and you can press charges and sue for damages. Do you know a lawyer up here?"

He watched as she stared off into the valley. Bella didn't respond. *I don't want to talk about this. Bad enough someone died on my property.*

When she didn't speak, Chad continued. "We have two in the valley. Of course, there are others in Round City and on over in Maryville or Knoxville."

She turned towards the house. "May I get you something to drink while we wait for Detective Williams?" She walked about six steps and stopped. "I didn't think to ask if you had something specific you wanted to ask me."

"No, nothing specific, but we'll wait on Billy. I'd love a glass of tea."

Bella picked up her glass off the step and walked into the kitchen as Chad held the screen door open. She decided not to push the point. *Gender rules. Guess there's another mountain man that needs to be asked why he has to open the door.* She walked to the sink to wash her hands, then took out three clean glasses, ready to offer something to the detective when he arrived.

In a lighter mood than she felt earlier, she pointed to the chairs at the kitchen table. "Were you able to have the birthday party you postponed because of all this mess?"

Chad was surprised she remembered the phone call. "Yes, my lovely daughter, Nora, is a saint, unlike my ex-wife who never liked the hours my job..." he trailed off. "Sorry, that was inappropriate. I don't usually say things like that." He watched her face for a reaction.

Bella handed him the tea. "No apologies necessary. We're all human." She tried to deflect from his comment. "How old is Nora?"

Relieved, he tried to recoup. He couldn't figure out why he had said such a thing to Bella—or to anyone. His always tried to keep his conflict with Mary just between them; there was no point in dragging innocent bystanders into the fray.

"She's thirty-two. She was teaching music at the high school, but she and her husband, Fred—he's the local doctor here—have two little ones. She's staying home with them for now."

He stopped abruptly. *What in the world am I doing? I don't know when I've ever talked about my family so much to anyone.*

Bella realized this was an awkward moment for him, but before she could salvage the conversation, they heard Detective Williams drive up to the cabin.

"Sounds like a lovely family. Here's Detective Williams. I'm guessing you don't want to keep him waiting."

They headed for the door. She smiled and made a point of holding it for Chad.

Inspecting the Shed

"Afternoon, ma'am. Afternoon, Sheriff."

Chad nodded.

"Afternoon, Detective, may I get you something to drink before you head to the shed?"

"No, ma'am, thanks just the same. I need to do some poking around in your shed, if you don't mind unlocking it."

"It's unlocked." Bella walked towards the door of the shed.

"Have you driven your ATV since the wall was busted?" Billy said.

"Why, no. No, I haven't. It never occurred to me to check and make sure it wasn't damaged." She reached for the door to the shed.

"No problem, Dr. Anderson. We can start it up and run it after I poke around. We walked in here getting the plywood down to close it up, and what I'm looking for could easily be kicked under something."

She looked at him then at Chad. "Sure. I understand." She stood back and let the two men enter.

"How long has it been unlocked?" Chad had to hold back his steely stare.

"I unlocked it this morning." She looked from Billy to Chad.

Chad studied her face. "Okay. It might just be a good idea until we have this all wrapped up to keep it locked unless you're moving back and forth regularly."

She didn't respond. She flipped on the light in the shed and turned around. "I'll leave you gentlemen to it." She walked toward the cabin.

Billy watched her walk away and gave a shrug to Chad. Chad just stood there. Billy knew to move on to the work.

"How sure were the deputies about the kid losing a ring when he hit the wall?"

"They didn't say it was when he hit a wall specifically. Seems he told the kids the ATV got banged up a bit when he had a little accident, and his class ring flew off his finger in the wreck. Apparently, the boy from the private school loaned Nick the money to buy the ring. Nick didn't get the right size and it was too big." Williams was blunt and to the point.

"That's not on the kid who loaned him the money."

"You need more time around teenagers, boss. Nick, according to the kids who spoke to the detectives, said the boy who owns the machine isn't upset about it being wrecked. Steve's upset that Nick thinks with no ring, no money's owed."

Chad just shook his head.

Both men put on gloves, pulled out their high-powered lights, and agreed on a plan for the search by splitting the shed down the middle, north to south. Each man started in a corner of the shed, grateful there was no real clutter. Bella's ATV was on the southwest side of the shed, with a work bench on the northeast side.

"Sure hope this light..." Chad hesitated.

"Find something, boss?"

"No, no. Just a nail that must have fallen off the workbench."

They continued their search.

"Hey, boss, looks like there might be something just to the inside of the tire of the ATV on your side." Being careful not to touch anything, Chad bent down on one knee and aimed his light underneath the tire closest to him, and Williams looked from the opposite side. "I'd say it looks like we found our ring, boss."

"Get your camera and let's get some photos before we move it."

Billy walked to his SUV and grabbed his evidence bag.

Bella was sitting on the steps drinking her tea. "Find something?"

"Making sure we're prepared to photograph anything we do find, ma'am."

She accepted his response and stared off at the maples and oaks on the northeast side of her land. She could envision the current tinge of orange on the leaves of the maple as it fully blossomed into a fiery orange red.

Reentering the shed, Billy said, "Boss, Dr. Anderson is one interesting woman."

"Yes, Billy, I think you've already made that observation. Something up?"

"Nah, just not used to folks being so curious. I don't mean she's trying to butt in where she doesn't belong—plenty of folks do that. Just seems she wants to know the answer to things."

"Guess that's why she has a doctorate." Chad leaned over the ATV. "Now, let's get this ring out, and let the good lady get on with her day."

Billy just looked at Chad. *Are you interested in her or aren't you?* Billy wondered why he was suddenly so focused on the sheriff's personal life. Sure, the two men got along well together, but they weren't exactly personal friends.

It turned out to be a challenge to get his camera under the Outlander at a good angle to see what he was shooting, but with Chad's light on it, and the fact it was sitting with the ring side up, they managed to get enough for proof of location.

Billy then went to Chad's side and used his phone as well as his camera to get pictures from another angle. Chad had carefully placed the yardstick, so they had measurements from both sides. Billy added his metric tape so they also had that measurement. Then he handed Chad a small stick, allowing him to reach the machine and lift out the ring. He dropped it in the evidence bag that Billy held open. After labeling it with the date, time, and location, both men took off their gloves and Billy turned the bag over in his hand.

"Look at this, boss. How convenient for us that Nick Brown had his initials engraved inside the ring. NB!"

"Good thing *only* if he was the only junior last year at the high school who bought a ring that size and has the initials NB"

"True that, boss. True that."

Billy put the evidence in his case. "I told Dr. Anderson I'd start up her ATV and make sure it's running. I'll go ask her for the key."

Chad nodded and opened the two doors on the shed used to get the Outlander in and out. He saw Bella walking back to the shed with Billy and handing him the key. *Guess I'm a little surprised she didn't insist on starting it herself.*

"Thanks, Detective, I appreciate knowing you're finished here. I fully expect the Outlander to start, just not sure why I haven't been out to try it."

Chad stepped over beside her. "The front of the Sportsman didn't push far enough through the wall to move your Outlander, so I think it should be fine."

Billy hopped on the Outlander, started it up, and put it in gear to back up.

Bella watched. "Are all your employees so helpful?"

Chad responded lightly, "Part of the job description, ma'am."

"Good to know." She smiled. "Good to know."

Billy pulled into the shed and turned off the engine. "Well, ma'am, pretty sure this machine will continue to be faster than a frog catching a June bug." He handed her the key.

Bella laughed. "It can move out, but not much flat land up here to be *that* fast!"

The two men nodded in agreement.

"Thanks for letting us drop in on short notice," Billy said as he closed the double doors.

Chad and Bella were already standing outside the shed. Billy walked out the single door, shut it, and asked Bella if she wanted to lock it.

"I'll get it later. Need to do a few things out here yet this afternoon."

"Fine, ma'am. Just remember to lock it until we have this case wrapped up."

Why do they keep warning me to keep it locked?

"Sheriff, may I have a minute more of your time?"

Billy walked to his SUV. "Afternoon, ma'am. Catch you at the station, Sheriff."

What's Next?

"Sure, what's up, Bella?"

She noticed he didn't say anything about the fact that she addressed him as sheriff, instead of Chad. *Wonder if he even noticed?*

"Want to finish that glass of tea?"

"Sure, I can get it." He walked towards the screen door. He opened the door and walked in ahead of her.

Well, well. Was that because he expected me to stay out here? Or was he making a point? She shook her head, knowing she would drive herself crazy if she continued making something of gender roles. *You established the ground rules, and he isn't stupid.* She followed him into the kitchen.

"Please have a seat, if you have a minute."

Chad pulled out the kitchen chair and sat. "What's on your mind, Bella?"

She sat down opposite him, took her time setting her glass on the table, and looked at him. "Any idea when I'm going to get my life back?"

"Get it back." He echoed her words but said it more as a statement than a question. "It will never be back, Bella. Back implies it will be the same as it was before. It won't."

She looked at him. "I'm guessing you're not giving the English professor a vocabulary lesson, are you?" There was sadness in her voice.

"No. No, I'm not." He let it hang in the air. "Look, Bella, I don't know the pain of losing a spouse through death, like you and Joshua, but I went through a pretty ugly divorce about fourteen years ago." She sat quietly, surprised he was continuing to reveal so much about himself after his earlier awkwardness. "That's a form of loss in and of itself. Loss of what you thought your life was, who you thought your spouse was, loss of what you thought you had together, and loss of what would never be. Not saying it's the same kind of grief you know because, well, I don't know. What I do know is the kind of loss you've had, and the kind I've had, are not the same as the loss that comes through being victimized." He let it hang in the air.

"I suppose not." She sat quietly. "I hadn't thought about it in terms of needing to grieve. I'll think about that." They looked at each other.

Chad spoke first. "We think we're close to wrapping up this part of the crime, and I promise you that as soon as we do, you'll be the first to know about it. Outside my station at least."

She nodded. "Am I understanding things correctly if I assume there is more to this crime than the ATV wrecks here?"

He nodded. "*The Tuesday Tattler* will be all abuzz tomorrow with the weekly news. Part of that news will include that the fire was definitely a meth lab. What they don't have is the connection to the ATV activity."

"Just a minute, Chad." Bella walked over to get *The Tuesday Tattler* she had picked up at the Valley Store on Saturday. She put the paper in front of Chad. "It was in last Tuesday's edition."

"What's this?" He read the headline and then looked up at the masthead. Extra Edition was written in small print, and he ran his finger under it. It was published on Friday. "Does it mention the ATVs or location of the fire?" His face was focused as he skimmed the article.

"No. I read the article to see if it mentioned my property—it doesn't. I didn't see that it was an 'extra edition.' I didn't even know papers published 'extras' anymore."

Chad looked up. "Well, at least they don't have the ATV information or location. We didn't reveal the specific location of the fire to them, although it wouldn't be hard to find if someone sends up a UAV."

"What's a UAV?"

"Unmanned aerial vehicle. What most folks call a drone."

She nodded. She knew she would do some research to learn more about these UAVs and how people used them. Suddenly, she felt like someone was looking right through her. She looked up to find Chad waiting expectantly. She shook her head slightly and said, "Sorry, my mind can go wandering on questions of curiosity, and I zone out."

"Zone out?"

"Ahhh, another man who doesn't spend much time around teenagers and young adults. To 'zone out' suggests your mind is off somewhere else..."

He interrupted her. "Oh, like we used to say tuned out?"

She started to laugh so hard that tears ran down her face.

"Glad I could be your amusement." The hard look on his face relaxed, and there was a hint of humor in his voice.

"Sorry, it's just that Joshua used the same phrase the other day."

Chad knew the laughter might be at his expense, but it also carried some relief of tension that can come with the trauma of being victimized. He was trying to ignore his reaction to being compared to Joshua.

"Just so you know, it's true. I don't have much time around what might be considered normal teenagers. Most of the ones I encounter have moved well beyond being normal when they end up on my radar."

Bella became more somber. "Yes. Yes, I suppose they are..." trailing off, she recovered quickly, "but no one is beyond saving. Right?"

"Another project you'd be willing to take on if you decide to stay full time?"

She looked at him quizzically. "What?"

"Well, you said you could get into promoting recycling in the area. I thought maybe recycling might extend to helping these kids reverse course. After all, you have experience with the teenage and young adult mind."

She just sat there shaking her head. "Sheriff Chad Oliver, you have a clever way of turning an off-hand remark into work."

"Suppose I do. I need to head back down the mountain." He stood.

"Oh, I'm so sorry. I certainly didn't mean to take so much of your time."

"Here to serve and pleased to be of help. That's why I took this job." His tone was sincere. "But, just as I've heard said that people who teach 'stomp out ignorance,' I have to go stomp out crime."

"Good. Then I'll get to work on deciding what my normal life here on the mountain is going to be."

"Maybe you'll even decide to come off this mountain on occasion and see what happens in the valley. With some luck, I may persuade that daughter of mine to start Friday night music at The Corral again."

"Oh, that would be awesome. Does she play bluegrass?"

"Absolutely!" His pride in his daughter was evident.

"Then please let me know if she starts up again. For that, I would come off the mountain on a Friday night."

"Good." He smiled with a hint of approval, and maybe even a bit more interest than she realized. "That would be good. Stay safe, Bella. I'll be back in touch."

He walked out the door, held it open for her to walk out, but she just stood in the doorway.

"Be safe down that mountain, ya hear?" Her drawl was full blown.

He smiled as he walked away. *She really is from these mountains. That's good—really good.*

4

Comes in Many Forms

Joshua checked the stair to see what had caused Joe to slip. A smooth, shallow depression was hollowed out on the bottom step. *I guess that's what happens when people have been stepping on a piece of wood for fifty-plus years.* He became more somber. *It could have caused Dad more serious injuries.* He made a note to call Arthur Gillett, the local carpenter, to check all the treads and provide a quote for replacing the dangerous ones. In the meantime, he would make sure he brought the cash drawer down before his dad arrived each morning.

He was surprised at how much business there had been for a Monday. *Or does it just seem that way with Monday deliveries and dad being home? I don't remember last year's leaf-lookers giving us so much business this early in the season. Helped having Doug here for a few hours.* The clock showed three o'clock.

Harold, the county manager, walked in. "Hey, Harold, good to see a friend. It's been a few weeks."

"Yeah, I think we've both been busy. Your response to my text for a get-together sure was vague. What's going on?" Harold looked around. "Hey, where's Joe? In the back?"

"Dad fell this morning."

"No! Is he okay? Where is he? What can I do?"

"Harold, slow down. I was able to get hold of Doc Fred and he stopped by. Doesn't appear he has any broken bones and apparently there's no danger of a concussion. Dad agreed to go home and put his foot up. I've talked to him a couple of times." Joshua looked at his watch. "Last time was about one thirty and he sounded fine."

"Okay, why are you here all alone?"

"Doug was in for a few hours, and Melody will be here at three thirty. I'm good."

"Well, least I can do is stop by and check on Joe for you."

"Thanks, Harold, appreciate it."

"Now, about the vagueness of that text?" Harold pushed.

Joshua was generally comfortable with silence and almost always contemplative, but he spoke quickly. "Truth is, I've been helping Bella Anderson—"

Harold interrupted. "The mysterious woman who is *of* these hills, but not *from* these hills?"

Joshua laughed. "She was raised in North Carolina, but trust me, my friend, she's *of* these hills."

"So, tell me more."

The bell above the door jingled as three customers walked in.

"Afternoon, folks," Joshua said politely, "thanks for shopping with us."

He turned back to Harold. "Look, it's been a couple of weeks since you and I had supper and agreed to get together again to discuss your concerns about the goings-on in the valley. Give me a day or two to make sure Dad's okay, then we'll sit on my porch and catch up."

"Fair enough." Harold looked at him with raised eyebrows. "Fair enough. I'll just grab the bottles of tea I promised I'd bring to the office. Then I'll check on Joe and let you know if I have any concerns. Otherwise, I'll check in with you on Thursday and see when we can chat. Deal?"

"Deal."

Pleased the customers seemed to be shopping for more than an item or two, Joshua's thoughts drifted to Bella. *She seemed in good spirits on Saturday, but I still don't understand why she's avoided us the last two weeks. Dad's comment about her needing some breathing room, makes sense, but. . .*

"Joshua," Harold said, "I have county business to conduct. Do you want my money or don't you?"

Joshua scanned the four bottles of iced tea. "Don't know where my mind goes sometimes, Harold."

"Well, I might!" Harold said playfully. "We'll sort it out over a beer. Talk to you on Thursday, if not before." Harold slapped Joshua on the shoulder as he walked out the door.

Joshua stared at Harold. *What did he mean by that?* He shrugged and was about to pick up the phone to call Arthur Gillett when Melody, his high school worker, walked through the door. *Arthur might not even be in range of a tower. I'll call him later.*

"Hey, Mr. Joshua."

"Hey, Melody." He was deep in his thoughts and answered on autopilot. *I'm worried about Dad, trying to figure out Bella, and already needing to stock some shelves.*

Back at the Sheriff's Office

Detective Williams pulled into the back parking lot at the sheriff's office, grabbed his evidence bag, and headed for the lab. Although he knew it was unlikely, he wanted to see if there were any usable prints on the ring. Even if that didn't pan out, he might be able to swab for DNA.

Wonder how long the boss stayed up on the mountain with Dr. Anderson? Foolish man if he doesn't show some interest in her. There's not many single women in these parts; well, ones that would interest Chad Oliver anyway.

He swiped his keycard on the back door and did a mock salute to the camera that he knew would get him some teasing from the desk deputy monitoring the video feed.

Elizabeth Alexander looked up from her lab table as he walked in. "Hey, Detective." Looking to see if someone was behind him, she shifted to "Billy" when she saw he was alone.

"Just finished up at the Anderson place." He sounded a bit boastful.

"And?"

"Patience, young lady, patience!" He swung his evidence kit up on the empty lab table. Pulling out the evidence bag, he swung it back and forth from the top of the bag, "Look what we found!"

"We?" She raised her eyebrows. "*We?*"

"Yes, we. The boss was up there too." Billy was a bit too mischievous for Elizabeth to ignore.

"He was?"

Billy nodded but didn't say anything.

"So, where did you find the ring?" She was anxious to hear the details.

"Spotted it next to one of the front tires of Dr. Anderson's ATV. It was a bitch—uh, a bit difficult to get the camera under the Outlander, but I managed to get good pictures." He walked to her table and turned the bag over so she could see. "And look how convenient for us, two initials: N.B."

"Well, well. That *is* convenient, isn't it? So, how do we find out if it was really his, aside from maybe a print from putting it on or DNA?"

"Of course, our best option is that we find both, and if we do, we'll try to get the records from the company that sold the senior class rings..." he stopped. With a quizzical look on his face, he said, "I never understood why you bought your senior class ring when you were a junior."

"I think there are several reasons. It gives the company making the money another year to convince you to buy one, telling you it will be such an 'important marker of your life—'"

He interrupted her. "Seriously, my pappy was pretty mad when I lost mine two months after he bought it."

"See, that's the point. Lots of kids would convince their parents to buy them another one. More sales."

"Okay, I get the profit motive. What's the other reason?"

"Not that I think most kids think about this, but when will you care more about having a senior ring than when you're a senior?"

He didn't say anything.

"Most of the kids in my college put them away by the end of first semester. You know, like a kid's toy. Anyway, boss—"

"Slow down, Alexander, I may be in charge of this lab, but I'm not the boss. We have one boss, Sheriff Chad Oliver."

"Fine. Fine. Will the company give us the records without a search warrant?"

"Always easiest to ask. But if they refuse, and particularly if we have DNA or a fingerprint, we'll just get a warrant for their records. Some places would rather give you the information with as little fanfare as possible to keep more of their records from possibly becoming public. You know, in the interest of helping law enforcement."

"Yeah, right." Elizabeth shook her head. She extended her hand. "Well, give it to me, I have work to do to see if there's anything we can use."

Handing her the ring, Billy went to get a cup of coffee and see if the sheriff was back in the house yet. In the break room, he heard the deputies talking about the Culverson kid.

"Afternoon." Billy was cordial but not interested in a conversation at the moment.

The three deputies looked up from the table where they were sitting.

"Hey, Billy, doing okay?"

"Doing fine, thanks. Y'all?"

All three men nodded as Billy walked towards the coffee pot.

They returned to their conversation. One of the deputies started to speak and then said in a little louder voice, "Hey, Detective."

Billy suspected they wanted to know something about a case. Given their earlier conversation, he assumed it was about Justin Culverson.

"Yeah, what's up?"

"Well, some of us have dealt with ole man Culverson before, and we were just wondering what the likely charges are going to be on his boy? There's some concern it might take his ole man over the edge."

Billy stopped just beyond their table, making it clear he was headed out the door. "Well, boys, guess that's why there's a district attorney, and we're just lowly law enforcement officers on the beat. We'll all have to wait and see what the DA does." He shrugged his shoulders and walked out. He turned the corner towards the sheriff's office and almost ran into Chad.

He was clearly startled. "Hey, boss, just headed your way to see if you were back yet."

"What's the matter? Phone in your section not working?" Chad was half reproving and half joking.

"Well, yeah..." Billy had always been quick at getting himself out of trouble's way except, of course, when he was creating it. "Got Alexander working on the ring. Just wanted to know if you had anything from Dr. Anderson I might need to run down."

"Nope. Not a thing. Aren't you headed up to Nick Brown's place with the deputies?" Chad asked flatly. "About now?"

"Sure thing, boss. On the way. I'll let you know what we find out."

"Counting on it, Detective. Counting on it." Chad continued down the hall. He assumed Billy was curious about why he had stayed behind to talk to Bella. *Aside from the fact that she asked to speak to me, I might be asking myself the same question.* He walked into the break room; the three deputies stood up and started to head out. "Afternoon, boss."

"Afternoon, men. Anything I missed?"

"Same ole stuff. Leaf-lookers having wrecks, petty thieves, and domestic abusers. Other than that, just an ordinary day here in these hills," said the deputy closest to the door. "Catch you later, boss."

They kept walking.

"Go get 'em before they do any more damage," Chad called to their backs. He always found it interesting who would just sit and continue their conversation when he walked in, and who would stand up and leave, as if they were headed out anyway. He filled his coffee mug and returned to his office. *Fascinating creatures, these human folks... not the least of which is Bella Anderson.*

Top on his list was trying to wrap up a couple of loose ends on the boys in the meth case, but he was still trying to make sure the unidentified light was accounted for in the fire at the meth lab. He would need to peruse the reports from the last several nights, particularly from Sector Two to see if there were any further sightings. *In all honesty, I hope not.* Sitting down at his desk, he wrote:

1. Justin Culverson
   a) Where's DA on charges of transporting meth? Any culpability in the wreck where WRH died?
   b) Any evidence of him selling meth? Using?
2. William Rutherford Hansen, III
   a) DEA still have remains or were they released to the family attorney?
   b) Any evidence of meth use by WRH?
3. Meth confiscated
   a) How much from the backpack?
   b) Verify amount from ATVs was eight pounds.
4. Medical reports on meth use in valley? (Nick Brown?) Town? Region?

He sat back in his chair to think. *I just haven't seen any evidence in the valley that we have heavy meth use. Of course, it could be inside people's houses and just not seen in the general public. That's a challenge in these hills—lots of closed doors.*

A Visit from the Sheriff's Office

"Crime lab, Alexander speaking."

"Hey, Elizabeth. Billy there?" She recognized the deputy's voice.

"Yep, just walked back in. Hey, Detective, it's for you."

"Williams here."

"Hey, Billy. Norris here. Tried you in the detective bullpen, but they said you don't come to work anymore."

"Ha ha, Norris. Too much to do in the lab and not enough of us to do it."

Elizabeth rolled her eyes in the small lab where she couldn't help but hear his side of the conversation.

"Yep, I'm ready to roll. I'll meet you at the Browns. Let's just hope they're back from wherever they went today."

Twenty minutes later the deputies pulled up and blocked the driveway of the Brown residence, one of three houses on Dickson Road, a single-lane dirt path leading off of Route 54 through the valley. The front door was open behind the screen door, which generally meant someone was home. Even though most folks didn't lock their doors, they closed them if they weren't home. One of the deputies walked out into the side yard like he was on an afternoon stroll, but his job was to make sure no one bolted from the back door. Billy pulled up on the road facing the opposite direction from the deputies to cover the road in case they had a chase. He and the deputy walked to the door. Billy rang the doorbell.

A man's voice called, "Yeah, what do you want? Nick ain't coming out to play, got it?"

"Mr. Brown," the deputy said quietly through the screen. "It's Deputy Norris and Detective Williams. Need to speak to you and your son, Nick."

They couldn't help but hear the man yell. "Carol, get that lazy no-good brat of yours out of bed and out here right now."

Billy shook his head. *Always the wife's kid when something is wrong. One way or the other, he's your kid, buddy. Got your name leastways.*

They could hear a woman calling for Nick; the sound echoed. Billy assumed she was walking down a hallway. "Nick, get out here right now. Your pappy is not joking around. The sheriff is here."

As he always did, Billy shook his head over how little understanding most people had about the people in the sheriff's office. *There is ONE sheriff. Sheriff Chad Oliver.* He figured out long ago there was no sense trying to explain the difference between the sheriff, deputies, and detectives. Local folks would still call them all "sheriff." Billy nodded to Norris, who stepped off the porch and headed to the end of the house opposite his partner to see if there was a window the kid could get out.

"Mr. Brown, you and the boy need to be out here on the porch in two minutes, or we'll need to come in and get him." Billy's voice was strong and clear.

"Be my guest. The no-good, lazy piece of trash. He may have my name but he sure as hell ain't got my blood. Carol, get him now or the sheriff will. Which you want?"

Billy already knew Nick was eighteen, so they didn't really need the parents, but it was always better to try and get their cooperation, especially when you wanted to enter their home. "Anyone else in the house, Mr. Brown?" Billy couldn't believe the man was still not coming to the door.

"Nah, my little girl done went home from school with her cousin."

"You and Mrs. Brown need to come out into the front yard. Then we're coming in to get Nick."

"Carol, you done screwed it up this time. Let's go. Ain't no sense in you and me getting in trouble over whatever foolishness that boy of yours done got into. Now!"

A short woman with disheveled red hair reached the screen and opened it. Billy saw that her dress and sweater were faded to such an extent he couldn't have guessed their original color, and her sneakers were nearly worn through at the toe. "Come in, Sheriff. Nick ain't goin' to listen to me."

A man wearing torn jeans and a plaid shirt with an obvious cigarette burn on the front followed right behind her. *Mr. Brown, I presume?* Billy's observation was quickly confirmed when the man opened his mouth. "Now get that piece of crap out of my house, Sheriff and, far as I'm concerned, you can keep him."

The detective saw that Carol had tears in her eyes, but she didn't say a word; she just kept walking towards the road. By now the neighbors on the other side of the road were looking out their windows, and a man was standing in the front door with a beer in his hand.

"Which room is he in?" Billy asked as Deputy Norris walked towards him, shaking his head to indicate there were no windows on the end of the house.

"Front room on the corner," Mrs. Brown said. Billy nodded and the other deputy pulled his service weapon and moved closer to the house. Mrs. Brown raised her voice, almost to a scream. "No, please don't shoot him."

Her husband grabbed her arm. "For God's sake, Carol. Let the sheriffs done do their job. You done know'd he's been up to something."

Norris took the lead and started down the hall, his weapon raised. "Nick! Nick Brown, come out—now!" He shook his head and looked over his shoulder to Billy, who had checked the other rooms of the house to make sure they were empty. They were.

Norris reached the door and tried the handle, grateful to see the door opened in from the left side, which meant he could throw it open without having to be in the line of any potential fire. The doorknob didn't turn. "Just need to talk to you, Nick. Need to know who your buddy is… the one giving you a Polaris Sportsman 850. That's a pretty nice machine." Norris shook his head at Billy and tried one more time. "Nick Brown, last warning. Come out or I'm breaking down the door." There was nothing but silence.

Billy called the other deputy to the door of the house and asked him to relay to the Browns they were going to break down Nick's bedroom door. Billy could hear Mr. Brown when the deputy told him, "Fine with me. Haul his butt out of there in handcuffs. Serve him right!"

Mrs. Brown just stood without saying a word. The other deputy moved back across the yard to cover the bedroom window.

Billy moved in close to Deputy Norris. "Think you can take it down?" No sound came from behind the bedroom door, and Billy began to wonder if Nick was even there. It wouldn't be the first time that a teenager had snuck out of the house without a parent knowing about it. Had he somehow been a step ahead of them?

"Yeah, I can get in with one good kick on the upper panel, assuming he doesn't have a gun."

"Betting if he had a gun, we'd already know it. Got you covered, give it what you've got."

Deputy Norris was well-built and one of the more avid weight trainers on the force; he kicked in the lower panel first without much effort. Now, knowing how much force he would need, he braced himself against the back of the hall wall and kicked higher, shattering the door. They stepped inside. Nick was lying on the bed, not moving.

Norris rushed towards the bed and reached for Nick's neck to check for a pulse. Billy saw the yellowish pallor of Nick's skin and feared it was too late. As Billy pulled his radio to call dispatch for an ambulance, Norris turned around and said, "Make it a wagon. He's gone."

Both men knew the stillness of a corpse.

Billy hoped to have enough time to get out to his SUV and call dispatch before the morgue van arrived to alert the Browns. Billy walked out the front door. "We're in the room. You folks might want to have a seat on the porch for a bit."

He nodded to the other deputy to follow them. He could see by the look on Mrs. Brown's face she suspected the worst. *The worst may be more than she expects.*

Getting in his SUV, Billy called dispatch and asked to be put through to the sheriff.

"Oliver here."

"Hey, boss, Williams here. Nick Brown's gone, likely overdose. Had to break the door down. Got the morgue van on the way. I'll call Alexander to work the scene so we can get him on his way and find out what happened."

"Parents know yet?"

"Not yet, wanted you to have it first. Neighbors are standing in the doors and windows across the road, so once activity starts, all hell might break loose."

"Think you need backup?"

"Probably only a grief counselor for his mother. Seems the father must have adopted the boy and clearly had no use for him."

"Never easy, is it, Billy? Never easy. Okay, thanks for the heads-up. Holler if you need anything."

"I know it's my job, but since I have you on the phone, could you send Alexander out? I want to tell the folks before the wagon gets here."

"Done. Thanks." Chad hung up and called Alexander to head out.

Simple Truths

Bella stood in the doorway trying to figure out what she wanted to do. *I have choices. My land is free from the crimes, more or less. I can finally create how I'll live during this extended stay.* The late afternoon sun would be fading soon. She already had her boots on and decided to head out for a short hike. She checked her pocket to make sure she had the key to the kitchen door and shed. She checked the lock on the shed door and decided to walk the tree line on both sides and head down the county road a bit so she could look back at her gate and see if she really wanted to install a fence.

She inhaled the fall air and saw that the sugar maples lower down the mountain were breaking into full color: oranges, yellows, and reds. *How could you not feel joy with such a gift of color?* She resolved that she would work in a hike or a ride on her Outlander every day. *This is, after all, my land.* Hearing the "drink-your-tea," "drink-your-tea" call of the eastern towhees, she decided a cup of tea was a good idea and turned back towards Drellag Caban. At the crest of the road, she realized she could see out across her land from this point when she was driving. She hadn't really considered the difference in height sitting in her Jeep compared to standing here. Even at five foot eight, plus a little extra for her hiking boots, she couldn't quite see the flat of her land.

Once back at Drellag Caban, she decided to check the double doors on the shed to make sure they were secure. *I remember Detective Williams shutting them. Why am I still so jumpy?* At the steps to the cabin, she untied her boots, pulled them off, and set them by the kitchen door. *I'm not sure I've paid attention to how ritualistic I am.*

There had been so many people in the cabin over the last few weeks that she had mopped her floors several times. Determined to work on her compulsive behaviors for cleanliness, she decided she could just sweep up from the dirt she and Chad brought in earlier. She put the kettle on to boil, grabbed the broom, and swept out the kitchen. As she propped open the screen door to sweep the dirt off the steps, she stopped. *How many times did my mother or Grandmother Hazel sweep dirt out this door?* She folded her hands across the top of the broom and stood there, visualizing the two most important women in her life standing in the same spot.

The whistling of the tea kettle snapped her back to the moment. Bella put away the broom, turned off the kettle, and grabbed the wooden box in which she kept her tea bags. *Maybe some green tea this afternoon.* She started to pick up the tea bag and realized she hadn't washed her hands. She stepped over to the sink, washed them, and then put a tea bag and boiling hot water in a mug.

Bella looked out the window. A broad smile spread across her face as she saw four deer running quickly down the other side of the shed, headed into the valley to the northwest. *This is why I'm here.* Without much thought, she decided she would make macaroni and cheese, ham steak, and broccoli for supper.

Her meal decided, she picked up the book by Susan Conley, an author new to her. She was looking forward to the peace and quiet to read *The Foremost Good Fortune,* and walked out to the porch with her tea and stretched out on one of the chaise lounges. Opening the cover, she wondered why Dona had recommended it as a new book. It was published several years ago. *It must be that Dona just found this author and she's new to her.* Bella sat for a minute to look out over the Great Smoky Mountains National Park to the south of her land. The view was breathtaking, with the color beginning to pop on different trees. Chad was right; soon there would be a painter's palette of color. She took in a deep breath and read the first line: "It's late on a cold April night..."

Tough Truths

Billy stepped out of his SUV and headed for the porch where Mr. and Mrs. Brown were sitting. Mr. Brown was holding an empty beer bottle and wearing a scowl on his face. Mrs. Brown sat with downcast eyes and her ragged sweater pulled tightly around her. The second deputy, who had been standing at the bottom of the porch steps, stepped back for the detective. "Mr. and Mrs. Brown, I'm sorry to inform you that upon entry into your son's room, we found him nonresponsive."

"What the hell does that mean?" Mr. Brown snarled. "Speak simple words, she ain't so bright." He nodded to his wife. Detective Williams could see by the tears running down her face that Mrs. Brown understood perfectly. *It's this jerk who should have paid attention in school.* "We have called for a—"

Mr. Brown interrupted him, "Hey, wait! You mean he's going to the hospital? We ain't paying for that. Whatever done caused him to go to the hospital ain't our fault. We ain't paying."

"Mr. and Mrs. Brown, I'm sorry to inform you that your son is deceased. We will be taking his remains to the morgue."

Billy watched as what little color there was in Mrs. Brown's face drained away and the tears began to fall faster. She made no sound but held her arms tightly to her chest. "Mrs. Brown," he said softly, "can we get you something?"

She just shook her head and stared at him.

"Deputy, would you please go inside and get Mr. and Mrs. Brown a glass of water? That all right with you, Mr. Brown?"

"Yeah. Yeah, but hell, I need a beer."

"The deputy can't bring you a beer, but he can bring you water. You'll be able to get whatever you want once we're finished."

"How long'll that be?" Mr. Brown's hands and voice trembled in unison.

"Might take a few hours, maybe longer." Billy knew they would have to search the whole house for drugs.

"I need to talk to each of you alone. Do you have somewhere you can stay tonight?" *He said his daughter was at her cousin's house, so let's see what he owns up to.*

Mr. Brown was getting more and more agitated. "Look here, Sheriff, ain't neither of us done nothing we shouldn't."

Billy's face was impassive as he looked at Mr. Brown. *Maybe other than beat your wife into submission?*

"Just need to ask you a few questions. So, how about you come with me over by my SUV and we'll have a chat and let your missus drink some water. Then she and I can talk, and you can decide if you want to wait out here until we finish inside, or if you have somewhere you want to go."

Mr. Brown knocked over the glass of water the deputy had set on the plastic table in front of him and stomped down the stairs. "Come on, I ain't got all night."

Elizabeth Alexander and the morgue wagon arrived, and Billy walked over to tell them what was going on. "I need Elizabeth to get some evidence and photographs. It may take a while. Then you boys can go get him."

"Used to it, Detective, used to it." The driver of the morgue wagon looked at Billy. "Was this one with the guy we picked up a couple of weeks ago?"

Billy was not pleased with the question. "We're all in these hills, except when we're not."

The morgue tech just looked at him and shook his head. "Whatever you say, boss."

Billy decided to ignore his use of "boss" since this wasn't his technician. "Relax, boys, we'll let you know."

He turned and walked to the SUV to talk to Mr. Brown.

After about ten minutes of listening to Mr. Brown bluster about Nick's shortcomings and how worthless he thought he was, Billy raised his palm. "So, you haven't met any of his friends?"

"No! Hell no. Didn't you hear me tell you he couldn't come out and play?" He let out a big huff. "Just know'd some boy done come to the door. Like before, when I hollered for Nick and they done gone off together."

"Okay, Mr. Brown." Billy saw the neighbor from across the road was now sitting in a lawn chair in his yard and drinking a beer. He had an empty chair beside him with a beer sitting on it. Billy knew as soon as he told this clown he was free to go, he wouldn't go check on his wife. He would walk across the street and drink the beer.

"If we have any more questions, we'll be in touch. Do not to discuss any of this with anyone. I'm sure you don't want to muddy the water while we figure out what happened to your boy."

"Ain't my damn boy. Not now, not ever. Dumb wife just convinced me to adopt him 'cause he was a baby and said he'd never know I wasn't his real pappy. Well, I damn sure know'd it from the time he was three. Always was trouble." He almost growled the last words, and Billy recognized the interview was at an end; there would be no more useful information from Mr. Brown—not that he had provided much in the first place. He also observed that Mr. Brown's hands were starting to shake. *I'd bet my last dollar that's from withdrawal rather than the cold or nerves.* It didn't take long for his suspicions to be confirmed.

"Thanks, Mr. Brown. I'll go up and talk to your wife now. I'll ask you to wait down here."

"If you're done, I'm going over yonder to sit with my buddy across the street. That far enough away for you?"

"That's fine, Mr. Brown. Thanks for your cooperation." Billy tried not to convey the disgust he felt.

As he walked up to the porch, Billy could have sworn Mrs. Brown actually seemed relieved when she saw her husband walk across the street. *Guess when you live with an alcoholic you know what they need in order not to take it out on you.* He shook his head slightly as he pulled up the chair vacated by Mr. Brown and sat down.

Tougher Truths

"Mrs. Brown, I need to ask you some questions." She nodded her head and started rocking herself slightly, even though she was in a straight back chair. "I need to know whatever you can tell me about the boys."

"It was only one boy." Her voice was barely above a whisper. "Stevie."

"Thanks, do you know Stevie's last name?"

"Not really. He wasn't one of us. He done come from them Villages. Y'all know... over the highway."

"Did you ever hear his last name? Do you know what he looks like?" Billy tried to be gentle with her.

"First, I done thought there was two boys, 'cause sometimes my boy said Phillip, or maybe it was Phillips. Then I thought to myself, maybe that boy Stevie's last name is Phillips. I never saw but the one boy, Stevie." She trailed off and the tears fell silently down her cheeks. The detective picked up the glass of water and handed it to her. She took it and sipped. "He was about Nick's size and had brown hair. That's all I really know."

"When was the last time Nick was with Stevie?" Billy proceeded to ask her for as much specificity as she could give about the times they were together, how long, time of day, how Stevie picked Nick up, and if Nick had an ATV.

"Nah, my boy don't have no ATV, but here lately, two weeks maybe... since the accident..." She stopped talking.

"Is that why you took him to Knoxville?"

Her head jerked up. "We ain't never gone to Knoxville. Who said that?"

Billy didn't answer the question. He now assumed the note to excuse Nick from school, because he had a doctor's appointment in Knoxville, was forged. "Where were you this morning around seven?"

"Me and my ole man done took our girl to my sister's house to go to school with her girl and then spend the night. Nick was still sleeping."

Billy made a note that the boy was home when they had come earlier in the day. He would check the actual time of death to see if he was already gone then. "Did you see or talk to Nick at all today?"

She just shook her head.

"Mrs. Brown, we're going to need to search your house for any contraband. Things like drugs or guns. Do you or Mr. Brown own a gun?"

"Only his huntin' rifle. I make him lock that in our bedroom closet so my girl doesn't get hurt with it. There's a latch high up on the door." Billy knew that meant it was likely just an old- fashioned barn door latch with a hook and eye.

"Does it need a key?" She shook her head. "Is there anything else you can tell me?"

She shook her head and continued to hold herself while rocking slightly.

"I'm sorry for your loss, Mrs. Brown, and we will try to be out of your house as soon as we can. Can you go to your sister's home?"

"I s'pose. He ain't gone like it, but he'll go if I can take his beer. Can you get it for me?"

"No, ma'am, but I can let the deputy take you inside to get it yourself. I'm going to ask you not to take anything else at this time. Can you drive?" She nodded. "Then I need you to be the one to drive you and your husband, and I'll need your sister's name, address, and phone number." She gave him the information then stood up and walked inside with the deputy.

As soon as she appeared on the porch with the beer, Mr. Brown returned from across the street. "Woman, what you doin' with my beer?"

"Come on, we're going to our girl." She handed him the six-pack and walked with her purse and keys to the car, getting to the driver's door ahead of him.

"What the hell... heck! Oh well, can't drink while drivin' now, can I?" Mr. Brown winked at Billy.

Billy finished his notes, ignored the man, and headed in to help the two deputies with the search already going on inside the house. One of them said they found what looked like a shaving kit in Nick's room filled with small packets of white powder. Billy suspected the powder was meth, but it would be confirmed at the lab. They had already searched the parents' bedroom, found the rifle locked in the bedroom closet with ammunition in it but no drugs. There was a tiny third bedroom that was clearly the daughter's room. It was painted pink and had a frilly bedspread; piles of dolls and toys confirmed she was likely still in elementary school. The room looked like it had been created by putting a plywood wall through part of Nick's bedroom. It was in stark contrast to Nick's dark room, decorated only with a few posters of heavy metal bands on the wall.

A deputy told the detective they were ready for the morgue techs. Alexander would take pictures and check the body temperature. It was the job of the morgue technicians, on behalf of the coroner, to remove the body while verifying and documenting the location and state of the body at the time of removal. The remains of Nick Brown were moved to a gurney, covered with a sheet, and taken out. The neighbor who was drinking beer with Mr. Brown remained in his lawn chair and was joined by an older teenage boy. Detective Billy Williams knew he would need to talk to them before the night was over.

Several hours later, at almost 10:00 p.m., the team agreed they had everything they could get from the house, and Billy had talked to the family across the street. Mr. Kirk claimed he and his son hadn't noticed a thing they thought was suspicious or unusual at the Browns' house. Ever.

The deputies who overheard the conversation in The Corral had called to tell Billy. He had sent a detective to visit the couple earlier in the day. There was no indication they knew anything about the activities Nick may have been involved in. Seems the girl had a crush on Nick, but had never really dated him. They were just neighbors—like the Kirks. So he didn't think he needed to follow-up unless something else came up. The mother wouldn't have to worry about her daughter riding an ATV with Nick.

Inside the house, the only place they had found drugs was in the shaving kit in Nick's room. There was no attic access and the house sat on a crawl space. Although Billy doubted there were more drugs squirreled away in the crawl space, he sent one of the deputies to check.

After walking the entire perimeter, the deputy returned.

"Detective, there's no way to get into the space. There's a small door, about one foot square, next to the water line coming into the kitchen. I opened it and looked in with my hand light. I could see from corner to corner. Clean as a whistle."

Billy nodded. "Okay, we can always check it later if we get more information. Let's wrap this up."

One of the deputies said, "Sure thing. Meet you at the station."

Billy called Mrs. Brown at her sister's home. "I can wait at the house if you're planning to come back tonight."

"Nah, thanks, sheriff. The ole man's asleep on the sofa and I'll just sleep on the floor. Ain't ready to go back in yet. I need my sister to help make 'rangements. We'll go home in the mornin' after dropping my girl to school, if'n that's okay? My hubby will need to shower and get to work over on the construction in those villages..." she hesitated. "Sheriff, when can I get my boy?"

"Someone will call you when Nick's body can be released. It may not be for a few days, so they'll call you at home. I'll be sure they have your sister's number too. We may have a few more questions for you, but that's all for tonight. Again, I'm sorry for your loss."

"Thanks." She hung up the phone.

The detective turned out the lights and pushed in the button on the door handle to lock it. He stared at the yellow crime scene tape then headed to the sheriff's station. *All that and I still don't know if I can find out who Stevie is. I know the principal of that private high school isn't going to be as cooperative as our Dr. Bennett. Oh well, tomorrow is another day.*

Simpler Times

Bella's afternoon was exactly what she had hoped. After reading for several uninterrupted hours, she stretched and put her book down. It was time to fix supper. *Funny how the meals of my childhood bring me the greatest comfort. Grandmother Hazel loved mac and cheese.* Forty minutes later, she had the mac and cheese made, the broccoli steamed, and, best of all, the ham steak ready. *There's a taste you get with ham steak cooked in an iron skillet that you just can't get any other way.*

As she gathered everything she needed for the meal, she caught sight of the mustard jar. *Mother would have never let me put the jar on the table as is.* She decided this might be something else she now allowed herself: salad dressing and condiments on the table in their original jars. She tried to smile as she thought of this as finally breaking free from the formalities of her childhood. The hard part was she felt the grief when she realized there was no one there to know the difference. *I think I might rather have the comfort of someone I love with me, so I care to put the condiments in nice jars or salad dispensers.* She compromised by putting a spoonful of mustard for her ham on her plate before putting the mustard jar back in the fridge.

Bella decided to put on her sweater and eat on the porch to watch the light drop behind the mountains. She stared out at the mountains as she ate. She had been back in her beloved cabin for three weeks. *Is my life back to normal? I need music.* She realized she hadn't heard any music since arriving and would try to find out what all was going on in the community. She was curious about the music Chad had mentioned. Her meal finished, she watched the sky turn the blue-black color she loved. The waxing moon held the promise of light at night; the full moon would follow in a couple of weeks.

After leaving the freshly washed dishes to dry in the dishrack. Bella quickly closed the windows in the kitchen and bedrooms to ward off the chill that would come earlier each night as autumn crept towards winter. She showered, put on her nightgown, and decided on an early night. She wanted to get up in the morning and put some serious thought into what she was going to do with the shed. If she waited too much longer, she would have to wait until spring if she was going to build something rather than just fix the shed. As it was, she realized it might already be too late in the season to do everything she wanted.

Bella looked at the picture of herself and Matt in the silver frame by her bed. She missed him and wanted to tell him things were finally getting back to normal at the cabin. She had the feeling he knew… somehow. As was her nightly ritual, she tried to recall if she had anything on her Not-So-Good List tonight. She thought about the detective and sheriff coming to search her shed. Even though she believed they had found something, she didn't know what it could have been. Either way, it served as one more reminder of the death and injury on her land. She was relieved when she realized there really was nothing new to put on this list.

A slight smile crossed her lips as she moved to her Good List. This one would be much longer. She had put together her writing table, spent some time reading emails from friends, thought about the possibilities for the shed, read for several hours, took a hike, and visited, yes, *visited* with Chad. She smiled, thinking he might become a more frequent addition to her Good List. She wondered why he had been so talkative about his personal life; regardless of the reason, she was pleased he had felt comfortable enough to share with her. Feeling herself drifting towards sleep, she finished up her Good List knowing she had thought about Matt, Grandmother Hazel, and her mother. *Hmmm… maybe I should put* myself *on my Not-So-Good List since I was critical of Mother's expectation for more formality in meals.* Her last thought before falling asleep was that tomorrow would let her start a new day in Drellag Caban.

Dawn Breaks

Chad woke up early on Tuesday morning and decided to go in later than his usual six-o'clock start to finish reading the report he had been trying to complete about human trafficking. One of the benefits of living in a small valley, off the beaten path, was knowing when there were folks who weren't from here. Most of the prostitution was off the highway exits and in Knoxville. He had no doubt there were women—and men—from the valley who visited or worked in those places. But, so far, they had not brought it into the valley and surrounding hills in a way that was evident. He particularly wanted to see what the report recommended for additional training on human trafficking. He would follow up to remain informed and help his leadership team stay alert. *I used to think we didn't have the drugs being home grown either. Can't assume anything.*

Chad finished up by completing some emails from the day before. He was ready to head out and planned to stop in at the Valley Store to see if he could talk to Joshua for a few minutes. Joshua deserved to know they were finishing up the Culverson case; he had been helpful when Chad needed him.

Chad knew the district attorney finally had what she needed from Justin Culverson. He had confessed, although likely not to everything, but they made a deal on his jail time. He would go to the Bledsoe Complex in Pikeville for assessment and further assignment. *Could be the boy will come out with a skill and a chance to live a decent life.* He sighed. *Well, I can hope.* He took his service weapon out of the gun safe by the back door, put the magazine in it, and stepped out the kitchen door into his boots while strapping on his weapon and opening the garage door. *Can still do it all in one fell swoop.* He drove out of the garage smiling to himself.

Chad arrived at the Valley Store right at seven thirty and was relieved there was no one in the parking lot yet. Joe looked up from the stool he was sitting on behind the register.

"Well, well, our esteemed sheriff. Good morning to you, sir."

"Good morning to you, Joe." Chad looked at him quizzically. "I'm trying to remember if I ever saw you sitting down on the job. Can't recall it."

"Observation is an important skill in a sheriff, and easier to take from you than from someone just being nosy." Joe had a twinkle in his eye. "Had me an encounter with that bottom step yesterday morning. Your son-in-law, the good Dr. Smith, stopped by on his way to the hospital and said I'd be right as rain in a few days... nothing broken and no concussion."

"Didn't know Fred made house calls. Thought the Medical Association would frown on that—"

Joshua walked up and interrupted. "And aren't we lucky they don't even know our little valley exists?" He reached out to shake Chad's hand. "Get you something? Coffee? Don't sell it yet, but I have some in the back that's not too bad."

"Well, maybe you should put in a coffee bar. It shouldn't be competition for The Corral and might be nice for folks who are doing their shopping." Chad returned the handshake. "Had my early morning caffeine limit, though, so no thanks. Wondering if you could give me five minutes, Joshua?"

"Sure," Joshua said amiably, "we can go sit in the back. Dad's good here and he knows how to holler if he gets busy."

Joe nodded his head.

The two men walked to the storeroom. "Seems you're getting more and more products and even more people shopping. Getting any from the Mountain Villages or are you just benefitting from the autumn leaf-lookers?"

"A bit of both, I suspect. I can usually tell by their clothes. The autumn leaf-lookers are more casual in their dress, like vacation clothes. Levis, sweaters, some kind of boots. The newbies dress up more; usually khakis and an open neck shirt on the men, and the women in nice slacks and sweaters, nice jewelry. Jan used to refer to them as prissy. Don't know if that defines them but, either way, we'll drop down to only the locals when the snows start. That's just fine with me. Have a seat."

"Pretty good observations, Joshua." They were sitting at the table in the storeroom and work area of the grocery store. "I just wanted to let you know we're wrapping up the case with the Culverson kid."

"Good to know. Bella's safe now?" Joshua said, trying not to show his concern.

Chad felt himself bristle a bit at the way in which Joshua asked. *Concerned friend? Or is there more in Joshua's question?*

"Saw her yesterday afternoon. There was a piece to the case we had to wrap up and—"

"Yesterday? What could have involved..." Joshua stopped. He realized he was sounding a bit possessive and wasn't quite sure why.

"Just finishing up on some evidence from the shed." Now Chad was intrigued. *Does this woman have a way of casting a spell on single men? I'm not sure, but maybe I'm under that spell.*

He sat up a bit straighter. "Anyway, I just wanted you to know we have one or two more things to wrap up with the second set of ATVs, but we should get that in a few days."

Joshua relaxed and sat back in his chair. "Good to hear." He nodded. "Good to hear."

Chad had a feeling Joshua was a bit uncomfortable with the conversation.

"Just wanted to stop by and tell you I appreciate all your help in this case. It was good you were at Bella's and called me. Thought you deserved to know directly from me it made our jobs easier and helped us catch, and hopefully stop, some pretty bad stuff from coming into our valley."

"Always happy to help, Chad, you know that." Joshua paused for a moment. Both men were comfortable with silence, and Chad waited until Joshua went on. "I've been thinking about starting to attend the county commission meetings. Just wondering if you have any thoughts on that?"

Surprised by the comment, Chad took a moment to think it through. "Well, Joshua, I think it would be good for our valley and good for you. It would give you some perspective on what some of the commissioners are hoping to develop that could affect your store. And, to be honest, it would be good for me to have another community member hear it. It will also help us make sure we have as much input to the growth going on around here."

Joshua nodded his head.

Chad continued. "I think growth is going to be inevitable, but if we don't have a say in how it happens, we could lose more than our land."

"I hear you, Chad, I hear you. Okay, thanks for your thoughts. If I can help by just knowing what's going on and maybe run anything by you I think you should know, I might just do it."

Chad relaxed and decided any questions around Bella were settled. For the moment at least. He stood up and extended his hand. "Good deal, Joshua. Looking forward to your return to being more involved in the community."

They walked to the front. Joshua extended his hand to shake. "Thanks for all you and your officers have done to settle up that mess, Chad. Hope we've seen the last of that kind of thing."

"Me too. For a while anyway. Suspect it's inevitable we'll see more changes with people finding out how special these mountains are. They bring their own brand of trouble, and we have our own right here."

Chad shook Joe's hand before leaving. "Always grateful for the Johnsons in our little valley. See you soon. I'll need some groceries in a few days."

"Look forward to selling you some." Joe winked at him. "Be safe, now."

The door shut behind Chad, and Joe looked at Joshua with a sympathetic look. *I hope you know I'm here for you, son. I know you'll tell me when you want to talk.*

Joshua leaned against the wall next to the stairs going up to his loft office. He happened to look down and remembered he hadn't done anything about getting them repaired. "Dad, as soon as I call Arthur about looking at these steps, I'll catch you up."

Joe nodded his head, knowing Joshua would tell him when he was ready. Joshua had always been that way and Joe knew it wasn't going to change now.

The Sun is Rising

Bella awoke early and ate a quick breakfast before washing up the dishes to leave in the drainer on the counter. After putting on her hiking boots, she made sure the key to Dellag Caban and her phone were safely stowed in a pocket. Since there was no cellular signal on her land, the phone was useless for making calls; it was, however, a perfect lightweight camera for snapping photos of the landscape and anything else that caught her interest. *Hopefully I won't have to worry about documenting any more ATV tracks.* She pushed the thought aside and headed out for a hike.

She liked this time of day in the mountains. There was still a nip of cool air from the night, and the blue-gray color of the sky showing through the mist revealed the first light of day that preceded the sun climbing over the mountain. She stopped at the gate to take in the little creek that ran under the cattle grate: Bella's Creek. She always thought it would serve as a deterrent to trespassers. Now she knew that wasn't true. She felt a moment of gratitude that Arthur Gillett had been able to quickly repair the gate after the ATV damage; if she decided to go ahead, she hoped he could finish the fence before the snows started.

Walking over the cattle grate, she ended up at the crest of the hill to her property and decided to walk down the county road. She saw some leaves had already started to drop with early color, but thanks to her former colleague, Wes, she knew the real color on the trees would emerge in the next few weeks as the amount of sunlight began to dwindle. She had always heard the folklore that the leaves started to turn after the first freeze. *I'm so glad Wes explained that it's a function of the reduced sunlight; the leaves made less chlorophyll in preparation for winter. I need to send him some photos next time I have a computer connection.*

Although she liked the colder weather of fall and winter, Bella was hoping for an Indian summer. She stopped in her tracks. *Indian summer, should I call it that? How did that start?* She decided the next time she saw Sam Nations, the special agent from the Drug Enforcement Agency, she would ask him. She had learned he was part of the native tribe from these hills. She made a mental note to do some research when she was next at the library. In the meantime, she would be careful in her use of the term to mean the warm weather that could come after the first cold snap.

Continuing on her hike, she stepped off the road and walked down a trail she and Matt had used a number of times. She knew the trail ended at an outcropping overlooking the valley below. Sometimes, after a lot of rain, there was even a waterfall that flowed gently over it to the rocks beneath. She allowed herself to be lost in the experience of the rocks, the trees, and the solitude of the forest. She perked up to the chirping and calling of the birds welcoming the morning. She heard the eastern towhee call "drink-your-tea," "drink-your-tea" and felt at home.

Mid-morning: Things to Do

Nora loved her children immensely. She believed the playgroup they joined on Tuesdays and Thursdays was a great learning experience for them, and she could already see they were learning about sharing and getting along with others. *They start to figure out friendships quickly, don't they?* Of course, the playgroup also gave her a little time to herself to get things done.

She had several things to do today, and the first was a stop at The Corral. She had spoken to James, one of the owners, yesterday, and he was excited to hear she wanted to restart the Friday night music fest. The weather was still good enough they could gather on the large grassy area behind the restaurant. Once the weather changed, they would move inside to the community room at the back of the restaurant. It was used for meetings and personal events, like her wedding reception six years before. *Hmmm, Mother was none too pleased about that. Oh well, it was my wedding. Even if she doesn't like this valley, I do.* She refocused on her meeting.

She parked in the side lot and waltzed through the locals' door. Carla was wrapping silverware on the back counter in preparation for the lunch rush.

"Hey, Nora, long time no see. Cup of coffee?"

"I might just take you up on that. I'm here to see your charming brother. He's still the owner, right?" She winked.

"So he tells me," Carla said in her usually blunt, playful way. "Truth is," she looked around, "I don't think he likes it known that *the family* owns it—that would be the two of us." She looked conspiratorially at Nora. "Far be it from me to burst his bubble or dash his ego, though. We both work hard and split the profits, so it makes no-never-mind to me."

Nora smiled at Carla, knowing she loved joking about her brother. *I hope Mac and Lilly have the same ease as they grow up.* Sitting down at the table closest to Carla, Nora saw the fish catch score board behind the bar. She gasped. "Wow, is that right? I can't believe Mr. Walter out-fished Chief Whitehorse."

Carla laughed. "Yep, we'll never hear the end of it from Walter. You know how he loves to talk; now he has a legitimate claim to fame." She shook her head in disbelief.

"Now, Carla, even Mr. Walter deserves one chance to share something worth hearing."

Both women laughed. Everyone knew Walter loved telling tales.

"Fair enough, Nora. You're right. Sure *will* be a nice change." She let the topic drop. "So, my brother tells me you're ready to start singing again on Friday nights."

"Thought we might give it a try before the cold sets in. What do you think?"

"We talked about it. Music has always been good for business, though it's not the only reason to do it," she said. "I told him we should go for it."

"Okay, tell me where to find the elusive James and I'll see what we can do."

Carla pointed towards the kitchen. "He'll be in his office. He said he was expecting you."

Thirty minutes later, Nora walked out humming to herself. She loved all kinds of music, but she really liked singing bluegrass. The Greg Brothers, a local bluegrass band composed of four brothers who played guitar, banjo, fiddle, bass, and, occasionally, the dobro, were always willing to play when Nora could join them to sing.

She knew they would be thrilled to get together again on a Friday night.

"See you soon, Carla. We're going to try this Friday just as a test run."

"Get me some of those posters you make up and I'll see we get them put up around here. Be sure to drop some off at the library..."

"Yes, ma'am. Your wish is my command." She gave a mock bow. Both of them laughed as Nora walked towards the door. "See you soon, Carla. You take care."

"You too, Nora." Carla waved goodbye.

Another Lead on a Nagging Case

Billy had not left the station until almost eleven the previous night. On his way back the next morning, he drove by the Browns' house to see if they had returned. The family car was in the driveway, so he assumed they were home, or at least someone was. He felt an urgent need to find this kid Stevie.

"Morning, Detective. Heard you had a late night?" The desk deputy nodded at him.

"Yep, that's the stuff you can hear when you listen to folks who have nothing else to talk about."

The deputies were accustomed to Billy mouthing off for no particular reason and most took it in good humor.

"Boss in yet?"

"I think he's in his office, want me to check?" The deputy had the phone in his hand.

"No, thanks. I'll check in at the lab then give him a call." He got the message loud and clear yesterday about using the phone. He walked down the hall to the lab and saw Elizabeth was already busy at work.

"Morning, Alexander."

"Morning, Detective, got a minute before you start your day?"

"Sure, what's up?"

"Medical examiner said they're backed up in the lab in Knoxville, so toxicology on Nick Brown could take ninety days..."

"Ninety days! Legislature hasn't heard there's a meth crisis in this country. How about some more help?"

"Finished?" She gave him a look—*don't blame me!* He had taught her to banter, so he couldn't get upset. He nodded at her to continue.

"The ME found some powder under Nick's nails. We didn't search the shaving kit at the house last night once we saw possible drugs. I went through it when I got back, and there was a syringe for meth powder and a pipe for smoking meth crystals."

"Well, that's interesting, but if he took a big enough dose to kill himself with a syringe, he didn't have time to get the syringe back in the kit." Billy was mostly thinking aloud.

"Right! Score one for you. And we didn't find another syringe or a pipe for smoking anywhere else. So, want to know what I think?"

"Sure, always want your opinion. And, who knows, you might even be right." Billy said it playfully, but she knew he meant it as a sign of respect for her work.

"I think someone else was in that room when he died. ME should give us the official time of death this morning. Given when we found the remains and the body temp, he was gone long before we got there."

Nodding his head, Billy didn't say anything to her as he turned and walked over to the lab table. *Was that Stevie kid at the Browns? Mrs. Brown said they took the daughter to her sister's house about the time we went by. Could that kid have been there and them not know it?*

"Good work, Elizabeth. Good work. Anything on the class ring?"

"Working on it. No finger prints, so hoping for some DNA. It must have skidded through the dirt quite a ways."

"Yep, it did. Thanks. Let me know if you get anything else." He turned to walk out the door, but did a U-turn back to the phone.

"Morning, Sheriff, got a couple of minutes? Okay, be there in ten. Thanks." He told Alexander he would see her later, took his coffee mug off the shelf by the door, and headed to the break room.

Finding Stevie

Chad stood up to stretch and decided he might need another cup of coffee this morning after all. Picking up his mug, he walked to the break room. As he approached, he heard Billy talking to someone. "Trust me, when we know something, you'll be the first..." Billy stopped talking to one of the deputies from the previous night as Chad walked through the door. He continued, "... to know after the sheriff."

Both men said, "Morning, boss."

"Morning, good work last night." His coffee mug filled, he nodded to Billy. "Ready, Detective?"

Billy knew it was time to quit gabbing and head to Chad's office. He stepped to the side so Chad could enter first, then followed him in sitting at the round table.

"I read your notes this morning, and it looks like there will be a busy day of trying to track down the other boy."

"Yes, sir. I asked to talk to you because there may be more to this than we thought."

Chad sat quietly and waited for the detective to continue.

"Alexander just told me it looks like Nick Brown might have had help taking an overdose."

Chad was good at keeping his emotions in check., but Billy saw his mouth twitch. Murder in the valley was rare and almost always from domestic abuse. When Chad spoke, his voice was calm but deliberate, and his words direct and authoritative.

"Run that by me one more time, Detective. What is your evidence for murder?"

Billy sat up straighter in his chair and told the sheriff what Alexander had found. He explained her evidence for suggesting there may have been someone else in the room when Nick Brown overdosed.

"I'm headed over to the private school as soon as we finish here to see if I can find out anything about a Steve Phil—"

"Have you found a last name? What's your evidence for someone at the private school being involved?" Chad looked at Billy, and it was clear he expected a definitive answer.

"Well, boss, if you remember, the kids at the high school told us about Nick getting a Polaris Sportsman 850, that fancy ATV ... hey, the Sportsman was Hansen's machine too. Must be the machine of choice for the rich kids. Anyway, the high school kids said Nick was getting it from a boy at the private school. Never can remember the name of it."

"The Mountain Villages Academy. Go on."

"As I put in my report, Mrs. Brown told me the only boy who had been around was someone named Stevie. She did say..." Billy hesitated, feeling pressure he wasn't used to from the sheriff. "She also heard the name Phillip or Phillips. Her take on it was that it might be Stevie's last name since she never saw any other boys. Sheriff, I know it's bad enough the kid got drugs and OD'd, but we may have more to this whole mess. I'm on it."

Chad relaxed his shoulders and looked at his detective. "Billy, there's a reason you're lead detective. You have good observation skills, you're thorough in your crime scene work, and you ferret out information, which no one else does as well. So, what I'm about to tell you is just another step in your training. Understand?"

Billy nodded his head. "Yes, sir."

"We haven't had to spend much time in the Mountain Villages because they have their own security and, for the most part, folks are law-abiding. This is possibly the second boy from there involved in running drugs and, for all we know, using, selling, and cooking meth. Now you're telling me there may be murder involved. This cannot be handled in the same way we deal with mountain folks. Mountain folks know when we show up at their door that we're from the same roots they are. We all have family here for many generations and that counts for something in this part of the country. They can often be surly and belligerent, but they don't usually put roadblocks in our way of getting to the bottom of the situation." Chad's tone was serious. "It worked to send deputies to the home of the first kid, the Hansen boy, who was killed on the Sportsman 850. We knew his name, so we knew where to find him. This is different."

Billy waited until Chad stopped. "Boss, I fully plan to go myself. I'll even put on my new Ralph Lauren sports coat and my LL Bean chinos. You won't have to worry about me embarrassing the department. I'll be discreet. I know I fool around, and God knows in this work it helps me deal with the stuff we see, but I know when to be serious too."

"Wasn't asking for a defense, Billy." Chad realized his own dismay about a murder in the valley had heightened his resolve to find out the truth. He was determined to see that all involved were brought to justice. "I already told you I know how good you are at your job, just needed to speak to the situation we might face. The principal—"

Billy interrupted. "The information I looked up last night says his title is headmaster."

"Fine, the headmaster of this school is not going to be like our own principal. She knows her responsibility as a school principal, but she also knows what she can do to help us. Not likely this *headmaster* will be so cooperative. He has bosses who don't necessarily see things the same as those of us who are public servants. Not saying we don't have our own bureaucracy, but the livelihood of a private school relies on folks being willing to pay for their kids to have what exclusivity they think their money buys. So, tread lightly, but leave no stone unturned, Detective."

"Got it, boss. Got it. I'll be in touch as soon as I know more." Billy knew Chad's use of his title was a sign of dismissal.

The End of a Hike

Bella reached the crest of the hill where her land began. She stopped at the grate and looked towards her cabin which was surrounded by pines, sugar maples, and oaks. *My great-grandfather knew what he was doing when he picked this spot.* She could barely see the top part of the shed because of the angle at which it was set back from the cabin and the rise in the road. She tried to imagine what building a larger structure to replace the shed would look like. She would need a garage for her Jeep and Outlander ATV, and she was still strongly considering a small residential space the size of an efficiency apartment in the city. *I guess in the mountains we would call it a bunk house. I want to think of it as a guest cottage. But I do like the idea of a writer's retreat!* She created a picture in her mind of a small building that wouldn't detract from her cabin and would enhance the setting. She was still deep in thought as she walked up the hill.

At the step up to the kitchen, Bella knocked the dirt off her boots before she unlaced and slipped out of them. She unlocked the door to the kitchen and set her boots just inside. In warmer weather, she would have slipped her socks off and walked inside barefoot, her favorite form of footwear, but the floors were cooler now as autumn took hold. She hung her red down vest on the coat hook behind the door. She decided to leave the door open to bring in more direct light now that the sun was lower in the sky. She was ready to sit at her new desk and do some serious thinking about the fence and the shed. *Might need some Earl Grey tea to help me think.* While the water boiled, she opened the window in her bedroom to get the mountain air flowing through the cabin.

Bella made two columns on her pad of paper. She wanted to keep the ideas separate in her thinking, along with the pros and cons of both the fence and the shed. Her list of pros for building the fence were pretty basic: it would provide a little more security from different kinds of vehicles coming onto her land, and Arthur said he could install it right away. *What are the cons?* After several minutes of thinking, she decided the two cons she could define were cost and changing the view when she drove up to the crest and first saw her land. She drew a line through the cost; she was on solid financial ground. She decided to accept the difference a fence would make to her view as part of the new reality of the changes happening in the world, even here in the mountains. She had already told Arthur she wanted the fence to be as natural to the setting as possible, and he had shown her a picture of a design that would blend in with the trees and wouldn't prevent the wildlife from roaming freely. At the bottom of the fence column, she made a note to call Arthur and tell him to get the fence done as soon as possible. *No time like present I suppose.*

She got up and reached for the phone. "Hi, Arthur, it's Bella Anderson. Have a minute?"

"For you, always have a minute, ma'am."

"Let's do the fence. Just let me know what you need from me; I'm ready when you are."

"I can come out and get final measurements tomorrow, sometime after three. Should be no problem starting on Monday. That suit you?"

"Perfect. I'll see you tomorrow."

Before returning to her writing table, she poured more hot water in her mug and dunked her tea bag into it. *Wonder when I first started saying "I like my tea bag to dance through the water, not steep in it?"* Shrugging her shoulders, she took out the tea bag and grabbed a protein bar.

She looked carefully at the sketches she had done the day before. The most important thing she had to decide was how she would use the space if she did more than repair the shed. If she could decide how to use it, she could talk to Arthur about the best way to get a final design. *In the city, I think I would go to an architect or someone who does design-build like our friends did. I don't know how something as simple as this gets done in the mountains. I'll wait and talk to Arthur.*

She put the drawing down, tore the sheet of paper off her writing pad, and put the two together in a folder. After labelling it "Shed," she set it aside. Bella took a new piece of paper and listed the pros and cons of what she viewed as the potential options of either a garage/storage area or a guest quarter/writer's retreat. She looked at the options and decided she should treat the guest quarters and writer's retreat as separate ideas. *It's pretty unlikely this can be done before spring anyway. I'll have to remember to ask Arthur if the roof on the shed is strong enough to hold snow with just the plywood they used to close up the hole from the wrecked ATV.* She put her pencil down and put the list of pros and cons in the folder. She knew just the act of starting to think about the problem would help more ideas percolate.

After putting the folder aside, Bella lifted the top of her laptop and looked at the virtual folder that held her short story. She decided to put the final polish on it. The writing she did the day after the explosion of the meth lab would be a good start because she could finish it without much more work. *If I'm going to go down the mountain on Thursday, I can send it off and see if it can be published.* Bonnie, her editor at *Stories to be Told,* would be the first to look at it.

Bella looked out the dining room window. The last story she published before retirement had been one of her favorites. *I'm glad "My Grandmother's Hands" was published; it's a nice way to end my career... or start my new life as a writer? If I build the writer's retreat, perhaps I can...* She shook her head to clear her thoughts. She needed to focus on the task at hand and stop letting her mind drift.

Opening the document, she began to reread her text, correcting a few typos as she went and revisiting her ending. *I need to get an inexpensive printer so I can have a hard copy to edit as I read.* The thought of waiting to get one delivered meant she knew she would print this particular story at the library.

She made a note to look online while there and perhaps order a printer. *Hmmm... I guess I could just drive to one of the big box stores off the highway and buy one.* She finally concluded there was no need to make a decision today. *After all, slowing down is why I came to the mountains, isn't it?* She continued to read the story, making edits as she went. She then read it aloud from the computer screen and only made one change as a result. She added a note to Bonnie regarding the draft title—"High on a Mountain: Altitude and Drugs"—and hit save. *I think I'm done. I'll send it when I go to the valley. She'll be straight with me about whether the title is suitable and if there are any flaws.*

The Mountain Villages Academy

The receptionist looked up at the man who had just walked into the office.

"Good afternoon, ma'am. I'm Detective Billy Williams from the sheriff's office..."

She jumped up from her desk as someone else walked in the office. "Right this way, sir." She hurried through a nearby door that read conference room, and Billy followed her without another word. *Guess she didn't want someone else to hear a detective was here.*

"Please have a seat. Our headmaster will be with you in a few minutes. Would you like some coffee?"

"No, thanks, ma'am. I'm fine." *Interesting. She didn't ask me if I have an appointment.*

He pulled out a chair facing the door as he handed her his card. He was hoping the headmaster would be cooperative, but he also knew it was close to dismissal time. If he needed to, he could just wait across the street and talk to the kids as they streamed out after the final bell. He would find out who Stevie was, one way or the other. He knew he had to make sure he talked to a kid who was eighteen or older since he wouldn't have parental permission since that kid wouldn't be a suspect when the age of a high school kid didn't matter. He had read on the school website that one of the senior privileges was getting out thirty minutes before the other classes. *I'm more likely to get an eighteen-year-old out of that group.*

The door to the conference room opened and a man entered. He was of average height, with dark hair and brown eyes. He wore a gray suit, white shirt, and red tie; a lapel pin with the school crest completed the outfit.

"Good afternoon, Detective Williams. Welcome to the Mountain Villages Academy. I'm the headmaster, Anthony Sanders. How may I help you?"

Billy wore an open collar gray shirt with a blue blazer and his new gray chino pants. Even though he knew most folks in the valley were pretty informal, he liked having the chance to dress up for something other than church. He was not surprised at the formality of the headmaster.

Billy stood. "Nice to meet you, Mr. Sanders." He shook his hand and waited on the headmaster to have a seat. The headmaster sat down at the head of the table as Billy had expected. Billy took his time sitting down. He wanted to see if Sanders was going to be uncomfortable with silence. He was.

"I don't believe we've met before. Do you have a son or daughter who might be interested in joining us? I could arrange a tour of the academy if you're interested. I'm sure one of our seniors would be willing to stay late and show you around."

Billy gave him a little more time. *Wish the sheriff could see me now. I'm learning from him the value of just keeping my mouth shut. I should have thought about the possibility of a tour by a student; it might have made this easier.*

"Detective, is there something more serious you're here to discuss?" There it was. An opening.

Billy looked at Mr. Sanders. "I would like to see your school some other time; it looks like a nice place. Unfortunately, there *are* more serious matters I would like to discuss with you."

The headmaster shifted and rolled his shoulders. He had a slight twitch to his left eye.

"I don't have much to go on right now other than a first name. We have a little problem in the valley, and the boy from one of our families said that this boy, Stevie, was a friend of his." He could almost see the headmaster's wheels turning in his brain. "The information we were given is that the young man is a senior." The headmaster looked crestfallen. Billy knew there must be only one boy named Stevie. This was, after all, a pretty small school.

"Detective Williams, it's against our policy to discuss our students without parental permission. While I'm aware you have the right to question a student, I would have to see if we have anyone who meets your description—" the headmaster stopped as Billy interjected.

"Oh, sorry, I should have told you. He's about five foot ten, perhaps up to six feet tall, average build, with dark brown hair." Billy wanted it to sound like he had forgotten to mention these details; he had not.

That clinched it. Sander's eyes betrayed him. "If you'll excuse me for just a moment, I need to check and see how I can help you. Coffee? Water?"

Billy saw glasses and mugs with the school crest on a highly polished cabinet at the back of the room. "Sure, water would be great." *Can't rush off someone you just offered a drink, can you?*

The headmaster took a green glass bottle out of a small fridge set in the cabinet. He poured it into the glass and set it on a coaster in front of the detective. "I'll be back in a few minutes."

Billy sat back and drank the water.

The headmaster used the time to recover his composure and figure out what he was going to do. He told the receptionist not to disturb them and reentered the room five minutes later.

"Detective, Steve Phillips is an eighteen-year-old senior. Based on our school policies and state law, I have to inquire if your investigation potentially involves a crime?"

"Yes."

"I've sent a student to bring him to the office, but I must tell you even though you may ask him questions here, I need to be in the room if he requests it. Otherwise, I can call his parents and they can come." The headmaster tried to mask the nervousness in his voice.

It's pretty clear he doesn't deal with lots of crime here. Billy nodded. He decided to wait until Steve, or Stevie, arrived and assess the situation. Parents did not legally have to be present if a student was eighteen. *Actually, it's over twelve in this state. Guess I don't need to educate this man.*

Billy looked him directly in the eyes. "Thank you for your cooperation. We'll check with Stevie when he arrives to see what his choice is. I should warn you the potential crimes involved may result in arresting him here and now." As he finished speaking, Billy was sure the headmaster's complexion couldn't turn any paler. The phone on the fancy side cabinet rang. The headmaster excused himself and answered it.

"Please send him in."

The secretary opened the door. "Mr. Steve Phillips, sir."

Billy knew that not wearing a uniform meant the boy was not likely to panic, or even be suspicious. "Please come in, Mr. Phillips," the headmaster said.

Billy had never heard a student addressed that way. *Think I prefer the informality of our little school in the valley.*

As the headmaster started to make introductions, Billy stood to shake hands while he moved to position himself between the boy and the door. "Detective Williams, this is Mr. Steve Phillips. Mr. Phillips, this is Detective Williams."

Billy put his hand out, and the boy shook it with practiced ease.

"Mr. Steve Phillips, you're legally an adult in the state of Tennessee, and you have the right to make your own decisions about talking to me. Those decisions are the following: you may have a lawyer present, you may have your headmaster present, or you can talk to me on your own. Your headmaster has agreed to stay. If he does not, he has indicated he'll call your parents to let them know you're being questioned. Do you understand those options?"

Billy watched as Steve weighed up the choices. He was a much more polished eighteen-year-old than Billy normally had the chance to interrogate; there were no flashes of sullenness, anger, or even fear in his face, just simple calculation. *He doesn't exactly appear surprised.*

"Sir, I cannot imagine why you'd need to talk to me, but I'm more than willing to talk to you on my own. I'm sure our headmaster has many things to do, and there is no need to clutter his day with this."

As Stevie turned to Mr. Sanders, Billy could have sworn the headmaster glared at him. "Thank you for your time and the use of your conference room, Mr. Sanders. I'll talk with this fine detective by myself."

The headmaster nodded but seemed to struggle with whether he should really get up and leave. After a few seconds, he stood and offered his hand to Billy and exited the room.

Leaving School

Billy took a recording device out of his pocket and set it on the table. He hit the record button. "This is Detective Billy Williams of the Valley Sheriff's Office. On this date, I'm at a conference room of the Mountain Villages Academy with..." he paused and said, "please state your name and date of birth."

"Steve Andrew Phillips," he said with confidence, then gave his birthdate.

"Steve Andrew Phillips, you have the right..." and Billy repeated the Miranda warning. "Do you understand your rights and responsibilities?"

"Yes, I do."

"As an eighteen-year-old, you are legally an adult in this state. You dismissed the headmaster of your school from being present during this interview, is that correct?"

"I did."

"Do you wish to have an attorney present?"

"As I told you before, I'll talk to you by myself. And you better hurry up because as soon as my mother gets a call telling her you're here, she'll be calling my stepfather. He's a county commissioner, so he isn't going to be happy to find out he wasn't notified." Steve's cocky tone was accompanied by a slow grin.

Billy ignored Steve's comments and what he could choose to perceive as a threat. "Tell me how you know Nick Brown."

"Who?" The boy feigned total ignorance.

"Nick Brown. You were at his house recently over on Dickson Road. Does that jog your memory?" Billy kept his voice flat.

"Oh, that Nick. I thought you meant a boy here in school. I don't know anyone here by that name."

"Yes, that Nick. When did you see him last?"

"He wanted to buy an old ATV I have. Had a little accident with it, so I don't want it anymore."

"When did you have the accident?"

"Hmmm ... I think it was two, maybe three, weeks ago. I took Nick, nice boy, for a ride up in the mountains and we bumped a tree. Scratched the Sportsman up quite a bit. I don't mind a dirty ATV, part of the fun, and, besides, our gardener keeps them washed. But once they're damaged, I get a new one." Billy thought Steve sounded like he was the lead in a school play; his delivery was as slick as grease on a pig.

"Is the damaged Sportsman the only ATV you own or have owned?" Billy asked, keeping his tone and face neutral.

"No, Detective, I've always had two or three ATVs. However, to be specific, I have three Polaris Sportsman 850s. There's my old one, the one that's damaged, and the one I bought to replace it. I like the look of matching ATVs sitting next to each other. You can understand that, I'm sure. As soon as I sell the damaged one, I'll have a nice set up with two fine machines. Also, just to be clear I *had* to buy the replacement, well, my stepfather bought it, because my mother wouldn't want me on a damaged machine. That could be dangerous."

The smugness in his voice was so blatant that Billy wondered if the newcomers on this side of the valley got lessons in speaking like that. "Mother was relieved I wasn't on the one we smashed in the woods. She was upset enough knowing I could have been hurt on the one damaged when we hit a tree." He paused. "Oh, and I don't think Nick is going to buy the damaged Sportsman. Do you know anyone who might be interested?"

Billy wanted to wipe the smirk off his face. He changed subjects to see how Stevie would respond.

"This Nick Brown, the nice boy from the valley, said you bought him his class ring, is that right?"

"*Bought it*? He—"

Billy saw he was on the right path; it was the first flash of authentic emotion Steve had displayed.

Catching himself before he swore, Steve continued, "He must have misspoken. I loaned him the money for it. Kid can't help it that his family is poor and his stepfather is a drunk. We have that in common." He stopped, cleared his throat, and said, "What I meant is, we both have stepfathers."

"Mr. Steve Andrew Phillips, please stand." Billy used a more authoritative voice than he normally did. At first, he thought the boy would refuse but Steve stood.

"Please place your hands behind your back." He pulled his cuffs out. "You're under arrest for suspicion of trespassing and destruction of private property. . ."

Steve just smirked.

"For suspicion of participating in transporting and possible sale of a controlled substance. . ."

The smirk turned to a look of *not-this-one-buddy*, which Billy had seen before.

"And for suspicion of murder in the death of one Nick Brown." Billy was watching him carefully. If he didn't know better, he could swear there was a bit of quiver in the boy's bottom lip.

As Billy stepped beside him to walk him out, the conference room door opened. The headmaster led a man and woman into the room.

"Detective, are you leaving?" he asked, not seeing Steve had his hands behind his back. "Mr. and Mrs. Zimmerman, this is Detective Billy Williams, Detective Williams—" he never finished.

Mr. Zimmerman, also known as Commissioner Zimmerman, said calmly, "What are you doing with our son, Detective?"

"Mr. and Mrs. Zimmerman, with all due respect, your son is an adult in the state of Tennessee, and he is under arrest. He has been read his rights, refused an attorney or any other adult to be present, which is his right. He has provided sufficient information for an arrest. So, if you'll step to the side, we will be leaving now."

Mrs. Zimmerman pulled out a chair, sat down, and looked up at Billy. "Officer ..."

"Detective," Billy said flatly.

"Detective, surely we can work this out? Stevie is a good boy. The headmaster can vouch for that. He's an excellent student and has already been accepted into one of the top colleges in the nation." She sounded just as rehearsed as her son had earlier.

"Ma'am, there is nothing to be worked out here; that is not my job or that of any other law enforcement officer. Our job is to investigate crimes, gather evidence, and make arrests based on that evidence. Any formal charges against your son will be brought by the district attorney. Should Mr. Phillips decide he wants an attorney, and you wish to help him get one, it's your choice and your right to do so. If you'll excuse us, we will be leaving now. If you do not wish to cooperate, I'll find it necessary to call for backup." Pausing deliberately, Billy looked over at the headmaster; he looked as though he might faint. "I'll have no control over how many deputies show up here."

Mr. Zimmerman nodded to his wife and then stepped out of the way. The headmaster was standing in the corner, almost cowering.

"Mom, Pop, give me a little help here," Stevie said. The polished voice was gone, replaced by the whine of a petulant teenager.

I see he has lots of practice getting his way. Billy walked past the county commissioner and couldn't help thinking he was witnessing another stepfather who was not going to help a son in trouble. *Interesting. He never once spoke in his defense or tried to use his position on the county commission to get me to release him.*

The receptionist tried to appear as if she wasn't paying attention, but Billy could see her eyes darting to them as he marched Stevie out of the main office. He was grateful the boy wasn't giving him any grief. Just as they reached the front door of the school, Billy realized it was dismissal time for the seniors, and they were heading out to the parking lot in pairs and groups.

A lagging student saw Steve and called out, "Hey, Stevie, how you doing?" Then the boy saw Steve was handcuffed. He called to him. "Taking a little ride, are you? Don't worry, your old man will take care of it."

The boy started calling out to the other students to look at Steve going for a ride. Those who were not yet in their cars turned to look, but no one said a word. After glancing back, they kept walking.

Billy never stopped moving. Once they reached his SUV, he opened the back passenger door for Steve. He wasn't really worried the boy would hit his head, but he cautioned him to duck and Steve did. Once he was seated, Billy buckled the seatbelt, closed the door, and locked it before walking around to the driver's door. In an ideal world, he probably didn't need to handcuff the boy, but it was protocol once he told him he was under arrest. He admitted to himself he thought it could serve as a deterrent to the other students who saw them. It might also prompt them to talk as the investigation continued. It should be clear to them that they could also find out what it was like to be arrested, regardless of their parents' wealth or connections.

It never occurred to Billy that the students' lack of interest was because Steve was an outcast. He would learn that later.

8

The Day Passes

Joshua was in the back of the Valley Store organizing the things he needed to finish stocking the shelves. He heard the double doors swing open.

"Just came back to say good night, Mr. Joshua." Melody had a big grin on her face.

Looking up from where he was stacking items on his rolling cart, he returned her smile. "Melody, as soon as we can tomorrow, I want to talk with you about the bookkeeping work I mentioned a couple of weeks ago." Her face lit up even more. "Something you could be interested in doing?"

"Sure, Mr. Joshua, sure. I like learning new things, and if I can help you and Mr. Joe, I can do anything you need."

"Good deal," he nodded. "Good deal. See you tomorrow, Melody. Have a nice night."

"You too, Mr. Joshua." He was pretty sure he heard her humming as she turned around and headed out.

There were not many shoppers this late on a Tuesday, so he was able to get the stock work done quickly. Joe was being cooperative about elevating his foot and sitting on a stool to run the cash register. Joshua noticed earlier that his dad didn't seem to favor the ankle when he was walking. *At least he didn't break anything. I just hope he stays as healthy as he is for a long time to come.* As Joshua returned the cart to the back room, he checked the locks on all the doors, stopped at the sink to wash his hands, and headed to the front.

"Dad, it's seven o'clock on the dot. Let's lock this place up, what do you say?"

"I say that's a grand idea. I made some vegetable soup on Sunday. Planned to have some tonight with some of that good bread we've been selling. Want to join me?"

"Soup sounds great. Have you grabbed a loaf yet?" He saw his father shaking his head. "Okay. I locked up the back. I'll grab the bread and pick you up at the front door." He stopped himself and turned around. "First, give me the cash drawer and I'll put it upstairs. I closed up things in the office when I went to stock. It'll just take me a minute to put this away." *I have no doubt Dad would have gone right up those stairs if I hadn't thought of it.*

Joe handed him the drawer. "Fair trade. I counted the drawer against the sales since things were quiet. The drawer is set up for tomorrow and the cash for the safe is on top. I'll grab the bread. Good for me to walk after sitting most of the day."

Joshua didn't argue.

A Thoughtful Dinner

Joshua was quiet as they ate. When they finished, he looked at his dad. "Dad, I think I'm going to start attending the county commission meetings."

"Good idea, son."

"Harold's going to let me know when he's free, and we'll have supper tomorrow or Thursday so he can help me start to understand what I need to do to be prepared. I don't mind listening, but I sure would like to know what's happening. I assume the official agenda is available ahead of time, but I suspect it might be harder to figure out the hidden agendas."

"Back in the old days, you got the agenda by asking for it. Of course, in those days I think you got most of it by listening to the gossip from the people who walked through the store."

They both laughed.

"I suspect there are more rules in government today than when we were a sleepy valley." Joshua sounded wistful. "And we both know the gossip was usually just that, gossip. I, for one, am thankful we're a bigger store and have more customers so we don't get so much of the gossip."

"Unless Walter comes in," Joe chuckled. Most people in the valley, the true locals anyway, knew Walter loved to talk and share whatever he thought he knew, regardless of its actual veracity.

Joshua nodded as he stood up and carried the dishes into the kitchen. Opening his dad's dishwasher, he saw there were actually dishes in it. "These clean or dirty?"

"Dirty. You can start it when you put those dishes in."

Joshua was concerned. He could hear a tiredness in his dad's voice that wasn't there before. *It isn't just weary like after a long day. He sounds tired.* Not washing his dishes by hand, which he usually did, was another sign.

"Hey, Dad, why don't you sleep in tomorrow. Come in late morning. I'll be fine. The stock work is done and deliveries on Monday have us set for the week."

"I'll think about it," Joe said. "I'll think about it."

After loading the dishwasher and setting it to work, Joshua turned to find the dining table empty. He was surprised to see Joe had moved into the living room and was already in his recliner. "Okay then, I'm headed home. You get some rest. Call if you need anything." He stopped at the door and looked at his dad. "Hey, Dad, I know I don't say it very often, but I hope you know I love you."

"Never a doubt, son. Never a doubt. Maybe we could both get better about saying it. I love you too." The timber of his voice was warm and enveloped Joshua.

"See you tomorrow, Dad."

Walking out to his Tahoe, the new moon was creeping above the mountain against the blue-black sky. *I wonder if Bella is watching the moon over the mountain. She commented once before about the difference in seeing the moon here and at her place. Maybe I should invite her over for supper soon.*

Every Case Has Its Quirks

The clock on his computer showed six thirty. Chad was wrapping up a call with Special Agent Sam Nations from the Drug Enforcement Administration, better known as the DEA. They were talking about UAVs. Chad glanced at his page of notes, which was peppered with assorted acronyms. *It's like a bowl of alphabet soup around here at the moment.*

Sam had indicated the DEA was not interested in putting up a UAV over the meth lab site. Chad suspected it was because of Special Agent in Charge McMullen; Chad knew there was no arguing with the SAC. Chad asked Sam a simple question, hoping to convey he thought there was more Sam wasn't saying. "Sam, any explanation for why the official language is UAV, and most folks call them drones?"

"Just one of the mysteries of life, my friend. One of the mysteries of life. Somehow I have the feeling you'll figure it out and educate me." Sam sighed through the phone, pretending disinterest.

Chad smiled at the double statement, a reassurance about Sam. He was concerned earlier that Sam was getting too far from his roots here in the valley. The unspoken message from Sam was that he was on the side of Chad, not McMullen.

Chad saw a message from Billy pop up on his computer screen. "Arrested Mr. Steve Phillips, booking complete. Got a minute?"

"Sam, thanks for this discussion about UAVs and the update on the Hansen boy's remains. Fast work for a toxicology report. Did I understand you correctly that the lab verified the weight of the methamphetamine in the backpack was thirty-two pounds, but the ME in Knoxville didn't see any signs of drug use in Hansen?"

"Yep, you got it. There were no indications of drugs in his system or signs of past use. You'll get the full report as soon as it works its way through the system." Sam knew how much Chad hated bureaucratic hold-ups, especially when they affected his ability to close a case.

"Next year, then?"

Sam laughed. "In good humor this evening, I see. While I have you on the phone, Sheriff, do you have any more intel on who rammed the ATV into the Anderson shed?"

"Are your psychic abilities heightened this evening, Sam?"

"Why?"

"Just had a message on my computer screen from Billy. Arrest and booking of one Mr. Steve Phillips. . ."

"Since when do you guys give perps a title? Mister? How old is this guy?"

"Eighteen. And Williams is clearly trying to make a point. Hard enough sometimes to get him to address me as anything but 'boss' when we're around others. He has his own style, that one. Good thing he's so good at what he does. Somedays it's hard to believe I have such a good resource in this small community."

"So, you cut him slack, eh? That's not like you when it comes to work."

"I'm getting wiser in my old age. If he isn't disrespectful and it helps break the tension, I let him go with his own brand of humor.

He knows when not to use it. Anyway, I'm going to call him in for a chat. Want to hear what he has to share?"

"Wouldn't miss it for the world. Okay with you?"

"Wouldn't have asked if it wasn't. Some things don't change, Sam. Look, I need a coffee refill. I'll give you a chance to do what you need to do, and I'll tell Williams to be in my office in twenty. I'll call you back. That work for you?"

"Yep, didn't I tell you I was on the road while we were talking? I'll be there in twenty myself. Later." Sam hung up.

Chad just shook his head. *I guess when you don't ask, you don't always know where somebody is these days. Mobile phones. Gotta love 'em.* He messaged Billy to be in his office in twenty minutes, then he headed out to splash some water on his face and get some coffee. *I'm not sure how much longer I can keep doing this job for over ten hours a day, sometimes seven days a week.* He couldn't shake the concern he had about UAVs doing something unlawful in the area, perhaps separate from the meth lab. His talk with Sam didn't allay his concerns.

Twenty minutes later, almost to the second, the desk deputy rang Chad. "Sir, Special Agent Nations is here."

"Send him back, thanks." At the same time, there was a knock on his door. *Hmmm... such promptness must mean I still have a reputation for expecting folks to do things right.* He stood and opened the door.

He did a double take. "Detective Williams, dressed for the occasion, I see. Nice look on you. Might interest some woman if you dressed like that more often."

Billy was about to say something when Sam walked up.

"Got a date, Williams?"

"Fine, fine," Billy said. "I'm always thrilled to be the object of derision and ridicule..."

Sam made a low whistle. "Whoa! Since when did someone complimenting your look *and* being interested in your welfare make you the object of derision and whatever else?"

"Since you didn't hear the comment from the boss. Besides that, Nations, I dish out enough sarcasm to know it when I hear it."

All three men laughed.

"Come in, gentlemen. Have a seat. Coffee or water, Sam? I see Billy has his coffee."

"I'm good, thanks."

Shifting directly to the matter at hand, Chad said, "Okay, Detective, update us on the arrest of Steve Phillips."

"You might not be ready for the best part." Billy paused, looking back and forth between both men; each wore an identical neutral expression. "Mr. Steve Phillips, that's how the headmaster addressed him, is the son of... drumroll, please." They remained expressionless. "The son of our own Commissioner Zimmerman."

Chad and Sam continued to show no reaction.

"Well, stepson, actually. Claimed it was a connection he had with Nick Brown, stepfathers." Getting no response from either man, Billy described his visit to the Mountain Villages Academy, his meeting with the headmaster, and his interview with Steve. "Or Stevie, as he's apparently called."

He told them about the reaction and comments of Steve's parents and Steve's polished demeanor until he asked his parents to help him get out of trouble. "And Mr. ... er... Commissioner Zimmerman only asked me what I was doing with their son. When he realized I had Steve handcuffed, he stopped. Come to think of it, his mother only asked what kind of deal we could make."

Chad finally spoke. "So, what is he booked on?"

"Suspicion of trespassing and destruction of private property, suspicion of transporting and possible sale of a controlled substance." Billy was all business now. "The look on his face with both of those suggested he wanted to say, 'fat chance', but when I told him suspicion of murder, I think he blanched a little."

"Slow down," Sam said. "Suspicion of murder? I thought this Stevie kid was just involved in the second set of ATVs on Dr. Anderson's property and destroying her shed. Who is he supposed to have murdered?"

Chad spoke up before Billy could say anything, "I'm assuming you don't yet have any clear-cut evidence of murder? Is that right?"

"Right. I sent some deputies back to the Brown's house to look for a syringe that might have been missed in Nick's room. Mrs. Brown was cooperative but told the deputies before they went to check that her hubby had taken down the broken door and moved the one from his little girl's room and she'd already painted Nick's room pink. She claimed there was nothing unusual in there when she cleaned it. One day seems pretty fast grieving to me."

Sam put up both hands. "Okay, I know I came late to the party, but could I have a quick update so I'm at the same table?"

Billy quickly gave him the details about the events surrounding Nick Brown: finding his class ring at Dr. Anderson's, finding him deceased—likely from an overdose—and finding meth packets in a shaving kit along with a pipe and needle.

"Our very competent forensic tech, Elizabeth Alexander, made a brilliant observation. Based on not finding another syringe in the house at the time, and evidence that the one in the kit hadn't been used, somebody had to have helped him out. Literally right out of this world."

Sam whistled. "Whew, things are moving fast in our little holler in the mountains."

Chad ignored Sam. "Since you didn't find anything in the house—"

"Knew you'd ask, boss. Deputies have been out checking along the edge of the woods outside the family's home and checking the trash barrel out back."

Chad gave Billy a hard stare. "Since you didn't find anything in the house, I assume you didn't just take his mother's word for it. What was your read on her?"

Billy cleared his throat. He knew he had interrupted the sheriff and promptly toned down his response. "Mr. Brown appears to be an alcoholic. Apparently, the little girl is their child together. Mr. Brown made sure we knew Nick was his son in name only. So, with Nick gone, he probably insisted on getting his girl into the bigger room. Mr. Brown definitely jumps when he says jump. I suspect her sister helped her because that room was finished in less than a day, and the girl's things were already in it, according to the deputies. I think Mrs. Brown told us the truth. She'd be terrified we would come back when her husband was home, so I don't think she would risk it."

Chad nodded.

"If there is evidence to connect Steve Phillips, we'll do everything we can to find it. On the trespassing and property damage, he admitted to being in an accident with one of his Polaris Sportsman 850s. He told me his stepfather had bought him the new 850 after the one was wrecked. Right proud he had two new Sportsman ATVs sitting side by side. He was pretty cocky when he told me he didn't think Nick would buy it, and he wanted to know if I knew someone who might want the damaged one. I didn't bother to tell him we did."

Chad looked at Billy.

Billy toned it down. "We picked it up at the Zimmerman home this afternoon. Alexander is on it with a fine-toothed comb."

"Anything else, Detective?"

"No, Sheriff, I think that's it." Billy stood.

"Before you leave... Sam, any questions for Billy?"

Sam just shook his head.

"Nice work, Detective. Keep me in the loop. Now, go home and get some rest."

"Night, boss. Night, Sam." Billy shut the door gently as he left.

"Whew, I guess you can still be tough as nails! Hope he appreciates it when you cut him slack."

"I'm a pretty good read of people, Sam, and when or if I think he can't handle it, we'll be talking about it." Chad's tone made it clear he was finished with that part of the conversation.

"Now. You know my office isn't bugged..." he knew Sam was about to say something important, "as far as we know. Tell me what your evasiveness was about UAVs when we talked earlier."

"Don't miss much, do you?" Sam said with admiration.

"Try not to. In this business, it can cost a life," Chad said, his voice quiet and sincere. He knew Sam was careful about what he could share from the DEA side of things, so he waited.

"First, to answer your question about the use of the terms UAVs and drones. In official circles a drone refers to those used by the military in surveillance and assault situations. The media seems to prefer drone. The FAA seems to prefer UAV. I guess to distinguish them from aircraft which have a pilot. They're interchangeable, so I don't think anyone will get their nose out of joint if you use either one. That said, there is nothing in my area that anyone is sharing. Even in our agency, where people are pretty tight lipped, it's hard to keep everything quiet. I just don't think there is anything in the drug trade or we'd be on it."

"But. . ." Chad let the word hang in the air, a clear indication he expected there was more to the story.

"But... there are rumors. Chad, you know I wouldn't use that word if I could help you out with something more definitive. There are rumors the Immigration Enforcement Agency might be doing some sniffing around in the woods. The IEA uses UAVs to help cover the vast territory they don't have the manpower to survey. Those moving illegal immigrants rarely follow the same path two days in a row."

Chad sat for a moment, processing what he just heard. *My instincts told me not to assume the meth lab was the link to the UAVs. Now I have to figure out how this impacts our community. I'll go back and reread the human trafficking report.*

Chad looked at Sam. "You're a local. Your roots go back far longer than those of us whose ancestors settled here and took your tribe's land. I have every confidence this valley means as much to you as it does to me. Probably more." He took a deep breath. "Sometimes in this work you just have gut instincts, and even if it *is* Immigration, I need to figure out how it affects us locally."

Sam nodded agreement. "I know you do. I can sleep at night knowing my folks, and my tribe, are protected by you and your team. I want to help any way I can. There just isn't anything in my agency that connects to your light. I know a couple of folks in Immigration who might talk to me, but the only way I can hope for that is if I happen to run into them. They're pretty careful too. Know what I mean?"

"I do."

"Best I can do is tell you I'll keep my ears open and my mouth shut. If I learn something that can help you in any way, I'll let you know."

As he thought about the reports on human trafficking, illegal immigrants, and drugs that were moving across the state, Chad couldn't keep the weariness out of his voice. "Thanks, Sam. I appreciate your help."

Sam slapped him on the shoulder as he stood. "Just returning that little slap from a few weeks ago. What do you say I spring you out of this joint and let's get something to eat? My folks aren't expecting me until late, I need to eat, and I need to hear the latest on Dr. Bella Anderson. Come on, my treat."

Chad looked at him, wondering what he meant. *Bella?* "You're on. Meet you at The Corral in fifteen minutes?"

"Works for me." Sam was out the door.

Supper at The Corral

Chad saw Sam's SUV on the side of The Corral when he arrived. He parked and headed for the side door. Sam was already sitting in a booth in the far back where no one normally sat unless the restaurant was really busy.

"Hiding from the law, sir?" Chad wasn't usually one to tease.

"I *am* the law, sir. What's your excuse?" Sam threw back at him.

"No excuse for me, no excuse at all," Chad said as he sat down. He smiled as Carla walked up to the table.

"Well, look at this, SA Nations, we get the finest server in all of the valley, Miss Carla. Evening, Carla."

Carla set menus and two glasses of water in front of them and smirked. "And I'm thinking you might consider it a privilege for me to serve the finest sheriff in the valley, and our own special agent?"

"Not sure if he's the finest sheriff, but he *is* the only sheriff in the valley." Sam winked.

"Well said. Well said. Now, what can I get you boys?"

"I'll have whatever lager you have on tap. You, Chad?"

"Carla knows what I'll have." She walked off, nodding her head.

Back with Sam's lager and Chad's iced tea, she set them in front of the men and asked if they needed some time. Both ordered the special.

"Now, Chad Oliver, catch me up on that pretty and highly intelligent woman who has descended upon this great land of ours. Well, that land of ours includes that land of hers, too."

Chad filled him in about the search of Bella's shed and the class ring. He didn't tell him about the conversation he had with Bella nor how much he enjoyed having a normal conversation with a woman, particularly *this* woman. "So, you see, not much. I think she thought she was done with us. Felt bad we had to go back up and bother her. If we can make the trespassing and damage charges stick on this Steve kid, I'll let her know. Then she can talk to an attorney about filing her own charges and trying to get him to pay for repairing or replacing it."

"Sounds like you have it all covered. Any DNA on the ring?"

"Last report I had our tech is still working on it, but we don't really need it. Steve Phillips acknowledged buying the ring for Nick."

"Got it. Now—topic change. I know you're literally old enough to be my father, being as Nora and I went to school together. I also know it's hard to have personal friends in the jobs we have. So, no offense, grandpa—" Chad started to say something, but Sam went on, "Well, you are, you have two really cute grandkids, right? I think you might need a friend to think this through. I know there are times I could use a friend as a sounding board."

"Think what through?"

"Your interest in Dr. Bella Anderson." Sam didn't bat an eye.

"Look, Sam, she's a lovely woman, clearly well educated, and smart as a whip. She was a great help in the crime, uh ... crimes, we're now wrapping up. That's all there is to it."

"Except... if I had put a mirror up to your face, my friend, when you just talked about her, even you might have seen your eyes light up. So, I'm going to leave it at this. There aren't many eligible women in this valley and my advice, free though it is, is that you should invite her out to dinner... oh, and go to town, not here in the valley." Sam intended to leave it at that, but he saw the expression on Chad's face and continued, "Unless, of course, going to town means you don't ever ask her. I'll give you permission to come to The Corral."

"Thanks for your concern, Sam. This is one I have to figure out myself. But I appreciate your advice." He was grateful to see Carla walking up with their food. "Here's our supper, let's eat, and you can fill me in on *your* love life."

"Guess we'll eat in a hurry then, because I have no love life, only a love of the job that consumes me every minute of the hour and every day of the year. One thing working the meth case with you reminded me was that I need to do better about seeing my folks. That's why I happened to be on the way here when you called."

"You should have had dinner with them, not sitting here with me trying to create trouble."

"Nah, they had a dinner planned with the chief. Something to do with the powwow in November. I'll be at the house before they are."

Chad let the remark about the powwow go and focused on eating. Sam insisted on paying the check and convinced Chad he had paid for the last meal they had together.

"Catch you soon, Sam, and thanks." The two men shook hands in the parking lot.

"Back atcha, Sheriff."

Chad called Nora on his way home. He hoped the kids were in bed and she could talk a minute. "Hey, honey, good day?"

"Sure was, Daddy, hope yours was too."

"Good as it gets in my business. Kids okay?"

"Fit as fiddles, and as active too."

"I wanted to talk to you about my question the other day. The one about you returning to teaching. It's none of my business, I just miss—"

"My music, Daddy?"

"Yes."

"Well, relax. I got the message. I was at The Corral today, and I've talked with the Greg Brothers, and we're going to try a bluegrass jam and sing-along out back this Friday night. Think you can make it?"

Chad smiled from ear to ear. "Wouldn't miss it for the world, my special daughter."

"Daddy, I'm your only daughter."

"Doesn't mean you're not special. Tell Fred I send my regards. Love you, honey. Go hug my grandkids for me."

"Done and done. Love you too, Daddy."

Chad was whistling as he backed into his garage. *I love that my daughter's voice can sing the high lonesome voice of bluegrass, or sound like velvet when she sings country. And I've heard it sounding as sweet as a nightingale when she sings a lullaby to my grandkids. I'm one lucky man.*

He was out of his boots and into the kitchen with his service weapon apart and locked in the safe box by the door in a record time of less than three minutes. He showered, put on a pair of boxers, and took a Fat Tire Amber out of the fridge before sitting down in his favorite chair to think in the dark. *Wonder why Sam is pushing me about Bella? Crazy thing is. . . he's right. She does intrigue me.* He stopped his musings and ran through the events of the day. He made a plan for what was left undone. He sat there for several minutes trying to figure out the actual reason Chief Whitehorse wanted to talk to him. It was more curious for the fact the chief was meeting with Sam's parents tonight. He knew he would find out more tomorrow at lunch. He walked into the kitchen to rinse out his beer bottle and put it in the recycling bin, then he headed to bed. He fell asleep wondering if he should invite Bella to the bluegrass jam and sing-along on Friday.

The End of Bella's Day

At the sound of the tea kettle, Bella looked up from reading *The Foremost Good Fortune*. She sat there for a moment trying to figure out how the tea kettle was singing since she still had a half full cup of tea on the table next to her. Suddenly she realized it wasn't the kettle, but the whistle of an osprey flying close by. She looked up to see two of them as they caught a thermal above the mountain and soared up, down, and around above the broad vista provided by her view from the porch. Their call sounded just like her tea kettle. She sighed. *I love this place. My Drellag Caban. I still have to figure out how I'm going to revive the spirit of this land after having such tragic things happen last month. I will though, I promise.* As she watched the birds soaring in patterns of swoops and dips, she hoped whatever the detective and sheriff were looking for in her shed was the end of this tragedy for her.

Even with the light from the lamp on the porch and the warmth of a cotton throw over her legs, the growing darkness and chill in the air indicated it was time to head inside and call it a day. She turned out the lamp, locked the French doors, put her empty mug in the kitchen sink, and headed towards the bathroom. She was just about to flick on the bathroom light when she decided she didn't want to get in the habit of leaving dirty dishes. Leaving them in the rack to drain in the second sink was one thing, but she didn't want to wake up needing to wash dishes from the day before. *This seems a fair compromise with myself.* She chuckled as she washed out the mug. She returned to the bathroom to shower. She towel dried her long hair before climbing into bed.

Thinking about her day, she was pleased there was nothing to put on her Not-So-Good List. With a relieved sigh, she considered what to put on her Good List. She had several things: her memories of Matt while on her hike this morning, ordering the fence and having Arthur tell her he could measure tomorrow to start installing it next week, her time spent on her short story and feeling it was ready to send to Bonnie. She was pleased how methodical she was being in thinking about what she might do with the shed. She listed her conversation with Chad. *Wait a minute, that conversation was yesterday.* She stretched, rolled over, and looked up at the ceiling. *Why am I still thinking about that conversation with Chad?* Just before she fell asleep, she smiled. *I'm one lucky woman.*

9

Carpe Diem

Bella woke up at seven and walked out to her front porch. When she breathed in the morning air, she knew she was on the mountain. The smell of autumn trees, with the mix of moisture in the air, was the precursor to winter's arrival. The scent of smoke was carried upward to her as well, and she could tell folks in the valley were starting to burn wood in their fireplaces and wood-burning stoves to ward off the chill. The blue-black sky of night was fading to an almost greenish blue; the stars were still visible. She knew this color generally meant a sunny day. *Maybe I'll just go to the valley today. I think I'm ready to send my short story and it might do me good to see people.* Walking back into the house, she looked at her get-when-you-go-down-the-mountain list and set it on the table in case she remembered anything else.

After showering, she dressed in her jeans and one of the new plaid shirts she bought before coming up to the mountain. For breakfast, she scrambled an egg and made a piece of toast, covering it with blackberry jam made by the same woman who baked the

French bread for the Valley Store. She ate standing at the counter while checking the cupboards for any needed supplies. Once she finished, she washed up her dishes and left them in the dish drainer. *I wonder why we say "washed up?" Mountain speak?* She smiled and started packing up her computer when she suddenly remembered that Arthur Gillett was coming today to measure the fence. She relaxed. *He said he would be here after three this afternoon. I'll be back in plenty of time.* She double-checked that she had everything including her laptop.

Bella checked the doors and automatically started to put on her hiking boots. She stopped when she realized what she was doing and laughed. She didn't need such heavy boots in the valley. She grabbed her loafers and took her red down vest off the hook. *Hmmmm… I like the red of this vest with the red in the plaid of this shirt. Lucky match.*

As she headed out, she made sure the door was locked and the key safely in her pocket. *After the events of the last month, I don't think I'll ever feel comfortable leaving the door unlocked again when I'm off the property.* It was another reminder of how much things had changed. However, remembering she had lots of cardboard and paper in the shed, she loaded it into the Jeep to drop off at the elementary school recycling bin. She was pleased that the packaging from her table would have the opportunity to get reused and made into something new. *I have to remember that not all change is bad!*

She turned the key in her Jeep, but it didn't start. She sat for a moment. *Patience. This is not the first time this has happened. I just drove it on Saturday, so it should start with no problem.* She counted to ten, turned the key again, and the Jeep started right up. *I need to go to Round City and get it serviced. Maybe Joshua or Chad know a local mechanic?* She liked the idea of getting someone local. She made a mental note to check on the servicing later.

She knew she could be at the library before eleven but saw no use in hurrying. Instead, she enjoyed the ride down the mountain. Along the county road, she looked for the spot where Chad had seen a stove thrown over the hillside but she was on the wrong side to see it. She decided she would look on her way back. With her window down, the smell of smoke was even stronger as she descended the two thousand feet; the cold air trapped the smoke in the valley. *How much of starting a fire is a habit by some folks just because it's autumn?* She reached the paved road and headed for the elementary school to drop off the recycling before visiting the library.

It was almost noon by the time Bella pull into the parking lot at the library. Bella grabbed her laptop bag and saw Dona stacking books.

"Dona, I'm so enjoying the Susan Conley book. Thanks for recommending it. I haven't had much time for reading, but it's a nice way to end the day on my porch."

"Thought you'd like it. What brings you to the valley?"

"I needed to send some emails and get a few things at the Valley Store. And, truth be told, I've only been down once in the last few weeks to get groceries. So, I decided I needed to see some smiling faces... like yours."

"Good enough reason. Good enough. Nothing like friendly folks on a beautiful autumn day, is there?"

As they walked in and Bella headed for her favorite table by the window, Dona said, "There's coffee in the machine in the break room and it's not too bad." She hesitated. "Oh, I think you drink tea, don't you?"

"I do, and thank you for remembering, but I'm fine right now. Thanks anyway."

"Anytime, Bella, anytime." Dona sat down at her desk.

Bella settled in with her laptop and quickly sent the emails she had written over the last few days. She pulled up the short story and reread it once more to make sure she was ready to send it. She was satisfied. She hoped Bonnie would think it was appropriate for *Stories to be Told*, the journal that had published her previous writing. If not, she knew Bonnie would recommend another place if she thought it worthy of publication. In her email, Bella reminded Bonnie to use the landline number and not to rely on her mobile. She retyped the number to be on the safe side, even though she knew she had given it to her before leaving North Carolina. Rereading her email, she attached the story, remembered to send herself a blind copy, and hit send. She sat back as the email disappeared from her screen. *I've actually written something creative since I arrived on the mountain and sent it to my editor. Okay, it's not a novel, but it* is *something.*

Leaning forward, she scanned the emails she could delete, downloaded the ones she could read later, and took time to read the ones that needed an answer. All of her payments for her credit cards and her utilities in her North Carolina home and the cabin were on autopay, so she didn't have to worry about not being able to get down the mountain to pay bills. The emails confirming her payments and her bank statement were in the emails she downloaded. She could balance her checkbook when she got around to it. *I know I'm fortunate not to have to worry about money. My university pension, the money Matt and I worked hard to save, and my inheritance from my parents is something I'll never take for granted.* She looked out the window across the valley and could see The Corral in the distance. *I went to sleep thinking I was lucky. Time to celebrate my good fortune. I'll have to figure out how to do that.* Looking out the window at the changing leaves reminded her she wanted to look up Indian summer to learn why people used it. She put the question into a search engine and switched into research mode.

The most consistent explanation she could find online was the use by Europeans in the United States in the late 1700s to describe the warmth in September through November in temperate climates. She learned some regions didn't use the term unless the warmth came after the first frost; she knew that to be true in the mountains. One article she read suggested simplifying things and not making the time tied to a term that could be offensive, even if unintentional. They recommended calling it second summer. *I like that idea. Second summer. I still don't know how native tribes feel about it.* She decided she would try to find out from someone in the local tribe. She decided that was enough research for the day; she was ready to get her groceries and head back up the mountain. After finishing up the few emails that required attention and sending her pictures of the autumns leaves to a few friends, she packed up her things and decided to stop at the post office to get her mail. It was already 1:30 and she was hungry. She pulled a protein bar out of her bag to eat in the car.

"Dona, I'm heading out, but wanted to thank you again for the book recommendations. I'll have those back before you have to come looking for me." She smiled.

"I'm not worried about it. I know where to find you," Dona said. "See you soon."

"Later." Bella walked to her Wrangler and was grateful for the beautiful day. Bella quickly went through her mail while sitting in the elementary school parking lot so she could put the things that didn't need her attention in the recycling bin. When she was done, all she was left with was a two notes from friends, both of whom mentioned the novelty of actually writing a letter instead of an email. *It's almost like having a pen pal again. . .*

Emails and mail finished, she headed to the Valley Store. *Wonder if it will surprise Joe and Joshua to see me again so soon?*

Joe Sleeps Late

Joshua was at the store at his usual early hour and grateful for the morning sky that promised a beautiful autumn day. He knew this would mean the leaf-lookers would be out in abundance. He almost called to tell his dad not to come in early but stopped himself as he didn't want to wake him. *I'll call if I haven't heard from him by nine or so.* He went up to his small office in the loft over the cash registers to decide what he would need to teach Melody about helping with the bookkeeping. He knew he could use help reviewing the inventory and the data entry that didn't come from the bar codes. He took a pad of paper and started making notes. A text came in on his phone: "Be by before noon to check those steps. A. G." He had finally remembered to text Arthur Gillett last night about the steps. He was relieved Arthur could fix them and he wouldn't have to worry about his dad slipping again. Sitting back, he heard a knock on the front door and saw on the wall clock that it was after seven thirty. He ran down the stairs and opened the door. He was surprised to see Dr. Smith.

"Hey, Doc, sorry, I got caught up in some paperwork. Thanks for knocking. Might have lost other folks who tried the door handle and left when they found it locked. Come on in."

"Actually, I just stopped by to see how Joe is this morning."

"I encouraged him to sleep in today and come in late. I was a little worried when I left him last night because he seemed really tired. It wasn't like him."

"Did he come to the store yesterday?"

"Yep, full day too. Think that was it?"

"Likely so. Even when you don't have any serious damage to the body from a fall, it's harder to bounce back from the adrenaline rush and the following let-down when you're his age. Plus, his body is adapting to changes in how he walks, the sprain of his ankle... well, you get the picture. Suppose you don't want a medical lecture this morning."

"I plan to call him around nine if I haven't heard from him." Joshua sounded worried.

"I suspect he'll be fine. A good sleep will help. I see there's a stool by the register, so I'm assuming he'll sit when he needs to rest."

"Yep, his idea even! I was surprised he was willing to consider sitting down."

"Okay, sounds like nothing to worry about. If you're still concerned after you talk to him, just call my office. I'll see him anytime."

"Thanks, Doc. Thanks very much. I'll be in touch if we need you. Oh, and Doc, make sure your office gal sends me a bill for your time. Hope you have a good day."

"Not to worry, Joshua. We're good." He was down the steps and gone.

Several people walked in the store shortly after Doc Smith left, but not enough to make Joshua feel he needed to call Doug. He brought his notepad down from the office. He continued to work on his list for Melody between customers. He made a note to budget a higher wage for her for the hours she was doing bookkeeping work versus running the cash register. *I didn't think about her needing money to go to college when I decided to ask her to help out. This will give her some extra she wasn't planning to have. That's good.* He looked up when he heard the bell above the door jingle. His dad walked in.

"Morning, son. Fine day, isn't it?" Joe acted as if nothing had ever happened.

"Dad, you look great. Good to know you slept in."

"Good suggestion, son, good suggestion. Slept like a baby without colic. I'll be fine now, the good Lord willing and the water don't rise."

Joshua shook his head. "Now I know you're better: mountain talk!"

"You like hearing I'm better than a pig in a poke?"

Laughing now, Joshua relaxed. His dad was back. No need to call Doc Fred. "Well, I'm fixin' to dock your pay if you don't get to work." Joshua grinned.

Detective Billy Williams entered the store. Joe and Joshua looked at him, and all three said, "Morning!"

Checking on the Prisoner

Billy decided it would be easier to stop by the Valley Store on his way to the station. He knew his day often went haywire. "Just picking up a few things I need before I start the day."

"Pleased as punch to have you." Joe gave him his usual smile.

I haven't heard dad use so many mountain expressions in years. Chuckling to himself, Joshua shrugged. "Let me know if you need help finding something."

After grabbing essentials to keep his larder stocked for at least a few days, Billy headed back to the counter and paid for his groceries. He thanked Joe and nodded to Joshua before starting towards the door. Joshua followed him. "How're things going, Billy?" They walked out onto the porch in front of the store.

"Good, Joshua, good. About to wrap up the second set of ATV drivers."

"Yeah? That's good to hear. I'm sure Bella will appreciate it too." He wasn't about to tell Billy the sheriff had stopped in to tell him.

"We won't be bothering her anymore. Well, I won't be bothering her anymore leastways." *Bettin' the sheriff might.* But he didn't say it aloud.

Wondering what Billy meant but aware more customers were driving up, Joshua just said, "All good to hear, Billy. All good to hear. You have a nice day now." The two men shook hands and Billy got in his SUV.

Billy drove to the station thinking about how oddly Joshua had acted when he mentioned Bella Anderson. *Guess I forgot he's single now. Might be more than one man in this valley interested in the lady.* He parked at the back of the station, scanned his ID card on the entry door, and did his mock salute to the camera. He didn't know which deputy was on the desk, but he knew it would get him a ribbing sometime today.

He scanned his card on the lab door and the lights came on. Alexander wasn't in yet. She worked long hours yesterday. He'd told her to put the ring aside and focus on the ATV the deputies had picked up from the home of Steve Phillips. *Well, actually Commissioner Zimmerman's home. Surprised the boy's mother didn't fuss about the deputies taking it. Of course, she may have wanted to be rid of it, just like her son. It leaves him his two shiny ATVs.*

Picking up the phone, he called down to the holding pen where prisoners were detained until formally charged. After that, they were taken to another wing of the county jail if they confessed and were awaiting a hearing, or to a regional prison to await trial once they were indicted. Elizabeth Alexander had called him last night to say the medical examiner had confirmed Nick Brown's official time of death as 6:45 a.m. on Monday. He had some questions for Steve, or Stevie, or whatever the name of the day was.

"Mornin', Williams here. Just lettin' you know I'll be down shortly to interview the Phillips kid. Have a room available?"

"Yep, Detective. See you soon."

When he reached the holding pen, he saw the deputy had Steve sitting on a hard chair with his hands cuffed behind his back. "Thanks. I'll take him from here."

"Mornin' Steve, or do you prefer Stevie?" Billy asked nonchalantly.

"I prefer for *you* to call me Mr. Phillips."

Billy wanted to wipe the smirk off Steve's face.

"Well, Stevie, I can see you had a rough night on that fine cot. Not used to our accommodations, I guess. We're going down to this room here on the right." Billy was still trying to decide how he was going to treat this kid. *Truth is I'd like to jerk a knot in his tail!* He snapped back to business, opened the door, and ushered Steve into the interrogation room. A deputy followed them in. Billy had arranged for a female deputy so they could play good cop/bad cop if needed.

Billy turned on the audio recorder, knowing the room was being video recorded as well. He decided to humor the boy. *Catch more flies with honey than vinegar.* He sounded respectful. "Mr. Steve Phillips, I'm Detective Williams and. . ."

"Deputy Thomas," she said and stated the time and date. Susan Thomas was the lead deputy and experienced in the interrogation of suspects.

"Yeah, yeah, I know, let's get on with it." Steve rolled his eyes.

"Please state your name and date of birth." Billy was staring at Steve.

"You can't be serious! You *just* said my name."

"I did, indeed, say your name, Mr. Phillips, but as far as this recorder knows, I could be making it up. Please state your name and date of birth."

"Steve Phillips," he said then gave his date of birth.

"Mr. Phillips, you were read your Miranda rights yesterday. Do you understand these rights and your responsibilities, or would you like me to repeat them?"

"Listen, Williams..." Steve tried to rise out of the chair, but it was awkward with his hands behind his back and his ankles chained.

Looking straight at him, without blinking, Billy said, "That's Detective Williams to you, Mr. Phillips. I'm sure you understand if we're going to stand on formalities, I expect the same show of respect I'm giving you."

"Sure, *Detective* Williams. *Got* it. I know my Miranda rights, and I do not want a lawyer or representative."

The deputy raised her eyebrows. "Detective, can we get on with this?"

"Sure, sure. But first, Deputy Thomas, please state your name for the record."

"I'm Deputy Susan Thomas." She knew she had stated her name already. *Is this idea of frustrating the suspect?*

"Deputy Thomas, please remove the handcuffs from Mr. Phillips. I'm sure he'll be more comfortable without them." The deputy asked Steve to stand and turn around. Her tone was serious but caring. She uncuffed him and he sat down.

"Better?" Billy said, feigning concern for the boy's welfare. Steve nodded.

"Tell me about this university you're accepted to. Excited?"

"Anything to get out of this hick place. It's an Ivy League. Know what that is?"

Billy ignored the response and continued throwing questions at Steve about how long had lived in the valley, what he liked to do outside of school, and other benign questions. He felt like he was playing a cat-and-mouse game trying to get the boy to loosen up.

"Now, Steve... okay if I call you Steve?"

"Whatever, Williams."

"Where were you Monday morning, the day before yesterday, between six and eight?"

"Asleep."

"Asleep where?" Billy saw the look of surprise on Steve's face.

"Do you know where you are when you're asleep, Detective?"

"Yes. Yes, I do," Billy said as if they were buddies.

"Well..." Steve hesitated, then quickly continued. "I sleepwalk, so I've been known to wake up somewhere different than where I went to bed." Steve gave his soon-to-be trademark smirk.

"That's interesting. Don't you think that's interesting, Deputy Thomas?" She just nodded. "Is there someone who can verify where you were when you went to bed, and where you were when you were asleep between six and eight on Monday?" Billy had his own smirk.

"Well, I crashed at a friend's house. He was... uh, gone, when I woke up, so guess there's no one who can verify where I was when I woke up." Steve sounded proud of what he viewed as a clever response.

Billy gave the deputy an imperceptible nod. "What is the name of your friend?" Deputy Thomas asked, her voice motherly. She waited a second. "I would hope your friend would want to corroborate your whereabouts. Don't you think so?"

Steve just sat there.

"Did you happen to see Will Hansen at school on Monday?" Susan changed tactics as smoothly as a sharp blade slicing ham.

"What are you talking about? I..." Steve started to say something else and then stopped. "Come to think of it, he hasn't been in school for a while. Guess his old man must have changed his school. Don't think he ever graduated. His dad didn't like him hanging around with valley kids." His attitude was cycling between agitation and back to cockiness. Billy had seen this before. *It's one of the challenges for an eighteen-year-old who has some brains but not enough life experience. Doesn't know which game to play.*

"Deputy, I think we could give Mr. Phillips, Steve, a break. Get him some water, maybe? What do you think?"

Susan smiled at Steve. "What can I get you to drink? Water? Tea?" She thought he could probably use some coffee but wasn't going to offer it, hoping to let him know he was in the Tennessee mountains, where people drank tea.

"Water! Who can drink tea at this hour?"

Billy and Susan stood up. "Detective Williams and. . ."

"Deputy Thomas exiting interrogation. Suspect Steve Phillips remains in Interrogation Room 1."

Billy stopped the recorder and put it in his pocket. He turned to Steve. "Feel free to get up and stretch. We'll be back shortly." He and Susan stepped out of the interrogation room, allowing the door to lock automatically behind them with a solid click.

"Detective, do you think you can get him to say he was at Nick Brown's house?"

"You never know, Deputy. Right now, he still thinks he's pretty clever and we're dumber than rocks. He's been a privileged brat for a long time. . ." An interesting idea for a question occurred to him. He would ask it when they returned to the interrogation. "So, we'll see. Good call on asking him about Hansen. Did you think he was going to say he's dead?" Billy stopped walking.

"Something up, Detective?" Susan watched Billy carefully.

Billy spoke slowly. "We don't get many local kids who have as much experience with people playing word games as Stevie has likely seen. His stepfather is Commissioner Zimmerman."

The flash of disgust on the deputy's face did not escape Billy, but he didn't question it. Many folks were not pleased this man was on the commission nor with his comments, particularly when he referred to locals as "mountain dopes."

Ten minutes later they reentered the interrogation room to find Steve drumming on the table with both hands. Deputy Thomas set the bottle of water in front of him and sat down. Billy leaned against the wall after starting the recorder. He and the deputy stated their names and Steve gave his information. Before Billy could ask, Steve said he knew his rights and didn't want a lawyer. Billy just smiled. *Gotta love a kid smart enough to hang himself out to dry.*

"Hope the break helped, Steve. I haven't met your dad…"

"*Step*dad. Get it right!"

"So, I was wondering what brought you to Tennessee from…" Billy let the question hang hoping to get at this boy's privilege. He knew full well they had come from somewhere near Detroit.

"Michigan. What's it to you? Still have a home in Grosse Pointe. Doubt you know where that is."

"Just nice to know what people leave behind to come to these lovely mountains."

"Left all my friends behind. That's what! Only thing good about these mountains is riding my ATV. It's a Polaris Sportsman 850, the top of the line. Did you know that, Deputy?" Steve looked at Deputy Thomas.

She sat without saying a word as Billy acted like he didn't know what Steve was doing. Billy said sternly, "That's detective, remember?"

"Wasn't talking to you, was I? I was talking to this lovely lady here. She's pretty. Even for a cop. She could be my mother's younger sister."

Billy and Susan worked hard not to roll their eyes.

"Well, you see, Steve, I have lots to do today, so it would help me get on with it if you answered the question. Where were you between six and eight on Monday morning?" Billy deliberately paused. With a hint of pity in his voice, he continued, "Or we'll just let you return to your cell and—"

"All right, all right. Just shut up for a minute and let me think."

Billy was quite sure Steve had used the same tone with his parents many times. He was hoping to get a report soon from the deputies who had gone to interview Steve's parents. He sent them because he thought it likely the Zimmermans would be flustered by two uniformed officers appearing at their door. The officers were warned about the ploys Mrs. Zimmerman was likely to use. Billy was also hoping for some results in the hunt for another syringe at the Browns' property in order to nail this kid. *Lots going on, but we're going to get him, one way or the other.*

Steve opened his mouth. Deputy Thomas interrupted him. "Did you know Will Hansen very well?"

"Yeah, what's it to you?" He apparently decided he was not so enamored with the deputy. "We hung out. No one else in that snooty school wanted to be friends. Too bad about Will."

"Too bad about Will?"

"Yeah, I thought I was going to save—" he stopped abruptly. "Uh, see him before he was sent home to Michigan for good. I was out looking for him the night of the little accident that damaged my ATV." He squirmed a bit. "So, I need to get out of here and see if I can find a buyer for it. Pop will want that trashy thing out of the garage."

Susan completely ignored that bit of information, "Oh, so he's not coming back?"

"No. What I heard from his folks' housekeeper is he won't ever be coming back." He trailed off and crossed his arms on his chest.

Billy stood for a moment, just looking at Steve. *Soooo... That explains why he and Brown were on the Anderson property. Just as we suspected. He knows Hansen is dead. Doubt we'll get any more out of him this round.*

"Deputy, cuff this young man and return him to his cell."

"Hey, wait! You can't do that. I want out of here."

"I look forward to being notified by the warden when you're ready to talk."

Billy recorded the date and time, he and Deputy Thomas gave their names, and said they were terminating the interview and escorting Phillips to his cell. Susan handcuffed his arms behind him then walked Steve through the door as Billy held it open for them.

He could hardly wait until this interrogation was over so he could update the sheriff.

10

Lunch at The Corral

Chad pulled up to The Corral and entered through the side door just before one o'clock. He hadn't noticed who was walking in the front door, so he was surprised when he looked to the front and saw Chief Whitehorse entering. *Oh no, don't tell me he doesn't feel comfortable coming in the side door! Has someone said something to him or some other tribal member?* There were not many people in the restaurant. He saw the chief heading to the far back corner. *Hmmm... He wouldn't sit there if he didn't feel like he was a local. Have to figure out what coming in the front is all about.*

Chad walked towards the back and greeted the chief just as he approached the back booth. "Tom, good to see you." Chad shook the chief's extended hand.

"Good to see you too, Chad. Thanks for meeting me. Sit, sit. This booth fine with you?"

"Just fine."

Carla was at the table as soon as they were seated. She smiled and nodded, welcoming them with more enthusiasm than she greeted most folks. "Chief! Sheriff! What can I bring you to drink?"

Chad nodded to the chief, "Please. . ."

"Unsweet tea, please."

"The same. Thanks." Carla turned and walked away. "How are things in your world, Tom?" Chad knew the chief would get to the reason for the lunch in his own time.

"Well, Chad, I suspect my world is not nearly as big as yours. Mine's the usual: family, tribe, neighbors. All of them need something most of the time." Tom had no dissatisfaction in his voice. "How about you and yours?"

"Mine's about—" he stopped as Carla set their drinks down and waited on their orders. *Southern comfort food seems the order of the day for me.* He nodded to Tom to go first, but Tom gestured for Chad to go ahead. In the end, they both ordered the lunch special: fried chicken, mashed potatoes with gravy, and green beans. "Thanks, Carla."

"My pleasure," she said cheerily as she walked away.

"That food will be in front of us before we can start any meaningful conversation, so suppose you finish what you started saying about your corner of the world, Chad."

"Nora and her family are doing well. It's been nice to have Sam Nations working with us on a case; it gets him home and gives us the benefit of his intellect and skills. Other than that, everyday life in the valley."

"Good to hear about Nora. You know my youngest daughter was in the same class with Nora and Sam. Seems Nora was the one content to stay in the valley."

"I had forgotten about your daughter being in the same class. Is she still in Atlanta, or has a bigger fishing hole caught her interest?"

"Still in Atlanta, but poverty law is her passion, so you never know where it will lead her. Always nice to know one of our own could be of help. Just sorry Sam is in Knoxville so much. I understand if you can't tell me, but I'm assuming he was here on the case written up in *The Tuesday Tattler* yesterday."

"Actually, it was an extra edition put out on Friday. Did you know that?"

"No. I didn't even look at the date when I finally had time to read it."

Chad nodded. Everyone knew it was a meth lab; it was the biggest news around the valley in a while. It was also an obvious link to Sam. Carla put their food in front of them and walked away without saying a word.

"Enjoy," Tom said.

"You too." Chad cut up his fried chicken so it would cool.

They exchanged pleasantries about the weather, high school football, and general talk about the community. As they were finishing up, Carla was there to take their plates and offer coffee. Both men accepted and they chatted until she put the cups in front of them.

Then, without much shift in the tenor of the conversation, Chief Whitehorse spoke. "Let me get to the reason I called you. The powwow this year is going to be the first weekend in November. We'll do it on our tribal grounds as usual. I wanted to know if it would create problems for you if we add all day Friday to the agenda. You already know we do the big opening on Friday night, but the tribe wants to extend the time during daylight hours."

Chad took a few minutes to run through any potential concerns in his head. "If it's just extending the time and not increasing the number of participants, I don't see any problem. It could actually spread people out, although I'm sure you're hoping it will increase visitors. The issues for us to consider are usually traffic and handling folks who let their ignorance and bigotry affect the activities."

Tom nodded in agreement. "I don't know if it will bring many more people, but I want to honor the tribal council's perspective. They feel it would enhance our visibility, and perhaps get some of the tourists who normally don't come because they leave their rentals on Saturday."

Chad smiled. "That makes sense. I think we're good. Just give your projections and time frame to Sergeant Whitehorse. You know her, right? She manages events we need to cover."

"We'll see that she knows." The timbre of his voice changed. Looking around to see if anyone was close enough to overhear, Tom said, "The other reason, the real reason I wanted to talk to you, is I've heard some talk, pretty creditable talk, about one of our county commissioners. I can't get anyone to give me anything specific, but the chatter has certainly heightened since that meth lab exploded. You know if I had knowledge of something specific, I would have been in touch sooner."

"Would this be a commissioner who's a local or a newcomer?"

"The latter. The only one."

As sheriff, Chad had a serious concern about where this might be going, but, as a member of the local community, he wondered if people just disliked having someone on the county commission who wasn't one of them.

"Do I assume since you're talking to me that the chatter involves illegal matters, or are you just talking as one citizen to another?"

Tom Whitehorse took a deep breath. "I'm talking to you, off the record, as sheriff. Look, I know how people gossip and how they complain if they don't like something. I have to say I'm glad the rumors don't directly involve my people, nor yours locally, but it could affect all of us in the valley."

Chad decided it was time to get out of a place where the walls could have ears. "Don't know about you, but this fine lunch has me needing to walk a bit. What do you say we get some fresh air? Maybe take a little ride together up to one of the lookout areas and see this lovely piece of paradise we call home?"

"Sounds good. Let me get the check and stop by the men's room, then I'll meet you up front."

Chad laid money on top of the check for his portion. In these situations, Chad always insisted on paying for his meals. He believed it made it clear he wouldn't be compromised as a sheriff by someone thinking he owed them a favor. "I'll drive. I'll pick you up in the front." *And I'm going to find out why you use the front door.*

The chief walked out the front door just as Chad pulled up.

"This ought to start some gossip. Folks will have me arrested and in prison before sunset." The chief gave a belly laugh.

Chad laughed too. "And there will be those who'll say I'm showing you favoritism because they don't get to ride in this fine police-equipped Ford Interceptor."

"True that," the chief said. "True that."

"So, Tom, I have a question for you. Noticed you came in the front door like the newbies but sit in the back like the locals."

"Observation is a good trait in a law enforcement officer, Sheriff Oliver."

"Second time I've heard that this week."

"Oh, and may I ask who else is speaking to your powers of observation?"

"Joe. I stopped in the Valley Store and saw him sitting with his foot elevated. Told him I had never seen him sitting down on the job before."

"So that rumor is true? He did something to his foot? Leg?"

"Seems he slipped on the steps up to the loft they use as an office. But he's fine now. No breaks or anything critical."

"Well, that's good to hear. See how fast the news about Joe spread in this valley? Same as all the things I hear on any given day."

"Guess I need to get out and about more." With a more serious timbre to his voice, Chad said, "I'm curious why you use the front door at The Corral."

"Because for so many years we couldn't go in the front door of most places owned by European descendants. Simple as that."

There was no rancor in his response. "I think we get along with most locals and they get along with us. But, you know yourself, there are a few boys running around who would like us to still be on the reservation. I'd like to tell them we might if Tennessee had one. Anyway, going in the front is to show respect to all my family members who never got to enter a business through a front door. At the same time, I know I can sit in the back. Not just because no one can stop me anymore, but because we work together in this valley to get along and show respect. For the most part."

Chad just nodded his head. They had reached the lookout on the northeast side of the valley. It was the first place on the ascent up the mountains with a place to pull over and view the landscape. Each man, without seeming to consult the other, walked over to a bench near the edge of the rock outcropping. They sat silently looking out over the valley. The spot was close enough to the valley to clearly see each of the buildings that made up their little community. The changing leaves would soon fall, and more of the cabins, houses, and mobile homes would become visible through the trees.

Chad spoke first. "Tell me what you know, Tom. I need everything you can give me so I can see if there's a pattern to what I'm looking at. And so I know if there are things I need to get some eyes on, sooner rather than later."

Tom spoke seriously for several minutes. He laid out the details he had heard involving the county commissioner and some mysterious light observed in the area. Chad knew he was referring to Sector Two, one of the six sectors the sheriff's office used to define precise regions within the county. "There's also some talk the commissioner is involved in brothel activity in Round City."

Chad was looking down wistfully at the valley he loved. *This small place is not likely to be found by very many, other than the curious. But I'm going to do everything I can to keep folks with ill intent in line.* He nodded at the chief. "As a customer or proprietor?"

"Procurer from what I hear." The chief's voice had a mixture of sadness and disdain. "Could be a proprietor too, but I'm guessing that would be at arm's length, if it's true."

"Thanks, Tom. I mean it. People aren't known for sharing facts or gossip with the sheriff." Chad had the flat voice he often used in his work. "Any gossip on the explosion of the meth lab? Anything that suggests this same county commissioner could be involved?"

Tom looked at him carefully, studying Chad's eyes. "Haven't heard anything like that. Folks seem to think it's mostly kids, well, older kids of eighteen or twenty. But, believe me, I'll let you know if I do hear anything else."

"Thanks, Tom. In the meantime, I'll get my better deputies to keep their eyes and ears open in that sector. All my deputies are good, but some are better at ferreting out things than others. Different skill sets needed for different things."

"Guess that's why my daughter is so good at her job. She can do it all."

"Yes, Chief Whitehorse, Sylvia is definitely a chip off the old block." Both men chuckled as they walked back to the Interceptor. They continued to make small talk while they rode back to the valley, and as they pulled into the parking lot at The Corral, Chad thanked the chief again for his time and the information. "We'll cover the powwow however you need, just let Sylvia know."

"Probably never told you this, Sheriff," the chief said, his tone suddenly more formal. "Real glad you're our sheriff." He shook Chad's hand and got out of the SUV. Chad watched him walk to his Chevy Silverado truck and drive off.

Now I'm going to have to get eyes up on the hill again for what I still think is a UAV. I'll also need to talk to the police chief in Round City and see what I can learn. Meantime, since I'm out, I'll stop and get a few groceries and drop them off at home before I head back.

The Valley Store

As Chad pulled into the parking lot at the Valley Store, he noticed there was only one other vehicle in the parking lot. He was pretty sure it was Bella's. He glanced in the mirror and ran his fingers through his hair. *When was the last time I did that? This woman is getting under my skin for sure.* He exited the SUV and took long strides up to the steps into the front door of the store. Bella and Joshua were talking to Joe, who was sitting on a stool but without his foot elevated.

Chad looked admiringly at Bella: tall, slim, and comfortable in her jeans and plaid shirt.

"Oh... hi, Chad," Bella seemed surprised to see him, but smiled. "Good to see you today. I have a question for you and didn't know if it was appropriate to call you or stop by the station with it."

Her smile was not missed by any of the men, especially not by Chad or Joshua.

Joe said, "If you need some privacy, you can go to the back."

Bella looked perplexed. "No, no. It's nothing serious." Turning to look at Chad, she said, "I saw a sign at the library for a bluegrass jam this Friday night. Is that Nora's?"

Chad answered as he watched Joshua's face out of the corner of his eye. "Yes, just as I said when I invited you." Joshua looked at Bella and then moved towards the stairs to his loft office. *Hmmm... giving me space but not out of earshot, interesting.*

Confused, Bella started to say something and then stopped. *Okay, it's been a long time since I've had to figure out advances by a man, but I've never been in a situation like this. There is clearly some alpha male interaction going on between these two.*

Then an idea struck her. "I appreciate the open invitation you extended. I was just about to ask Joe and Joshua if they knew about it."

All of them turned and looked at the door as the bell above it jingled. Nora Oliver-Smith walked in, totally oblivious to the tension in the air. She made a beeline for Chad and kissed him on the cheek. "Hey, Daddy." He smiled and kissed her back. "Oh, I'm sorry, I didn't know someone was behind you." She looked at Bella and extended her hand.

"Hey, I'm Nora Oliver-Smith."

Delight showed on Bella's face as she shook Nora's hand. "Oh, hey, it's nice to meet you. I'm Bella, Bella Anderson. I was just talking with your dad about the music on Friday."

"Serendipity then, isn't it? I just stopped in to ask Joshua and Mr. Joe if I could put a poster on their door." She looked at Joe and then realized Joshua was standing on the steps to the office area. "Oh, hey, Joshua, didn't see you when I came in. So, what do you think? Any problem putting up a sign about the bluegrass jam and sing-along?" Her blue-gray eyes and shiny blond hair perfectly set off the smile she gave him.

"Hey, Nora. Of course you can put up a sign. Usual start of seven or so?"

"Yes, the Greg Brothers are going to play, and we'll be warming up by six thirty or thereabouts. That way Fred can bring the kids for a little while before he takes them home to bed."

Bella listened to the enthusiasm of this young woman and the velvet tones of her voice. She could see why Chad was excited about her starting up the musical activities in the valley again.

"Am I safe in assuming you're the vocalist?" Bella said.

"Love to sing. Do you?" Nora's warmth radiated.

"I do. I can hear you have a lovely voice for singing. Mine is more the sing-along type. But I love good bluegrass, gospel, country, and have even been known to attend an opera." All three men looked at her, which she noticed but ignored. "Your dad was up at my cabin the other day, and he sounded very proud when he told me you were restarting the sing-alongs."

Chad looked at both women, not knowing if he should smile or not. *Score one for me. But now my daughter's going to be asking a whole bunch of questions.* He noticed Joshua was looking back and forth between him and Bella. Chad decided to stay quiet and keep his face neutral.

"I was just about to ask Joshua and Joe if they knew about the bluegrass jam and were planning to attend." Bella paused and, without looking directly at any one of the men, she asked, "Well, are you?"

"Absolutely!" Joshua said, jumping in quickly. "Wouldn't miss it for the world. Bella, you've never heard bluegrass or gospel sung by a voice as perfect as Nora's."

"Aren't you the gentleman, Joshua! Thank you." Nora's voice was a soft croon. "Well, if y'all excuse me, I have two little ones to pick up from a play date, so I'll put the sign on the door and say that I hope all y'all will come on Friday. See you then."

She kissed her dad on the check again. "Talk to you *soon*, Daddy, love you."

"Love you, Nora. Hug the kids for me." *And, yes, I'm absolutely sure you'll be talking to me soon.*

Nora waved goodbye to all of them and headed out the door. Joshua stepped off the stairs, experiencing how easily his dad could have slipped on the last step as he almost did himself. *Why am I so distracted?*

Chad realized he needed to recover the situation. "Well, that's just great. Bring a folding chair, some bug spray if mosquitoes like you, and don't forget your thermos of coffee or tea. It can get cool in the evening this time of year."

He was walking towards the center of the store when he said, "And, Bella, I can pick you up." He did not look back at the three of them. *I cannot for the life of me remember what I stopped in here to get. Guess I'll get my usual staples, and at least I'll have something to eat at home.*

Bella looked at Joshua and Joe and smiled. "It's great you'll attend. I haven't heard good bluegrass, well, except on the radio, in a long time. Certainly haven't heard live bluegrass in far too long. Nora seems like a nice young woman."

Joe realized his son was struggling with something. He thought the something might just be Bella Anderson, and it might just be complicated by Chad. He decided he better step in and try to save the day.

"Listen. I think Joshua and I can close up the store a bit early, even though it's a Friday night. Once the word is out, most folks will be headed to The Corral for the music. How about we bring some picnic food to share?"

Chad had just returned to the register.

"What a great idea, Joe, that sounds perfect," Bella said. "I'll make some brownies and can bring something to snack on. What about you, Chad?"

Caught totally unaware, Chad looked at her. "Yeah, sure. Let me know what I can bring."

Joe saw Joshua was standing back observing. It was his usual way of handling situations he hadn't figured out yet.

"Work for you, son?" Joe said to Joshua.

"Sure, Dad, sounds like fun. If y'all excuse me, I have work to do in the back."

"Oh, Joshua, I'm so sorry. I didn't know I was keeping you from work earlier. I should have realized. I'll just get my groceries and head out." She tried to ignore the growing tension in the air.

"*You* were no problem, Bella. Not *ever*. See you Friday." Joshua walked to the back.

Chad paid for his groceries and took his time chatting with Joe while Bella got the things she needed. He was still standing there holding his grocery sack when she put her things on the counter for Joe to ring up. Chad picked up a paper sack and started to put her groceries in it.

"Whoa, Mr. Sheriff, I recycle and reuse. I finally dug my shopping bags out of storage," she said, pulling two neatly folded canvas tote bags out of her shoulder bag and handing them to him. "*Now* I would be honored if you bagged my groceries."

Joe was doing all he could to keep a straight face. He felt like he was watching two high school boys posturing over the homecoming queen they wanted to invite to the prom. *I wonder if either Chad or Joshua know they're smitten with Bella Anderson. Just hope they sort it out in a way none of them gets hurt.*

"Thanks, Joe. Tell Joshua I'll see him soon." Bella leaned over and gave Joe a kiss on the cheek.

Joshua heard her as he watched Chad carry Bella's groceries out to her Jeep. He saw them standing outside talking. He turned around, walked into the storeroom, and started stacking boxes of cans to stock the shelves. *Dad always says work is a good antidote for what ails you. Not sure what's ailing me, but something sure is. I think it might be Chad.*

An Urgent SOS Call

Bella smiled at Chad as he held her door open after she got in. "You really don't need to pick me up on Friday, Chad."

"I'd feel better knowing you had a ride back up that mountain after dark. So, maybe you'll humor me. Mountain man, you know." He hoped she wouldn't say she could drive herself.

"Okay, if you insist. Just give me a call when you're leaving the valley and I'll be sure to have everything ready. Does that work?"

"Perfectly." He closed her door as she lowered the window. "See you Friday evening then."

"See you then, Chad. Have a good couple of days." She started the Jeep and drove off with a small wave.

He lifted his hand to wave and almost dropped his own sack of groceries. *Women. Can't live with them. Can't live without them. Although I have to admit I've done okay without Mary.* He set the groceries on the back seat of his SUV and headed home to put them away before returning to the station. He needed to talk with Detective Williams and make sure Sergeant Whitehorse knew she would be getting the request for services for the powwow. *I have things to do between now and then if I'm going to be free to take Bella to hear Nora sing.* His phone buzzed with a text. "Call me. ASAP. SOS." He chuckled because Nora used her middle name, Sarah, when she wanted his attention: Sarah Oliver Smith—SOS. *Good thing I know it means* she *views something as urgent. Might as well get it over with.* He pushed the button on his steering wheel that dialed her number.

"Hey, sweetheart, you wanted to talk to me?"

"Daddy, why haven't you told me about Bella Anderson?"

"I think that would be Dr. Anderson to you, daughter."

"Really? *Dr.* Anderson," she said, a pause suggesting she was thinking about it. "She introduced herself as Bella. So, in case you've forgotten, that's an invitation to use first names. So, quit procrastinating! How do you know her?"

"She owns a cabin up in the higher elevations."

"Yeah, yeah, still procrastinating. Spill."

He started laughing, "Nothing subtle about you, is there? I just met her about a month ago when Joe introduced us at the Valley Store. She owns a cabin her family built over a hundred years ago. She was a professor of something, English I think, in North Carolina and just retired. She's now thinking about being up here year-round." *The sheriff part of me is not going to tell you Bella's land and shed were involved in the drug crimes last month. The dad part of me doesn't want you worrying about things like this happening.*

"And do I sense you're trying to encourage that decision?" Nora had something of a command in her voice. She was also surprised her dad knew so much about Bella.

"What if I am?" Chad said quietly.

"I'd say it's about time. I thought she was a lovely person. She has southern charm, sounded like she was pretty well educated, and you just confirmed that. So, what's your problem?"

"Whoa, slow down. First of all, I'll admit she intrigues me. But, beyond that, I'll let you know if my intrigue becomes anything more. Fair enough?" He realized he said it in his sheriff's in-control voice. "Sorry, honey. Too much on my mind. And, I'll be honest, this is a distraction I probably don't need right now."

"Hogwash, Daddy. She might be *just* the distraction you need. Period." Nora had her own authoritative voice.

He recognized the tone. He also knew where she learned it. "Thanks, Nora, thanks for caring about my social life. I have to run groceries in the house and get back to the station. Hug the kids for me. Look forward to seeing them on Friday night. Love you."

"Slow down a minute. No one is going to dock your pay for five minutes with your daughter on the phone. I love you, Daddy. In case you haven't noticed you're a smart and caring man. And, in addition to that, you make sure we're safe in our community… and, if I do say so myself, you're quite handsome as well. But all that aside, I know what it's like to have a man in my life who I love and respect, and who loves and respects me. I actually have two: one is my husband, and one is my daddy. I would love for you to know what it is to have a woman in your life that you can respect and, who knows, maybe fall in love with. So, as your loving daughter, I'm telling you to step up your game. If you need lessons, I'll get Fred to coach you. Now, go save the planet. At least our little corner of it. Love you, Daddy."

He pulled into his driveway and shook his head in amazement. "Love you too. Now and forever. Thanks, sweetheart. Now don't forget to hug the kids and tell them I love them and a shout-out to Fred."

"Done and done. Bye. Love you." She hung up.

"Love you." Chad wasn't sure if she heard him before she hung up, but he was confident she knew it. He sat there trying to figure out all that had happened in the last half hour. *I may be way too old for this. Courtin'. Isn't that what Grandpa called it? And who could get used to having his child trying to fix him up with a woman?* He set the groceries in the house and headed to the station. *What am I walking into?*

11

What to Do?

Bella arrived home later than planned, but she hoped she would have time to put her groceries in the cabin before Arthur arrived to measure for the fence. She put the two tote bags of groceries on the counter and immediately started to put things in the fridge. She stopped. *Why did I buy more eggs? I just bought some on Saturday.* As she emptied the bags, she was relieved to see she had bought all the items on her get-when-you-go-down-the-mountain list. As she folded the tote bags to put back in her Jeep, she thought about the exchange at the Valley Store. She was delighted to have met Nora and enjoyed learning about the music on Friday night. She pulled out a chair at the kitchen table and sat down. The tension between Chad and Joshua was crowding her thoughts.

Am I flirting and don't realize it? I've been alone for almost five years now. What is happening with Chad? Joshua? Me? Anything? She shook her head trying to clear her mind. *I was surprised at Joshua's reaction to Chad. He's usually much more placid. . . like Joe.*

After pondering the interactions for several minutes, she was no closer to an answer than when she started.

Bella heard the sound of a vehicle coming up the road and pushed her confusion to the side while she laced up her boots. She walked out the door just as Arthur stepped out of his truck.

"Good afternoon, Arthur."

"Afternoon, ma'am." Arthur touched the brim of his hat as he walked towards her. "Fine mountain day, isn't it?"

"Fine day, indeed! Thanks for coming. I know you're a busy man, but I was wondering if I could talk to you again about my shed before you take the measurements for the fence?"

"Splendid idea. I've been thinking about what it would take to repair it ever since you showed it to me. Let's do it now so I won't have to disturb you after I get the fence measurements." He walked towards the shed. Bella followed.

"Sooo..." Bella said slowly. "I'm thinking about not fixing the shed."

"Oh, Miss Bella, you have to fix the shed! You could get a snow load in the winter that would bring the whole thing down."

Looks like he answered my question about the snow load on the roof.

Bella laughed lightly. "Thank you for caring about making sure the shed is safe. I should have started by telling you I'm thinking about expanding or replacing the shed." She saw she now had his full attention. "Here's what I've been thinking." She proceeded to tell him her ideas about how she might like to build an addition or maybe even a new structure to include a guest cottage. She didn't mention using it as a writer's retreat.

"How quickly you wantin' to do this? Winter will be coming in a couple of short months, sometimes sooner as you know. It might have to wait to spring, especially if you want it stick built."

"Sorry, stick built?"

"Carpentry talk, ma'am, I apologize. Means we build it from the ground up." His eyes seemed to search her face to see if she understood. "It's true right now that we're a bit slow, mostly doing odd jobs like the fence and fixin' the stairs at the Valley Store—"

She interrupted him. "Oh, Arthur, that's great news to hear you can fix them. I've been so worried about Joe since he slipped. I'm so thankful he's all right."

"Yes, ma'am, me too. Yep, that one's an easy fix. Now, as for your work here, I'd need some time to turn it over in my brain, and on paper, but if you wanted to think about a prefab—"

She interrupted him again. "Oh, no, I want it logs, or at least wood; something that'll fit in with being on this mountain."

"Yes, ma'am, I understand. This isn't a prefab like those trailer homes you see everywhere. This is a prefabricated log cabin. They have them up on the highway on the way to Knoxville. You could go there and take a look. Of course, they can design one the way you want, too. My initial thinking is the quickest way to get something built is if you choose one of them. You'd need to have someone do the foundation work and install it. I could do that for you if you want. Then we could either do a stick-built extension on it for your garage and shed storage, or we could fix or replace this one."

"Hmmmm. . . it never occurred to me that I could get something that was ready to put on the ground, so to speak."

"Some folks just do more of a carport for their cars and close in another part for a shed. Sort of like a double garage, but one with no door. Then the doors on the other side could be an actual garage door, or swing doors like you have now on this shed." He stopped and walked to the shed door.

Bella patted her pocket. She had been so distracted thinking about Chad and Joshua that she had forgotten to take the key off the hook by the kitchen door. "I'll run and get the key so we can go in."

"Fine, fine. I'll do some head scratchin.'"

As she went inside to grab the key, Bella's head swam with possibilities. *It sounds like there are more options than I originally thought. Maybe something good can come from all this.* Returning with the key, Bella opened the single door on the far side of the shed.

"Just curious, ma'am... any idea why the double doors are on this side?"

"I really don't know. I was young when my daddy passed away. He built this in the 1950s. The story I was told was he wanted a solid wall facing the road to paint a message or picture, like people do on barn sides. I just never knew what he planned to put there ..." Her voice trailed off as she thought about all the things she would never know about her dad.

"Sorry to conjure up sad memories, ma'am."

"Oh, not at all. No apologies needed. It's good to be reminded of his dreams. Now, what did you want to see here?"

He walked into the shed and checked the concrete floor. "Seems he did a pretty fair job of concrete work for that many years ago. In those days, it cost plenty to use rebar, the steel bars in concrete. That's what makes it more stable. This floor is pretty good; looks like he used rebar."

"What does that mean for making changes?"

"Well, wouldn't know for sure unless we take this shed down completely, but right now it looks like we could use this foundation, leastways for part of what you want to do." He headed out the door again and looked towards the cabin and then out towards the valley to the northwest. "Something you might want to think about is moving the whole thing forward on your land, then you'd have even more of a view from that window over yonder." He pointed to the kitchen window on the cabin.

"Whew! So many things to consider. I appreciate it. Thanks for clarifying I'd be taking a big chance with snow load if I don't fix the shed right away."

"We could go in and do some more reinforcing. Those boys who put up this plywood just closed the hole. It's not a bad job, just not enough to keep that wall up under snow."

"Okay. If you tell me where I can go see those cabins, I'll try to do that before you come back next week to fix the fence. Then I'd like to finalize a plan. Does that work for you?"

"Yes, ma'am. I'll bring an extra boy to help with the fence, then I can break away when you want to talk."

"Thanks, Arthur. I appreciate your time and the ideas. How long would it take if I do a prefab cabin?"

"Depends on the one you choose. They usually have some of the smaller ones ready to go. If it's one of the bigger ones, they tend to do those when you order it, and it can take a couple of weeks or months depending on how busy they are. Just ask them. I'd appreciate it if you tell them I sent you, and I'm available to do the work to install it. Could be, depending again on your choice, we could do it before heavy snow."

"Of course, I'll tell them you sent me. We can talk again on Monday."

"Thank you, ma'am." He gave her directions to where she could view the prefab log cabins. "I'll be going now to get the final measurements and be out of your hair. Be here first thing Monday morning. Thanks for your business." He stopped and turned around, "Oh, ma'am, I forgot to tell you. I can do the repair work with a simple permit that I can get the same day. Been some changes on our county commission and a new build takes a bit longer. The prefab permit is easier than the stick built. Just wanted you to know."

"Thank you, Arthur, that's all helpful information. See you Monday." Bella was relieved the fencing would be up soon and excited by the ideas for her cabin, shed, and garage. She would definitely take a ride to look at the prefab cabins before Monday—no matter what she decided to do about the shed.

Back in the cabin, she put away the last of the groceries, fixed a glass of tea, and headed to the porch. She wanted to finish reading the Conley book, even though she knew her mind would play around with the ideas Arthur had given her. She would let the thoughts incubate then continue with her sketches.

Several hours later, she realized she had goosebumps from the chill in the evening air. Looking at her watch, she was surprised it was already seven. The light was fading quickly. She checked the hook-and-eye latch on the screen door and wondered who the latch was intended to keep out. *Not anyone who was determined to get in, that's for sure. Probably has helped keep out some critters over the years if the screen door had blown open. Though I doubt that solid door would blow open in anything less than a gale.* She walked in and put her book down on the table before locking the French doors; she quickly closed the windows in the rest of the cabin. *Fall air is definitely here. I have to remember to close up the windows a bit earlier or I'll be starting that fireplace sooner than I would like.*

Bella's stomach growled. *Guess my protein bar is wearing thin.* Chili warmed on the stove while she placed some cornbread in the oven to reheat. She wondered why she thought she needed a microwave. She knew how to do many of the things a microwave could do. *Did advertising convince us we needed the microwave? Save time. Perhaps. Save energy? Does it? I'll check that out one of these days. Time is not an issue for me anymore, so I'm fine reheating in the oven for now.*

After supper, she cleaned up the kitchen before taking a shower and crawling into bed. She looked at her 25th anniversary picture. *I know you told me you didn't want me to spend the rest of my life alone. I don't know what to make of the things happening around me with Joshua and Chad. They both seem to be really nice men. They're different too. Was Chad's invitation a date, or just a friend asking a friend to a local event? I can't sort it out.* She stared at Matt in the picture. *Please send me a message so I know what to do.*

Hoping he would, Bella thought about her Not-So-Good List. Another day with nothing to put on it. *Hang in there, Drellag Caban, we may be on the way to bringing good memories back. I'll ask Sam if it's possible to have a tribal blessing of my land when the construction is finished.* She remembered there was one thing, even though it wasn't really her *own* not-so-good item. She learned Joe had fallen on Monday. She prayed he would be okay.

Then she started her Good List: she'd sent off her short story to Bonnie, she saw lots of happy faces today, she met Nora Oliver-Smith, she was going to a bluegrass jam and sing-along... with Chad. She had thought of her daddy, the shed he built, and considered what she would do about repairs to the ATV damage—in fact, she had the opportunity to do more than just repair it. She smiled at having time on the porch to almost finish her book. *I wonder what I've done in life to deserve so many good things?* She turned off the lamp, rolled over, and pulled up the quilt. She was ready for sleep.

What Do You Think?

Towards the end of the day, Joshua spent an hour teaching Melody the basics of the software he used for inventory. He decided to have her work on the things that needed to be hand entered, like the bread they sold from Diane's Home Cooking. "Good job, Melody, you caught on quickly. Keep track of the time you spend on the cash register, and the time you spend on data entry on your timesheet, please. Let me know if you have any questions or need help. Okay?"

"Sure, Mr. Johsua, I think I understand what you need me to do, and I'll ask if I have questions. Thanks for the opportunity to learn something new. I'll see you tomorrow. Night, Mr. Joe." Melody waved as she headed out the front door.

Joshua and Joe finished their usual end-of-day activities, and Joshua offered to drive his dad home. Even though Joe only lived a few minutes' walk from the store, Joshua knew Joe had been on his feet most of the day.

"Dad, Harold sent a text a little while ago saying he can't get together tomorrow, so he wanted to drop by tonight."

"That's good, son." He wanted his son to have time with his friend; he knew Joshua needed it. He was still concerned about Joshua and his interest in Bella. *If he's interested, and after all these years I think I know him well enough to know he is, I just hope he doesn't get hurt.* "It'll give you and Harold a chance to catch up and see if he still has concerns about things going on in the valley."

"For sure, Dad, for sure." Joshua looked past his dad, rather than at him, as Joe got out of the Tahoe. "See you tomorrow."

"Have a good evening, son. Call if you need anything." *My son is sixty-three. I guess you don't ever get over worrying about your kids.*

Joshua watched Joe walk up the ramp as easily as he had before he fell. He gave a sigh of relief and headed to his own cabin. He knew he was going to need to think about what was going on with Bella—and Chad. *Well, I guess I won't know unless I ask Chad his intentions, but it seemed pretty clear he was asking Bella to the blue-grass music as a date.* Harold was sitting on the front porch waiting for him.

Joshua rolled down his window and waved. Harold waved back as he stepped off the porch. "I'll just come in through the garage if that suits. No sense letting this food get cold."

"No problem. Come on in." Joshua entered the kitchen and Harold set the food he had picked up from The Corral on the counter.

"Hope this is okay with you. Easy enough to eat out of the containers and not dirty dishes. Unless, of course, your formal ways require it?" Harold's ribbing was evident in his quiet chuckling.

"Containers are fine. Do we need forks?"

"Only if you want to eat coleslaw. I had Carla do barbeque sandwiches so we wouldn't have to pull it off the bone."

Harold walked on through the kitchen as if he owned the house and opened the doors to the back porch. He hollered at Joshua, "Too cool for you on the back porch?"

Joshua reached the door with the forks and their beers. "Fine with me. I could use some fresh air." He set a Chimay Blue in front of Harold and his own pale ale on the table.

Harold thought he heard sadness in the silence. *Sometimes you just know when a man needs silence, and sometimes you have to shake him out of it. Which is this?* He watched Joshua unwrap his barbeque sandwich and decided on the former—for now.

Harold unwrapped his sandwich and put some sweet barbeque sauce on it.

"Carla marked the little plastic containers. This one's sweet and that one's tangy. Choose your poison."

Joshua reached for the tangy sauce.

Harold fell silent. He decided talk could come after they ate.

Joshua ate his sandwich, taking in the quiet of the mountains. "Ever notice the change in the sky when the moon is in this phase?" He glanced at Harold. "When I was up at Bella's—"

Harold interrupted him.

"Whoa, is that what this morose man silence is all about?" He looked at his friend. "You'll have to excuse me. I don't have much experience with how a man feels when he loses his wife. I know less how to talk about it. I was just waiting on you to work through whatever you needed to work through. But it's for sure I didn't think it was Bella Anderson." He shook his head wondering how he could have been so unaware. "Come to think of it, I don't know anything about being interested in a new woman at this age either. I'm grateful for Julie, that's for sure." He could see Joshua was alternating between looking at him and the sky.

As he stared off at the rising moon, Joshua said, "Would you think less of me for being interested in a woman so soon after losing Jan?"

"Hey, I'm not here now, or ever, to judge you. I'm your friend. Jan was sick for a long spell and really sick for the last two years. I could see you were struggling with your worry over her and how she felt. I can't imagine what you felt when the woman you loved was changing in ways neither of you could do anything about. Don't know what I would, or will do, if something happens to Julie. I think the important question is whether you'll think less of yourself? For me, that is the only question—" Joshua started to interrupt him. "Give me a second to finish my thought. Likely to lose it if I don't say it."

Joshua nodded, understanding.

"So, I was going to say, what anyone else thinks or says is their business. And, unless they support your decision, they don't matter anyway. Now, what did you start to say?"

"Not sure what to say, I guess. I like Bella as a friend and have for a long time. The fact she and Matt invited me and Jan up from time to time when they were at the cabin was always appreciated and enjoyed. Aside from you and Julie, I don't know any folks our age who don't have kids; most have grandkids."

He stopped and looked at Harold. He realized he had never made that connection before. Julie and Harold didn't have children, he and Jan didn't, and Bella and Matt didn't. Strange when he thought about it. *I never thought about why someone else didn't have kids. Guess I just assumed it was like us. With several miscarriages, we didn't talk about it with others. Hope I didn't say something that would make Harold feel bad.*

"Hey, look, Joshua, this isn't stuff most folks here talk about unless they live their lives engaged in gossip. I think our wives probably knew how each other felt about not having children, but... well, us men folks just don't talk about those things. Not saying we shouldn't, we just don't." Harold realized that was something in itself to think about. *Why don't we? Afraid we won't look very manly if we acknowledge we can't or didn't produce a kid? It just never happened for me and Julie. Is that what Joshua's thinking about? Kids?*

Joshua stood up and took Harold's empty beer bottle and his own. "Another?"

"Sure, time to put our feet up on that rail. Let me throw everything but your forks in this bag and we'll sit a spell. I have something I need to talk to you about too. And, who knows, maybe we'll come up with a plan for Dr. Bella Anderson, the new lady in town." As Joshua stepped away from the table, Harold slapped him on the back in a friendly gesture.

Harold took the beer, and they propped their feet up on the railing. "I really like how you can see the evening sun go down with the silhouette of the trees and mountains from here. My view is a bit different but still a good one. I like when cabins are placed on the land to take advantage of the view and not just plopped down, like those on the streets in town. Now, tell me… what has your shorts in a wad over Miss Bella, or do I say Dr. Bella?"

Joshua laughed. "I would love to see what she says if you ever call her Dr. Bella. Wish I could tell you what's got me agitated. Who Bella Anderson is as a person is pretty obvious: good looking, intelligent, strong willed. In many ways, not too different than my Jan was, and those two loved talking together. I always felt like the time Jan had with Bella filled a void women like Jan and Julie have…" he trailed off. Regaining his composure, he continued, "But she's as different as day and night from Jan in other ways."

"Like what? Is that what's bothering you? Don't know if the difference is good or bad?"

"No, no. Jan expected me to treat her as an equal, and I think I did on matters of living life and the things we did together. But Jan also expected me to open a door for her. You know, our mountain men ways."

"So, what's the problem with that?"

"Bella and I had a discussion about gender roles and how they have evolved and if they should still exist. Simple things, like opening a door for a woman."

"Gender roles, eh? Pretty fancy way of saying differences between men and women. Did you sort it out? I expect a number of folks would be interested in getting that one right."

"No. I don't think we did sort it out, but I enjoyed the conversation and wasn't offended or afraid of the discussion."

"Well, I think that's good. Look, I admire you for thinking with your brain about this, but don't get too carried away inside that head. Ask the nice lady out for dinner," he hesitated, "or, hey, I saw a poster at the The Corral that Nora is starting up the bluegrass jams again on Friday night. Ask her to that. Easy, non-committal, and it'll be good for her to get to know the community."

Good friend though you are, Harold, I'm not ready to tell you Chad Oliver beat me to it. "Good ideas, Harold. I'll see what I can come up with. Thanks for letting me get that off my chest."

"That's what we do, right?" Harold thought Joshua looked a little more like himself. "Now, I'm going to switch subjects on you. Remember how I told you I wasn't quite sure, but I felt Commissioner Zimmerman, the one who refers to locals as 'mountain dopes,' was up to something but I couldn't figure out what?"

"What do you say we don't use his phrase anymore. Even in joking we run the risk of it spreading even more." Joshua's tone was serious.

Joshua's back. Harold smiled inwardly at hearing the determination in Joshua's voice. "Good deal. Got it. Anyway, he's still pushing to widen the road and thinks it would speed up development in the valley. His words, not mine."

"I've been thinking about what you said about attending the meetings. When's the next one?"

"We meet every Tuesday evening at seven, as long as the weather allows." *Boy, you have been out of touch. You used to know that, Joshua.* "Wouldn't expect you to remember that with all you've dealt with the last couple of years."

"Something said last night that's got you worried?"

"It just felt like Zimmerman slipped up a bit when he was talking about what he sees as development for the valley."

"What did he say?"

"Not sure what he was *trying* to say. Here's what I heard. 'I have some business opportunities for this valley that I think the men are really going to like.' Sounds weird, doesn't it?"

"Any idea what he meant by it?"

"No, and probably wouldn't have thought much of it except one of our local commissioners snickered and said, 'You got that right.' Somehow I didn't think they were talking about carpentry work."

Back to his normal contemplative self, Joshua stared out at the moonlight. Harold knew not to interrupt his train of thought; Joshua would speak when he had something to say.

"You know, Harold, I'm going to think on this one. Maybe between us we can see what the gossip in town throws around and if there's anything to this." *And I need to talk to Chad about it. Can I talk to Chad without asking his intentions about Bella?*

After several minutes of silence, Harold said, "Look, it's getting late. I'll let you get on with your evening. Thanks for letting me get that off my chest. I'll stay in touch. And, as for you and the lovely lady, ask her to dinner. Soon." Harold automatically started for the kitchen door since he had come in that way. "Oops, I'm not superstitious. No sense in opening the garage door. I'll just let myself out the front."

Joshua walked with him to the front door and flipped on the porch light. "Thanks, Harold. I value having a friend I can trust." *I'm not worried about Harold drinking and driving with two beers, but I didn't even offer him coffee. Idiot! You have to get over being distracted.*

Harold reached out to shake Joshua's hand. "Glad to be of help!"

Joshua slapped him on the back. "Night, Harold. Give my best to Julie."

"I will. Talk to you soon. Night."

Joshua waited until Harold was down the drive. He turned off the porch light and locked the front door. He locked the slider to the back porch and forgot there were dirty forks in the sink. He was ready for bed. After showering and brushing his teeth, he looked in the mirror. *Maybe you're too old to think about having a woman in your life again.* He turned out the bathroom light, and automatically walked into the guest room. He still couldn't bring himself to sleep in his and Jan's bed.

Joshua rested his forearm on his head. There were two things caught in his mind like a fish on a hook. Bella, first and foremost, and what Harold said about Commissioner Zimmerman. Tomorrow was another day. He would try to figure it out then. For now, he knew he needed sleep.

12

Sorting Things Out

The station was humming when Chad pulled into the back parking lot. He realized it was just after four o'clock. and the shifts were changing. He didn't have many deputies compared to other sheriffs, but the recent federal funding increase had made it possible for him to hire more, providing better coverage on the many roads across the mountains. *Might be needing to cover more than roads. Bad enough some of the things people choose to do of their own free will, they don't need things forced on them. I'll do everything I can to keep human trafficking out of this valley, so help me God.*

One of the newer deputies was about to exit the building as Chad approached it. The deputy started to open the back door, stopped, and looked at the sheriff. *I imagine he can't decide if he'll be in trouble for not opening the door for me or for opening it, which will mean I didn't log in with my card.*

Chad scanned his card to open the door. "Afternoon, deputy. Good thinking to wait and see if I had my card. . . or if someone had a gun to my back." He moved on down the hall. *I'd give anything to see his face.* Chad just kept walking to the front. *Might as well greet the troops before I dig into the things that need my attention before the day is done—whenever that's going to be.*

"Evening, Sheriff."

"Evening, Sergeant Whitehorse. Coming on for the night shift?"

"Yes, sir. Switched with Sergeant Eddie."

"Appreciate the flexibility. Give me about twenty minutes, then stop by my office if you have time."

"I'll be there."

Chad made the rounds of deputies going off the day shift and those heading on to the night shift. He mostly shook hands, exchanged greetings, and asked about family and how things were going. Light banter. But he never missed anything in the eyes or voices of his deputies. He was pleased they all seemed in good spirits. "Thanks for your work. Now, go get them before they take over the valley." It was a quip he always knew was a hit with them. He heard a ripple of laughter among the deputies as he walked away. Chad smiled at their responses.

"You bet, Sheriff."

"Right, sir."

"Got it covered."

He swung by his office to grab his mug then headed for the break room. It was a rare occasion to find it empty, but he was grateful for the brief pause in small talk while he filled his mug. He walked back down the hall and shut his door. He needed to gather his thoughts, but a note on his computer screen caught his attention. Chad wasn't sure how he felt about this modern version of notes that used to appear on a clip outside his door; it seemed much harder to get away from the virtual ones. "Need to update you on Steve Phillips. BW." He picked up the phone and called his lead detective.

"Williams here." Billy was not looking at the display on his desk phone or he would have addressed the sheriff.

"Sheriff here." Chad loved to fluster Billy.

"Sheriff. Of course, I knew it was you."

"Hmmm… do I have worry about the veracity of your comments from now on?"

"No, sir. Nooo, sir! Just checking to see if you were… Guess I better quit while I'm ahead?" Billy hoped he sounded somewhat contrite.

Chad did not want to extend the conversation. "See you at five o'clock. That work for you?"

"Yes, sir. Thank you, sir."

"Later, Williams." Chad hung up the phone. The knock on his door had to be Sergeant Whitehorse. He stood up and opened the door. "Thanks, Sergeant, come in."

"Here to serve, boss." She walked to the round table and waited for Chad to sit.

"Sit. Sit. Day's young for you." She sat. "Had lunch with your father today. It was nice to see the chief. He said he'd get you the powwow information about additional security. Seems they're going to try adding daytime on Friday."

"My dad is nothing if not one to observe protocol. He called me *after* he talked to you and gave me the update. I asked him why he couldn't have told me at Sunday dinner. He gave me a simple response, 'Because I hadn't spoken with your boss yet.'" She laughed.

Chad smiled. "Sylvia, all those things he taught you about protocol help make you the great sergeant you are."

She appreciated the sheriff for calling her by her first name when they were at the round table. It showed her he understood the talking circle of her heritage. "Now, boss, if I didn't know better,

I'd say you were trying to butter me up for something." She didn't call him by his first name because even though the tribal chief's position was one of equals in the talking circle, he was still addressed as chief.

"Not a thing. Doing my job on the follow-up with the chief. Anything going on I need to know?"

"Nothing in the valley. Always lots of gossip here, there, and yonder. But nothing that makes my ears perk up. Do you know something we need to be on the lookout for?"

"Nothing specific. I'm still trying to run down the light that seems to appear and disappear. I've rechecked the FAA to see if there is a Part 107 permit issued for night flying of UAVs in the area, but I can't find one. I'm heading up to Sector Two tonight to see if I can find any mysterious lights. The DEA team is finished in the area around the meth lab explosion, so I need to reassure myself the lights were related." *Or not, if DEA Special Agent Sam Nations was right.*

"Want someone to ride with you? I think I can spare a deputy tonight."

"Thanks, but no need. I'm good. I'll call in if I need backup for anything. So, if you have nothing else..."

"Sheriff?"

He looked straight at her.

"You know I don't cotton to gossip, but there's quite a bit of chatter about our non-local county commissioner. I haven't paid it much mind other than to note it in case something reliable comes along."

He knew her using his title meant she might not know anything specific but was concerned enough about it to bring it up. "What kind of places are you hearing things?" He wondered if her source was her father.

"Mostly it's the deputies. There was some talk after choir practice at church last Thursday night. It's always a good source for what's happening around the valley. Some of it's even worth hearing." She tried to make light of criticizing her fellow choir members.

"Any talk or speculation about what's going on?"

"Nope. Just sounds like they're planning something big 'for the improvement of life in the valley.'" She used her fingers to put air quotes around the gossip.

"Thanks, Sergeant. Keep your eyes and ears open. I count on you for that."

"Will do, sir. Let me know if you need help up on that mountain tonight."

She closed the door on her way out, and Chad refocused on the possible link between the unidentified light, the Immigration agents if they were involved, and... *heaven forbid, human trafficking*. From the reports he had read recently, he knew human trafficking was a common way immigrants were brought into the country, with people on both sides of the border involved. He also knew young people, boys and girls, were being targeted for trafficking in the sex trade. *I really may be too old for this job.* He was not aware how long he had been at the table, but he stood when he heard the knock on his door. *Yep, five o'clock on the dot.*

The Meth Case Hangs On

"Come in!" Chad walked to his desk chair. *Might be time to slow Billy down a bit.* He knew Billy would expect him to open the door. Billy opened the door a little when he heard Chad tell him to come in. The perplexed look on his face amused the sheriff. "Have a question, Detective?" *Hmmm... this could be fun. I could use some humor today.*

"Sir, shall I close the door?" Billy tried to sound all business.

"Sure, thanks." Chad sat down in his chair.

Billy stood there. He expected to be sitting at the table, so he wasn't sure why the sheriff stayed at his desk.

"Something to report, Detective?"

Billy was trying to figure out what was going on. It wasn't like the boss to be so stiff. "Yes, sir. May take a bit of time, sir." He hoped that would get him an invitation to sit.

"Too out of shape to stand now that you're out of uniform, Detective?" Chad decided he was enjoying this.

"Sir, no, sir. It's just..."

"Just what, Detective?" Chad said, trying not to laugh.

"Nothing, Sheriff. Earlier today Deputy Susan Thomas and I interrogated Steve Phillips. In the interview—"

Chad interrupted him. "Sit down, Billy, take a load off," Chad said with less authority in his voice and stood up to join him at the round table. "How did it feel?"

"How did it feel, sir?" Billy tried to figure out the question, "How did it feel to interrogate a suspect?"

"Billy, you're smarter than that. But if you need me to spell it out..."

"No sir, I got the message loud and clear. Guess I've been getting a bit too loose in my joking around. Probably acting too familiar on the job too. I'll get it in line. I will."

"Good. That's all I need to hear. Now, tell me about your interview."

Billy told him how he and Deputy Thomas had handled the interview and Steve's reaction to the deputy's question about Will Hansen. "It seems pretty clear to me that Stevie knows Hansen is dead. He just didn't say the words. He told us the Hansen housekeeper said 'Master Will' was never coming back. I suspect she confirmed what he already knew or believed. He admitted he was out looking for Hansen the night of 'the little accident' with his Polaris Sportsman. Seemed real important to him to make sure I knew it was an expensive ATV."

"Think he'll lawyer up?"

"Don't think so. The interview our deputies had with his mother, seems the commissioner was unavailable, was just more of her trying get some kind of deal to let him out. You know, 'Can't we work this out? He's just a boy.' The deputies didn't think she had any idea how serious the charges were and didn't indicate she had any concern. What I find curious is that his father hasn't been beating the door down with fancy lawyers. Think they know what he was doing?"

Chad was contemplative, carefully turning his thoughts over in his head. *I think his stepfather doesn't want us snooping and is hanging the kid out to dry. And I suspect his mother knows which side her bread is buttered on.*

"Though I don't know for sure, I suspect that they're waiting to see what charges are brought against Steve. Then, depending on what they are, they might jump in and try to save him. It seems pretty clear from his whining they have done that a time or two."

"True, boss, but they don't know he was arrested on suspicion of murder," Billy said. "The tough thing is, even if we find a syringe with his prints on it, there's no guarantee the DA can prove Steve actually administered a lethal dose. I'm sure hoping we can get him to confess... if he did it."

"I know you'll do everything you can; just keep it clean. Make sure you have a deputy with you. I like the idea of Deputy Thomas being there. Good call."

"Yep, she's smart and a quick study." He was trying to figure out why Chad was staring at him. "Did I screw up, boss?"

"Let's save the 'yeps' for The Corral or station annual picnic, shall we?" Chad's flat voice made his intent very clear.

"Sorry, Sheriff."

Chad was worried that Billy was getting too free with his offhand comments, and he didn't want to give a defense attorney, especially a bigshot like this boy might get, any reason to convince a potential jury to dismiss the charges.

"Anything else I need to know, Detective?"

Billy stood. He knew he was on the sheriff's radar. As he headed for the door, he turned back. "I forgot to tell you the lab reports on the ATV we picked up at Steve's home and the paint we scraped off the gate pole at Dr. Anderson's should be ready shortly. That'll help." He decided it was best to go. "Good night, sir. I'll leave you to it."

Chad was struggling with whether he should cut Billy some slack and tell him he was using his comments to help him learn the importance of when you can tease and when you shouldn't. In the end, he decided to let the detective stew on it for a while. *He's a bright man. He'll figure it out.*

Chad stood up from the table and checked his mug; his coffee was cold. He pushed the coffee aside and did a quick review of the notes had made about what he decided to call the meth case since Justin Culverson wasn't the only one involved. A quick glance of his notes showed he had checked off Justin Culverson (in prison), William Rutherford Hansen III (deceased), and the weight of the confiscated meth (a total of forty pounds, seven ounces). The latter information was verified by a note from his own lab techs about the drugs confiscated from the ATVs driven by Culverson and Hansen: eight pounds, seven ounces. *Didn't need it for Culverson since he struck a deal with the DA. Did Nick Brown die from meth? At his own hand or someone else's? It may turn out we still need it with Phillips, then I want it out of our secure storage.* They were close to wrapping up the meth case, but he still needed to do some poking around to find out about methamphetamine use in the valley and surrounding areas. That would have to wait for another day.

He called the police chief in Round City to see when he might have time to get together or chat on the phone. Chad needed to know what was happening over the mountain, particularly if anything involved human trafficking. The police chief's administrative assistant said he could talk by phone at eight the next morning. "On my calendar, eight tomorrow. I'll call him then. Thanks so much." *One more puzzle piece.*

He stood up, stretched, and decided to pick up a sandwich at The Corral on his way out of the valley. He was headed to look for mysterious lights in Sector Two.

Surveillance

Before he left the station, Chad stopped in the men's room to wash his face and hands. It had already been a long day and, depending on what he encountered, it could be a long night. After his last time up on the hill overlooking Sector Two, he had bought a pair of long-range binoculars with a tracker, spending over three thousand dollars for the Zeiss Victory RF 10x54. *Sure appreciate Sam showing me the new technologies. I'll get Sylvia Whitehorse to do some research on what we might need beyond the info Sam shared. She's methodical and might enjoy the challenge.*

Once he was in his SUV, he called The Corral and asked Carla to fix him his usual fare for the road: barbeque sandwich, chips, water, and a big coffee. He always marveled that in the five minutes it took him to get to The Corral and walk in the side door, Carla would have his food ready to hand to him. "Appreciate the efficient service, Carla."

"I know, I know. Next you'll tell me it would be even faster if we put in a drive-up window."

"Hey! Now that's not a half-bad idea. Why not?"

"My brother will have none of that. Doesn't matter if it would increase the bottom line. He always says, 'If they're going to eat country food, they need some exercise.' Sounds just like him, doesn't it?"

"Well, he does have a point. Seems my exercise routine has taken a back seat recently, at least. Guess I need to get up a bit earlier and not miss so many days."

Carla looked him up and down, her admiring look not missed by him. "Look just fine to me, Chad. Just fine." She turned and walked off with a wave of her hand.

He turned, shaking his head. *Maybe I do need lessons on modern women. Wonder when I can get my son-in-law over for a drink?*

He headed out of the valley towards the outcropping that gave a perfect view of Sector Two. In a rare move, he turned on his SUV's radio and popped in the CD of gospel music from Nora's concert in Knoxville last year. He was proud of his daughter for so many reasons, but he liked that she was known throughout the region and invited to sing at different events. *Glad I made sure she learned the ins and outs of copyright. Could be embarrassing if she got caught for copyright infringement with her daddy as a sheriff.*

Then he lost himself in one of his favorite songs: "I'll Fly Away." It wasn't about losing himself in the music, but rather losing himself in his daughter's voice. By the time the song finished, he was almost to the outcropping. He pulled over, parked facing the valley, and decided to eat his sandwich as he waited on dusk to settle in.

As he took the first bite of his sandwich, he remembered telling Sam Nations that if he could run a string from Bella's place to this spot, the light would be in the middle of it. *Wish I could. Even with these fancy binoculars, if I could run a string it would mean I would have to go to her place. Don't think Friday evening can come fast enough.*

He pulled himself back to the task at hand. The waxing crescent moon meant he could have trouble with too much light. He knew it would be worse next week as they moved towards a waxing gibbous moon. He also knew it meant he had to be very diligent tonight. There was a bit of a cloud cover—could be good, could be bad. He followed a grid pattern as he looked through the binoculars. He stopped. He thought he saw a light. Then he moved on. The blue-black color of the night, combined with the deep darkness of the valley, promised a good backdrop if the light appeared.

After almost an hour, his neck was stiff, and he wished he had taken Sergeant Whitehorse up on her offer of a deputy. He walked around the SUV a few times to loosen up his muscles then started the search again. This time he started with the coordinates from the last time they saw the light. While the coordinates had helped find the meth lab, it was not the exact coordinates of where he and Sam had seen the light a few weeks before. *I guess that's why it's still nagging at me. Those coordinates were close to the meth lab, but not exactly where it was.* Then he saw two lights, one after the other. He checked the coordinates on the more distant light, writing them down using his pocket light. *Good start. I'll stick around a while and see if there's any pattern.*

He had three more sightings of a single light, each roughly forty-five minutes apart. He wondered if the light revealed an encampment rather than a night flying UAV. *It seems strange it would always be in the same general vicinity if it was a UAV carrying out a search. It would be moving in a grid pattern. That's the challenge of mountains and forest. It's not possible to look down a straight line.* He stood up from leaning on the front of his SUV and decided to head home. He might come back tomorrow night, depending on what he learned from the police chief in Round City.

End of a Long Day

On the drive home, Chad did not listen to the CD again. He wanted to use the silence to try and figure out what was going on. An encampment would explain the occasional light. It was highly unlikely an unmanned aerial vehicle would stay in the same spot all these weeks. *If I don't learn anything from the police chief, then I'll decide what makes the most sense to try and get in there to see what's what.* He backed into his garage, left his boots on the kitchen step facing out, and put his service weapon and ammunition in the safe box by the door.

He didn't even bother to turn on the kitchen light. He walked straight through to the bathroom, undressed, and stepped in the shower. He let the water wash over him and closed his eyes. *Wonder if it's possible to fall asleep standing up?*

Afterwards, he put his dirty shirt, socks, and boxers in the hamper, and his slacks and tie in the pile to go to the cleaners. He put on clean boxers, walked back to the kitchen, and took a Fat Tire Ale out of the fridge; it was the one beer a day he allowed himself. He sat down in his recliner to process his day and plan for the next one. *I wonder if other people have rituals like this? Or do they just go to bed and fall asleep? Wonder if Bella has a ritual before she goes to bed?* He sat up straight in his recliner and put his feet on the floor. *Get a grip! You may or may not ever find out the answer to that question. Now, sort out the work.*

He ran through his workday trying not to let the encounter with Bella and Joshua interfere. He decided his folks had made good progress on wrapping up the meth case and, hopefully, the overdose as well. He would have a whole new problem if the county commissioner was involved in activities that were immoral, illegal, and, perhaps, very dangerous. He knew he could start fitting some pieces together once he talked to the police chief. It was possible that adding time to the powwow could bring a new set of problems, but they just had to be prepared to try and avoid any. The source of the light—well, it was going to take a little more time to figure out the light. Lifting his beer bottle in the air, in a mock toast, he felt pretty good about following his instincts. He decided he had enough stuff rolling around in his head for tonight.

He leaned back in his recliner. *May need to rethink the interaction with Bella today.* After several minutes, he stood up and rinsed out his beer bottle in the kitchen before dropping it in the recycling bin. He walked into the bedroom, pulled down the covers and all but fell into bed. *Friday night bluegrass jam and sing-along and I'm picking up Bella. I think I'll fall asleep on that fine idea instead of work.* He knew the desire to have something pleasant on his mind as he fell asleep didn't mean he wouldn't dream about work. But he was hoping for sixty-forty odds on dreaming about Bella.

13

In the Middle of the Night

Detective Williams was startled awake at three in the morning by the ringing of his work phone on the nightstand. He fumbled for it, managing to answer the call on the fourth ring. "Williams here."

The matron for the holding cells said, "Sorry, Detective. Steve Phillips asked for you and said he was willing to talk. Actually, his exact words were, 'Get Williams here right now!'" She stopped for a moment, and Billy could hear the suppressed laughter in her voice. "Do you want me to tell him to sleep on it, and you'll see him in the morning?"

"No. Thanks, though. Maybe the cot got to him after all."

"More likely it was the drunk I put on the top bunk who just shared his drink and dinner all over our fine Mr. Steve Phillips."

"Oh, I see he's given you his preferred form of address—comes from that fancy private school he attends. Seniors get addressed with titles: Mr. Smith, Ms. Smith." Billy paused, finally catching sight of the time. "Argh... three o'clock in the morning! Okay, be there in less than fifteen."

Billy splashed water on his face, dressed, and decided to get coffee at work. It would be better than the instant he would fix at home. Twelve minutes later he walked in the back door of the station. He didn't give his usual mock salute to the camera. *Maybe the sheriff heard I was doing that. Gotta clean up my act. Time for something new.* He opened the door to the lab to get his mug for coffee. Elizabeth Alexander was bent over the evidence table working on something. "Alexander, what are you still doing here?"

"Oh, hey, Billy." She looked over his shoulder to make sure no one was behind him. She didn't want to get in trouble for calling the detective by his first name in front of a superior. "What are you doing back here?"

"I asked you first."

"Running what I hope will be the last analysis on the paint from Phillips' banged-up Sportsman 850 against the paint on Dr. Anderson's gatepost. It looks promising."

"Good work. Don't let me distract you. Appreciate you taking the night shift tonight, although this is the late-night shift!" His satisfaction with her work ethic was evident in the warm tone of his voice. "I have to go see the young Mr. Phillips. Seems he has requested the pleasure of my company."

"At three in the morning?" Elizabeth looked up at him.

"Ye..." he stopped himself from saying yep. "Yes, three in the morning. Worse yet, I had to call Deputy Thomas, who is due back in here at eight. Guess she'll have a long day too." He turned to walk out the door. "Catch you later."

"Maybe much later. I'm headed home in about fifteen."

"Good enough."

Deputy Susan Thomas was coming down the hall as he headed towards holding. "Sorry to get you up in the middle of the night."

"It's okay. I had to get up to answer the phone anyway." She covered a yawn.

"Humor at this hour of the morning?"

"Beats screaming and having my husband think I'm dying."

They walked up to the matron. She had Steve Phillips sitting on a wooden chair. His jumpsuit was covered in wet spots from where he had likely tried to clean up the free gift he got from his bunk mate.

Billy looked at the boy. *Smart move on the matron not to give him a clean jumpsuit. Don't know how long Thomas and I can take the smell, but maybe his tolerance is less than ours.*

Billy nodded to the matron. "You called, Stevie?"

"Damn straight. What took you so long? Tell this. . . this woman to get me a fresh jumpsuit. Better yet, get me my own clothes."

"Oh, I'm so sorry. Our matron is busy and doesn't have the time to get you one of those lovely orange outfits. I'm sure once the new matron does her check-in duties, she'll get to you. . . at some point later today." Billy kept walking towards the interrogation room. "Let's get this over with. I want to go home and back to my nice, comfortable bed."

Deputy Thomas and Billy took their time getting the room open and walking in. Billy gave the deputy a look that she knew meant to leave the cuffs on.

"Have a seat, Steve. We'll get this little recorder set up and be right with you." Billy nodded towards the chair.

"Well, hurry up. I'm giving you one chance and one chance only."

"Oh, Stevie, I have nothing but time tonight. You see someone woke me up in the middle of the night, so my day is just starting. We can spend all day together. Isn't that right Deputy Thomas?"

"My time is your time, Detective."

Billy pretended to have trouble starting the recorder. "Testing, testing." He stopped to play it back. Starting it again, he stood against the far wall. "It seems to be recording. This is Detective Billy Williams and. . ."

"Deputy Susan Thomas," she said before Steve could speak.

Billy gave the date, time, and location, trying his best to drag it out. "State your name and date of birth, please." He stared at Steve.

"Steve Phillips." He gave his date of birth.

"Steve Phillips, you were read your Miranda rights. . ."

"Yes, yes! I know my rights! I don't need them repeated! I do not want a lawyer! I want to tell you what I have to say and get the hell out of here."

Deputy Thomas ignored the profanity and pulled up a chair at the table where Steve was sitting. Billy didn't object but wasn't sure how she could stand the smell that close.

Billy spoke slowly. "Just to verify, Mr. Steve Phillips, you're in no way being coerced or threatened to share the information you're about to give us. Is that correct?"

"Yes, yes. How many times do I have to tell you? I don't want a lawyer, I know what I'm doing. Let's get on with it."

"Very well. Deputy, are you ready?"

"Yes, sir, Detective." Her words dripped with respect.

"Okay," Steve said. "Well, we had a little accident up at some old, abandoned farm, or whatever you want to call it. We were looking for Justin and Will. They told us the general direction they were going, and we were supposed to meet them down the road from that place. We waited a long time. Before they came back to our meet-up place, cops and ambulances came up the road. So, we waited on a path we found where we couldn't be seen. We were afraid to leave because those ATVs are so loud that we thought the cops might hear us." He stopped and took a deep breath.

Deputy Thomas had brought a bottle of water in with her, and she offered it to him. He pulled his hands up behind his back with a gesture of "How"?

Billy nodded to her; she asked Steve to stand then uncuffed him. He grabbed the water bottle and sat down again.

"We knew something was going on. We were there for a long time. Once it was good and quiet, we went back up the road, but it was really dark and the damn gate was locked."

"Language, Stevie, language. There's a lady present." Billy stated it simply, as if a friend reminding a friend.

"Sorry, Deputy. Anyway, we went around the gate and headed down the trail that Will had told me to follow if they didn't meet up with us. It was along the creek. Our lights didn't help. We went real slow around the side of that hill and all of a sudden we saw the two wrecked ATVs. We knew it had to be Will and Justin. There was yellow police tape everywhere. So, we hightailed it out of there and went up over the hill like we did the first time we were up there. Nick swerved out and ran right into that big barn." He went quiet again.

Billy realized the days of locking a gate and not leaving a deputy were over. *Hard to learn big city lessons back in these hollers.* He and Susan just looked at Steve and waited.

He took another sip of water. "Nick jumped off the ATV faster than a flea gettin' on a cat—"

Billy interrupted him. "Why, Stevie, you *are* adapting to our ways here in Tennessee. That line about the flea was pretty good. Didn't you think so, Deputy?"

"It was. I'm impressed."

Billy knew the sarcasm was totally wasted on this kid. He was on an adrenaline high, and it was best to let him talk it out. He knew once Steve ran down, he would be finished.

"Yeah, well, anyway, I was pretty mad at Nick for wrecking into that building. That was my ATV, not his. Anyway, he hopped on the back of mine and we were moving fast to get to the road. Like I said, it was dark. I didn't see the post for that gate. We were lucky it didn't flip us." Then after a deep breath, like he'd been running a marathon, he said, "Don't you think it was lucky?"

"Oh, yeah, real lucky. Not so lucky for the owner's shed and gate post, though, was it?"

"How much can it cost to fix it? I have plenty of money of my own, and if I don't have enough, good ole Pop will pay up I bet, just to keep it out of the papers." The smugness was returning.

Billy pulled up the chair by the wall and sat facing the back of the chair, resting his forearms on it. He watched Steve start to squirm.

Steve looked from Billy to Susan and back to Billy, "So, now you know everything. I want out of here."

"Oh, Stevie, Stevie, Stevie. If only it were that easy. You see we have this little matter of the murder charge."

"I didn't kill Will. I didn't."

That threw Billy because he wasn't expecting it. "Which Will would that be?"

Starting to get agitated, Steve blurted, "Will Hansen!"

"Deputy Thomas, do we know anything about Will Hansen being deceased?"

Susan feigned a look of confusion but said nothing.

Billy took his time. "I need you to tell me where you were on Monday morning of *this* week between six and eight a.m."

Steve tapped his heels on the floor. "Okay, okay, I was at Nick's, but I didn't kill him either. He OD'd on his own and I hightailed it out of there. His folks weren't home, and I didn't want to be accused of something I didn't do."

Deputy Thomas made sure he was looking at her. "That's all very interesting, Steve. First you tell me Will Hansen is dead. And now you're telling me you didn't kill Nick. I'm assuming you mean Nick Brown. Is that right?"

Billy had conducted interrogations with Susan before and she definitely knew how to play the motherly "I'm here for you" card. Billy sat perfectly still so as not to distract Steve's gaze on her.

"Could I have some more water and another jump suit? *Please*? It would help me relax. Then I'll tell you what you want to know."

"Well, here's the problem with that, Steve," she said in a soft voice. "If I do that now, it's going to look like it was *quid pro quo*. I do something for you—"

"I know what it means!" he snapped. "I'm going to an Ivy League university, remember?"

"You tell us what else you have to say, and answer any questions we have for you, and then maybe we can arrange more than clean clothes. We can probably convince the matron to let you shower. Wouldn't that be better?" Susan sounded very sincere.

Steve's shoulders slumped. He took the last swallow of water, lowered his head, and softly said, "What do you want to know?"

Billy purposely let the question hang in the air for a few seconds. "We'll come back to Will. Will Hansen, was it?" He didn't wait for a response. "First, how did you get both your ATVs over here to the valley?"

Steve kept his head down. "I have a truck, so we brought my other ATV here and locked it behind Nick's house in the woods. I didn't trust his stepfather not to sell it if he knew it was there. Then I went back and got my newer ATV."

"Good, Stevie, that's helpful information. Now, I just need you to verify that you were at Nick Brown's residence on Dickson Road on Monday of this week between six and eight in the morning."

Steve dropped his eyes from the deputy and looked at his feet, which were still bouncing on the floor. "I was at Nick Brown's house on Dickson Road. But I didn't kill him. He put the needle in his own arm. I don't do that sh– ... sorry, Deputy. He like took this deep breath, let it out like one of those accordions, and then he just lay there. I thought he was dead. I was scared. I grabbed the syringe and pulled that rubber band off his arm and ran out the door. I threw it in the bushes near the corner before turning on to the main road through the valley." He seemed to slump down even further down in the chair.

Billy was concerned Steve was going to fall to the floor, but he slowly sat back up. There were tears streaming down his face.

"Were you driving your truck on Monday morning?"

"Yeah, what did you think I was driving?"

Billy ignored his sarcasm. "What did you get out of this friendship with Will and Justin? And Nick?"

Steve sat without speaking for a minute. When he finally spoke, his voice was barely above a whisper. "See, I met Nick at a party and we kind of hit it off. Truthfully, the only thing we had in common was having stepfathers. I always knew Pop was my stepfather, but Nick thought that crazy man was his dad until one night his old man was so drunk that he told Nick the truth. Then Nick told me he just didn't care anymore. He couldn't figure out how his mother could let a man like that be his father." He slowed down. "And I told him I didn't know how my mother could let a man like Pop be my dad either."

"And Will Hansen? How do you know him?" Deputy Thomas asked quietly.

"I *knew* him. I told you his housekeeper said he was never coming back. So, I figured he was dead... well, at least I think he's dead." Steve's voice was even softer. "We both went to the Mountain Villages Academy. Will left more than a year ago. We met up one day in the summer while riding our ATVs and I found out he'd been in juvie. It was stupid to get caught. He told me he had a friend from the valley, and I told him I did too. He asked me some questions about Nick and then told me he wanted to meet him. Will met Justin in juvie, so I guess he wondered if Nick had been in juvie too. I never had any friends at the Academy, so I was happy to have Will talk to me."

Deputy Thomas asked, "Did Will tell you what he and Justin were doing?"

"Not at first. But then I found out. One day Justin told Nick he could help him out of his misery with his dad. I told Nick I thought he was crazy to use that sh–... stuff, but he wanted it."

"Justin already knew Nick 'cause they went to the same high school, the one here in the valley. So, when Justin started giving Nick some meth, I asked Nick if he was paying for it. Nick said Justin told him it was 'extra' from some work he was doing for Will."

Steve sat back and Billy was afraid he would stop talking.

"So, I told Will what Justin had said to Nick, and Will got really mad. I think he was afraid I'd tell my dad. So, he gave me… I think you call it hush money."

"Hush money for what?" Deputy Thomas asked sympathetically.

"I called Will up and asked about the drugs Nick had from Justin. He acted all surprised, but I think he knew I knew the truth. He asked to meet me at this place on our side of the valley where we all rode ATVs. So, I met him there."

Hesitating a few seconds, Steve plowed on. "At first Will tried to get all tough, but he was like me. He came from Michigan, rich family, and he wasn't tough at all. He was just doing the meth runs for the fun of it. At least, I think he was. He offered me $500 a week if I would keep my mouth shut. He joked that the rich boys get richer, and the poor boys get hooked on drugs."

The tears had stopped, but it was clear Steve was coming off his adrenaline high.

Billy had been listening carefully, but he had also been considering there might be more the boy could give them to help make sure they had all of the parties involved with the meth lab. He also had to see what the DA wanted to do about charges. They at least had him on failure to lend aid, but Billy knew Steve could also be criminally charged in Nick's death.

"Listen, Steve, it's been a long night. What do you say we get the matron to let you shower and put on a clean jumpsuit? We'll see if she's got a clean bunk and you can get some rest. Then we can talk later in the day." Billy tried to sound like he was doing Steve a big favor.

"Yeah, yeah. Okay. Don't know what else I can tell you."

"Deputy, please cuff Mr. Phillips and walk him back to the matron. I'll catch up with you shortly."

"Can I go home later today, Detective Williams?"

Billy almost laughed. *Did this boy think he was going to get on my good side by calling me Detective Williams? Or be able to go home without any consequences?*

"Let's take it one step at a time, Steve. One step at a time."

"This is Detective Billy Williams, and. . ."

"Deputy Susan Thomas."

"Returning Steve Phillips to holding and exiting the interview at four thirty-four a.m." He gave the date and turned off the recorder. They walked Steve back to holding and Susan spoke privately with the matron.

Detective Williams said, "Catch you in a bit, Deputy Thomas. Good work in there."

Looking for Her Own Answers

Bella followed a flatlander out of the valley and didn't really mind the slow speed. She opened the window as she usually did when driving in the mountains. *Too cool to open all the way. Even cracking the window makes it cool enough to make sure I stay awake.* She shook her head. *Why in the world do we use the word "crack" to describe opening the car window?*

She had awakened early and decided to go look at the prefab log cabins. The traffic would likely be worse on the highway if she waited until Saturday. Besides, she didn't really have any plans for today since she'd gone to the valley yesterday.

After fifteen minutes of following the flatlander, she hoped the driver knew about the pullouts along the road: areas that allowed people unaccustomed to driving on the steep, curvy roads to pull over and let others pass. She didn't consider herself a speed demon, but she knew how to take the bends and when she needed to slow down. She was hopeful he would pull over when she saw the blinker flash on the car with Louisiana license plates. He did. She passed, honked, and waved, not sure if he would see her friendly gesture through her back window. She took the next curve and started the descent to the highway. Listening to Alison Krauss on one of her CDs, she settled in to enjoy the drive. As the sun hit the trees through the gaps in the sides of the mountains, they glowed with reds, yellows, and oranges.

Thirty minutes later, she saw the GPS on her phone light up with a signal. She was approaching the exit for the prefab log cabin company. A large billboard just before the exit pointed the way: "Buy YOUR Log Home Here." The arrow indicated a right turn off the highway followed by "1/2 mile on the right." *Simple enough. I'm not crazy about dealing with people who are trying to sell me something. Hope they're not too high pressure.* Turning right at the light at the bottom of the off-ramp, she felt like she was putting on armor not to bend to the pressure, if it came.

Well, there's no one standing in the parking lot hustling you like at a car dealership; hopefully that's a good sign. She pulled up in front, parked, and entered the front door of a large, modified A-frame cabin with a sign on the door indicating it was the show room. A tall young man, casually dressed in khaki chinos and a blue pullover sweater, greeted her.

"Hey, how are you today? Interested in building a cabin in our fine mountains?"

"Hey! It's right possible I could be interested in building a cabin." *I can slip into that mountain drawl in a heartbeat. Wonder if it will become routine the longer I stay up here?*

"Well, that's just great. Just great." He extended his hand to shake hers. "If you know what you want, we can talk about specifics. If you need some ideas, I can show you our models, then we can go from there. What's your pleasure?"

Bella decided she liked this young man's approach; she could let her guard down a little. He didn't seem likely to be a high-pressure salesman. "I would like to see any models you have that are 600 to 800 square feet."

"So, basically sleeping space, a sitting area, and a bathroom?"

"Yes, that would work. I'm Bella Anderson, by the way."

"Nice to meet you, Ms. Anderson, I'm Macklin Evans. My dad and I are the owners. Feel free to tell me what you like and don't like about what I show you and we'll figure out the best way to help you."

"That sounds perfect."

It took nearly forty-five minutes to look through the models they had on site. Bella was surprised how much she liked the one that included a large room with kitchen and eating area, one bedroom, and a bathroom. It was called the Overlook. As she walked through the models, she could see there was good attention to the detail on the logs and, even though the distance between the logs would mean more chinking than Drellag Caban had, she didn't think it would look out of place. Her mind felt like it was working overtime trying to sort out whether she should tear down the shed and put one of these up, or have Arthur do a stick-built garage and shed. *Maybe I'll set this cabin closer to the gate and just have him repair the shed.* She suddenly realized Macklin was holding the door to the showroom open for her. She didn't even remember walking back to the large building, but she walked in and he followed her.

"Thanks for the information. By the way, Arthur Gillett sent me. He's available to install the cabin for me." She watched his face.

"Mr. Gillett has installed a number of our cabins. He does good work."

"Yes, he does. If you could give me some literature on the Overlook model along with pricing and ordering time, I would appreciate it."

"Yes, ma'am, no problem at all. Feel free to look around and I'll get that together."

Bella nodded her head and walked over to a wall of the showroom that displayed different floor plans. She saw that it was possible to get any of the models with different window and door configurations. She would have to make sure she had all the information on that too. A few minutes later, Macklin returned.

"Would you like to sit down and go over this?"

"Sure. That would be great."

Fifteen minutes later she had all her questions answered. Bella was impressed when Macklin told her the first fifty miles of transporting the logs was included and quoted the amount for the distance to her land. *I like that he pointed out that service. I wouldn't have thought to ask.*

"Ms. Anderson, the logs are delivered on a truck that can offload them onto the foundation. Of course, Mr. Gillett will know that. Do you have any questions?"

"I think I have enough information to discuss with Mr. Gillett. I'll be in touch soon."

As Bella pulled out of the parking lot and turned left to head back to the highway, an office supply store caught her eye. *Perfect! I'll get a printer, ink, and some paper, and then I'll be ready to read my work as I write.* She enjoyed the nip of fall in the air as she returned to the Jeep, the printer and its accessories in tow, but she left her windows up until she reached the Route 54 exit and was headed towards the valley; she really didn't like the windows down at seventy miles an hour on the interstate. Winding up the mountain on the way to Drellag Caban, she was pleased it would still be early afternoon when she arrived.

14

Decisions to be Made

Chad was dressed and at his desk in the station before six, feeling more rested than he had in a long time. *I either had really pleasant dreams or I slept like a rock. At least I didn't have work rolling around in my head all night. That's a good thing.* He knew the morning would require his full attention—and then some—depending on what he learned from the police chief in Round City.

Despite the early hour, Chad really liked this time of morning. Whatever activity requiring deputies during the night had generally died down and shifts weren't changing yet. He filled his mug with coffee in the break room, shut his door, and started going through his messages and emails. He saw Billy Williams had been called in during the night and interrogated Steve Phillips. He would catch up with Billy later.

He walked over to the board showing the sector maps to study the topography where he had noted the light the previous night. Assuming the coordinates were accurate, the topographical markings indicated there was a rock plateau tucked under an outcropping. It was a large enough plateau to safely have twenty to thirty people moving about on it. The outcropping above it, particularly when the trees were covered in leaves, would provide good shelter and could affect its visibility when looking down on it. It was in the same general vicinity of the meth lab, but not close enough to be visible. *Maybe the plateau's elevation would have prevented whoever was in the meth lab from seeing anyone on the plateau itself. I have to figure out how they could get there.*

The road used by the DEA and sheriff's ATVs to get to the site of the meth lab explosion was marked on his map. The road was not adjacent to the plateau. He was still trying to figure out the possibilities of access points when the timer set for his call to the police chief chimed. He walked back to his desk and scanned his notes.

"Good morning. Chad Oliver calling for Chief Nelson."

"Good morning, Sheriff. Chief Nelson is expecting you. Please hold."

"Morning, Chad. How are things over in the valley these days? Settling down from the explosion?"

"Hey, hope you're well. I'd like to tell you we have that behind us and that we're back to our usual autumn leaf-looker accidents and petty theft, but unfortunately no such luck. How are things in the big city?"

"As you know, the use of city in our title is a bit of a misnomer. Thankfully, I have no interest in big city policing. That's a promise."

A chuckle escaped Chad. "So, when you get recruited to Knoxville or Chattanooga, I should remind you of that?"

"Puh-leez! Enough to do right here! Pretty sure you didn't call to talk about my career path, though. What's up?"

"Looks like we're about to wrap up the meth lab distribution, but in the process of that investigation, we've had some curious activity involving random lights concentrated in a single sector over here. I've followed up to see if they disappeared with the explosion. They haven't. I've been trying to figure out the source. I've checked on FAA Part 107 certificates for night UAV flying, but none have been issued for this area. I wanted to check in with you and see if you have anything going on that might overlap our areas."

Chad left it at that, trying to give Chief Nelson enough to latch onto without giving him something that would elicit a pat affirmation. *I don't have anything to affirm anyway.*

"You know that we get some challenges on this side of the mountain that haven't reached your neck of the woods yet. Well, I suspect not anyway. Not sure what you might be tracking, but we've got some uptick in human trafficking activity. Some of it's coming across the border from Mexico, and the rest through an internal network, mostly moving young people north. As I'm sure you know, the main corridor for trafficking teens in our own country used to be I-95 between Miami and New York. When the numbers built up around Jacksonville, the traffickers started moving out I-10 and then up I-75 and I-65. Most of I-65 is hitting Nashville, but I-75 is starting to branch off on I-40/81 and coming east." The police chief stopped for a moment.

"Getting any help in dealing with either issue?" Chad asked. He knew Immigration would be the agency to deal with people being moved across the border and the FBI with domestic trafficking.

"Most of the federal agents are pretty tight lipped. If I go to them with a specific situation, or when I actually have arrested someone, they're cooperation personified. When I ask for information so I can to be on the lookout, I get the general bulletin they put out to the world. So much for interagency cooperation, right?"

"I hear you. I hear you." Chad tried to decide if he wanted to push and ask specifically about immigration.

Then the police chief spoke. "I do have to say the legislators are starting to put some money behind trying to stop human trafficking. I think that's a good thing."

"Absolutely! I just read a bulletin that Tennessee is number one in the country for this year in combatting human trafficking. I'm just hoping that means some resources will be flowing our way when we need it."

"I hear you, Chad." The police chief paused. "I'm not one for gossip myself, and I know you aren't either. That said, some of the folks in our restaurants lately pretty much scream immigration enforcers. Too much English to have just come across the border, and too much Spanish not to be suspicious."

Chad waited to see if he was going to share anything else. When he didn't, Chad asked, "Any increase in by-the-hour motel traffic?"

"Hard to catch it without having someone sitting in a parking lot twenty-four seven. So, outside of complaints and routine patrols, hard to track. Just don't have enough resources. Two new low-end motels went up last year. Some developer from Michigan, I think. Seems an unusual number of cars in and out of it, but—"

Chad interrupted him. "Mind giving me the names of those hotels?"

"Got something in mind, Chad?" Chief Nelson asked, the concern in his voice evident.

"Just rumors on this side of the mountain, but I promise you if I find out anything, I'll let you know." *If I was a betting man, and I'm not, I'd bet our county commissioner is behind them one way or the other.* "Tell me, were those motels the new modular buildings they're doing now? The ones that go up pretty quickly?"

"Yep. I'd say it was less than a year from going before our city council, to permitting, to doors open. That ticking a box for you?"

"Right now I'm just trying to fit the pieces together, as it were. I'll do some research on instant motels, for sure. I'm still trying to sort out what this elusive light is. If you hear anything you think might fit, please give me a call."

"Sure thing, Chad. I look forward to what you learn that could help me out over here. I, for one, am fine with folks who come here legally, wherever it's from. What has me concerned is that we don't know about who is behind the illegal immigrants. And, worse than that, what I'm reading says American boys and girls are swept up by some of these clowns as soon as they post online that they're unhappy at home. I'd appreciate help in catching any that come through our fair city."

"Sure thing. Appreciate your time, Chief. Stay in touch. I'll let you know one way or the other what I figure out."

"It's a deal, Sheriff. Just hope the aliens are human and not the green men from Mars." Chief Nelson laughed uproariously at his own joke.

"Gotcha. Hang in there. Catch you later."

"Later, Chad."

Putting down the phone, the only thing Chad felt he got out of the call was the possibility that the two new low-end motels might be connected to Zimmerman. He picked up the phone again and called Harold Cooper, the county manager.

"Hey, Harold. Chad here. Got a minute?"

Chad asked to be informed of any building permits for anything outside the Mountain Villages that was more than a twelve-hundred square foot cabin. "And, Harold, I particularly want to know if Commissioner Zimmerman starts talking about doing any building in the valley."

"Chad, got time for a coffee at The Corral this morning? Say around ten?"

"I'll be there." Chad didn't hesitate. He knew Harold wouldn't have suggested it without having something important on his mind.

Tying up Loose Ends

Billy left a message for DA Peggy O'Haire to call him. He spent the next three hours in the lab going over Alexander's reports about the evidence related to all four boys on the ATVs—two dead and two locked up, at least for the time being. Alexander's work verified the paint from the damage on Steve Phillips' Polaris Sportsman 850 was a match to the paint on Dr. Bella Anderson's gate post. There was a less than one percent chance it came from some other object. *Doesn't get any better than that.* There was a sudden knock on the door, and he got up to open it.

"Hey, Detective, I checked with my sergeant and I can head back over to Dickson Road if we need to keep looking for that syringe."

"Tell you what, Deputy, I'll meet you over there. Park just off Route 54 where it meets Dickson Road. See you there in ten."

"Good deal, Detective." The deputy headed out without further comment.

Well, Stevie boy, let's see if you hit any bushes with that syringe and rubber band. Of course, if we find it, likely means your prints are on it and we may not be able to tie it back to Nick Brown at all. He picked up his evidence kit, checked the battery in his camera, and called dispatch to say he was headed out.

When he arrived at Dickson Road, the deputy was waiting in his SUV and stepped out as Billy drove up and parked. As he looked around the area, Billy started feeling frustrated; leaves had already started to fall, which would make it harder to search.

"Well, Deputy, this little task may literally be trying to find a needle in the proverbial haystack. Or, in this case, fallen leaves."

The deputy didn't respond. He stood waiting for directions.

"The suspect says he threw the syringe and elastic band in the bushes as he turned off of Dickson. So, theoretically, we should be able to assume it would have been to his left. I think you'd have to preplan to roll down the passenger window and hope you could throw it far enough. My gut feeling is this kid was just trying to get rid of it. Let's start over here." Billy handed the deputy one of the two yardsticks from the back of his SUV.

Carefully moving leaves aside with the yardsticks to ensure they didn't inadvertently step on the syringe, they each worked in a pattern side-by-side, moving the stick left to right. When they reached the bushes and had not found anything, they walked back to the edge of the road: one stepped to the right and one to the left and they went towards the bushes again. Once they had a six-foot swath from the road to the bushes, Billy said, "Okay, let's get down and look through the base of the bushes. You start on the far left side, and I'll start here." He indicated the far right side of their swath. "Remember, this is a syringe we're looking for, so don't stick yourself with it."

"Got it, Detective." The deputy watched his steps going to the assigned area.

Wearing gloves, each man started sorting through the leaves, working towards the middle of the area they had cleared up to the bush line. Moving a few leaves at a time, each man was methodical in his search.

Billy didn't mind the exacting work, but the frosty chill on this autumn morning was not his cup of tea. *Stevie boy, you better hope this pays off. 'Cause if it doesn't, you haven't begun to see how tough I can get in an interrogation.* He heard the deputy clear his throat.

"Detective Williams, I think I have it."

"Don't touch anything. Let me get my camera. Be right there."

He walked back to his SUV and got his sketch pad, the high-powered camera he used to document crime scene evidence, and his markers. The first thing he did was take a picture of the street sign, dilapidated as it was, on the corner of Dickson Road and Route 54. He then took a picture of the area they had been searching, using the deputy as a marker for the area he was about to photograph. They both had yardsticks to help with measurements, but he also had his tape measure to get the distances in metric as well. Billy was always careful with his crime scene sketches. He wanted to be sure the triangulation, baseline, and polar coordinates indicating the evidence would hold up in court. One of the things he liked about being in a small sheriff's department was being able to do far more technical work than if they had several forensic techs.

"Okay, Deputy, show me what you found." The deputy pointed with his yard stick to the lower branch of the bush and, sure enough, there was a syringe. There was no elastic band, but the syringe was as clear as day. As he did his preliminary sketch on paper and then took photographs, he double-checked his measurements and made sure his digital images had readable numbers.

"Looks good." He pulled a pair of bamboo tweezers out of a sealed plastic envelope, although he always thought they looked more like tongs than tweezers. "If you'll hold this evidence bag open, I'll grab it and drop it in." Being careful to grab the syringe by the outer edges of the very top of the plunger, he hoped he wouldn't damage any potential fingerprints.

"Got it, Detective. Good job. You barely touched it with the tongs."

"Good job finding the syringe, Deputy. Now we can move around a bit more and see if we can find the elastic band. It's not as critical, but I'd sure like to find it if possible."

After an hour of rustling through the leaves and pulling back branches of the bushes, Billy sat on his haunches and sighed. "Let's go with what we have for now. Some critter may have found that elastic band and taken it who knows where. If the syringe doesn't pan out, then we may need to come back with a team and really search for it." *I don't like not having it, but I don't think it would have traveled as far as the syringe. It's likely long gone.*

"Go on back to the station and clock out. Thanks for your initiative in getting us out here this morning and for finding this evidence. I'm going to take some pictures from here to the Browns' residence, and then I'll head in myself. Get some rest."

"Sure thing, Detective." The deputy headed off with a smile of satisfaction at a job well done.

Billy finished photographing and measuring the distance from the Browns' driveway to the corner since he didn't know where Steve's truck was parked when he was there. He put everything back in his evidence kit and headed for the station. He'd already been on the job almost six hours and the day had just begun. There was work to be done when he got to the station to see if there were any prints to be pulled from the syringe. *I sure hope so.*

Meeting at The Corral

Harold was sitting in a back corner booth when Chad entered. He was talking with Carla and both said good morning to Chad as he walked up to them.

"Fine company you're keeping this morning, Mr. County Manager," Chad said as he smiled at Carla.

"Yeah, yeah, get on with you, Sheriff," Carla said, pointing to the seat on the opposite side of the booth. "Having breakfast this morning, or just taking up space drinking coffee?"

"Come to think of it, Carla, I got up before breakfast this morning. Might just have some scrambled eggs and grits. How about you, Harold?"

Harold held up his hand. "Coffee is good enough for me at this hour."

Carla poured coffee for Chad and walked away.

"Thanks for meeting me, Chad." Harold looked around at the surrounding booths. There was no one on this side of the restaurant.

"Been too long, Harold. Guess it's a good thing, us not needing to meet too often in our official capacities. Did I present you with a problem earlier?"

"No, not really. Just thought I might need to run something by you." Harold told Chad about the comment Commissioner Zimmerman had made at the last county commissioners' meeting regarding something "new" coming to the valley. He watched Chad's face but was not surprised there was no visible reaction. "Nothing I can pinpoint, just thought it was strange."

Chad remained silent. He was trying to determine if he could find a connection between what the Round City police chief had told him and the commissioner's comment. "Harold, these are the puzzles I try to put together—a piece of information here, a piece of information there. Just trying to make sense of it all."

Harold nodded his head. "Get that in my job too. There haven't been any agenda items at this point that would suggest someone was planning to build anything more than a residence. However, I've heard talk from other county managers that just before an agenda deadline closes, a commissioner will submit something for the agenda that seems benign. In the end, it leads to a building permit and, before you know it, you have a new business in town."

"Not opposed to progress, Harold. Just don't want to go the way of the highway and end up with troubles none of us want."

Harold did not respond; he just nodded his head in agreement.

"Do you have any idea of the businesses the non-local commissioner owns or has a partnership interest in, anywhere other than the Mountain Villages?" Chad watched Harold's face.

"Directly, no. His financial disclosure of interests filed for this year lists a couple of companies, but they're not located in our county."

"Okay, thanks. I'll check those out with anything else I come across. Meantime, if you can let me know of any unusual agenda items or unusual building permits, I'd appreciate it. I try to follow your agendas each week, but some weeks it just gets by me."

"Still not considering a personal assistant?"

"No more than you are," Chad said quickly. "I think both of us know serving the folks in the valley is a better use of state and federal money. For me, it's more deputies on the road. For you?"

"Just good ole everyday life: pre-kindergarten programs, health department, waste disposal... when it's not earmarked for something specific by folks in Nashville or Washington who know nothing about our needs"

Carla brought Chad's breakfast, filled their coffees, and disappeared. Suddenly, she was back again, pretending like she was filling their coffee mugs. In her trademark nod to the folks in the sheriff's office, she indicated the two people who had just entered The Corral through the front door. Chad was facing the front, so he did not have to move to look. Chad listened as Harold continued to talk about county management matters. Chad looked past him to see Commissioner Zimmerman and a very young woman enter and sit down near the front. *She could be older than she looks, and she could be a native woman. But, dollars to donuts, she's neither. I might just need to exit through the front door.* He suddenly realized that Harold had stopped talking and was saying his name.

"Sorry, Harold. Got a bit distracted there. Thanks for getting that stove off the mountainside up by the Anderson place. By the way, she said if she ends up staying here full time, she could get interested in helping promote recycling."

"That would be great. I haven't seen Bella in several years. Met her and her husband… sorry, her late husband… but I don't really know her. Apparently, she's causing quite a stir in the valley, especially the Valley Store." Harold stopped. He didn't want to divulge anything Joshua had said to him.

"That so?" Chad said. He waited to see if Harold would say more.

Stammering a little, Harold said, "Yeah, Joe was talking about how nice it was to have an intelligent conversation with her a few weeks back."

"Likely so," Chad said. "Likely so. Well, I hate to eat and run, but duty calls. Thanks for the heads-up and sharing the comments from the meeting the other night. I'll let you know if I hear anything we need to address at your level."

"Thanks, Chad. With Abigail's help in the office, I'll be on the lookout for those things we discussed."

Carla reached the table and handed them each a check. She knew better than to give one check to two government employees. Both men laid cash on their checks and stood up to walk out. Harold was closest to the side door and Chad followed him. As soon as they reached the door, Chad said, "Think I'll stop off at the men's room before I hit the road. Thanks again, Harold. Catch you later."

"Yeah, take care, Chad." Harold walked out, apparently not seeing the county commissioner.

Chad walked past Carla on his way to the front door and just nodded. The young woman was facing his direction and the commissioner was facing the front door. One look at her confirmed Chad's suspicion that she was probably not more than fifteen or sixteen. She glanced up as he walked past and he saw her dark brown eyes, which perfectly complemented her jet-black hair and light caramel colored skin. She was silent, but Zimmerman was talking to her in short simple sentences—in English. Chad heard him say, "You'll love it here," and "Nothing to be afraid of." *Except maybe you, Commissioner. I may need to see where he heads when he leaves here.*

Bella's Not-So-Simple Afternoon

It was a little after one when Bella descended into the valley from the highway. She felt foolish having to stop at the Valley Store two days in a row, but she forgot to get brown sugar and pecans for the brownies. She pulled in front of the store and saw there were several cars; she hoped it wouldn't take too long. She saw Joshua opening the front door as she walked up.

"Hey, Joshua!"

"Hey, Bella." A slight tremor in his voice made her look up at him.

"Are you okay, Joshua? Not getting a cold, are you?"

"No. No, I'm fine. Just saw you drive up and hurried to get the door."

"Thanks for that. Long time no see," she said lightly, hoping he would relax.

"Real long time, it seems." Joshua tried to hide his hangdog look.

She couldn't tell if he was trying to make a joke or was troubled. "I just need a few things to make those brownies I promised for Friday night. I won't keep you." She walked through the door. "Afternoon, Joe," she said as she walked by the cash register.

"Afternoon, Bella, nice to see you again. Hope this becomes a pattern." Joe smiled at her then turned his attention to a customer who had approached his register.

Joshua was right beside Bella. "Anything I can help you find?"

"Think I'm good, Joshua. Thanks all the same." Not sure if she should stop and talk with him or just keep moving, she asked, "Busy day?"

"Off and on, pretty typical for Thursday. This is the end-of-lunch crowd. Lots of folks come on their lunch hour so they don't have to stop by after work." He paused. "I know we're going to see you on Friday, but we won't really be able to visit then. So, I was wondering if you'd like to come to lunch on Sunday?" The words seemed to tumble out of him.

Bella stopped. She turned and looked up at him. "Why, Joshua, I hadn't considered the bluegrass jam and sing-along wouldn't really be a chance to chat and catch up. Guess we'll all be singing some of the songs, right? Maybe even some dancing. Do I remember hearing you're quite the dancer?" She cocked her head and looked at him, trying to figure out what was behind the invitation. "I think I could do lunch on Sunday, but could I call later today and confirm?"

Joshua looked over the top of her head to the wall behind her, trying hard not to let the disappointment show on his face. He was afraid she would say she couldn't come. "Sure, Bella, that would be great." He stepped back. "Look forward to hearing from you. I'll let you get on with your shopping." He walked to the back of the store.

Bella stood perplexed. *Date? A friend asking another friend to visit? Matt, if this is a sign, I need it to be clearer.* She picked up the brown sugar and pecans, relieved they were both on the same aisle. Not able to think of anything else she needed, she walked to the front and watched Joe and listened to his interactions with the customer ahead of her. *Joe reminds me of one of the things I remember about my daddy—neither one ever met a stranger. Wish I felt that comfortable with people I don't know.*

"Well, that was some quick shopping, Bella! Find everything you needed?"

"I did, thanks. Need to get those brownies made. They're always better the second day, don't you think?"

"How do you resist brownies for two days? I need lessons on that!" He winked at her.

Bella laughed. "I have to say, 'get thee behind me Satan,' often!"

Joe laughed nodding his head. "See you tomorrow night."

"Oh, just so you know, I also decided to make deviled eggs. Seems I bought eggs yesterday and last Saturday." She shrugged her shoulders.

"Sounds delicious. Haven't had homemade deviled eggs in a long time. Drive careful now. See ya Friday evening."

"Have a good afternoon, Joe. Tell Joshua goodbye. See y'all soon." She opened the door and headed to her Jeep.

It was almost two o'clock when she reached the crest on the county road where she could see her land. She stopped and sat for a few minutes, looking at possible locations for a cabin. She considered Arthur's suggestion about moving the new structure more to the east-southeast and opening up more of the view from her kitchen and dining room windows. *Lots to consider. I'll just play around with my pros and cons list and see what I decide.*

Bella backed into the carport and unloaded the printer and groceries onto the kitchen counter until she took off her boots. She stepped into her slippers; she knew she would be wearing all the time now. The colder air made the floors too cool even with socks, much less to go barefoot. She put the printer on the floor next to her writing table. *I'll set it up later.* She remembered to take the informational leaflets about the log cabins and set them on the writing desk. Now to bake the brownies.

She walked into the kitchen. As she opened the boxes of the brown sugar and pecans, she stopped to think about Joshua's invitation to lunch. *He said, 'Come to lunch'. Does that mean at his cabin or come to the valley? I don't know if I'm ready to navigate the life of a single woman and the potential dating scene.*

Putting Joshua's invitation to the back of her mind for the moment, she pulled out Grandmother Hazel's recipe box. Flicking to the "B" tab, she browsed through the hand-written cards until she found the one she was looking for. She loved the fudgy taste of brownies made with a combination of white and brown sugar, but it had been a while since she had used this particular recipe. *I got into such a bad habit of using instant mixes for faculty meetings. I'm looking forward to having the time to prepare homemade treats now.*

She carefully measured and mixed the ingredients, enjoying the same feeling of achievement as when she put together the writing table. *It's nice to use my hands for something other than typing.* She poured the brownie mix into a large baking pan, then scooped a bit of the batter onto her finger before transferring it to her mouth. The rich chocolate flavor melted on her tongue. She smiled, remembering how Grandmother Hazel had always let her lick the bowl. *Yes, I could definitely get used to this!*

Once the double batch was baking in the oven, she washed up the dishes, poured a glass of tea, and headed to the living room. Although she thought she would hear the timer on the porch, she didn't want to risk it, so she grabbed her book and curled up on the sofa instead. She looked at the cover of *The Foremost Good Fortune* and considered how the elements of the memoir could also play out in a book of fiction. The focus of the book was the author's bout with cancer while living in a foreign country. *Matt and I were also traveling when he got sick, and we had to fly home to find out what was going on. It was so easy to think he was tired from work when he said he was too tired to walk around Prague. What if we had been living there, instead of just visiting?*

She settled into learning how Conley dealt with breast cancer and her move to China with her husband and two young children. She was nearing the end of the book when the timer on the brownies went off. She checked the brownies with a toothpick; the wooden surface emerged cleanly—they were perfectly cooked. She set them on a wire rack to cool before returning to finish the book.

An hour later, she closed the cover and hugged the book to her chest. She tried to settle the feelings swirling inside her head. She knew her own emotional struggles were nothing compared to the author's. *I'm retired, living in a familiar place, and I've had more than four years to settle into losing Matt. I'm free to do what I want, when I want. Matt would want me to do that. So, why am I so unsettled by Chad and Joshua?* With Joshua on her mind, she had to make a decision about lunch on Sunday. She walked to the kitchen and called the Valley Store.

"The Valley Store, how may I help you?"

"Hey, Joshua. Bella here. I just wanted to confirm lunch on Sunday."

Joshua stammered, "Oh, that's great. How about..." she could hear the hesitation in his voice. "How about a late lunch? Say, two o'clock? At my place?"

She was pretty sure he was making it up on the fly. "Two is great. Let me know what I can bring. See you tomorrow night."

"Sure, Bella, sure. See you then."

Well, that was awkward. I guess it's a date. Too much hesitancy to be a friend inviting a friend. Time will tell what the future will bring. Isn't that what Grandmother Hazel always said?

Returning to the cooled brownies, she picked up a knife and sliced them into squares before putting a lid on the tray. She then pulled out a bottle of sauvignon blanc out of the refrigerator and poured herself a glass. She preferred Kim Crawford, but even this off-brand was fine for watching the afternoon pass over the mountains. The autumn colors were blossoming more quickly than spring flowers. She lifted the glass in a toast: "Drellag Caban, we're truly starting to build new memories. I plan to enjoy every minute of it."

She walked out to sit on the porch, drink her wine, and think about the book she had just finished. She wanted to relax and try not to over analyze the weekend activities, but instead take it one step at a time.

15

Long Morning, Longer Afternoon

Peggy O'Haire listened intently as Billy reviewed the evidence from the crash of the ATV into Dr. Anderson's shed and the subsequent death of Nick Brown.

"I'll read the final report when I receive the results of any prints and DNA on the syringe. I'll contact you about charges."

"Thanks, Peggy." He knew how thorough the DA was.

"I know I cut a deal with Justin Culverson, but I still wonder if he was either directly dealing or using meth himself. Do you think Steve Phillips knows?"

Billy shook his head. "Hard to tell. I don't think Steve really knew Justin, but I can ask him. Do you think there's any advantage in telling him Justin confessed to transporting the meth?"

"I'll leave that up to you. Just don't like leaving loose ends."

"Me either. Thanks, Peggy. Talk to you soon."

"Later, Billy."

Case Review

Chad looked up as the message came on his screen. "Brown/Phillips case. Found syringe. No elastic band. Want to review?" Chad leaned back in his chair and stared at the ceiling. *I know Billy has this case in hand, so let's get the review done and then I can focus on what trouble others might be creating.* Leaning forward, he typed "See you in fifteen." He no sooner clicked send than a message popped up: "10-4."

Standing up, Chad looked at the dregs of coffee in his mug, walked down the hall to the break room, and poured the whole mess down the sink. He washed the mug in soapy hot water and decided it was safe to use again. After he dried the mug with the rough paper towels, he rinsed it with cold water. *Who told me rinsing the mug with cold water would take away the taste of these brown paper towels?* He shrugged. His mug refilled, he chatted briefly to a deputy entering the room then returned to his office. He made a few notes while he waited for Billy.

1. Sylvia - tech equipment for night surveillance, buying our own UAV(s)?

2. Put surveillance on house where commissioner took young woman. What's going on?

3. Check ownership on the two motels in Round City. Link to commissioner?

4. Review statistics for missing teens in the region.

The knock on the door stopped him. He opened the door and nodded for Billy to go to the table.

"Sheriff, I've never had to interrogate someone like Steve Phillips. He's as unaware as most teenagers on some things, but on others he's pretty slick." Billy gave the details of the early morning interrogation.

As his detective spoke, Chad could hear by the cadence of his words that Billy was excited about finding the syringe. Even waiting for Alexander to carry out the DNA testing didn't seem to faze him, despite his early morning start. Chad simply listened.

"Boss, this new DNA test can run in four hours or less. It will sure make it easier to hold a suspect. Alexander is amazing the way she keeps up with the latest research in forensics. Sure hope we can keep her here. Anyway, we should know pretty soon whose DNA is in or on the syringe, if it hasn't deteriorated too much."

"Good work, Billy. Let me know as soon as you have something definitive on the syringe. Do you think there's any more you can get from Phillips?"

"The DA is reviewing what we have so far. She asked if I thought Stevie might change his mind about a lawyer. She's filing charges based on his confession to the damage to the shed at the Anderson place. The paint samples corroborate it. We'll still hold him on suspicion of murder. Even if the syringe doesn't pan out, the DA may charge him with second degree homicide. I'm pretty sure she'll wait on all the evidence before deciding whether she can take it to a judge. She may need the grand jury. We'll just have to wait and see."

Billy recognized the look on Chad's face—pursed lips and slightly squinted eyes. It was the look the sheriff had when thinking.

Chad looked directly at Billy. "Any evidence Steve's parents have tried to reach him?"

"Boss, I'm still trying to figure that one out. Granted, this kid is eighteen, but he's still in school and lives at home. Most parents who have the kind of money the Zimmermans must have would be beating the door down, demanding to get him out; it wouldn't matter how old the kid is. What do you think?"

Chad nodded. "I think it's rather unusual we haven't heard from them. Do you have anything to suggest the parents knew what he was doing? Or if they were in any way connected to him... or the other two boys we know were running meth?"

The detective knew he better be precise when he spoke. No speculating, just facts. "At this point, no. I think Steve is a pretty unhappy kid with no friends. No reason not to believe his story that he latched onto Nick because they both have stepdaddies they don't like. He didn't seem to think there was anything wrong with telling us he was taking 'hush money' from Will. Do we know if the DEA are following up on Calhoun, the boy killed in the meth lab explosion? I think the link is more likely from him to whoever he was cooking for than these four boys. Looks like they were just pawns in someone else's game."

Chad waited for him to finish. "Sounds like we've both ended up at the same place. Sam Nations will let us know if they find a link to the other end of the supply chain. But it's likely a dead end..." he hesitated, "so to speak." *I just can't help but think Zimmerman might be involved in this, but perhaps he didn't know his stepson had linked up with those transporting the meth.* Deciding he would just need to keep following the various trails and see where they ended, he looked over at Billy. "Thanks, Detective. If that's all, we're good here."

"Uh, Sheriff," Billy said haltingly, "should I notify Dr. Anderson that the DA has charged one of the people who caused damage on her land?" Billy suspected the sheriff was going to do it himself, but he was not about to say so.

"Sure, Billy. Just confirm with the DA and let her know you're notifying Dr. Anderson." Chad stood up, clearly distracted.

Billy stood as well.

"Right, boss. Talk to you soon." As he reached the door, he turned back. "Hey, I saw the signs about the bluegrass jam and sing-along tomorrow night. Good to see Nora's name on the flyer."

"Right, thanks. See you there if you can make it."

Billy knew something important must be occupying the sheriff's mind. *I really thought he would want to tell Dr. Anderson himself.*

Connections or Not?

Chad sat down and looked at his list again before deciding to send a note to Sergeant Whitehorse. He wanted to determine what new equipment was needed. Since the DEA was apparently not interested in the source of the light still appearing in Sector Two, he wanted to figure it out and needed a drone to do it.

He decided to do a preliminary search himself on the ownership of the two motels on the highway and see if there was any link to the commissioner. As he stretched his arms above his head to ease his tight muscles, he wondered how it was possible to keep up with all the ways people could choose to do bad things, much less the ways they could hide or cover them up.

By mid-afternoon, Chad thought he was on the trail of owner-ship for the two motels. It was fascinating to see how someone had created a company name that was very similar to a well-known or-ganization. Anyone having a quick skim of the documents would assume the off-brand organization played by the same rules and would just look elsewhere. But Chad was not to be deterred. *I may need to put one of our other detectives on tracking addresses and po-tential owners, but this is a good start.* The knock on his door gave him a much needed break.

He stood and opened the door to Sergeant Whitehorse. "Hey, Sergeant, come in."

"Yes, sir. How may I help?"

"Just need some research and for you to arrange surveillance. Come in, have a seat."

"Whatever you need, Sheriff."

"We need to invest in some high-tech equipment, especially for night work. I think we will benefit from one or more UAVs. I'd appreciate it if you could get details on the best models for law enforcement work. I'll also need to know what it would take for the training and licensing of one or more staff. I'm quite sure I know just enough to be dangerous, so you might talk with Sam as well and see what he can share with you."

"Sheriff, I'll make sure I've covered all the parameters you mentioned. I've been learning about UAVs for a while. Since the challenges of the meth lab explosion, I've been doing specific research on law enforcement uses. I was planning to bring you a proposal for some equipment based on what I saw the DEA using. I asked Sam to send me some information too. I don't think it will take me long to get something together for you. Next day or two soon enough?"

Chad's expression was normally unreadable when he was discussing work, but Sylvia saw the sheriff's response written all over his face. She didn't know when she had seen such a big smile about anything other than his daughter or grandkids.

"Including drones... uh, UAVs?" Chad shook his head. "Drones is so much easier to say. Anyway, I'm really interested in how soon we can get someone licensed and get a UAV in the air."

"Yes, sir. My husband bought a drone..."

"He did? I assume he's licensed?"

"Yes, sir. We both are."

Chad stared at her. "Okay, give me a minute, please." Chad started considering the possibilities of immediate access to a UAV. "How long does it take to get licensed? Is it complicated?"

"No, sir. It's not complicated. You have to study, but my husband and I found the material interesting and passed the test the first time. As with most bureaucratic things, the most challenging part was getting the documentation we needed. It took us almost three months to get our actual licenses, so we played around with it in our backyard and didn't take it above our rooftop until the licenses were delivered. He wanted to get some experience as he's likely getting one for the fire department."

Chad nodded. "Sergeant, have you found any research on UAVs being used by law enforcement?"

"Yes, sir. More and more law enforcement offices are using UAVs. The earliest record I found was from 2005 when officers tried to find evidence of a young woman who went missing in Georgia."

"Did they find her with the UAV?"

"No. Still haven't found her. There have been other uses reported as well. Another interesting case involved cattle rustling out in North Dakota. I believe it was the first arrest assisted by a UAV. It was pretty controversial apparently, as the local law enforcement was using a UAV belonging to Customs and Border agents." She waited a moment to see if he had a question. "Sir, if the last couple of years is any indication, I think there will be more and more uses of this technology in law enforcement, and it could be a huge help here in the mountains where some areas are just impossible to access. I think it can help with both searches, like lost hikers, as well as what we encountered with the meth lab."

"Sergeant, I knew you were overworked and underpaid, but now I don't know if I could ever afford you." He sat back and the smile returned. "I need about thirty minutes to run some things through this slow brain of mine. Then I'd like to talk to you again, as soon as you're free. In the meantime, I need you to set up some surveillance on a house." He gave her the details of the property where he had seen Commissioner Zimmerman take the young woman. He suspected there was prostitution there, but knew they would need several days of watching the place to be sure it wasn't just a shelter for young women. "If we move too quickly, we could end up without sufficient evidence to satisfy the prosecutor. *If we move too slowly underage girls may be in peril.* He was not ready to share the last thought with her yet.

"Whatever you need, Sheriff. We'll get someone on the surveillance. I had my lead deputy cover check-in, so I'll just go make sure everything is running smoothly for this shift. I'll be available when you call for me." She stood up and left without another word.

Chad leaned back in the chair. Ideas were flowing through his brain at ninety miles an hour.

Considering Her Own Answers

The scent of smoke rising up from the valley, intermingled with decaying leaves on the forest floor, added to the total relaxation Bella felt sitting with her glass of wine and Louise Penny's book, *Glass Houses*. She made a note to thank Dona for the book recommendations. *I enjoyed the Susan Conley book, and she knows I'm a long-time fan of Penny's work. This is going to prove a fascinating read.*

As she picked up the novel, her phone rang. *Does the phone ring every time I start to read, or does it just feel like it?* Part of her wanted to let the answering machine kick in, but it had always been hard for her to ignore a ringing phone. *I guess Mother viewed answering the phone like answering a knock at the door—the polite thing to do. No neighbors up here to know I'm sitting on my porch.* She sighed and headed for the kitchen. "Drellag Caban, may I help you?"

"Good afternoon, Dr. Anderson. Detective Billy Williams here. Do you have a minute?"

"Yes, Detective. How may I help you?" She hoped there was nothing more he needed to search for on her land.

"I'm calling to tell you the district attorney has charged a young man with the damages to your property. If he accepts a plea deal, or even if he goes to court, the DA will include restitution of your damaged property in his sentencing."

"Oh, okay, thank you for letting me know."

"Well, ma'am, although that is normal procedure, it doesn't remove your rights to file charges against the young man yourself. You'd need to talk to—"

"Sorry to interrupt you. I sincerely appreciate the call and the information. Right now, I'm inclined to leave it with the district attorney. I'll certainly consider talking to my attorney. Is there anything else I need to know at this point?"

"No, ma'am, the sheriff just wanted to be sure you knew about the arrest and charges. Also, he wanted to make sure you know you have the right to file your own charges."

"Thanks, Detective. I appreciate it, and please tell the sheriff I said thanks. The professionalism of your officers has been evident throughout this ordeal. It makes me feel safe up here knowing you're all on the job."

"Why, thank you, ma'am. If there's nothing else, I'll leave you to the rest of your day."

"Have a good evening, Detective. Thanks again." Bella hung up the phone. She looked at the fading light and decided that a change of plans was in order. Walking over to the fridge she took out the pot of vegetable soup she had taken out of the freezer to thaw and put it on the stove to warm. *Now I know how the victims I read in mystery stories feel when they wonder if they can ever put the crime behind them.*

She took a shower and put on her nightgown and robe before closing all the windows and locking up the cabin. When she returned to the kitchen, the scent of the soup filled the space as she ladled it from the pot into a small bowl. She took it to the writing table. *I probably shouldn't get into the habit of eating and working, but I need to get my thoughts down.* She opened a new document on her computer and started making notes to capture the emotions she was experiencing around the events of the past several weeks. She saved the document as, "Perpetrators and Victims: The Suffering," and decided she had enough to write at least a short story. Checking that the new printer she had set on a TV tray table was ready she decided to print a copy to read tomorrow.

The darkness in the room made Bella realize the only light was from her laptop and the porch light through the kitchen window. She saved her document and shut the computer down before walking into the kitchen to wash her dishes. Leaving dishes in the second sink to dry was becoming routine; she decided she was fine with it.

She headed to bed, leaving her bedroom window open a few inches to enjoy the change in the night air, knowing it would be too cold before long to have them open at all. Crawling into bed, Bella pulled the quilt up around her neck and rolled onto her side.

She stared at the picture of herself and Matt. *Well, my love, I guess you've sent me some signals the last couple of days. I don't want to make more of Chad's invitation for Friday or Joshua's invitation to lunch than I should. But I would be less than honest if I didn't admit to a little flutter in my chest when I think about the weekend.*

She did a quick run through her Not-So-Good List. First, she thought about her emotions, with another day reminding her of the damage to her property and the young man whose life was lost on it. She was relieved there was nothing else. Her Good List was much more satisfying and longer; Joshua invited her to lunch; she saw a prefab cabin she thought might work on her land; she bought a printer; she was thinking of ways to tie the repairs and new construction together; she was able to sit on her porch and read; she made brownies for tomorrow night; she started a possible short story, maybe even a novel; and she thought of her daddy, mother, grandmother, and Matt. *All in all, a good day. I can sleep on these memories.* She touched the picture of herself and Matt in the silver frame, tucked her arm under the cover, and lay quietly looking at Matt until sleep came.

Let's Do This

Chad needed more than half an hour. He wanted to be sure about liability to all parties, to say nothing of the wisdom of his plan. He checked with the county attorney and was satisfied his plan was on solid ground. He called Sergeant Whitehorse to say he was ready to see her in a few minutes, then walked down to the break room to get a bottle of water out of the machine. The sergeant fell in step with him as he returned to his office. He closed the door behind them.

"Sergeant, first I want to make sure you know you can decline what I'm going to ask, and it will not negatively affect your performance evaluation."

Puzzled the sheriff felt he needed to say anything, she said, "I've always assumed so, sir, for anything not a direct command."

He nodded approvingly. "Good." He still wondered if he should ask. "I'm asking if you'd consider using your UAV to help check out a—"

She interrupted him. "Whatever is needed, Sheriff. Mike is off rotation at the fire department, so he could do whatever you need. Or I could."

Chad stood up and motioned her over to the topographical map. He explained how the coordinates seemed to align with a plateau that was covered by an outcropping. "I don't know where the nearest access point is, but if there's any chance of taking a look at first light, I would like to do it."

Sergeant Whitehorse studied the map. "Since I'm on nights, Mike and I could be here at six in the morning, lay out a plan with you, and go take a look."

"Good deal. I've approved funds so that we're renting the time of your UAV. I'll get someone to cover your night shift tomorrow so that you're on duty in the morning. Seems having you on duty will cover us legally if we find anything."

He looked at her, his gray eyes intense. "Sylvia, I know I don't heap praise on folks, but I hope you know you're invaluable to this organization. . ." He hesitated. "And you're a colleague I know I can trust and rely on. Means more than I can express."

Sylvia was not accustomed to anything like this from the sheriff. "Thank you. Proud to serve my community, and you, sir."

"Make sure you're out of here at shift change, or earlier if you need to be. See you at six."

She knew a dismissal when she heard it. "See you in the morning, Sheriff."

Pleased with the plan, Chad checked off his earlier note to talk to the sergeant about technology. He knew he would have a plan from her; her word was a promise.

It was already more than a twelve-hour day for him. He sent a note to dispatch to get a sergeant to do overtime and cover the evening shift tomorrow. He packed up his reading material into his father's satchel and notified dispatch he was headed home.

After a light dinner, he read two reports about sex trafficking and reviewed the data about missing children in Tennessee and surrounding states. He felt he was better informed to deal with wherever the Zimmerman thread might lead.

As was his habit following his shower, he took his Fat Tire Ale to his recliner and sat in the dark to review his day. He was excited at the possibility of knowing what the elusive light was. He was also satisfied he had a methodical plan to learn if there were any concerns with the new county commissioner. Thinking ahead to tomorrow, he could hardly believe the end of the week was already here.

I think we'll wrap things up with Steve Phillips tomorrow or the next day. With any luck, after our search in the morning I'll be able to relax and enjoy tomorrow evening with my grandkids and Fred, listening to my lovely daughter sing. Staring off into space, his thoughts moved away from work and family to Bella. *And, best of all, I may actually be free to enjoy the company of a lovely lady. Now* that *will be a pleasant change.*

He took his beer bottle to the kitchen and rinsed it out before putting it in the recycling bin. He went to bed, content to think about all tomorrow might bring.

16

The Early Riser

Joshua arrived at the Valley Store at six on Friday morning, trying not to think about all the day would bring: lots of customers, a late-day rush so folks could get to the bluegrass jam at The Corral, and Chad picking up Bella. He knew he shouldn't grumble about the additional business, but it seemed like the autumn leaf-lookers were greater in number this year. Many seemed to stop in even if they were staying near the highway. *Dad always said there was merit in retaining the original structure. Folks seem fascinated by the building and, once they come inside, they always seem to buy something.*

As he walked the aisles to check the shelves for any gaps in products, the bluegrass jam kept intruding on his thoughts. He enjoyed the music, the dancing, and the singing, but he couldn't remember the last time he'd been able to go to a community gathering of any kind. *I think it was more than three years ago when Jan was still trying to get out and about, even though her cancer was taking its toll.* He jerked his head when he heard the jingle of the bell over the front door.

"Morning, son."

"Morning, Dad. Sleep well?" He walked to the front and was relieved to see his dad sign on to the register. Joshua hoped it meant Joe knew the cash drawer would be in place before he arrived from now on.

"As snug as a bug in a rug. How about you?"

"Maybe not quite that well, though always grateful when sleep comes." A tinge of sadness colored Joshua's voice.

Joe tried to shift the tenor of the conversation. "I talked to Diane, and she'll drop off the picnic basket around six. I think all we'll need from here is some potato chips and the cooler with some waters and teas. Sound right to you?"

Joshua was completely baffled by his dad's comments. "For what?"

"Joshua, don't you remember? I said we would bring the picnic food for the bluegrass jam and sing-along tonight." He looked at his son, trying to figure out whether Joshua was just tired or if there was more on his mind.

"Oh, sure. Sure, Dad. Got it. I'll take care of the chips and water, and I'll grab plates and all that good stuff. If it's quiet by six thirty, we can head over. Work for you?"

"Perfect." Joe was still trying to figure out where Joshua's thinking was. "Well, let's get this store open so folks can shop and get themselves ready for an evening of good music."

Joshua unlocked the front door and headed up the stairs to the loft. "Oh, Dad, I forgot to tell you Arthur is coming Sunday morning around seven to fix these stairs. I'll meet him here, and he should have us as right as rain in a few hours." *Now I have to figure out how to tell you I invited Bella to lunch on Sunday.*

"Good deal. Guess it will take some getting used to. Those dips in the stairs took a long time to create." Joe had a cheerful lightness in his voice. "Morning, folks." Several customers entered the store.

Joshua turned on his computer and tried to focus on payroll and bills. *I'll have to tell dad about Sunday before we go to The Corral tonight in case Bella brings it up.* He shook his head. *Enough distractions! There's work to do!*

Early Morning Sightings

Sergeant Sylvia Whitehorse and Fire Chief Mike Smallwood, her husband, were at the station at five forty-five when Chad pulled into the back parking lot.

"Sorry to get you up before breakfast." Chad extended his hand to shake with each of them.

"We were up with the last singing of the whippoorwill," Sylvia said.

Chad looked at her curiously. "I never understood that saying. What does it mean?"

"No disrespect, Sheriff, but you need to get out and enjoy nature a bit more. Whippoorwill males sing through the night to protect and attract their mate. They stop singing at first light and then camouflage themselves in the trees and bushes."

"And, don't forget," Mike said, "it's early October, so we'll soon hear the last of their singing until spring. They choose to spend the winter in warmer weather and migrate to Mexico and Central America."

"Thank you both. Never a day wasted when you learn something new. I suspect this will be only the first of a number of lessons you give me today."

Sylvia called from the card scanner to tell the desk deputy that Fire Chief Smallwood was with her and the sheriff. She scanned her card and the door opened. "Welcome to *our* house, Smallwood," she joked.

They went to Chad's office to plan for the UAV search. They studied the topographical map on Chad's wall and a trail map that Sylvia brought with her. They discussed pros and cons of different access points.

Mike Smallwood was focused and deliberate in his comments. "Chad, I think we've identified a trail where we can use those fancy Renegade 100 ATVs you have. They will get us to a walking trail, which should get us close enough to send up the UAV. It should also keep the noise of the ATVs far enough away not to spook anyone who might be up on that plateau."

"I assumed we'd need the ATVs, so they're gassed up ready to go. The trailer will be hooked up to my SUV before we get outside."

The three headed out. They had the coordinates from the night sightings of the mysterious light, the plateau marked on Sylvia's trail map, and a plan they had reviewed and agreed was the most likely to yield results. The ATV trailer was attached to Chad's SUV when they walked out the back door. They had agreed Sylvia and Mike would take lead in the fire chief's SUV. Knowing their convoy would draw attention, Chad hoped anyone who saw the two official SUVs would assume it had to do with checking for fire breaks, a frequent occurrence this time of year.

"You know, Chad, I think with the leaves as colorful as they are, the UAV will be less noticeable than if all the leaves were green. The range of fall color makes it more difficult to detect things when you look into the trees. And there's still enough green to give some camouflage."

Chad shook his head and promised himself he would spend more time with native people and learn what he should have learned earlier in his life. He knew they had many things to teach him about the nature in which he was privileged to live. *I'm looking forward to what I'm going to learn today.*

"Lesson number two received, Chief Smallwood." Chad nodded at Mike. They each got into their respective vehicles and headed out.

Chad was grateful for the solitude of the drive up and over the mountain. He liked the pale light of morning which etched its way up the sky and over the hills. He knew they would have the UAV up in the air and likely finished with the flight before full sun. Autumn generally meant the sun wouldn't be fully visible much before ten. Plenty of time, he hoped, to get in and out; with any luck, undetected.

Pulling into the trailhead where they would offload the ATVs and head into the hills, Chad hoped anyone coming across the two official vehicles didn't cause a distraction or interfere. If someone asked what they were doing, he was prepared to tell them they were testing some new equipment. It was partially true.

Chad and Sylvia offloaded the ATVs from the trailer and secured their vehicles. Mike had the UAV in a plain, hard plastic carrying case that could have held any kind of equipment. Chad was relieved they wouldn't be signaling their intent to any passersby on the trail.

Sylvia had Mike on the back of her Renegade. Chad slapped Mike on the back before mounting his ATV and said, "Lead the way!" Although the ATVs had small logo decals identifying them as belonging to the sheriff's department, the three were in jeans and plaid shirts, looking like anyone else who would be out enjoying a morning on the trails. Of course, his and Sylvia's weapons were not visible under the wind breakers they wore. Chad shook his head in mock surprise at the speed at which Sylvia took off. *Not a race, Whitehorse, not a race.*

As they approached the hiking trail, Chad saw there were no hikers on the path yet, and there was no evidence of illegal camping in woods along the way. He did not want to be distracted by having to deal with people who didn't bother to learn the backcountry camping rules in effect in these mountains. He knew he might find an encampment on the plateau; that would be enough to manage for one day. The plateau bordered on national park land, so, depending on what they found, there could be multiple jurisdictions involved. *I know the feds always win over a local sheriff. Lucky for them I can generally keep my ego in check.*

Mike had straps on the UAV case that allowed him to wear it like a backpack. Chad and Sylvia had actual backpacks containing high-powered binoculars, canteens with water, bear spray, protein bars, and a first-aid kit. All three were trained in advanced first aid, and each had experience in treating the wide variety of things one could encounter in the backcountry. They had determined they should have cellular service in the open area where they needed to launch, ensuring the laptop Sylvia had in her backpack would receive real-time images from the UAV. Although Mike could see what his UAV was viewing, he had to focus on piloting and navigation. The laptop would allow Sylvia and Chad to look for detail.

"Ready for a hike?" Chad looked ahead to the trail and then to Sylvia and Mike.

"Ready," Sylvia and Mike said in unison.

Mike led the way. Chad noticed he had a digital device on his wrist that was clearly more than a watch. Chad stepped up beside him.

"Okay, my friend, time for another lesson for this old boy today. Tell me about that fancy wristband."

Mike glanced over at him. "Oh, that? It's some gadget Sylvia gave me for my birthday. I wear it to humor her. My feet know these hills like my family had been here for hundreds of years." The chuckle in his voice carried a pleasant lilt. "I think it can do everything but cook dinner for me. It has an altimeter, barometer, and compass, and it'll have GPS when we get cellular or a satellite signal."

"Well, Nora's always asking me what I want for Christmas or my birthday. Might have to put one of those on my wish list."

"Looking forward to hearing her sing tonight," Sylvia said. "Her voice is so lovely you know God was paying extra special attention to His work that day."

Chad stopped in his tracks. He turned and looked at Sylvia. She saw he had a tear in his eye.

"For sure! Nora is a blessing... far more than I could ever deserve. It will be great to hear the two of you sing. I do hope you'll do some duets with her."

"Might just do that," Sylvia Whitehorse said in a low voice, the contralto timbre obvious.

"We're about to reach that plot of open land we saw on those pictures. Let's hope it hasn't become overgrown since the last satellite photo shoot," Mike said.

They walked on in silence for another five minutes before an open patch of land appeared. It wasn't big enough to be considered a meadow, but it was obviously a spot reached by enough hikers to keep the grass tamped down and the saplings from taking hold. The location was a good site for them to send up the UAV and see what, if anything, was on the plateau.

Mike turned to Chad. "Any chance some piece of metal just got left up there and catches the light?"

"I thought about that," Chad said, "but most of the sightings have been at night, even when there's no moonlight."

"Curious." Mike nodded his head, suggesting Chad's comment was logical. "Do you think it's a signal?"

"I think we'll know more when we see what's up there. It could be a signaling device. That would suggest there's a pretty clear path from there to somewhere. I'm sure hoping the drone... UAV will give us more than we know right now."

"Okay, let's set up shop right here and get this baby in the air. We're not near any flight paths..."

"Except for birds." Sylvia's comment was not meant as a joke.

Mike shook his head and took out their UAV and the iPad that allowed him to run the controls and see through the UAV's camera. He began to set up for launch.

"We'll do a quick check to make sure we're receiving, and then wait to use the laptop once we're in range. We don't have any other programs on this laptop running in the background and draining power, so we should be fine."

Chad just looked at her bewildered. *Sam Nations was right to call me an old man. I can learn this stuff and I will. Not sure why I've avoided it for so long.*

"Anything you can't do, Sergeant Whitehorse?"

"She can't cook her way out of the kitchen." Mike laughed and never looked up from the work he was doing.

"He's right about that! It's part of my overall plan in life: he cooks, I benefit from it."

They all laughed.

In a few minutes, Mike was ready to go and the UAV lifted off the ground. Chad felt like he was watching a small alien spaceship. "Hope that thing doesn't cause someone to jump off a cliff thinking they're being invaded." He watched Sylvia's laptop as the UAV flew over them, and he could see on the screen what the camera was picking up.

"Good as the camera on your phone, don't you think?" Sylvia kept her eyes on the screen.

"Close enough for government work, for sure," Chad said in awe.

"Oh, boss, I don't think I told you Mike is licensed for BVLS with the UAV."

"Seriously, Whitehorse? You expect me to know what BVLS is?"

"Beyond visual line of sight. Most people are only licensed for VLS."

"I get it. Visual line of sight. Well, I'm not surprised. I would certainly expect you two to go above and beyond."

"Oh, I haven't taken that exam yet. Working on it, though." Sylvia was matter-of-fact in her reply.

Mike flew the UAV above the nearby trees and headed it towards the coordinates for the plateau.

Chad looked through his high-powered binoculars. At first he tried to follow the UAV, but it wasn't easy. He felt like he was on a roller coaster, so he focused on the outcropping over the area where the plateau was.

"Am I correct in assuming you capture the video?"

"Yes, boss. Amazing things you can do with all this technology."

"Well, at least you didn't call me Grandpa, like Sam did," Chad muttered, never taking his sight off what they thought was the target area.

Sylvia heard him but decided she would ask what he meant later, *if* the time was ever right.

"Sylvia," Mike said, his voice calm, "time to get some images on that computer. I want to know if what I'm following is a trail leading up to that plateau."

Sylvia brought up the image on her laptop. "Certainly looks like a well-worn path. May have been used for a long time. Doesn't show signs of grass being trampled... more like the grass can't grow for all the footsteps."

Chad moved over to look at the screen. "This must be what it's like for a bird to look down."

"Seems that way to me too. At first I assumed I would have the same type of view that I had when I look out the window of a plane, then you realize it's more like looking through a telescope. You can see what's in the immediate area, but the range is limited to about a mile and a half, depending on how high up you are."

"Thanks, Sylvia. It's helpful to learn more about the possibilities of this technology for our work while doing this search. I really appreciate it."

"Hey, Chad! Heads up. I'm almost up to the plateau, and there are people starting down the trail. Zoom in, Sylvia... Now!"

Both Sylvia and Chad looked at the screen and saw several people walking down the trail.

"Want me to drop closer to them?" Mike said.

"Can you get close enough without spooking them for us to see if we need to move in?"

"I can get close enough. Here we go. Watch the screen, boys and girls."

Chad stared intently at the laptop. Although the images were not close enough for facial recognition, he called out, "Mike, stay right there if you can."

"Oh, I can hover with no problem." Mike sounded sure of himself.

"Sylvia, I'm headed up that way. You should get a good signal here. Call dispatch and get backup, then you head up too. Mike, you keep that little device on the group."

Sylvia clicked on her handheld radio and called dispatch while focusing on the screen to see what had sent Chad off at a fast jog. "Mike, those people have their hands up!"

"Dispatch, what's the nature of your call?"

"Whitehorse here, get me backup to the location we left with you. Now."

"10-4."

"10-4, over and out." With that, Sylvia was headed up the trail behind the sheriff. *I think we've gone off plan. I pray I can catch up with him in time to help if something happens.*

Bella Starts her Day

Bella sat on the porch, drinking her Earl Grey tea and eating breakfast. The morning air was pungent with smoke and there was a chilly nip from the morning frost. Yet she was pleased with everything she had already managed to accomplish as the first hint of light began to play on the hillside.

She had awakened early and decided to make a small batch of biscuits. She carefully followed her Grandmother Hazel's recipe for buttermilk biscuits from the little box of recipe cards. She knew she would remember how important it was to fold the dough in thirds between each pass of the rolling pin to create the flaky layers. *Just enough, but not too many. Right, Grandmother? "And not too much pressure with that rolling pin," you'd say. I still miss you, Grandmother Hazel. I'm so grateful your spirit is here for me in Drellag Caban.* The buttery taste of the biscuit she was enjoying with her sunny-side up egg was proof she hadn't forgotten the lessons.

Once her dishes were washed and sitting in the dish drainer, she pulled out a large pot to boil the extra dozen eggs she bought when she was so distracted by Chad's invitation to the bluegrass jam. She added cold water until it covered two inches above the top of the eggs, then put the pot on the stove to boil. While waiting, she put the remainder of the eggs in a bowl in the fridge and washed the two egg cartons with warm soapy water and left them to dry. *Where did I learn to use egg cartons to transport deviled eggs? They sit perfectly in the egg cup and the lid keeps them from getting crushed. I love it when clever people figure out easy solutions to annoying problems like transporting deviled eggs—without using plastic!* Once the water was at a full boil, she set the timer for eleven minutes. Everything would be prepared in less than thirty minutes, and then she could think about making a decision about repairing or replacing the shed.

While the timer ticked down, she went to her bedroom to decide what to wear to the bluegrass jam. She had three cotton shirts from the Gap that she really liked, so she decided on jeans, one of the cotton shirts with a dark blue shell, and her blue and white sweater from LL Bean. She stepped back, looked at the outfit and decided it worked. She sat down on the bed and looked at the framed anniversary picture. She said aloud, "Matt, can you believe I'm actually thinking about what I'll wear tonight? How many times did you tease me because I just threw on whatever I put my hands on at the last minute?" She sighed and let her shoulders sag. "Is this a signal you're sending me to open up and accept the possibility of enjoying the company of another man?" The timer on the eggs brought her back to the moment.

She finished off the deviled eggs and placed them in their cartons in the fridge for later, then went to her desk to study the information she had picked up about the prefab log cabins. She was so accustomed to discussing big decisions with Matt that she found herself struggling to accept she could make a decision without having someone else weigh in on it. Drawing different layouts on her notepad, she looked back at the drawings she finished earlier in the week and compared them. She was becoming intrigued with the idea of repairing the shed, closing in the carport so she could park right at her kitchen door as she did now, and putting up a prefab cabin closer to the gate. She could use it as a guest cottage or writer's retreat. She was leaning more and more to the idea of a writer's retreat.

Bella leaned back in her chair and let her mind wander to the various ways, simple and complex, in which she could do writing retreats. She could just screen individuals and offer them a place to write for a period of time… probably no more than a couple of months, she thought. *I would really have to think about the conditions under which I would want someone up here on the mountain with me. Would I limit it to women? How can I make sure the person is not a risk to my safety? Would I need to carry out a criminal background check on them? I should ask Chad about that.*

The thought of asking Chad snapped her back to the moment. Bella had figured out long ago that when it came time for her to make a choice, it was rarely what people called a snap-decision. *After all, even Matt was happy just to serve as a sounding board once I had collected all the information I needed. He never actually told me what to do. I have to learn to trust myself. As it is, these ideas have been at the back of my mind for weeks, ever since the ATV ran into the shed.* She opened her laptop and started a list of her current thoughts.

Satisfied the list of pros and cons was complete, she read through it one more time. On Monday, she would ask Arthur to give her a quote on closing in the carport, repairing the shed, and putting a cabin up towards the front of her land. It didn't matter at the moment how the cabin would be used; she had time to figure that out.

Now it was time to clear her head. She filled her Yeti thermos with cold water, grabbed a protein bar and her phone so she had a camera, put on her boots and vest, and headed out for a ride on her ATV. It was time for her to get out and enjoy her eighty acres.

– John Muir, 1838-1914

17

Who are These People?

Sylvia was moving at a fairly fast pace. She could see the sheriff still jogging up the path, which appeared to be the same one the people were descending. *Why do they have their hands in the air? Was someone behind them with a weapon? Did they know they were wanted by law enforcement for something?* It just didn't seem to be the actions of a group of people who were simply camping out on a plateau, even if it was illegal to do so without permission. She knew she could pull her own gun on the move but prayed she wouldn't have to use it.

The incline of the path became steeper. Chad assumed he was nearing a point where the people would be visible. He slowed down. He wanted to be sure he was prepared to respond as needed when he met up with whoever was coming down the mountain. The ground cover on the path was turning to moss as he climbed, making the rock more slippery. He heard Sergeant Whitehorse behind him as she jogged up the path. He raised his hand to slow her.

Without either of them saying a word, she came within a few yards of him.

They approached an angle on the side of the mountain that Chad had seen earlier with his binoculars. He couldn't be sure how close to meeting up with the people he was, so he tucked in close to the side of the mountain. Sylvia saw his action and stayed back, closer to the outer edge of the path in case someone came towards them. Chad heard her stop, knowing she understood they would want to listen for footfalls.

A high-pitched whirr could be heard, and it took Chad a few moments to realize it was the UAV. He had been unaware how loud it was, or how much it sounded like the a helicopter. *Great! I wish I had paid better attention to the sound down below. I need to be able to distinguish footfalls on the rock.*

Mike concentrated on the screen but couldn't see Chad and Sylvia. The angle of the mountain between them and the people who were coming down blocked his ability to see where the two were in comparison to the others. He knew he would have to move the UAV out. Deciding the people only had two choices—to continue coming down or to go back to the dead-end plateau—he moved the UAV to see if he could pull Chad and Sylvia into view.

Fire Chief Mike Smallwood was a large man who had encountered his own kind of dangers, including saving people in burning cabins. This was a whole different scenario. He was watching the sheriff and his own wife approach potential danger, and there was no way he could warn them. It was unnerving. As the UAV pulled out, he was able to see the figures of Chad and Sylvia as well as the people with their hands in the air. They had raised their hands in response to the approaching UAV. It dawned on him they might even think the UAV was capable of firing on them. *I wonder if Chad or Sylvia has realized the raised hands may be from fear of the UAV?* He saw Chad start to move.

Taking his service weapon out of his holster, Chad made the decision to be in the low-ready position. It's not how he would approach a potentially hostile situation, but it had occurred to him the people may have thought the UAV was a weapon that could shoot them. He also knew he was capable of a fast aim and could shoot from this position. He did not need to lead with his gun. He looked over his shoulder to verify where his sergeant was positioned. She was ready for his decision: wait for the people to round the curve in the path or advance towards them. Chad raised his non-weapon hand with his palm out, signaling her to wait.

The UAV was less noisy now. Chad could see it had pulled out from the side of the mountain and it was now visible to him. It was slowly moving towards the angle in the mountain which protected him, and he slowly nodded his head. *I'll bet dollars to donuts Mike is moving the UAV towards us to signal the movement of the people. Son of a gun!* He wanted to tell Sylvia what he thought was going on but knew they needed to remain quiet. He raised his hand again to signal for her to wait. He backed up towards the wall of rock and made sure he could catch Sylvia in his peripheral vision. She had her weapon in ready position; she had no choice. She was an open target for anyone coming around the curve.

A short, mocha-colored man came into view. He saw Sylvia. "Espera! Espera!" He stopped, keeping his hands in the air and continuing to yell. "Espera! Espera!"

A much smaller voice, a child maybe, yelled "Stop! Stop!" Sylvia lowered her weapon and signaled the man to come towards her. Chad stayed in place, his gun drawn but aimed low. A woman with four children cowering behind her turned the corner and came into view. At that moment, the sound of pounding feet could be heard and the small family fell on the ground, arms outstretched.

Chad looked to his left and saw two deputies running up the path behind Sylvia. She had already put away her weapon and was moving towards the family. He holstered his gun and called out to his deputies. "Weapons down. Situation secure."

He saw the UAV pull away and start to drop down. As the other two deputies approached, he saw there were actually three people. Billy Williams was behind the deputies. *Oh, just wait, Billy. I'm going to razz you good about getting soft now that you're a detective—*

shielding yourself behind two deputies. He waved the three forward and then turned to the family.

Sergeant Whitehorse had the family sitting with their palms flat on the ground.

Chad approached. *I'm pretty sure they're speaking Spanish. One more thing I need to learn. Easy to forget how sheltered I've been in these mountains.*

He bent down and looked at the family. He wished he could speak their language, but since he couldn't, he said, "English?"

The older boy, whose voice was in the squeaky changes of puberty, said, "A little. Please. No hurt us. Please." The fear in his eyes was deeply disturbing to Chad.

"We won't hurt you," Chad said quietly. "How many people are with you?" He drew a circle in the air with his finger like drawing a loop around the group. He hoped the boy would understand.

"Six. Mi padre, mi madre, y mis hermanos." He pointed to his father, mother, and siblings. "No today."

Chad was now almost eye-to-eye with the boy, who sat beside his father. *No more today? How many have there been? When?*

Deputy Amy Murphy stepped forward. "Sir, I can speak a little Spanish. Do you want me to ask him any questions?"

Chad leaned back on his haunches, wondering if there was anything the two women up here with him couldn't do. "Please. Thanks, Murphy. Williams, Whitehorse, and I need to go check out the plateau. I need to know if we're likely to encounter anyone else. I'm also curious what he knows about anyone else who was here. Does his comment of 'no today' mean others were here? How long and when did they leave? I think that'll cover it. Then I'll have you two deputies take this family down to the area where you saw Mike Smallwood. Thanks, Murphy."

She nodded at her boss.

She smiled at the father and the boy. "Hola, soy Murphy, una diputada de la oficina del sherif." She pointed to Chad. "Tu familia está bien?"

All of the family nodded their heads to indicate they were fine. She asked how many people were left on the mountain, how many days they had been here, and when others had left. Everyone listened quietly as Deputy Murphy talked and the father answered. She asked them how they knew about this place and if someone brought them here. The father looked at Chad, fear evident in his eyes.

"What did you just ask him?" Chad looked at the father and at Murphy.

Murphy put her hand down by her side, indicating to wait.

The father started speaking very quickly.

"Despacio, por favor." Murphy indicated he should speak more slowly.

The father spoke a little less quickly, but even without translation the others knew he just had to get it out, or he likely wouldn't say anything.

"Dónde está el lugar donde recibió instrucciones?" Over the years, she had learned people were generally pretty forgiving when you tried to speak their language, but she knew she was stretching her knowledge of Spanish grammar trying to find out where they got directions to this location.

The father finally wound down like a clock. He just stopped speaking. He lowered his head and was silent.

Amy stood up to speak to the assembled staff from the sheriff's office. "The family has been up on the mountain for almost a week, he wasn't sure how long. When they arrived, there was one other family with two children, and they left when his family arrived. He said that was the plan they were given. Each family was to stay until the next family comes." She went on to explain they had been provided with water, what she assumed were protein bars, and toilet paper.

Billy Williams started to make a smart remark about the toilet paper and caught himself before he opened his mouth. "Not much to live on, is it?" He sounded concerned as he looked at each of the children.

"They're from Nicaragua. That's a long trek." Murphy went on to explain they were told if a new family didn't come, they should stay as long as they could and then return to the place where they got directions.

She looked at the sheriff. "I asked him if he could lead us to the place where he got the directions. I honestly think he doesn't know how to get there, but he said it was 'una iglesia,' which is a church." She took a breath. "I also asked him why they came down the mountain with their hands in the air. He said they saw the flying machine and were afraid they would be killed."

Chad rarely gave away his thoughts on his face, but his expression was one of grief. "It was certainly not our intent to scare them. Please be sure they know that." He quickly moved into his responsibilities as sheriff as Murphy told the family they were safe.

"Good work, Murphy. I'm going to take Whitehorse and Williams with me up to the plateau. You two take this family down to the area where Mike Smallwood is and get them some water from our backpacks. There are protein bars there too. We'll see about proper food when we get them to the valley. You can get through to dispatch on the secure radio when you get down. Have them see if they can reach Sam Nations." He saw the puzzled look on her face as she knew Sam was DEA, "Ask him to give me the name of the guy he knows at Immigration. I prefer to talk to someone I've been told I can trust."

"Done and done. I prefer to talk to someone on our side when I can as well."

"And, Murphy, just one question. How is it you know Spanish?"

"I do mission work with my church in Central America during my vacation time. Thought you knew."

"I knew you went on missions, just never occurred to me you learned Spanish. Good for you. Thanks for your help. Not sure what we would have done otherwise."

He watched the family go with the two deputies and was counting his good fortune to have a deputy who was able to communicate with these folks. *I think we may have a greater need of that from now on. I better start learning some basic words.* He was still trying to figure out why a family would be sent into this wilderness, especially by a church group—if it was in fact a church group. He almost stopped Murphy to have her ask if they knew anything about a light, but he would wait until he joined them at the bottom.

"Ready?" He turned to Whitehorse and Williams. "Let's move up to this plateau and see what we have there. Then we'll have to figure out what to do about it."

The three of them headed up with Chad in the lead. It only took them fifteen minutes to make it to the point at which they could see the plateau and the small outcropping of trees beyond. He had expected to see personal belongings, but the plateau looked as innocent as someone's camping area. There were blankets neatly stacked against the side of the mountain and three metal boxes with latches to secure them. The boxes had old US Army markings on the side. One of the boxes contained protein bars, a supply of toilet paper, and a trash bag holding empty wrappers. Another box had full and empty bottles of water. The third had a first-aid kit, a small battery powered lantern, extra batteries, and bear spray. Chad looked at Sylvia and Billy, shaking his head in bewilderment.

"Boss, do you think the lantern is the light we were seeing? It would make sense if they were using it to go into the woods for personal relief at night." Sylvia was scanning the area as she spoke.

Chad nodded. "Williams, do some reconnaissance over in that wooded area and see what you find."

Billy headed off to check out the wooded area, returning in only a few minutes. "Well, boss, this looks more and more like a well-planned hideout." He showed Chad and Sylvia the pictures on his phone. There was a crude, fence-like igloo structure sheltering a hole covered with small branches. The leaves were now mostly off the branches, revealing a modified outhouse.

"Looks like we have to figure out who's behind this hideout and why. Get as many pictures of this area as you can, then let's head down." Chad walked over to the edge of the plateau to see how dangerous a drop there might be if someone stepped too close. He could see the tops of the taller trees, along with the undergrowth, would actually save someone from falling all the way down the mountainside. *Still, it would be a rough tumble and some real damage could be done. I don't even want to think what it would take to get them out. No way a helicopter could get in here with the outcropping above the plateau. But the outcropping certainly created a secure open cave for shelter.* He shook his head in amazement at the planning that had gone into this refuge.

"Took all the pictures I think we need, boss."

"Sergeant, see anything you think needs our attention?"

"No, sir. In fact, I'm pretty amazed at the setup here. This took some planning, and it takes some work to replenish things. It sure wasn't what I expected to see."

"Me either." Chad walked towards the path. "Me either. I don't want to disturb anything. Immigration Enforcement will likely end up taking charge."

Then in a joking challenge, he looked at Billy and Sylvia. "Last one down the mountain in one piece buys a round tonight after the sing-along." He took off in a solid jog. Williams and Whitehorse let him go.

Autumn Leaf-Lookers Galore

Joshua looked down from the office loft and saw Doug and his dad had a steady stream of customers. He was grateful Doug was available or otherwise the payroll would have been delayed. Even though he and his dad didn't mind, he had to think of his part-time help who depended on their income from the work. In the old days, he would have just written out a check for each of them and sorted out the books later. Now, with the automated system, their checks printed on a form that also gave a breakdown of the hours worked, along with the deductions. *I do think it's more fair the employee can verify their work hours and know where their money goes. Just never quite sure that automation always makes things easier.*

It was almost two o'clock and neither he nor Joe had managed to get lunch. He walked downstairs and told his dad to go eat and he would cover the register.

"You haven't eaten either, son." Joe sounded concerned.

"Looks like we might be slowing up a bit. I'll join you when we get through these customers. Unless too many more come through the door, Doug can handle it. Right, Doug?"

"You bet. Go eat, Joe. You too, Joshua. I've got this."

Joe headed to the back while Joshua finished up the two customers in his dad's lane.

"Thanks, folks, hope to see you at the bluegrass jam and sing-along tonight." Joe chatted with the customers as he walked to the back.

"Planning on it," many of the customers said.

A local shopper looked at Joshua. "Certainly hope *you* intend to bring your dancing shoes!" Joshua smiled and continued to ring up customers—he loved to dance.

As the line dwindled, Joshua nodded to Doug and headed to the back. His dad was sitting at the table, eating a sandwich and drinking his tea.

"Might be time to bring out the ole crockpot and start having some soup or chili on these cooler days," Joe said.

"Good idea, Dad." Joshua sat down with his sandwich. "Want some chips?" Joe took a few and put them on his plate.

"Looking forward to the get-together tonight," Joe said. "Awful sweet of Nora to keep the community gatherings going. They get more important as other things change around here, don't you think?"

Joshua was clearly distracted. "Yeah, Dad. Sure." He was trying to figure out how to tell Joe about inviting Bella to lunch on Sunday; there hadn't been many Sundays recently when he and his dad weren't together. An idea occurred to him.

"Dad, any problem with missing our Sunday lunch this week?"

"No, son." Joe wondered what Joshua was trying to avoid telling him. "I thought you said it would only take Arthur a few hours early Sunday morning to fix the steps. Something you need me to help do?"

"No, no. It will only take Arthur a few hours. Even if he needed longer, I would have no problem leaving him here alone. With me to help get whatever he needs, it will go even faster." He hesitated. "Actually, I invited Bella to come down and have lunch with me."

"Did ya now, son? Did ya?" Joe smiled. "That's right nice." Joe stopped himself from saying anything else. He did not want to make more of this than Joshua wanted it to be. And he sure didn't want to put any pressure on him or Bella.

They finished their lunches in silence, as they often did. Cleaning up their trash, Joshua put it in the lidded trash can and started loading the cart with products to put on shelves. He wanted to be sure they could get out on time, or even a little early, and still be ready for tomorrow's Saturday rush.

Joe headed up front and left Joshua to his stock work and his thoughts. Melody was already at the register, and Joe said goodbye to Doug and told him to be ready for some good singing at the jamboree.

The steady stream of shoppers expected in mid-afternoon did not disappoint. Joe could hear a customer talking to Joshua as he was putting products on the shelves and decided all was right with the world. *I knew Joshua was trying to figure out how to tell me something. I just didn't know if it would be his disappointment about Chad taking Bella tonight or something he learned going on around the valley. Didn't figure it would be that he stepped up and asked Bella to lunch. Good for you, my son, good for you!*

This Land is My Land

After almost an hour riding on her Outlander ATV, Bella stopped to enjoy the peace and quiet. She knew she could wander away from the trail but still needed to be alert for bears. The females would start their winter sleep in mid-November, with the males following a month later. She stayed alert and carried the bear spray she purchased at the Valley Store, but also allowed herself to just be at one with the trees and hills. She had often thought she should hire a helicopter pilot to take her above her land so she could gain a full appreciation of the eighty acres. It was one thing to see the space on a map compared to everything around it, but something else to take it all in at one time. *Hmmm... I might have to figure out how I could place markers at the corners to know what I was seeing. I need to talk to a pilot one of these days.*

The colorful canopy provided by the changing leaves enveloped her in a calm she wanted to feel each and every day she was at Drellag Caban. Although she loved the autumn rainbow, she didn't need the color, or even the leaves, to feel the tranquility of these mountains. She equally loved the trees when they were bare. Bare trees had always been a metaphor for the cycle of life for her. The shedding of the old to be ready for rebirth in the spring, whether it was trees or life in general. She took in a deep breath and stretched her arms as far she could, inhaling the cool air. She stood for several minutes, then hiked towards an outcrop she and Matt had visited many times.

Once she reached it, she sat down and pulled her knees up, crossed her arms on her knees, and rested her chin on her arms. The vista made her feel like she could see forever. It was not the same as standing at the edge of the ocean looking towards the horizon and having the feeling of endlessness beyond. It was the variety of detail provided by the mountains: the trees, the sky, the occasional waterfall when it rained, and the streams that carried the water off the mountains. Today? Well, today she just enjoyed the vastness of the wilderness: imagining all the life on the forest floor, and the birds performing their daily rituals of calls, songs, and foraging. She knew the birds would soon be gone for another season. *I need to store the songs of the birds to recall after they have left the mountains for warmer climes.* She glanced at her watch and saw it was already three thirty. She avoided any quick moves that might draw attention of the larger wildlife as she headed back to the ATV and towards the cabin.

She put her Outlander in the shed, left her helmet on the seat, and made sure the window was locked, a habit started after the theft of the motor oil last month. She was hanging up her vest when she saw the blinking light on the answering machine. Thinking it might be Chad calling about the evening's plans, she walked over to listen before she headed to the shower. *Will I still go if something has come up and he isn't coming to get me?*

Bella pushed the button to hear the message. "Hey, Miss Bella, it's Arthur. Arthur Gillett. Just wanted to let you know, in case I miss you at the jamboree tonight, that I still plan to be there bright and early Monday morning. Let me know if you weren't able to get to the log cabin showroom and I'll try to get you some information. Otherwise, see you Monday." She erased the recording. She was relieved it wasn't Chad.

Bella didn't know what time Chad would call to say he was coming. Nora had said the children would be there at six thirty while she and the band warmed up, and then her husband would take them home to go to bed. She assumed he would pick her up before six.

She had never liked using a hair dryer, so she needed time for her hair to dry. Since she already knew what she was wearing tonight, she could take a leisurely shower, towel dry her hair, and make sure the house was closed up before she dressed. She relished the heat of the hot shower and the steam on her face. She wasn't sure how long she stood there, but the water started running cold, so she knew it was longer than normal. She was toweling off when she heard the phone ring. She threw on her heavy cotton robe and ran out, hoping to answer it before it went to the answering machine.

"Drellag Caban, may I help you?"

"Ms. Anderson?"

"Yes?"

"Hey, this is Macklin Evans..."

"Oh, hey!"

"Sorry to disturb you on such a fine afternoon, but I wanted to check and see if you had any questions about the cabins we considered yesterday, the Overlook in particular." He quickly went on, "Of course, we can do whatever you want. You just showed quite an interest in that particular model."

She really did dislike the work salespeople had to do. *Be calm.* She knew he was just being a good salesman—she didn't want to sound annoyed.

"Thank you for checking. I've reviewed my notes and the information you gave me. I'll talk with Mr. Gillett on Monday and hope to make a final decision soon." She waited a moment to see if he would say anything. "Was there anything else?"

"No, ma'am, just wanted to be of service if you need us. That's all. Have a nice weekend."

"Thanks, I appreciate it. You have a nice weekend too."

She plopped down in the kitchen chair. *Why am I running at every ring of the phone and blinking of the answering machine? It's not like I can't go to the gathering tonight on my own if Chad can't go.* She drummed her nails on the table. *Just take the days as they come. Quit trying to figure out who intends what under what conditions. It will be what it will be.* She started humming a song she had loved since her childhood: *Que sera, sera.*

Bella decided she had appropriately admonished herself and decided to let it go. She closed the windows, checked the hook latch on the porch screen door, locked the French doors, and walked into her bedroom. *Drellag Caban, new memories await.*

18

Wrapping Things Up

"Detective Williams, I'm sure all these fine officers of the law and fire service will be pleased to hear you'll be buying a round for all those who can make it to The Corral after the jamboree tonight."

They clapped, but Murphy quieted them with her hand. She turned to the family. "Disculpame. Perdóname." After her apology, she explained to the family that the detective was the last one down the mountain, so he had to treat everyone else to something to drink. She felt badly for the disrespect she felt the clapping showed to the family. She knew the sheriff had made the offhand comment without thinking. *If I know the boss, he'll be kicking himself all the way to the valley when it dawns on him the family might think we were clapping about capturing them.*

"Entiendo," the father said.

Chad knew his pronouncement was wrong as soon as it left his mouth. He walked over to Murphy. "Please extend my apologies. I meant no disrespect."

"I already explained it to them, sir. The father said he understood."

The family all had water bottles, and each appeared to be holding the wrappers from protein bars in their hands. Chad walked over and extended his hand to take the paper from them. He hoped it would convey the human decency he should have considered before his announcement to the troops about Williams.

He then called the team together.

"First, to Fire Chief Smallwood and Sergeant Whitehorse, I extend my deepest appreciation for the use of your UAV and the skill with which both of you helped navigate this situation. Deputy Murphy, your ability to talk with this family and hopefully make them feel safe is greatly appreciated. I want you two," nodding to Murphy and the other deputy, "to take this family to the station. Please call dispatch on your way and tell them to get a meal from The Corral ready. You can pick it up on your way. Were you able to get a name and number for me from Special Agent Nations?"

"Yes, sir." She handed him a piece of paper.

"Good work. Now get this family to the station." He paused. "Put them in the conference room to eat. They can wait there until I arrive. I need to see what the next steps will be. I'm going on the assumption they have no papers, so Immigration will be in charge..." His voice trailed off. He felt conflicted about his legal obligation and his wish for a humane way to deal with people just trying to be safe and improve their lives.

He waited to talk to the others until the family was headed out. Since Murphy didn't say otherwise, he assumed she had come in one of the larger SUVs and could transport all of them in one vehicle.

Before Chad could speak again, Billy Williams stepped over to him. "Sir, I rode with the deputies. Room for me with you?"

Chad just looked at him. Smiling to himself, he shook his head. He looked straight at Billy and acted like he couldn't believe what he'd just heard. "You don't think I'd wish you on the fire chief, do you?" He slapped Billy on the back. "You're good, Williams! Too far for ya to walk."

"Mike," he extended his hand, "I owe you big time. You helped me solve a problem that has been keeping me awake at night. You may well have also saved a family, and future families, from a lot of danger, at the very least from the wildlife."

"At your service, Sheriff," Mike said with respect. "Care to ride with me, Sergeant Whitehorse? I'll drop you off at the station."

Sylvia looked at Chad. "Work for you, boss?"

"Go home. Let's do this as overtime, if that works for you? You had a short night."

"Works for me, boss. Thanks." She spoke up again, "Sheriff, do you think we could hang around a few minutes and let the others get out? Don't want to pass them on our ATVs while they're walking out."

"How long did it take you to walk in?" Chad asked Billy, wondering where he had left his brain. *How have I become so insensitive to others? I need to regroup and remember to see the decent side of folks. So easy to lose it in this business.*

"About fifteen minutes, but we were moving at a fast clip. I'd say with the little ones, give them twenty or so, then we should be okay."

"Thanks, Billy. Let's use this time to learn something. Mike and Sylvia, how about a run down on how you used the UAV in this little operation?"

Mike talked them through piloting and maneuvering the UAV. He explained the challenges of getting up over the trees, and he answered Chad's questions about ease of handling. Chad also asked for Mike and Sylvia's recommendations regarding training others in the department.

"In this day and age, you want people to be able to fly BVLS. They have to have the video technology I was using today."

"BVLS?" Billy looked dumbfounded.

"Why, Detective, are you admitting you don't know the abbreviation for beyond visual line of sight?" Chad feigned surprise.

"No, sir. I did not know. Thanks for telling me." Billy tried to figure out if the sheriff was upset with him.

Chad slapped Billy on the back. "Let's go, hotshot. We have work to do."

Turning to the other two, he said, "Thanks again, Mike and Sylvia, for everything. Sylvia, on Monday we'll talk about your recommendations for what we need to purchase."

Chad put on his helmet and hopped onto the ATV; Billy hopped on behind him. He was hoping the sheriff wouldn't say anything about him not having a helmet. Chad took his helmet off and handed it to Billy. "Put it on."

The other sheriff's vehicle was gone when they arrived, and the lot was full of what he assumed were day hikers. He would figure out later how no one else had gone up the trail to the plateau. Once the ATVs were locked on to the trailer, Chad and Billy pulled out of the lot, waving to Mike and Sylvia as they got into their own SUV.

"I'm going to need to make a call here in a minute, but first have you found out anything on the syringe in the Brown case?"

"Yes, sir. Found one print that matches Phillips. Brown's DNA was apparently in the needle. I've talked to Peggy and she's considering further charges. She's going to let Stevie sit in our fine jail for the weekend and be ready to go with charges on Monday. She didn't say if she was going to the judge or going to convene the grand jury. Either way she's satisfied, at least at the moment, with what we have. She said she would let me know if she wanted me to take one more run at Stevie to see if changed his story in being a bystander to Brown's overdose."

"Good work. Sounds like we have this wrapped up. Still no call from Steve's parents? Has he asked to make a call?"

"Neither. I still don't understand the parents. I thought at least the mother would call. But once the DA files additional charges, things may change. Just don't know what to make of it."

"Me either," Chad said bluntly.

He hit the button on his steering wheel to dial the number of the Immigration Enforcement Agency official. He had no idea if Sam Nations had already called ahead to let the IEA agent know. He saw the name written on the paper was Quinn.

"Yes?" A female voice answered.

"May I speak to Quinn?"

"Who's asking?"

"A friend of Sam." Chad knew how this game went.

"My Uncle Sam or some other Sam?" The woman's voice was deadpan.

"Both. I've pledged an oath to Uncle Sam, and I'm a personal and professional friend of Sam Nations," Chad said, wondering how long this would continue.

Billy stared at him. Chad just shrugged and kept driving.

"I, too, have pledged an oath to Uncle Sam. And a Sam Nations told me I might hear from a strange man who needed my assistance." She chuckled.

"And I'm guessing he told you to string me along." He paused. "I'm going to assume I have the right person if you don't hang up when I tell you I'm Sheriff Chad Oliver."

"Quinn speaking. Game's over, sir. How may I be of service?"

Chad told her he had a family from Nicaragua at his station in the valley and would like to request her assistance. "Sam probably told you I need people who understand the uniqueness of the hollers in these mountains, not some card-carrying bureaucrats..." he trailed off. "Sorry, I don't usually go on a rant with someone who doesn't know me."

"It's okay, Sheriff, Sam filled me in. I know it's his neck of the woods and helping you out would be worth the adventure."

"Good. Haven't had any direct experience with IEA, so can you give me the right chain of command to call and end up with your help if you're available?"

She filled him in on the right contact and told him she would look forward to meeting him in person. "Anything else right now, Sheriff?"

"Good to go. Look forward to meeting you too."

He hung up and spoke the number she'd given him to his car phone. When the operator at IEA answered, he identified himself and asked for the director whose name Quinn had provided. He realized he didn't know if Quinn was her first name or last.

"Sir, if you'll give me your number, I'll have someone call you back and see if they can be of assistance."

Chad knew the drill. No one at any major federal agency was going to admit the person you thought you were calling was at their agency. He no sooner hung up than the phone rang.

"Oliver here."

"Afternoon, Sheriff, Agent Isaacs said I would be hearing from you." The director whose name Quinn had given Chad was all business. "I think she brought me up to speed on what's happening, as she understood it. I'll send her over. Do you need more than one agent?"

"Thanks, sir. I don't think so, but from a safety point of view it's not my call. This is a family of six, so I'll leave that to your discretion. There was no resistance on our approach, and they've been cooperative to this point."

"Got it. Unusual way of us getting involved, but I appreciate your effort to do this thing right. So, I'm going to allow it, this time. I hope I won't learn I made a bad decision." His officious tone was the same as all the mid-level bureaucrats Chad had spoken to over the years. *It must be a requirement for promotion.*

"Not on my end, you won't. Thank *you* for your cooperation. I look forward to meeting Agent Isaacs."

Updates

On the way back to the station, Billy said, "Boss, do you think the light you were monitoring was the lantern from the encampment?"

"Makes sense, Billy. Guess we could have counted the steps to the makeshift outhouse but given the time it took you to walk to it, take pictures, and come back, no reason to think otherwise. It explains why the light disappeared so quickly. Even if they used it to walk back to the plateau, we wouldn't have seen it from the pullout overlooking Sector Two. The plateau also fits the coordinates we had for the light."

"What will happen to the family?"

"Most of what I know about immigration is from reading official bulletins and reports. This will be my first, and hopefully my last, interaction with IEA. Nothing personal, just like to see a better coordinated immigration system. But we'll do our part. It seems pretty clear these people have no official papers. I suppose I could have Murphy inquire, but I don't want to mess up any investigation the IEA agent will do. I'll have to be pretty satisfied they'll get a fair shake before I'll release them from my custody, though."

"Is that why you wanted someone Sam knew?"

"One thing I've learned in this job is to trust people who are worthy of your trust. I trust Sam with my life, and yours. If he trusts Immigration Enforcement Agent Quinn Isaacs, then that's a good first step for me. Let's hope she's worthy of his trust and ours."

Chad went quiet, and Billy knew to be quiet too. Twenty minutes later they pulled into the station. "Coming in, Billy, or are you done for the day?"

"Headed in, boss. I spent so much time on Steve Phillips that I need to do some catching up with the other detectives on other cases. Never ceases to amaze me how many issues can need our attention in such a small community." He looked at Chad. "Grateful for the help, though, boss."

"Let me know if there's anything I need to know before Monday." Both men had their ID badges out and scanned them. Chad walked into the first men's room; Billy kept walking.

"Catch you later, boss. At The Corral later tonight, if not before." Billy started whistling "Turkey in the Straw."

Chad was still shaking his head about Billy's whistling as he stopped in the break room. He needed coffee and something to snack on while he checked messages. He hadn't paid attention to the time it was already nearing two. He wanted to see if the surveillance on the house where he had seen Commissioner Zimmerman drop off the young girl had any results last night. The deputy and dispatcher in the break room looked up and said good afternoon, then went back to their conversation. Suited him just fine.

He had several messages on his computer monitor once he fired it up: one from the detective he had checking on the ownership of the motels in Round City, and one from the sergeant who had last night's late shift to say the surveillance information was on the secure server. Chad opened the secure server while phoning the detective to ask him for an update about the motel ownership. The detective answered on the second ring. He informed the sheriff he was making progress, but the companies used some tricky maneuvers to hide ownership. He thought he would have something more definitive on Monday.

"Thanks, Detective, we can go to the FBI if there's something that suggests more than what appears on the surface, but they don't like fishing expeditions. So, let's see what you can find and then we'll meet Monday and go from there. Good work."

"Yes, sir. Hope you can get to the jamboree, Sheriff."

"Me too, Detective. Me too."

He sat back for a minute and thought about the data search on the motels while wondering what he would find when he opened the message from the sergeant. After he logged in to the secure server, he found the file and started reading. "Compiled report from Sergeant Whitehorse's shift and my own. Drive-by every twenty-five to thirty minutes by regular patrol. Unmarked patrol from eight p.m. Thursday night until two a.m. Friday morning. Frequent vehicles in and out of the driveway and parked on the road. No more than three vehicles at one time. No vehicles seen after two a.m. Longest time for vehicle was three hours. Only solo individuals seen exiting cars. All were men. Based on directive, deputies did not record any license plates or stop to observe. Unless notified otherwise, will maintain same routine tonight."

Well, well. I doubt there was a family gathering at that house. Part of me wants to jump right on it. I know in my gut that young woman was underage, but I need to do this one by the book. We'll just keep it under surveillance for the weekend and then I can put together a team next week. If my suspicion is right, I may need Immigration on this one too. He sat back in his chair, ran his hands through his thick salt-and-pepper hair, and took a deep breath. He felt he should go check on the family in the conference room, but he decided it was best to just wait until Agent Quinn Isaacs arrived to avoid causing any more stress to the children.

Cooperating with Immigration

His quandary was resolved when his phone rang and dispatch told him Agent Isaacs was in the lobby. "I'll be right up, thanks." Letting out a sigh behind his closed door, he opened it with his normal sheriff in-charge demeanor and strode up to the front desk. The deputy on desk duty buzzed the door before Chad could open it himself. He exited and walked over to the young woman.

Agent Quinn Isaacs walked towards him. "Sheriff Oliver?"

Chad extended his hand to shake and waved the other one indicating she should go through the open door. "Nice to meet you, Agent Isaacs, you must have been fairly close to get here so quickly."

"Just over in Round City, so it was an easy drive, even with the autumn leaf-lookers not knowing how to navigate the curves between there and here."

"Well, that's good news. Means we've kept the traffic and economy moving in the right direction."

He led the way back to his office. He noticed she was wearing the typical uniform of the Immigration Enforcement Agency: khaki slacks with a dark blue golf shirt and a windbreaker with IEA emblazoned on the back. Chad guessed she was about Nora's age, and she was all business without being stuffy. He wondered if her height, which he judged to be about five foot nine, would be intimidating to the family in the conference room. The oldest son was the tallest, and he barely pushed five foot two. He gestured for her to enter his office and offered her a seat at the round table.

"May I get you something to drink? Water, coffee, tea?"

"I'm good, Sheriff, thanks all the same."

He sat down and noticed her looking at the maps on his walls. "Good topo maps you have there, sir."

"They come in handy when most of our territory is up one side of a mountain or down the other. Actually, they came in handy when trying to get to the spot we found today. . ." he paused, thinking he should probably back up a few steps to bring her fully up to speed. "Over the last month or so, we have been trying to pinpoint the source of a light which has been repeatedly reported as 'there and then not there.' Sam and I were tracking a drug case—"

She interrupted him. "Word is you made a pretty big bust and had to deal with a meth lab blowing up."

He guffawed. "Well, don't be mistaken. It was no bust. It was purely accidental, literally and figuratively." He gave her a quick overview of the ATVs running drugs, assuring her they were all locals, at least on this end of the operation. "At this point, anything else is in the hands of the DEA. I hope they can find out who was the money behind it and where the meth was being delivered. Back to the light… I was not convinced the meth lab was the source. Quite frankly, I thought someone was flying a UAV at night without a Part 107 permit. Given what we found today, it appears much more simplistic than that."

"Really? What? No UAV?"

"Nope, not even any UFOs. But apparently a frequent site for aliens of the kind who come across our border looking for refuge for their families."

She was nodding her head. "Lots of those, Sheriff, lots of those."

"Are you from this area, Agent Isaacs?"

"Please, call me Quinn. Sam has filled me in that you're a by-the-book kind of sheriff." Chad looked at her quizzically, wondering what else Sam had told her. "Please, call me Chad."

She smiled. "Sam also made it very clear that you have a heart for your community hidden behind your bark."

"Well now, that's better." Chad smiled. He continued explaining how they found the plateau using the topo maps and used the UAV to check out the plateau. He then described the response the family had when they saw it. "I feel badly they thought it was a weapon."

Quinn shook her head, and her light brown eyes softened. "Doubtful they've ever even seen a UAV. They probably thought it *was* extraterrestrials. Chad, the reports we send you outlining what these folks are trying to escape don't begin to paint the full picture of deprivation, beatings, and kidnappings. And that's just what's done by their government."

She paused for a moment before continuing. "It was good to hear your deputy could speak Spanish. Helps in this business. I didn't answer your question earlier. Yes, I'm from Knoxville and my mother's family has been here for many generations, more than a century and a half. My dad's family is from northern Spain. My parents met at UT Knoxville and the rest, as they say, is history. My mother majored in Spanish, so it was inevitable that between them that I would grow up bilingual. Speaking the language makes this job much easier with most of the people we encounter in this part of the country, although I don't think I'd be much use to the IEA service out west with Asian immigrants."

"So far, my experience with IEA is in written reports. What are our next steps?"

"Well, first I'd like to know a bit more about the area where you found them and what you think was going on."

Chad told her about the plateau and said it was clear someone was supplying the people who camped up there.

"I have another car with two agents waiting outside. Do you have someone who can take them there now? I'd like to get the area identified and then secure whatever we can find useful there."

Chad stood up and called Billy Williams. "Great! Be here ready to go in ten."

"Do you want to bring your agents in? They may like to use the facilities as there's nothing but trees and rocks once they leave here, and it will take a good thirty minutes just to get there."

Agent Isaacs took out her mobile phone and called the agents. Chad called the front desk and asked to have the sergeant on duty escort them back.

"Listen, Quinn…" he said softly, wanting to use the right words, "I don't have any experience with modern day immigrants. I've learned many things in the last few years from my native neighbors about those of us who descend from European immigrants. It would sure help me sleep better tonight knowing what the next steps are for these folks."

"Assuming you found no immigration papers on them, we will place them in an immigration facility while we try to determine the validity of their claim for asylum, which is what we expect they will request. We try to determine if they already have relatives in the country, and we do a pretty thorough job of informing them of their rights and responsibilities under US immigration laws."

Chad listened silently.

"But I have to be honest with you. They will likely be deported. That decision happens way above my pay grade, but I assure you it isn't done as cruelly or wantonly as the media portrays. You might also like to know there have been families who have helped us identify and locate those who are moving people across the border, and those who are aiding them once they're here. It has happened where those families are given favorable consideration towards legal application for entry. So, it's not always a bad outcome."

"Thanks, Quinn, helps to hear that from someone Sam trusts."

She wondered what he saw in her eyes when he mentioned Sam.

There was a knock on the door. Both stood as Billy and the two IEA agents entered the room. Chad made the introductions and gave Billy his instructions. Billy was to get the other agents to the site and help with whatever they needed. Chad made it clear that Immigration was in charge. Within five minutes the two agents and Billy were headed out of the building.

"If you're ready, I'm going to take you to the conference room and introduce you to Deputy Murphy. She'll be able to tell you if the family volunteered anything."

"Very unlikely," Quinn said from experience.

"I imagine." When they approached the conference room, Chad said, "I'll call Murphy out and introduce you. Then I suspect you'd just as soon I disappear."

"Nothing personal, Sheriff, but might be easier all the way around. I have another agent with me. He's in the van. We generally don't encounter problems, but six people, even with four of them children, isn't a good plan for one agent."

"I'm actually relieved to hear that. How about I introduce you to Murphy and then see if your agent wants to step in before you hit the road?"

"That'll work. Thanks. Hope to see you under more pleasant circumstances in the future. This valley looks like a pretty nice respite from my day-to-day work."

"Well, I suspect it is. Starting tonight we're bringing back our Friday night bluegrass jams and sing-alongs. We're outside at The Corral restaurant for a few weeks. When it gets too cold, we'll move inside to the community room. Come anytime."

He shook her hand, opened the conference room door, and signaled Murphy to come out. "Deputy Amy Murphy, I'd like introduce Agent Quinn Isaacs."

He walked outside to offer the agent a chance to come in before they hit the road. He stood for a minute breathing in the fresh air.

He asked a deputy to escort the IEA agent and said his goodbye. He saw on the wall clock it was already a few minutes after four o'clock. *Guess I better finish up a quick scan of messages and emails then head home to shower and change. Do I have time to get a shower? I'll make time and just call Bella as soon as I get to the house to tell her I'm on my way.*

19

Ready to Go

Bella was dressed and sitting on the living room sofa reading *Glass Houses*. She knew she would have at least twenty minutes once Chad called to put the deviled eggs in the insulated carrier and set out the brownies. She learned long ago that picnic food was best when it was the cocktail party equivalent of finger food. From the walls of Drellag Caban, she could hear Grandmother Hazel saying, "We had fingers before we had forks." *I wonder if she said things like that to try and offset the formality of my mother? I don't think she would have ever openly contradicted Mother, but she wanted me to be comfortable in whatever situation I found myself. And, generally, I have been. Thanks, Grandmother Hazel!*

Deeply immersed in her book, she was startled by the ringing of the phone. She hadn't considered how much louder it sounded in the living room than on the porch. She placed her bookmark and set the book on the trunk she used as a coffee table before jumping up to get the phone. It was on the seventh ring when she answered. "Drellag Caban, may I help you?"

"Good evening, Bella."

"Good evening, Chad." *Is he being formal because I'm so often formal?*

"Been a busy day, and I haven't been sure whether I would be able to get away—"

With concern in her voice, she interrupted him, "Oh, Chad, I know your job requires—"

It was his turn to interrupt her, but his tone was playful. "If I may finish—"

Interrupting him again, she said, "Bad habit, sorry. Please continue."

He laughed. "Okay, let's not make this difficult. I'll be more direct. Maybe that'll help." He took a breath. "I'll bring chairs for us. I should be leaving my home in about ten minutes. That'll put me up at yours no later than six. Does that work for you?"

"Perfect. That'll get us down the mountain before six thirty."

"This isn't a gala performance, you know. Doesn't matter what time we arrive."

"Yes. Yes, it does."

"Why?" He sounded perplexed.

"I'll explain it to you when you get here."

"Fair enough," he said. "Fair enough. See you before six."

"Goodbye, Chad." There was a teasing lilt in her voice.

"See you soon, Bella."

Bella walked into the bathroom and looked in the mirror, brushed her hair, and then decided to pull her hair back in a ponytail. She walked back into the living room. She picked up her book to continue reading then set it down. *I'm as nervous as a schoolgirl on her first date. This is ridiculous. Chad is simply picking me up. This is not a date.* After sitting quietly for several minutes, she finally had to admit it to herself. *It's a date. I want it to be a date.* She picked up her book and started reading.

A few minutes later, she realized she had read the same paragraph three times without absorbing any of it. She was so distracted she knew it was futile to continue. *I may as well get everything ready.*

She went into the kitchen, put the small plastic container of ice in the middle compartment of the insulated carrier bag, then put the egg cartons holding the deviled eggs on either side. She knew Joe and Joshua were bringing everything they needed for a picnic, but she decided to put some napkins in the carrier for the brownies, just to be sure. She started to open the door to sit on the kitchen steps and then decided that would be a little too obvious. She plopped down on the kitchen chair instead.

Fast Clean-up

Chad was still shaking his head when he stepped in the shower. *I don't know if I'm quick enough to navigate interacting with a woman who is always thinking. I like her concern for others and not wanting to inconvenience anyone. But I'm not sure if I can figure out if she's just being polite, or if she could be interested in being more than friends.*

After a quick wash, he threw on his jeans and started reaching for a plaid shirt on autopilot. He stopped. *I may as well put a little more thought into this... just in case it's the second option.* He opted for one of his pale blue cotton shirts, then pulled out a navy-blue fleece vest to ward off the cool chill of an October evening and cover his service weapon. He slipped on his LL Bean camp moccasins and couldn't remember the last time he'd worn them. *I didn't even wear them to the picnic for Nora's birthday. Maybe it's time I remembered I can be sheriff and still have a personal life.* He walked into the kitchen, took his service weapon out of the gun safe, and placed it in his concealed holster. *Hmmm ... didn't wear a gun the last time I was on a date.*

He put the folding chairs in his SUV before remembering no one had told him what food to bring, and he hadn't bothered to ask. Trying to decide what to do, he remembered he had a fresh prepackaged veggie tray, one of several he kept in the fridge as a snack food. Perfect. He grabbed the veggie tray and headed out. He put on the CD of Nora singing; he couldn't believe he was actually going to pick up Bella for an evening of music and good company.

Joe Sends Joshua on His Way

Joshua peeked in the picnic basket Diane had dropped off. It had cold fried chicken, biscuits, and dill pickles. Diane had also given him potato salad and pasta salad to put in the ice chest. He already had the bottled water, tea, and ice. Joe had put plates, napkins, and forks in the basket—everything was ready to go.

"Hey!" Joe said as Joshua finished stocking shelves for Saturday's shoppers. "Like I figured, we're down to a trickle here. I think you should load up the things for the picnic, run home and shower, and head on to the jamboree. Melody's planning to stay here until it's time to go over to The Corral. I can walk over with her."

Joshua had not planned on that turn of events. He started to tell his dad he would just wait so they could go together, then changed his mind. He sure thought he would feel better if he showered.

"Sure, Dad. If that works for you, I'll take you up on it."

"Perfect, son. Now, get out of here."

"I've already locked up the back, so I'll pull up to the front to load this stuff then be on my way. Promise me you'll text or call me to come get you if you don't feel like walking."

"I promise. But Melody and I will be fine."

Headed to the Bluegrass Jamboree

Bella heard the SUV coming up the road. Tired of trying to decide whether to wait inside or out, she decided to leave the kitchen door open and stay inside. Chad pulled up so the passenger door was facing the kitchen door. She opened the screen and waved. Turning back, she picked up the brownies and deviled eggs. When she turned to the door, he was standing with the screen door open and his hands out to take the food from her. He leaned in and kissed her on the cheek.

"Looking lovely as ever, Dr. Anderson." Chad had a schoolboy grin.

She had turned too far to make a return cheek kiss seem anything but awkward.

"Good evening to you, Sheriff Oliver."

Then she looked him in the eyes and smiled as she handed the two containers to him. She flipped the switch for the porch light as she stepped out the door, then turned to lock up. When she turned back to the car, Chad was standing with the passenger door open. In spite of her continual push for gender equity, she was aware she didn't bristle when he opened the door for her. She walked over and got in. He waited while she buckled her seatbelt and then gently closed the door. She watched him walk in front of the truck and decided it might be the first time she had seen him so casually dressed. She smiled—she liked what she saw.

Chad reached over to turn off the CD of Nora singing.

"Wait, let's hear this song at least."

Nora was singing "Down to the River to Pray." Bella thought it was as lovely as she had ever heard it sung by Alison Krauss. Without realizing it, she sang aloud on the last verse, "And who shall wear the robe and crown? Good Lord, show me the way."

Chad stopped at the grate across Bella's Creek and listened. He clapped. "You've been holding out on me. You have a lovely voice. Can't wait to tell Nora." He saw the red of an embarrassed blush blossom across her cheeks.

"Whoa, I got a little carried away there." She felt the heat rising in her face. "I'll just enjoy the sing-along, and I promise not to belt the songs out too loudly."

He reached over to turn off the CD. "Okay if I turn it off?"

She nodded. Chad started down the mountain, keeping his speed safe and slow to watch out for leaf-lookers. At least that was his ostensible reason if Bella asked. *But we'll get to spend a few more minutes alone together.* He glanced over at Bella out of the corner of his eye; she seemed to be looking at the fall scenery. Suddenly, she leaned forward and pointed to something coming up the road from the other direction.

"Chad, look! Is that a dog?"

Chad stopped, and they both jumped out of the SUV. It was a dog; it limped slowly up the road in their direction. Chad knelt down on one knee.

"Come here, boy, what's the matter?" As it got closer, they could hear the dog whimpering. "Looks like he might be part lab and part German Shepherd. He's pretty young. Have you ever seen him before?"

"No. Look, he's favoring his front paw."

As the distance between them narrowed, Chad saw there was no collar or identification on him. He waited until the dog approached him, then he put his fist out slowly while talking quietly to the pup in a calm voice. The dog stopped at Chad's feet and sniffed his fist, then raised his right front paw.

"What are you trying to show me, boy? Let's see that paw." A gentle touch caused the dog to whimper and back away from Chad.

"Bella, we need to get this pup to the vet. I can call Doc Jim as soon as we get a signal, and we'll take him before we go to the jamboree."

"Please. He looks like he's in pain. I wonder who he belongs to. Is there a way we can find out?"

Chad coaxed the pup towards him again. "The vet will be able to tell if he has a chip. People around here usually only get a microchip if it's a hunting dog. He doesn't have a collar. Let's see if he's going to let me check his paw."

Chad paused and looked up at Bella. "To get him down the mountain, I'll have to put him in the back of my SUV. If he snaps at me, I'll have to do a makeshift muzzle. Is that a problem for you?"

"No, I understand. Let's hope it won't come to that."

The dog let Chad turn his paw over; there was a large gash down the center of his pad. "Okay, buddy, we're going to take you down off this mountain and get you to a friend who can help you. He'll know if we can do anything to find your owner. What do ya say?" The dog rested his head on Chad's knee. Bella watched as Chad picked him up, continuing to talk to him and stroke him the whole time.

She got in the SUV and watched over her shoulder as Chad placed the pup in the back. Chad's gentleness touched her heart.

"You'll be just fine back here." The wire guard between the back seat and the rear compartment would allow the pup to hear Chad's voice. "Okay, boy, here we go. Nice and easy now."

Running Late

Chad called Doc Jim, the veterinarian who lived in the valley. He was now retired from his practice in Round City, only doing emergency care of animals in the surrounding area and putting chips in for those who knew him. He was waiting on his front porch when they pulled up, and Chad made introductions.

Shaking Bella's hand, Doc Jim said, "Nice to meet you. What have you brought me?"

Chad opened the rear of the SUV to lift the dog onto the porch, and Bella explained the situation. "He came on my property when we were headed down the mountain. His right front paw is hurt, and we can't find any identification on him."

Doc Jim looked at the pup. "On first glance, it doesn't look he has a chip. Most local folks bring their pets to me for that, and I don't recognize this little guy. I'll keep him for a week or so to let that pad start to heal, and we'll see if we can find the owner. If not, I'll take him to the shelter in Round City and someone will adopt him."

Bella spoke up quickly. "Please let me know if you don't find his owner. I've been thinking about getting a dog, and I'd be happy to take him."

"Let's get him inside for a proper once over."

Chad scooped the dog up and followed Doc Jim into a small examining room. He placed the pup on the exam table. Now that he was off the injured paw, he seemed much calmer.

Bella reached out to scratch behind his ears. His tail wagged and he began to lick her hand. "Think you'd like to live up on my mountain with me?"

Chad rubbed the pup's rump, and the tail began to thump against the table. "Well, buddy, it looks like you have a proud parent waiting on you right here. We'll check back in a few days, if that works for you, Doc?"

"Good enough. He'll be fine. I'll give him a good going over and let you know if I have any luck finding an owner. If my experience counts for anything, Miss Bella, I suspect you have a new pet. If it turns out otherwise, I'll be happy to help you find a good one."

"Send me the bill, Doc. I've got this," Chad said. The vet nodded at Chad.

Bella thanked Doc Jim and they headed out to the SUV.

"Any thoughts about me getting a dog?"

"Good idea up there on that mountaintop. If this one doesn't work out, we'll see what we can do. Deal?"

"Deal! Music awaits. Oh, and speaking of music. . ." she paused.

He glanced at her.

"Remember I told you we needed to be there early? Well, I was surprised at your comment not to worry about being there by six thirty. If memory serves me, and sometimes it doesn't, Nora said they would be warming up then, and her husband would bring the children over. Your grandchildren, I believe?" She purposely sounded a bit like a schoolteacher chastising a wayward student.

"Indeed, they're my grandchildren, and I stand humbled in the presence of a great memory." He felt a rush of color to his face. "You haven't met them yet. And I don't believe you've met my son-in-law, Fred."

"Right on both counts. I'm looking forward to meeting all of them."

"Good. I think you'll like Fred. He's our full-time local physician, and a pretty good one if I do say so myself."

"Another good reason to meet him. It could prove helpful to know someone in the medical community. I haven't considered *how* important it might be now that I'm here for an extended stay. Thanks."

They were quiet as he pulled on to the main road into the valley. For two people accustomed to silence, they both started to talk at once. They ended up laughing and glancing at each other.

"Don't know why the silence seemed so deep. I'm not usually unsettled by quiet."

"Hmmmm… know what you mean," Bella said.

The parking lot of The Corral was already filling up as they pulled into it. Chad drove past the building. "Not many perks in this job, but I get my own parking space close up for these events. Carla wants to be sure there's clear evidence of the law being present."

He glanced at Bella.

"Not on duty, so don't worry. Just a presence. Most times that's good enough. And, just so you know, there are a couple of off-duty deputies who do overtime for these community events. We can get a big crowd out on a nice night like tonight."

He parked the car and turned to look at Bella. "I, for one, am here to have a good time. How about you?"

"Absolutely! Me too!" Bella's smile extended to her voice.

The Community Arrives

Chad was about to take the food out of the truck when he heard, "Grandpa, Grandpa!" A little boy ran towards him. Chad took a couple of long strides to meet the boy at the edge of the parking area.

"Mac, there's my boy! Stay right there. I'll come to you."

Mac stopped his run and waited. "I wouldn't run in the road, Grandpa, you know that."

Bella admired his confident assurance.

Chad picked Mac up and began walking towards her. She smiled at the man, the boy, and the sight of them together—she felt her heart skip a beat.

Chad put Mac down. "Mac, this is a friend of mine, Dr. Anderson. Dr. Anderson, this is my grandson, Mac Smith."

Bella squatted down so she was eye to eye with Mac and extended her hand. "I'm very pleased to meet you, Mac."

"Nice to meet you. Do you work with my daddy? He's a doctor too."

Bella smiled. "No, I don't. I'm a different kind of doctor."

"Oh, are you a speshulish? My daddy is a general practisher." Bella smiled at his confidence, in spite of how he pronounced specialist and practitioner.

"Well, Master Mac Smith, you're quite well informed. When you and I have time to talk, I'll explain what kind of doctor I am. Do you think it would be all right with your mommy and daddy if you call me Bella?"

Mac looked up at his grandfather. Chad said, "I think you could call her Miss Bella, if that works for her. What do you say, Mac?"

"Yes, I like Miss Bella." He reached out and took her hand. "Come on, I can help you meet my sister, Lilly. She doesn't talk much yet, but you'll like her. And you can meet my daddy too. My mommy is busy warming up her voice. Do you know how to do that?"

Chad laughed and shrugged his shoulders. "He'll wear you out. Have fun. I'll get our things and catch up with you. He knows where he's going."

Bella took Mac's hand and headed towards the gathering crowd. Mac chattered the whole way as Bella swung his hand. She was clearly enjoying every minute of it.

Chad watched them walk away, smiling at the picture the two of them painted. *I've never seen Mary hold her grandson's hand. Bella took it with no hesitation and with a sincerity Mac can feel.*

A slap on his back startled him, and he turned quickly to see Joshua standing there.

"Hey, Chad. Nice night for a jamboree. Sounds like Nora is in good voice already."

Chad shook Joshua's extended hand and realized he needed to put the little green devil of jealousy away. *Why would I be the only single man intrigued by Bella?*

"Good to see you, Johsua." Chad looked around. "Where's Joe? I thought you were closing up early tonight."

"Since we have the picnic food, he told me to come ahead, and he'll walk down with Melody. You know there's no arguing with him."

"That's as true as a preacher's sermon on Sunday."

Joshua laughed. "Guess we best get this food over. Doc and his kids will want to eat before he takes them home to bed."

Chad felt a bit sheepish. In the last half hour two people had remembered things about his own family that he hadn't. *I've let this job become all consuming.*

He looked at Joshua. "Let's do it."

It took them several trips to get the food, the chairs, and the card table Joshua had brought. Joshua put a tablecloth on it and started unpacking the picnic basket. Bella greeted him with a kiss on the cheek then started to set up the food so people could eat.

"How are you, Bella?" Joshua looked past her to Chad, who was watching them.

"Right as rain, Joshua. Where's Joe?"

"He'll be along directly. I'll get this food ready so Doc and the kids can eat. Nora said they would leave pretty early so he could get them to bed."

"Yes, she did say that. Here, I'll help." She saw Chad setting up the chairs. She noticed he put two by Fred's and the other two on the other side of the table. *What is that all about? I do not want to be a competition between these two men.* She hit the brakes on that train of thought and decided she was just going to have fun. She started whistling, "Que sera, sera." *What will be, will be.*

Chad approached the table.

Joshua said, "Best fix the kids something to eat. May I help?"

"Sure, that would be great, Joshua. I'll fix Lilly's plate and get her started. She's a slow eater. Mac can tell you what he wants. I see

Fred is walking over to speak to Nora before she starts in earnest. Thanks."

Plates filled and the kids seated on a blanket in front of the chairs, Chad motioned for Bella to sit down. Joshua brought Mac's plate over and grabbed one of his own chairs and pulled up beside them. Carla walked up just as they sat down.

"Private party or can a stray lady join?"

Both men stood. Joshua spoke first. "More the merrier! Right, Chad? Bella?"

"Absolutely," they said in unison.

Bella said, "I'll watch the children. Go fix a plate of food while the deviled eggs are fresh and before the delicious smelling fried chicken gets soggy. Besides, you'll need time for your food to settle if you're going to do some serious dancing."

Carla, Chad, and Joshua looked at each other, and then looked at Bella. Carla was the only one who spoke. "Well, don't mind if I do. Be nice to have something besides what comes out of our kitchen... good as it is, of course!"

They all laughed. It seemed an unidentified tension broke.

Nora came over just as the children were starting to eat. "Just wanted to kiss the kid's goodnight." She bent and kissed each of her children.

"Mommy, I need to tell you something." He whispered in Nora's ear.

She glanced at Bella as he spoke. "Mac, thanks for telling me. Normally it isn't nice to whisper in front of others but I'm glad you told me." She kissed him on the forehead. *So my son thinks Bella has a lovely voice.* She smiled as she quickly returned to the stage.

Chad reappeared and put two plates of food in front of Bella. "Only difference is whether you like white meat or dark. I'm good either way, so you choose." He winked at his grandson who was watching him like a hawk.

"Grandpa, is Miss Bella your wife?"

Chad almost dropped the plates. *Oh my gosh, it never occurred to me he's never seen me with a woman. Haven't been with one in umpteen more years than he's been alive.* He decided to see if ignoring it would work.

Bella reached for the plate with the smaller servings; she couldn't wait to see how Chad handled this. *Gotta love an inquisitive kid!*

Mac stood up between the two chairs where Chad and Bella were sitting. "Well, is she, Grandpa? Is Miss Bella your wife?"

"Mac, Miss Bella is my friend. Remember when I introduced you, I said, 'I would like you to meet my frien—'"

"I know, Grandpa, but mommy is daddy's wife, and they always tell me they're best friends, too."

Suddenly, the sound of "Rocky Top" was in the air as the band started playing. Within moments, the crowd was on their feet, hands clapping. Mac joined in, clapping with the beat. The question appeared forgotten, and Chad took a deep breath. *Saved by the music.* He looked over at Bella. She smiled at him and looked down at Mac and Lilly. Fred was sitting on the ground with his daughter to make sure she was eating. He had a look of sheer pleasure on his face when his wife started singing the wildly popular song, one of Tennessee's many state songs. It seemed to Bella that everyone joined in the chorus, whether they could carry a tune or not.

Bella leaned towards Chad. "Do you think most people know there are nine state songs in Tennessee?"

He spoke close to her ear. "I suspect most folks choose the one they like the best."

*Fresh beauty opens one's eyes wher-
ever it is really seen, but the very
abundance and completeness of the
common beauty that besets our
steps prevents its being absorbed
and appreciated.*

    – John Muir, 1838-1914

20

Let's Dance

As they sat down, Bella turned to Chad. "They have quite a setup for all kinds of performances. I could see the wooden stage the band and Nora are on, but I didn't realize there was a dance floor down below."

Chad cringed inside. *I really hope you don't want to dance, Bella. I did* not *get the dancing gene.* He wanted to change the topic and realized he had not introduced Bella to Freed. "Bella I'd like to introduce my son-in-law..."

"Thanks. We've met. Mac introduced us." Bella smiled.

Fred nodded as they heard Nora start to speak.

"Good evening, ladies, gentleman, and gentle young folks. The Greg Brothers..." Nora extended her arm with her palm out towards the band.

There was thunderous whooping and hollering from the crowd.

"Yeah!"

"Woohoo!"

"Let's hear it!"

"The Greg Brothers and I are—" Even louder whoops and hollers drowned her out. She laughed and took a bow, then put both hands in the air to signal for quiet. The noise gradually dropped to a murmur. "We are so thrilled to be back for what we hope will be weekly jamborees of good bluegrass music. For any of you who are new to our gatherings, we do a segment where all musicians are encouraged to bring their own instruments and join in to make it a proper jamboree. The rest of you, bring those fine mountain voices and we'll sing to the heavens tonight."

Another round of applause shook the stage.

Once it died down, Nora continued, "We wouldn't have this stage, electricity, and dance floor without the generous support of the fine owners of The Corral. A little bird told me Miss Carla is out here tonight. Where are you, Miss Carla?"

People clapped, shouted, and pointed. Carla stood and acknowledged the crowd with a wave and a flash of her brightest smile. Once she sat down, the crowd turned back to Nora.

"Now that most of you have eaten those fine picnics I can see out there, it's time we get some foot stomping going." Rhythmic clapping began throughout the crowd. "Who better to start the dancing for us than the two best cloggers in the valley? Come on up, Miss Carla and Mr. Joshua! Lead us off."

People cheered as the music started. Clogging was a wildly popular folk dance in the hills, and they all knew Carla and Joshua had won competitions in the dance. Carla stood up and put her hand out to Joshua. "No choice. They'll stop coming to our businesses. Let's go."

Joshua's face turned a deep shade of crimson as he glanced briefly at Bella, but he was smiling broadly as Carla acted like she had to pull him out of his chair. This pantomime won them another round of applause from those watching nearby. They both laughed and walked towards the dance floor as the banjo player began to pick out the tune to "Blackberry Blossom." As they stepped up on the stage, the band shifted to "Oh, Susannah" and hands clapped in time with the music. Joshua and Carla bowed to the crowd and started clogging.

Bella watched as the heels of their shoes either hit the floor or clicked together in time with the music. Bella turned to Chad and started to say something, then leaned close to him to be heard.

"I admire anyone who can do any kind of dance, but I think in order to clog you must have the energy of a chicken pecking for seed."

Chad laughed boisterously. "Oh, my dear Bella, you're as right as dew on the morning grass. Watching those two dance, you can't imagine anyone who could do it better."

They both looked at each other and then glanced away at his very southern term of endearment. *My dear Bella.*

Recovering after a moment, Bella said, "Well, they sure look like they go together."

Chad almost shouted to be heard over the noise of the clapping and the sounds of music and dancing. "We needed you to get out with the valley folks sooner."

"I agree." She looked at him. "Why do *you* think so?"

"You belong here among these folks. I can hear your mountain twang and all our great old sayings coming back to you."

They both laughed and started clapping again. Bella saw that Mac and Lilly were holding hands and dancing in front of their dad. She leaned forward and clapped so they could see she was clapping for them.

Mac ran over. "Come on, Miss Bella, let's dance."

She held her hands out to him and moved her arms from her seated position while Mac danced. She glanced over at Chad. "This is my kind of dancing." She threw her head back laughing.

"Mine too." Chad laughed. "Mine too."

The song ended and Bella bowed towards Mac. "Thank you for the fine dance, Mr. Mac Smith."

He looked at her in the way only a four-year-old can. "Aw, Miss Bella, you can just call me Mac."

Chad reached over and grabbed his grandson and swung him up over his head. Mac squealed with delight, and Lilly ran up and held her hands in the air for her grandfather to pick her up too.

Fred stood up. "Thanks, Dad. Need them worn out so they will go straight to sleep when they hit the bed." Realizing Fred was about to leave, Chad and Bella stood up to say their farewells.

"Nice to meet you, Fred," Bella said. She squatted down and told the children she enjoyed her time with them. Her smile lit up her entire face.

Chad looked at her in awe. The look of admiration was not missed by Fred.

"Nice to meet you too, Bella. I hope to see more of you now that you're here for a spell. Okay, kiddos, let's get this train headed towards home." He picked up Lilly, who leaned out for a kiss from Chad. As Fred started to walk away, Lilly stretched out her arms. "B'la."

Stepping up to Fred, Bella said, "I do believe she's calling my name." She kissed Lilly on the cheek. "Sleep well, sweet girl." She felt a tug on her jeans.

"Night, Miss Bella, come see us, okay?" Mac had the sincerity of a long-lost friend.

Bella squatted down again. "I'd be honored, Mac. I hope you'll come visit me too. Sleep well, and I hope to see you soon. Good night." She and Chad waved as Fred walked off with Mac holding his pant leg and calling "Toot, toot," like a train.

"You're a very lucky man, Chad Oliver. You have a lovely and talented family." There was a bit of a catch in her voice on the word "family."

Folks Start Drifting Off

Bella noticed Carla swinging Joshua's hand as she pulled him off the dance floor and headed back to their seats. Joshua didn't let go as they all but skipped up to the table. Both picked up a napkin and took one of Bella's brownies.

"If your brownies as are as good as your deviled eggs," Carla said, "I'll have to fire our cook and give you the job."

"You'd be sorry at the first meal," Bella laughed. "Those are both recipes from my Grandmother Hazel. It just happens that I'm a pretty good reader and can follow directions."

Joshua and Chad both looked at Bella and then each other.

Joshua muttered, "Yes, ma'am, but you may not follow directions outside of cooking."

Chad chuckled and thought it was probably a good thing Bella didn't hear Joshua.

She saw the looks on their faces and said, "Mostly."

That brought a round of laughter from her and the men but a puzzled look from Carla.

Carla grinned. "Are you telling me you speak your own mind and don't let these mountain boys take charge?"

"YES!" Bella, Chad, and Joshua said in unison.

Looking around, Carla asked, "Where's Joe? Didn't he come over?"

Bella and Chad realized they had not seen him. Bella felt badly she hadn't thought to check on him. Joshua pulled his phone out of his pocket.

He let out a long sigh. "Guess I didn't hear the text come in over the music and dancing. Dad decided he was too tired tonight and was going home. He said Melody was headed home too. They'll both be in the store tomorrow."

Joshua looked around the group. "Speaking of tomorrow, I have a full day of propane deliveries, so if you fine folks will excuse me, I'm going to head home myself."

Carla joined him. "No rest for the working stiffs. Let me help clean this up and I'll be heading out too. I'll be needed in the bar when this crowd breaks up." She nodded towards The Corral.

Joshua looked at the group as all four pitched in to clear the scraps from their meal into a trash bag Joe had tucked into the picnic basket. All but two of the chairs were folded up, the remaining food put away, and Bella's containers stacked to go back into the SUV. While cleaning up, Joshua found himself thinking about how much he enjoyed Carla's company. They had been default dance partners at the jamborees for years because Jan claimed she couldn't keep up with his fancy footwork; it felt good to be back in step with someone.

Carla turned to Chad. "Heard some of the deputies are stopping in for some libations after the last song. You two joining us?"

Chad shrugged. "We'll see how the night goes."

"Ummmm…" Joshua cleared his throat. "This is kind of spur of the moment, and I know Sundays are busy at The Corral, Carla, but I was thinking maybe we could all have a late lunch at my place on Sunday afternoon." The words were out of his mouth before he had the chance to think about them further or change his mind. His face reflected some of the shock he felt at acting before fully contemplating the idea.

Bella spoke quickly, "That's a great idea, Joshua."

"Turns out I'm off on Sunday this week," Carla said.

"Count me in," Chad responded.

"Just bring yourselves then. Two o'clock." Joshua tried to act like he invited people to lunch all the time.

"Here, Joshua, let me help you load up this stuff. I'll be right back, Bella." Chad smiled. He was not at all unhappy about what he saw as a change of fortunes when it came to courtin' Miss Bella.

The Evening of Music Ends

Most of the families with children left, and the remaining crowd moved closer to the stage. Nora started a sing-along. Over the next half hour, some people danced while others belted out the old mountain tunes. They had come to sing, whether they could or not. It didn't really matter whether they could carry a tune or if their voices fell flat. What mattered was they were a community: they were bound together by their families and their traditions.

Finally, Nora stepped forward. "We're going to end this lovely evening tonight with two of our all-time favorites. The boys and

I want to thank you for joining us and hope you'll be here next Friday night. For our next to last number, I'm inviting two women from our great little community to come up and join me. One y'all know… Sylvia Whitehorse." The crowd started clapping. "Come on up here. And the second is rooted in these hills but has only recently been able to be here for a spell. Miss Bella, please come up and join us. A little boy who is very special to me said, 'Mommy, Miss Bella has a voice like an angel.' Come on up, Bella Anderson."

Bella looked at Chad, feeling a flutter of nervousness and excitement in her stomach. After teaching students for decades, she didn't mind being in front of people, but she had never considered singing in public before. He shrugged and gestured towards the stage. "You better go, or they will start chanting your name!" He winked at her.

The fiddle player started playing "Amazing Grace" as Bella and Sylvia walked towards Nora. The other instruments joined in. Nora met them as they stepped onto the stage, taking each woman by the hand. She turned them around to the crowd and started singing. "Amazing grace, how sweet the sound…" Bella, who was also a soprano, joined her along with Sylvia's contralto singing harmony. Everyone in the audience let them sing the first verse, then most stood and joined them. As the last verse was being sung, Bella kissed Nora on the cheek and stepped away and down the stairs. Sylvia followed her.

"Lovely voice, Dr. Anderson," Sylvia said.

Bella stopped, "Oh my, I was thinking about your beautiful voice." She slowed her pace as Sylvia fell into step with her. She turned to look at Sylvia and said, "Hey, I'm Bella."

"I know," Sylvia said, smiling and extending her hand to Bella. "I'm Sylvia, and I'm a sergeant at the sheriff's office. Nice to finally meet you."

Chad watched the two women talk as they walked towards him. "I see you two have met."

"Yes, Sheriff, and I'm glad to finally make her acquaintance. You two have a nice evening." She kept walking and did not look back.

While they were singing, Chad had responded to a text on his phone. He knew how quickly the crowd would jam the parking area as soon as Nora finished, and he needed to be able to get out quickly. He folded the remaining chairs and took Bella's hand. As they started walking towards his SUV, he leaned in and whispered in her ear, "Thanks."

Nora went into her final song of the evening, "Goodnight, Irene." The crowd joined in at full volume, and Bella and Chad sang along too. They reached the SUV and headed out before the crowd dispersed, the last of the music fading in the background as they drove away.

"I thoroughly enjoyed meeting your grandchildren."

"Oh, I'm pretty sure you'll have a fan for life in my grandson. He was smitten with you." The smile in Chad's voice carried throughout the vehicle. "Sure glad you went up and sang with Nora and Sylvia. That was a highlight of the evening."

They chatted about some of their favorite folk songs as they headed up the mountain, and Bella could hardly believe they were already home when they pulled up in front of Drellag Caban.

"Smart move to leave the porch light burning," Chad said.

"Surprised I remembered with us leaving before dark." Bella chuckled with a nervous quiver in her voice.

Chad was out of the SUV and at the passenger door before she realized it. He opened it, and she was probably as surprised as he was that she didn't comment on it. He let her step out and then opened the back door to get her containers. Bella had her key out but waited on him to walk to the door. She opened the screen, unlocked the door, and stepped into the kitchen. Chad set the containers on the kitchen counter and then turned to Bella, who had stepped out of his way.

He leaned in and kissed her. She did not pull away.

"Do you have time for a drink?" She sounded out of breath.

"There is nothing I would like more." He was a bit breathless himself.

"But?" she inquired, dragging it out with a bit of a tease in her voice.

"Well, this is not the way I had hoped this night would go, but I'm needed in what looks like a break in a case we've been monitoring, which could involve the trafficking of young girls." He bit his tongue as soon as the words were out of his mouth.

A look of shock and dismay flashed across her face.

"Sorry, Bella, I shouldn't have said that, and I didn't mean to ruin your evening. You're just so easy to talk to. . ." he hesitated. "I didn't mean to take advantage of that."

"The evening was wonderful, no apologies needed. I have to admit it makes me very sad to know you have to deal with such things. Truly, that anyone has to deal with it. But I know you'll get those involved."

He nodded. "I plan to do just that."

She leaned forward and kissed him. "Then go fight crime. Thanks for a lovely evening and for sharing your very special family. I'll see you Sunday at Joshua's."

"It's a date," he said. "So to speak." They both laughed. He kissed her gently, leaning his forehead against hers. He knew he had to leave. Now.

He quickly walked to his SUV whistling, "Goodnight, Irene," and called out "Good night, Bella."

She stood in the open doorway and returned his farewell, "Good night, Chad." Sadness and disappointment were evident in her voice as he drove away.

The End of Bella's Evening

Bella did not turn on the light in the kitchen. She slipped out of her loafers and put her sweater on the hook behind the door. She knew all the brownies and deviled eggs were gone, so she left the containers on the counter and walked into the living room. She was about to sit on the sofa when she turned abruptly and walked into the bedroom. She undressed, crawled into bed, and found herself looking at the picture frame. "Well, Matt, I think you sent me a sign." *You did if that kiss was any indication.* She had no trouble at all remembering Chad's lips on hers.

The only thing on her Not-So-Good List tonight was the ending; girls possibly being abused and Chad having to go. *Even though I would want him to go try and stop it. Thankfully, my Good List is much better.* She recalled the ride on her Outlander and the scenery across the valley. She smiled as she thought about meeting Chad's delightful son-in-law and grandchildren. She stared at the ceiling as she hummed "Amazing Grace" and thought about her first per-formance as a singer on stage. She decided it wasn't too bad—Nora made it easy. She had thought about Grandmother Hazel, mother, and Matt today. *And a very handsome and interesting man kissed me. I hope I can sleep on that memory.*

21

Back in the Valley

Chad drove faster on the switchbacks down the mountain than he knew was wise. He needed to get down far enough for a cell signal so he could call the night sergeant. He would have to make a decision about whether to raid the house they had under surveillance.

"Dispatch, Sheriff. Need me or someone else?"

"Give me Sergeant Douglas, please."

"Hey, boss. Sorry to interrupt your evening. This is important, but it isn't life and death."

"The message said that but, given the subject, it's urgent. What's going on?"

"You told us not to intervene at the scene, but our routine patrol up by that house encountered a little situation. I put two deputies in the car, what with the surveillance and being Friday night, and they happened by at the time a woman looked like she was being forcefully taken out of the house. The deputies stopped and asked if help was needed. The man said, 'No,' and the woman continued to pull back from him."

Chad listened but was already driving towards the road leading to the house under surveillance.

"They made both of them show ID. The man was none too happy. Turns out the young woman was nineteen and it was her pappy who was dragging her out. She was yelling at him that she was old enough to do what she wanted and he couldn't stop her." Sarge waited to see if the sheriff had a question, then he continued, "The deputies told them they could each step apart and talk with them separately, or they could go to the station for disturbing the peace."

"Good move. Tell them I said so."

"Sure, boss. Anyway, the father was none too pleased, as he put it, to have his daughter hanging around with a bunch of 'whores.' His word, boss."

"Sadly, I've heard it before."

"He told the deputy as long as she lived under his roof, she would live by his rules. Then he quit talking. The young woman apparently tried to sweet talk the deputy, telling him if he didn't make her go home with her pappy, he could come in the house and she would show him a good time." Eddie Douglas cleared his throat. "The deputy asked her how many other girls were in the house. That's what made me get a message to you."

"Go on."

"Well, at first she said none of them were girls, 'If you mean under eighteen.' The deputy pushed a bit more and she said, 'Promise not to arrest me?' He let her stand there, and finally she told him, 'There are a couple who don't speak English and I don't know how old they are.' Her words were, 'One of them sure looks like she's fifteen.'"

Chad slammed his fist on the steering wheel. "What did the deputies do?"

"The deputy told her if she went back in the house, she would be arrested on charges of solicitation. He said his best advice to her was to get in the car and go home with her pappy and not do whatever she was doing in that house again. He made the point to her that they could be coming back to talk to her, so his advice was to find other things to do with her time."

"Did she go?"

"Yes, sir, without a peep. The deputies moved on, but our plain-clothes guys are sitting outside the house waiting on any further instructions. Didn't want to go in given your earlier direction about observing."

"Sounds like it was handled well. I'm almost up there now. I'll check in with our guys on watch. Go ahead and send the deputies on patrol back to the area. We may have to go in. I wanted to try and get more intel, but we can't take the chance if there's the likelihood of an underage child being present. I'll be in touch if I need anything else."

He saw the black sedan parked off the side of the road and drove past it, then turned around and parked behind it. There were days in the summer when he wished his SUV was white, but at night he knew the value of being in a black vehicle. He turned off the inside light, stepped out, and both of his deputies exited their vehicle at the same time. As they approached each other, a car stopped on the other side of the road just past the driveway up to the house. A single male stepped out of it and started towards the driveway.

The deputies on patrol drove up behind him and blocked the driveway. The one on the passenger side stepped out. "Evening, sir. This your home?"

"What's it to y'all?" They couldn't see his face, but the tone carried irritation.

"Had some complaints of trespassers. I need to verify this is your home."

The man turned and started back towards his car. The other deputy stepped out of the car. Then the man saw Chad and two more men on the other side of the road. Even though Chad was in civilian clothes, most people in the valley knew who he was.

"Evening, Sheriff," the man said with a husky voice.

Chad walked across the road and recognized the man. "Evening, Mr. Turner. What brings you to this side of the valley tonight?"

"Uh, must have the wrong address. I was going to see a buddy of mine. Looked like his house, but he's further up the road."

"Visited him up here before, have you?"

"Uh, yeah. But it's easy to get turned around in the dark."

"Now, Clyde Turner, you seemed pretty sure about where you were headed 'til my deputy over there stopped you. At this moment, it doesn't look to me like you've done anything wrong. And, who knows, maybe our well-trained deputy over there may have saved you from doing something wrong. So, maybe you could help us out."

"Yeah, how?"

"Why don't you tell me who's in charge inside that house, and how many people there are besides the gentlemen like you who come visiting in the evening?"

Chad was good at waiting. He could see the indecision in Clyde's eyes even in the pale moonlight. *One of the good things about country policing is no streetlights to mess with your night vision. Come on, Clyde, you could help make a really risky operation a whole lot safer.*

"You promise no one will know I talked to you?" Clyde spoke very slowly, and his eyes darted around the five men.

"Now, Clyde, you know I can't make a promise like that. I don't know what you know, or what you might have done. But what I do promise you is this: if you don't help me and I find out you were inside that house and I can prove it, I'll make sure the district attorney has everything she needs to get a warrant for your arrest." He paused. "I have work to do here tonight, and anything you can tell me will help me keep my men as safe as I can. That's called co-operation. If you ever find yourself facing some charges before the law, cooperation can often prove to be in your favor. So, something you can tell me?"

"Okay, okay. There's a woman in there, least ways I think she's a woman. She sits in the front room. I was told you pay her, and she has four rooms with young girls."

"How young?"

"Don't rightly know. Honest, I was never here before."

"Clyde? You really don't want to lie to me."

Clyde was shuffling from one foot to another and biting his lower lip. He started to reach for the cigarettes in his shirt pocket and stopped himself.

"Listen, I don't know how old they are. I heard there was one girl, one of those illegal girls, who was fifteen or sixteen. But I never met her."

Chad could tell Clyde was trying really hard to think about the words he used. *I might not have given Clyde credit for being smart enough to try not to implicate himself. He had me fooled. Don't think we've arrested him before.*

When it was clear Clyde wasn't going to say anything else, Chad looked at him. "Thanks for your cooperation. I want you to go back over to the deputy and show him your driver's license. He'll make sure my memory is correct that you've never been in trouble with the law. If that's the case, he'll let you go. My advice to you is to make sure this is the closest—and last time—you ever approach something illegal. Understand that?"

"Yes, sir. I do." He stared at Chad and waited. "Go now?" he asked, nodding towards the deputy.

"Now." Chad shook his head as Clyde rushed towards the deputy.

Getting Ready

Chad walked back across the road and talked with the plainclothes officers. "The report I have from last night is one car was here three hours, but generally the cars are here less than thirty minutes. I'm going to call the sergeant and have him send me two more cars. One can stop anybody coming up the hill and check them out like I had to do for Clyde here. May prove to be a lucky night for those men. We'll wait until the owners of these two trucks come out. Then we'll let the other car take them to the station on suspicion of solicitation. The three of us will then go into house, with the two deputies here providing backup. Any questions or concerns?"

"Only one, boss."

Chad waited.

"Did you wear your Kevlar vest to the jamboree?"

"Appreciate your concern. I did not. But I have it in my SUV, so you can stop worrying. And thanks." He slapped him on the shoulder.

He called Sergeant Douglas. The sergeant said two cars and four deputies would be there in less than ten minutes. Chad told him he thought they had two men inside the house and, as soon as they exited, he would send them back to the station with one of the cars. The other car was to position itself below the crest in the road and stop all vehicles headed up.

"If the driver can prove residence further up the road, the deputies are to detain them until I call down and say it's safe for them to head to their homes. Get the license information on any they let leave in case they're needed for follow-up. Tell the deputies to act like it's a normal Friday night sobriety check."

"10-4, Sheriff. Think it's going to be a big takedown?"

"Sarge, if the information Clyde Turner gave me proves accurate, it may not take too long. But I always want to be prepared for what I can't know until I'm inside."

"Boss, you know you don't have to go in. You can send a deputy."

"Not on your life, Eddie. I'll get to the bottom of this one if it's the last thing I do."

Chad hung up and Eddie muttered, "I hope it *isn't* the last thing you do, boss."

Chad walked across and brought the deputies up to date. All five of them checked their weapons and their vests as Chad put on his own Kevlar vest.

Let's Go

There were now six deputies on the scene. Two men exited the house, and Chad told the most recent deputies to arrive to arrest the men on suspicion of solicitation and take them to the station. Chad called Billy Williams and told him to have one of the detectives at the station interrogate each man to see what could be learned about how they found the place and if there had been different people running it. He told Billy to tell the detective to be prepared for anyone else they might bring in tonight.

"Tell him if it's just the women, including the one running the house, I'm inclined to let them sit for the night. Sarge knows to separate them as much as possible when they get to the station. Make sure whoever we find running things is isolated from the others."

Billy told Chad he had a beer after the jamboree. "Remember, Sheriff, I had to buy."

"Right, I forgot you got to entertain the troops. Get some sleep. I suspect it will be Monday before we may be lucky enough to go after any bigger fish."

"No problem, boss. No problem. Call during the night if you need me. I only had one beer and I'll be fine."

"Night, Williams." Chad hung up and saw the deputies head to their SUV with the two men they had arrested.

"Since those two trucks belong to the two gentlemen headed to the station, I'm assuming there are no more men in there." Chad looked at the four men, pointing to each in turn. "I'm going in the front, you on the back door, you on the left flank, you behind me, and you wait here. Questions?"

Hearing none, Chad nodded to the deputy assigned to the back; he took off around the side of the house. His job was to stop anyone trying to get out the back, and he knew to wait to enter until called.

After waiting a minute to make sure everyone was in position, Chad and one of the plainclothes deputies walked up to the front door as if they were customers. He turned the doorknob and gave it an experimental tug; Chad was surprised the door wasn't locked and pulled it open. When he saw who was sitting behind the desk just inside the door, he signaled to the deputy behind him to slow down.

"Well, well, well, if it isn't Mr. Lawman himself! I kinda wondered what a good-looking man like you did for entertainment after your wife leaving all those years ago. Knoxville, right? She like the big city life?"

"Gertrude, I have to say it's been a few years since I last saw you. I kinda thought you might have taken up cosmetology while at Bledsoe. I didn't know they taught finance." He continued walking towards her. "Might be able to talk the DA into recommending another stint at Bledsoe, you know, keep you close to home. But I have no problem recommending the Deborah K. Johnson Rehabilitation Center in Nashville. Keep those hands on the desk and that'll go a long way in convincing me you want to cooperate."

She put her hands flat on the desk and did not resist when he stepped behind her and cuffed her. The deputy was in the room now and Chad told him to get the officer from the back of the house.

Gertrude sounded very cooperative. "I have three girls visiting with me here. They needed a place to stay for the weekend. Did have four, but one had to leave. I think her pappy took ill. Something like that."

"Yeah, we met them outside, Gertrude. I think her pappy was pretty sick about his daughter being here."

Chad signaled the two deputies to clear the house. They brought out three girls in handcuffs. One of them was the girl with dark brown hair and even darker brown eyes that Chad had seen at The Corral with Commissioner Zimmerman. The other two looked young as well. One was a blond with blue eyes; she was likely the oldest and potentially a local. The other was definitely young. She had red hair with hazel eyes, and deep copper skin to match. All three wore expressions of relief mixed with fear. Seeing them walking away together, each in handcuffs, he realized as he looked at the back of their heads that their hair colors were like the autumn trees—colors that were fading, just like the innocence these girls had lost.

Chad stepped out and called Sergeant Douglas. He told him to notify the car that was just below the crest to come up the road and sit outside the house in case any more customers arrived. "Pull the best female deputy on duty to meet these young girls when they get to the station."

"One more question… are the deputies coming up the hill on shift or overtime?"

"Overtime, Sheriff," the sergeant replied.

"Fine. Tell them to stay 'til first light and mark the house with crime scene tape. They should wait for the forensic team. They'll be up here at first light. No need to get them out of bed tonight."

He sent Billy a text. "Have your favorite madam in lock-up. Interrogate her tomorrow." Chad was sure Gertrude wouldn't enjoy a visit from Billy. Chad added a new message: "I want to know who is behind this operation."

Billy sent reply: "Gertrude?"

"None other."

Finally, he sent a text to Deputy Murphy to interview the young girls in the morning. *Glad she can speak Spanish, but we have to get folks up to speed—myself included.*

With everything organized for weekend and the two deputies set for the night watch, Chad got in his SUV and called dispatch to say he was heading home.

The Night: On Balance

It was after midnight when Chad stepped out of the shower. He wrapped a towel around his waist and got a Fat Tire Ale out of the fridge before heading to his recliner to sit in the dark to process his day. He was relieved to have solved the mystery of the light, although not thrilled to know that illegal immigration had invaded his territory. He suspected when the weekend's interrogations were finished, the young girl would be part of the movement of people from Mexico and Central America.

Just a fluke I spotted her with Zimmerman at the restaurant and followed him. He's connected somehow. Maybe he's just a customer, but I doubt it.

He knew the detective tracking down ownership on the two motels in Round City wouldn't stop until he had whatever it was possible to get. If they reached a dead end, he would go ahead and call in the FBI. As he knew from experience, the more information he had before he reached out to the FBI, the better the case was handled. *At least we're making progress.*

He stretched his hands over his head. *Well, this night did not quite end like I had anticipated. I have to admit, on the personal side, it was a pretty special night. Sure hope that won't be the last kiss I share with Bella. Been a long time since I imagined having a lady in my life, and I think I'm going to like it. More than I dared to imagine, truth be told.* He finished his beer and walked into the kitchen. After rinsing out his bottle, he put it into the recycling bin and headed for bed. *I don't have any plans for tomorrow, well, I guess later today. Maybe I'll call Bella and see if she wants to go out to dinner.* He settled down on his bed, locked his hands together, and laid the backs of his hands across his eyes. He took a deep breath and hoped for sleep.

22

Promises of a New Day

Bella sat at her computer, nibbling a piece of toast with blackberry jam and sipping her tea. Her sleep had been unsettling: a mixture of pleasant dreams and nightmares. She couldn't shed the thought of young girls being abused right here in the valley. *I'm not naïve. I know this goes on in the world. I just haven't allowed myself to think about it happening in my own backyard.*

She reread the short story she had sent to her editor about drugs being run across her property, then she opened the draft of the one started earlier in the week: "Perpetrators and Victims: The Suffering." She wondered how she could write something that she initially thought would be about her own reaction to what happened on her land: the boy who died, the boy in prison, and the damage to her shed and how it affected her. *Now it feels there's a much bigger story than my own. There's a story on this theme that needs to be told. Too many young lives being ruined by things in our modern world that too many adults, myself included, have been all too willing to ignore.* She made a list of what she knew about human trafficking and the questions she had. She wondered if Chad would tell her anything else—she doubted it.

The very question of whether he would tell her anything shifted her waking thoughts to her pleasant dreams and her memory of him kissing her at the door. She realized she had goosebumps, pleasant goosebumps, thinking about it. *The jamboree was so much fun. All those people from the community coming together to hear good music, sing and dance, and enjoy life. Why can't those kinds of things dominate our lives?* She finished her toast and tea and took her plate and mug into the kitchen. The phone rang. She was tempted to let the machine answer it.

She didn't.

"Drellag Caban, may I help you?"

"Morning. Did I wake you?"

"Morning, Chad. No, it's almost eleven, you know. Did you have a late night and therefore a late morning?" She had a mixture of concern and cheeriness in her voice.

"Late night, yes. Late morning, no. I didn't want to wake you in case you slept in. Fresh air can do that to you."

She liked how pleasant and easy going he sounded. "That's for sure. Fresh air can help you sleep better than a hound dog on a front porch on a summer afternoon."

He laughed. "Now, that's the gospel truth." He took a moment. "Aside from thanking you for a lovely evening, I'm calling to ask if you're available to go to supper tonight. We could take a ride over to Round City, if you like."

She started to speak and stopped herself. She couldn't believe she almost said she would see him at lunch tomorrow at Joshua's.

"Bella? Did we get disconnected?"

"No, sorry. Have I told you I sometimes get lost in my own thoughts?"

"Yes, believe you did. Been known to do it myself."

"Good. Helps that you understand the syndrome. Listen, I think your plate has been—"

He interrupted her. "Please, Bella, I really would like to have an uninterrupted evening with you."

"To quote a friend of mine, 'let me be more direct and see if that helps.'"

Oh no, that memory of hers can come back to bite me. Better be sure I don't say something I don't want to hear spoken back to me.

"Why don't you come up here? I can't promise a gourmet meal, but I can fix something that'll keep us from starving. In fact, if you don't have plans this afternoon, why don't you come up around two or three and we can take a hike? You might enjoy some of the places on my land where you can really see the beauty of this area."

"I'll be there at two. What can I bring?"

"Not a thing. Any food allergies or restrictions, or even likes and dislikes?"

"Pretty easy to please that way. Been eating out, or my own cooking, for way longer than I care to remember. That said, I'm a southern mountain boy and haven't met too many southern foods I didn't like."

"Fair enough. I'll hope the ones I fix aren't on the list. I'll keep it simple. I have beer and wine. If you want something particular, you can bring it."

"Got it. See you at two." He paused. "And Bella, I'm looking forward to it."

"Me too, Chad."

After hanging up the phone, she pulled the macaroni and cheese she had made out of the freezer and set it on the counter to thaw. She tried to decide what else she could serve.

The Day Flies By

Joshua was at the store at six and did one last look up and down each aisle to be sure they were fully stocked. He knew Melody was coming in for the whole day to help his dad. He heard the silver bell above the front door jingle. Melody and Joe walked in together.

"Morning, son."

"Morning, Dad."

"Morning, Mr. Joshua." Melody's voice had a lilt.

"Boy, I must have lost track of time."

"It's seven thirty straight up," Joe said. "I asked Melody to be here at opening because I knew you had lots of deliveries today. We're here and ready to go."

"Perfect. I'll be heading out in just a few minutes. We missed you at the jamboree last night. Sorry you didn't feel like coming."

"Oh, I decided next Friday's jamboree would be soon enough for me to have a really long day." *And I'm not about to tell you I didn't want to be in the middle of you and Chad sortin' out the courtin' of Bella.*

"Turned out to be a fun evening. Nora called Carla and me up to start the dancing."

"Did she now? Good to hear. No better dancers in the valley."

"Sorry I missed that, Mr. Joshua. I saw Miss Carla in a dance competition once. She's really good."

Joshua nodded. "Oh, yeah, she sure can cut a swath."

Melody laughed. "My daddy loves to say that. Miss Carla's dancing a swath doesn't cause destruction, though... well, except maybe to someone in a competition with her."

They all laughed.

"Okay, you two hold down the fort. I may need to stop back for a fill-up but won't come in unless you text. I'm mostly in the valley today, so should have a signal. There's a delivery up high over in the northeast section about four, so I'll be out of range for about an hour or an hour and a half. Need anything?"

"Nope. Good to go. Be safe out there."

"Sure thing, Dad. You two have a good day. Catch you later."

Joshua already had water in the truck, but he grabbed a few protein bars to take with him on his way out. He snacked on them throughout the morning, and he was surprised to see it was already nearing noon when he made his third delivery. He was headed to his next house when it occurred to him that he forgot to tell Joe that he had invited Chad and Carla to join him and Bella for lunch. *Oh well, I'll tell him when I get back.* As he continued with the propane deliveries, he planned the menu for the next day, starting with fixing burgers on the grill. *That's easy enough to do with salad and some of the locally made baked beans.* He was satisfied with how his list was taking shape.

A Great Afternoon for a Hike

Even with the prospect of spending the afternoon and evening with Bella, Chad never forgot he was sheriff and had to be reachable. Although it wasn't always possible, he made every effort.

"Afternoon," Chad said to his dispatcher, "I'm going to be out of range this afternoon, but you can leave a message for me at this number." He gave her the phone number at Drellag Caban. "Sergeant Whitehorse can handle anything that comes up if I'm not available. Call and leave a message if you need me." He listened to her repeat the number. "Right, thanks. If Detective Williams is in his office, put me through, please."

"Detective Williams."

"Have a minute?"

"Always for you, sir."

"Any luck with Gertrude?"

"As you suspected, Gertrude was not happy to see me. She's being stubborn today. I was even polite and called her Madam Gertrude." Billy paused but got no reaction from Chad. He cleared his throat. "I'm going to let her stew for a while and try again later in the day. I'll do everything I can to get her to tell us who was paying her and who's behind the prostitution operation." The tone of his voice had returned to business. Despite his frequent jokes, Chad knew Billy was determined to get the information from Gertrude in the right way.

Satisfied things were under control, Chad headed up the mountain to Bella's. He saw her silhouette behind the screen on the front porch, and she stood as he approached, waving out the screen door. He walked up, handed her a bottle of wine, and gave her a quick kiss. She put her hand around his neck and pulled him in for a longer kiss. He did not resist.

"Well, good afternoon to you, Miss Bella."

"Back 'atcha."

They stood awkwardly for a moment, then Bella turned around and walked into the cabin. "Hook the latch on the porch screen if you don't mind. Let's head out for that hike." She put the wine in the fridge and tried to figure out how he knew it was her favorite: Kim Crawford Sauvignon Blanc.

"Want me to lock the French doors?"

"Yes, please."

She slipped on her vest and was putting on her boots when he entered the kitchen.

He stood admiring her and wondered why some women squatted to tie their boots and some bent from the waist. He had to admit he liked that she bent from the waist.

Standing up, she said, "Okey dokey, let's go."

"Wait just a minute. Let's lock these windows. What do you say?"

"I say, it's not necessary. Next time you see the sheriff, you can tell him I learned a neat trick. I have these handy dandy window wedges. They work just like a door stopper. Good reason to have double hung windows." He noticed the impish smirk on her face. "Anyone who wants in is going to have to break the glass either way. So, let's leave the fresh air to Drellag Caban and go get some of our own on the trail. Ready?"

"Ready." *Though I don't know if I'm ready for a woman who is so positive, knows her own mind, and is a problem solver too. I'm pretty sure I'm willing to find out.*

They headed down the road towards the gate. Bella told him that Arthur was putting in her fence on Monday. She also talked about her options in fixing the shed or tearing it down and doing a whole separate structure. He listened as she outlined the pros and cons of each and couldn't find a flaw in her logic.

"Do you expect to have enough guests to need a guest cottage?"

"I could with my North Carolina friends, particularly if I decide to sell my house there."

Chad wanted to shout for her to sell the house and get a guest cottage. Instead, he kept his voice neutral and asked, "Is that a likely choice? Selling your home in North Carolina, I mean?"

She walked across the cattle grate and turned right, heading down a path Chad could see was well worn. The cop in him hoped the path was only from her hikes, not intruders.

"It's becoming more and more of a possibility. Drellag Caban is the one place that's been a constant home in my life. My parents' hearts were always in these mountains, but North Carolina was our home. It was also my home with Matt, and my professional life." She turned onto a small trail that led them down a steep incline. "It's true I have friends there, but most of them have children, and now grandchildren. As they retire, their lives are more and more immersed with their extended families." She looked back over her shoulder. "I'm happy for them, and they're generous to include me in their activities. But I've been up here over a month now and, for most of them, out of sight is out of mind." She stepped over a large boulder. "I don't have any family there... or here." He heard her voice trail off.

Chad kept quiet. It had not really dawned on him she was truly alone. *I think she passed the Mac and Nora test. Wonder if she could learn to see my family as hers?* "Happy to share mine," he said.

"That's sweet, Chad. You have a lovely, and loving, family. I do hope I get to see more of them."

"Me too," he said. "*Me* too."

They arrived at the outcropping. "Come, pull up a rock and have a seat."

"Sure, which boulder would you like me to move?" They both laughed. "You won't believe that I've heard more than one northerner think we actually mean 'pull up a rock!'"

Bella settled into her usual position, with her arms resting on her knees and her head propped on her arms. "As someone who has spent all my adult life studying the English language, I don't think we should be too hard on the 'Yankees,' as my daddy called them." She looked over at him and saw he was watching her. "Did I say something wrong?"

"No, nothing at all. I'm just admiring the view."

She turned her head to look behind her. "Nice trees."

He leaned over and when she turned her head back, he gently put his hand on the back of her neck and pulled her to him and kissed her. "This view, silly woman."

"Oh, that. My view is pretty nice too." She looked at him and kissed him back.

They both turned to look out over the valley. He took her hand, looked at her, and wiggled his eyebrows. "What else do you have to show me?"

Bella blushed.

"That, kind sir, may take a long time." She saw his smile fade. "Remember, I have eighty acres here." *Oh, Chad Oliver, two can play the flirting game.*

She stood up and pulled his hand to bring him into a standing position as well. They started back on the trail. "In the meantime, we should head back. It's well after four. I promised to show you that I'm a mediocre cook."

Bella walked first on the trail. As the trail widened, he stepped up beside her and took her hand. "May I?"

"By all means." They walked on in silence back along the jagged trail through the trees. When they reached the grate, she took off running. "Last one to the kitchen door has to do dishes." He let her go, following in long strides, but was more than willing to be last.

She sat down on the kitchen steps and untied her boots. He did the same. "Feel free to leave them on if you're more comfortable."

"Are you kidding? I'm a southerner." He let out a loud guffaw. "My favorite form of footwear is..." She joined him in the last part, "barefoot." They both laughed and leaned shoulder to shoulder to remove their boots. They left them next to each other on the top step and walked into the kitchen; Bella made sure she opened the door.

She pointed down the hall. "Feel free to use the facilities. Oh... I forgot you know where they are."

Chad stood there.

"I can't believe it's almost five forty. Are you starving? You're getting my simple go-to meal. I hope you like macaroni and cheese and ham steak. You have your choice of broccoli or asparagus."

She realized she was talking a mile a minute while washing her hands at the kitchen sink. She turned around to find him staring at her.

He approached her. "Am I being too forward if I do this?" He reached and pulled her into a strong embrace and kissed her. She returned the embrace and the kiss.

"Nope, not too forward. But thanks for asking."

He stepped back. "I'm fine with either green vegetable. You decide." He walked down the hall to the bathroom, feeling pretty self-satisfied that he actually remembered the fun of flirtation.

She finished drying her hands, put the macaroni and cheese in the oven, and pulled out the broccoli. She was cutting it up to cook when he returned.

Last Delivery of the Day

Joshua was on his last run, this one up a mountain where he knew he wouldn't have a signal. He called the store.

"The Valley Store, may I help you?"

"Hey, Melody, may I speak to dad?"

"Sure, Mr. Joshua. It's as slow as sorghum running up a tree in the wintertime."

Joshua laughed. *Good thing she wants to stay in the state for university. Can't imagine her having to explain herself in California or some such place.*

"Hey, son. What's up?"

"Just heading up to the Macaws' place and wanted to remind you I'll be out of range for about an hour and a half. Sounds like we might get to close up early tonight. If you want to go home, don't wait on me. I think most folks shopped yesterday before the jamboree."

"I think you're right. I'll see how it goes, but I'll likely send Melody on home and just wait for you."

"Good deal, Dad. Want to get a bite to eat when I get back?"

"Sounds like a plan. See you soon."

"Okay. Love you, Dad." Joshua was glad he remembered he wanted to tell his dad this more often.

Joe smiled. "Love you, too, son."

Joshua lost the signal as he took the slow, steep climb up the mountain. It took both hands to keep the big truck on the road. He always hoped there were no low hanging branches when he drove this route. The colors of autumn, which were approaching their most vibrant shades of orange, red, yellow, and even some pink, brushed against the truck windows as he climbed. The greens were all gone at this elevation.

As he approached the Macaws' property, he wondered how they could live this high up with absolutely no way to reach anyone. They were off the electric grid completely and used the gas he delivered to heat and cook. They had a large solar array that Mr. Macaw had shown him on his first trip up here, but they limited the use of it to lights and the refrigerator. The Macaws were on their front porch, waving as he pulled up.

Joshua finished filling and checking their propane tank. He took out a bill pad because the Macaws insisted on paying immediately, in cash. He had them initial his copy, so he had proof of payment. *Not sure why I feel I need them to do that. But I do. Better safe than sorry.*

"With those two large tanks, you should be good for quite a while now."

"Yep, we should be. But we'll have you up one more time before the road gets so bad you can't make it. Don't want you slipping down into the holler like a pig sliding in mud." Mr. Macaw slapped his knee and guffawed at his joke.

Joshua found northerners who tried to use southern expressions annoying; too often it felt condescending rather than as a way of adapting to the environment in which they now lived.

"Well, just send me a smoke signal and I'll be up." Joshua had his own way of making a point.

Mrs. Macaw laughed. "That may be what it takes to reach you. You take care, Joshua, thanks."

He waved as he walked back to his truck and headed down the mountain. It would be good to have dinner with his dad and get his head on straight. He was not usually disrespectful to native history or his customers. He decided he was just tired. It was five twenty when he reached the store. He went in the back door and called out to Joe to say he was back. He stopped in the bathroom to wash his hands before he headed to the front of the store. He didn't hear any customers.

The Unexpected Always Comes

Bella asked Chad if he wanted wine, beer, water, or tea.

"Good idea to rehydrate after a hike," he said matter-of-factly. "I'll start with water, thanks."

"Good plan. Mind pouring me one, too?"

She had set the dining room table earlier, so she was turning on the heat under her iron skillet to cook the ham steaks when she saw the blinking light on the answering machine. *Funny, I didn't see it blinking when we came in. Must have been distracted.*

"Chad, normally I wouldn't listen to a message with someone here, but I assume your staff knows where they can reach you?"

He hesitated. "They do. Should have asked if that was okay. Actually, could we just get that out of the way once and for all?"

"I know what you do for a living and the security you provide for everyone in our community. That help?"

"Yes. Thank you. I'll make you a promise. I'm going to work really hard at letting go of the reins..." he paused, "now that I have a reason."

She smiled and tried to lessen the electricity sparking between them. "Since very few calls come in for me, I suspect it's for you."

"Suit me better if it was for you."

She pushed the button.

"This is dispatch at the sheriff's office. It's five thirty-one p.m. Please have Sheriff Oliver call the station as soon as possible. Again, this is a call for..." He turned off the recorder.

He pulled her towards him. "Do you want to get mixed up with a guy whose life is like this much of the time?"

"I'll take my chances." She hugged him and then handed him the phone and walked back towards the bathroom.

"Oliver here." He listened intently and asked a few questions. He lowered his voice as he kept one eye on the bathroom door to see if Bella had stepped out.

"You're sure he's still alive? Okay, get word to his son that I'm on my way and I'll have Dr. Anderson with me. Please call Carla at The Corral and ask her to go be with Joshua." She was the only person Chad could think of who might know Joshua well enough to sit with him.

He turned off the burners under the broccoli and the smoking iron skillet. He moved the skillet to a back burner to cool down and took the macaroni and cheese out of the oven. He was pouring the water off the broccoli when Bella came back in the kitchen.

"Oh my gosh, I completely forgot about the skillet. I'm so sorry about the smoke." She realized he was closing the window, not opening it wider. Thinking he didn't know how to remove the window wedge, she reached across him to show him how to remove it. He turned her gently, pushed the window down, and locked it.

"I'm going to close up Drellag Caban while you put together whatever you need to stay down the mountain tonight." He looked at her expecting an argument, or at least some push back.

She knew by his tone this wasn't a request. It was something important.

"Chad, I'll do what you say, but tell me why. Please."

He was afraid she might collapse when he told her. He pulled her in close. "Apparently Joshua was out on propane deliveries, and Joe was at the store by himself."

She pulled back, started to speak, but stopped herself.

"It looks like a robbery. Someone hit Joe over the head and Joshua found him alive but unconscious. Joe will be at the hospital by now. Doc Fred will be there too." He waited to see if she was still standing on her own, then he gently stepped back.

"I'll be ready in less than five minutes. Can you get word to Joshua that we're on our way?"

"Already done."

Bella dashed to her bedroom and began to throw clothes and toiletries into her overnight bag. Chad put all the food in the fridge then pulled his SUV up to the door. He had the passenger door open and was standing in the doorway to take her bag.

Neither of them spoke. Chad's mind was divided between thinking about how on earth this amazing woman came into his life and how he was going to manage the logistics of the crime that was taking them down the mountain.

Bella looked at Chad, reached over, and squeezed his arm. Her mind was filled with emotions she had to capture. She pulled her iPhone out of her pocket, opened a note-taking app, and quickly jotted down thoughts that were coming faster than she could key them in. What she would do with these thoughts wasn't important. She just needed to get them down. Bella was still making notes when they reached the hospital. She closed the app, looked at the building, and hoped the night would bring some good news.

23

The Emergency Room

Chad pulled up to the emergency entrance. The front entrance was closed at this hour on a Saturday. "You go ahead and find Joshua. I'll be right behind you."

"Thanks, Chad, see you inside." Bella rushed through the doors and saw Joshua and Carla were the only ones sitting in the small ER waiting room. She went straight to Joshua, who stood and started to hug her, then pulled back. Bella could see the blood on his shirt. Carla watched them.

"Oh, Joshua, how is Joe? How are you?" Bella stretched up and kissed his cheek. She looked at Carla. Carla looked down at her feet. Bella stepped away from Joshua and towards Carla and sat down in the chair next to her. She touched her arm.

"I'll be back," Joshua said abruptly.

"How are you, Carla? I know Joshua is relieved you could come." The softness in Bella's voice disarmed Carla.

Carla looked at her, then up at Joshua who was walking out the doors of the ER. "I'm worried about Joshua. I wanted to take him home to change or get him to let me go get a clean shirt, but he refused. He said he needed to be here."

"And I'm sure he wanted you here with him."

Carla nodded her head. "I hope so."

Joshua and Chad walked back through the doors together. Chad nodded to the security guard on duty. The guard nodded back. Joshua was talking too softly to be heard by the women, but the agitation on his face was evident. The men stopped just inside the doors and stood talking.

Bella could only imagine that Joshua wanted to know if there were any answers to who did this and why. She, too, wanted to know. The two men walked towards them. Both of the women stood.

Joshua spoke in a more animated way than Bella had ever heard him. "Doc Fred sent word he'd be out as soon as he could. This waiting is awful. I hate it. What's going on? Is my dad going to make it?" The words seemed to gush out of him. He dropped down in a chair. At his 6'4" the chair was dwarfed by his height. Chad pulled up another chair from across the small room. They all sat.

Time dragged for each of them in different ways. Carla's parents had died in car wreck when she was in her late twenties, so she was not a stranger to this ER waiting room. Since Matt's death, Bella felt the stab of loss she had experienced so many times before. Chad went into his objective law enforcement mode, processing what needed to be done so his folks could solve this crime. At the same time, he knew he need to be a friend, something he was starting to realize he hadn't done well in many years.

"My dad loves this community, you know," Joshua said to no one in particular. "He's owned the Valley Store for sixty-two years. He started it when he finished his degree at UT Knoxville."

"Joshua, this community is here for Joe, and for you, whatever you need," Carla said. Bella noticed Carla was holding his hand.

Bella was about to speak when the internal doors to the ER opened.

Doc Fred walked towards them. "Let's go to this room over here." He pointed across the small lobby to a door marked "Private" on a frosted glass panel. "It's quiet and we won't be interrupted." The physician knew these situations needed to move at their own pace; they were never easy.

Chad moved towards the door and Bella followed him. She turned and saw Carla was still holding Joshua's hand. His shoulders drooped further as he walked towards the door, and it looked as if Carla were propping him up.

Chad opened the door and Bella walked into the room. Joshua followed her and dropped into the first chair inside the door. Carla sat next to him. Bella sat in a chair on the other side of Joshua. Chad gave his son-in-law, Fred, a soft pat on the back as both men entered. Chad quietly closed the door behind them. He created a bit of distraction by pulling over two more armchairs to form a lopsided circle.

Joshua's eyes implored Fred not to tell him what he didn't want to hear.

"Joshua," Fred began. The compassion in his voice was mirrored in the gentleness of his eyes as he looked at Joshua. "Joe didn't make it. He went very quickly." He stopped for a second. "The swelling in his brain was too much."

The room was silent. Doc Fred knew to sit quietly and wait for the inevitable questions that would come. He also knew sometimes they didn't come in the first moments of shock.

Joshua stared at the floor, elbows resting on his long legs in a chair that was far too close to the floor for his tall, lanky frame. Everyone in the room knew Joshua was a quiet, contemplative man under normal circumstances—these were not normal circumstances. Coupled with the loss of his wife a month ago, it made what was happening unimaginable. No one spoke.

"He was the best man I ever knew," Joshua said in a voice that cracked and was barely audible. "He never hurt another person in his life." He stopped talking.

Finally, Joshua looked at Dr. Fred Smith, a kind and caring young physician who chose rural practice for reasons like this. Fred liked that he knew his patients and their families; now, he knew he was looking at a man who had just lost his last family member.

"Thanks, Doc, thanks for taking care of him. It's what he would have wanted. He wouldn't have wanted to be in Knoxville. This was his home for eighty-five years. He was in the right place. Thank you for that."

"Joshua, it will take time, as you already know, to let this all sink in. I'm going to leave you with your friends. Anytime you want to talk or have any questions, call me. Anytime. Okay?"

"Sure, Doc. Sure." Doc Fred stood up and Joshua automatically followed suit. He shook his hand then dropped back in the chair. Fred nodded to Chad and walked out. Chad followed him. Bella saw the look on Chad's face and felt he must be struggling with rushing out to find the person who did this to Joe and being here as a friend to Joshua.

Bella had more experience than she might have wished at managing difficult situations, and she knew there were going to be many decisions to be made. She finally broke the silence. "Joshua, Joe was a kind and gentle person who only ever showed concern for others." She paused. "Do you think you want to see your dad now? Or do you want to wait until he's transported to the funeral home?" They all knew the funeral home was in Round City, some thirty minutes away.

Joshua looked up with pleading eyes, eyes that said, "Just tell me what to do." Bella knew the look—and the feeling.

"I think the best thing right now is to take you home. We can sort out what you need and what needs to be done." Joshua nodded and then his eyes darted around the room, looking from Bella to Carla, to the door and back to Bella.

Chad walked back in the room. Joshua's voice was shaking as he spoke, and his voice had a more demanding tone than any of them had ever heard from him. He said, "Chad, promise me you're going to find out who did this. My dad didn't deserve this."

Chad pulled his chair up in front of Joshua. "Joshua, finding out what happened and who did this to Joe is my top priority."

Joshua nodded and his shoulders sagged even more. His voice was barely audible. "I don't know if it really matters. Dad's gone, and it won't bring him back." He buried his hands in his face. His friends sat with him; each was lost in thought. The room was silent.

Bella thought about the story she was writing on perpetrators and victims—one more victim in these hills that connected all of them. She looked at her new friends with the understanding of someone who knew that loss exacted a price for each of them. *I know we'll get through this together. I also know that love and compassion from others helps you heal.* She reached over and touched Joshua's hand.

About the Author

Jacqueline Evans Jacobs, Ph.D., celebrates the opportunities offered in her life to serve as a teacher and educational leader on five continents. As a little girl, born of parents whose roots in the Smoky Mountains date to 1720, she dreamed of the journeys traveled in the books she read. She couldn't have imagined the places she would live, nor the amazing people she would meet. She gave each of her doctoral students at the University of South Carolina the book *Oh, the Places You'll Go* by Dr. Seuss in anticipation of their leadership to encourage another little girl to dream of the places she can go in life. *Life on a Mountain* is the second book in her series, *Love is a Cabin*.

Author's Note

A lifetime of reading and writing is invaluable. A lifetime of living is worth the experience.

December 2020